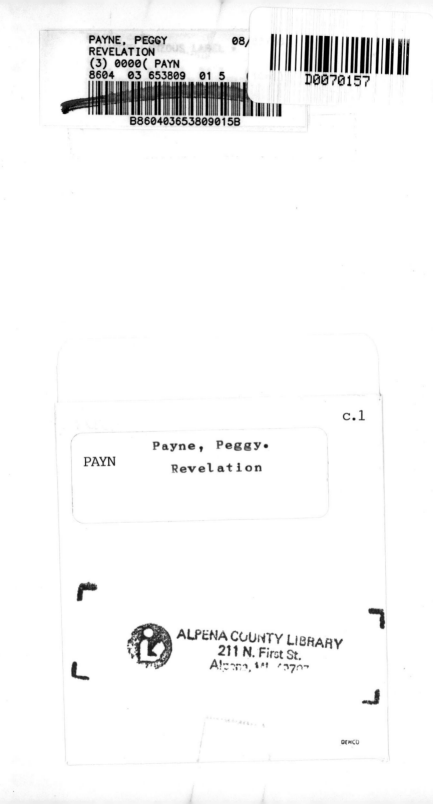

REVELATION

PEGGY
PAYNE

SIMON AND SCHUSTER

New York   *London*   *Toronto*   *Sydney*   *Tokyo*

Published by Simon and Schuster
A Division of Simon & Schuster Inc.
Simon & Schuster Building
Rockefeller Center
1230 Avenue of the Americas
New York, New York 10020

SIMON AND SCHUSTER and colophon are registered trademarks
of Simon & Schuster Inc.

Designed by Liney Li
Manufactured in the United States of America

3 5 7 9 10 8 6 4 2

Library of Congress Cataloging in Publication Data
Payne, Peggy.
Revelation / Peggy Payne.
p.   cm.
I. Title.
PS3566.A954R48 1988
813'.54—dc19
87-32621
CIP
ISBN 0-671-65252-4

The author and publisher gratefully acknowledge permission to quote from *The Minister's
Handbook* (*The Minister's Service Handbook* and *Funeral Services* by James L. Christensen;
Communion Messages, edited by Frank S. Mead) copyright © 1960 by Fleming H. Revell.

Lyrics from "Puff, the Magic Dragon" by Peter Yarrow and Leonard Lipton. © 1963
Pepamar Music Corporation.

For my husband, Bob Dick,
with love

ACKNOWLEDGMENTS

I am very pleased to thank a lot of people for the many ways that they've helped me with this novel: from editing and criticizing the manuscript to keeping me happy while I wrote it. For staying with me through every draft, I want to thank the small dedicated band of writers brought together by Laurel Goldman through Duke University's Division of Continuing Education. Angela Davis-Gardner, Georgann Eubanks, Peter Filene, Charlie Gates, Pete Hendricks, Carrie Knowles and Linda Orr, as well as Laurel, have offered the kind of insightful criticism that's hard to find. For keeping me happy while I wrote the book, I especially want to thank my husband and best friend, Bob Dick, who was also helpful in another way. Bob's skills in hypnosis, which he uses in his practice as a psychologist, helped me at times to get the creative juices going again.

There are so many others who have helped in very important ways: Malaika Adero, Bob Bender, Rev. Sam Burgess, John Cleaveland, David Eastzer, Rev. W. W. Finlator, Ethel Gilchrist, Ardis Hatch, Cynthia Hazen, Kent Jarratt, Rev. Collins Kilburn, Dan Leigh, Barbara Lowenstein, Mary Metz, Mildred Modlin, Dr. Larry Moore, Jr., the staff and students of The Governor Morehead School, Suzanne Newton, Harry and Margaret Payne, Franc Payne, Harry Payne, Jr., Dr. Bob Phillips, Rev. Ted Purcell, Larry Rice, Rev. Cally Rogers-Witte, Randee Russell, Dr. Nick Stratas, Brenda Summers and Harriett Taylor. I'm glad to have this space to say to you once again: thank you.

REVELATION

ONE

Swain hits the brakes and all the books on the car seat beside him shoot forward onto the floor. A Datsun swerves out around him, the driver yelling, but Swain can't hear a sound through his closed window. The last Swain sees as the car window flashes past is the guy's finger pointing him to look up. He does as he's told and looks: red light. When did they put a light in here? There was never a light here.

He sighs, shrugs, backs his car out of the intersection and sits motionless, his elbow on the hot window frame in the midsummer heat. Six o'clock and it's still this hot. The smell of the road tar rises up around him.

He stares for a moment at the books spilled onto the floor, then slowly piles them back on the seat. *Eschatology and Ethics. New World Metaphysics. The Science of Theology.* He shakes the cold coffee off the bottom book. Damn. He finds the mug, empty now, and puts it back on the seat. Somebody behind him honks. Okay, okay, he thinks, and pulls out.

I should have demolished the one in the Datsun, kept going and plowed right through him. Him and his window closed to keep in the air-conditioning. He could have looked where he was going. I should have bashed him, or at least yelled something. One good "fuck you." Once in my life I'd like to do that. The one time I ever do, it'll turn out to be somebody from the congregation.

He presses his head back against the headrest, trying to loosen up his neck muscles. Nothing is more irritating than sitting in a seminar with a bunch of other ministers all day. All of them working so hard at being warm and sensitive. They act as if they're teaching kindergarten for a living, not working with adults. I'd rather deal with my own congregation any time, he thinks. At least they don't expect me to act like Captain Kangaroo.

He pulls to a stop for another light, putting a hand out to hold back the stack of books beside him. He glances out each of the side windows, as if maybe somebody had been listening and heard what he was thinking.

In all his life, Swain would never have said that he was "called" to the ministry. After spending a day with his colleagues, he still occasionally questions how it happened. But in his heart, he knows.

He simply grew up certain that it would be so—that he would be a preacher. Not because of any belief he could actually pin down. Instead, it was because of a powerful lifelong desire that there be "something else." He wanted there to be more to life than he himself had seen or felt so far—something to ease his chronic vague dissatisfaction, something to subdue the irritation which he had always reined in . . . even in his moments alone in traffic. Some would consider that yearning a too-slim, or very selfish, reason for the choice he made, but it was enough for Swain. So, after Yale and one brief stint as an associate minister, he came home to Chapel Hill to be the pastor at Westside Presbyterian.

He and Julie live in a neighborhood a few blocks back from the fraternity and sorority houses along Franklin Street, the wide main street that divides the campus from the town. Turning now onto his own narrow shaded street, Swain feels the tension inside him let go a little. He loves it here. It's an old neighborhood. The houses all look different from each other, big white-columned ones next to more modest ones like his own. In summer, the big yards are lush and unkempt around the huge oaks and magnolias. He and Julie have left theirs wooded and no one around them seems to mind. He edges his car over to the side, and lets an old Mercedes pass.

Several other families from the church live in the surrounding blocks. Westside has a liberal congregation, full of academics from the university community. Lots of bright, interesting people, but as a group, they tend to be a bit stiff...like Swain, a bit overly intellectual. The church was an excellent choice for the careful, self-controlled man that Swain has grown up to be.

Now he pulls slowly up into his own gravel driveway, sits still for a moment to recover from the day, then gathers up his books and goes in.

The house is quiet. Julie is already out back on the patio, arranging skewers of pork and green peppers on the rack of the charcoal grill.

Swain gets a beer out of the fridge. He knocks on the kitchen window and waves to Julie.

Julie is a medical librarian at the hospital, though if you met her you would never think of libraries. You might think of Hayley Mills in those movies from her teenage years. She has the same full features and thick red hair. "I'll be out in a minute," Swain calls to her through the pane. He goes back into the bedroom and changes into shorts and a T-shirt. Their bedroom, shaded on two sides by a big oak tree, is cool and dim. He stands, damp still, in front of the rattling window air conditioner and feels the cold column of air wrap around his middle. He feels his mind slow down as his temperature drops. He takes a swallow of the beer and closes his eyes. A peaceful moment. Why can't it all be this way?

The backyard smell of lighter fluid and searing meat reaches him. He goes out to find Julie.

"Hey," she says, and still holding the basting brush, turns to kiss him. He holds on to her for a moment, until she pulls away to take care of the fire.

"What can I do?" he says.

"Set the table. Otherwise it's mostly done. I got home a little early."

"Lucky you. I wish I had." He unloads the tray of plates and silver she has brought out, then squints up the slight hill of their wooded backyard. There's a spot of color there he hasn't noticed before. "Isn't that a lady's slipper?" he says. "Was that out yesterday?" But Julie is busy. She doesn't look.

Swain's long white feet still bare, he carefully picks his way up the hill to examine the flower. It's then, as he stops yards away from the plant—not at all a lady's slipper—that he hears God for the first time.

The sound comes up and over the hill. He stands frozen and feels it coming. One quick cut. Like a hugely amplified PA system, blocks away, switched on for a moment by mistake. "...Know that truth is..."

There is no mistaking the voice. At the first sound, the first rolling syllable, he's swimming up out of a sleep, shocked into wakefulness. He stands where he stood, feeling all through him the murmuring life of each of his million cells. Each of them all at once. He feels the line where his two lips touch, the fingers of his left hand pressed against his leg, the spears of wet grass against the flat soles of his feet, the burning half-circles of tears that stand in his eyes. His bone marrow hums inside him like colonies of bees. He feels the breath pouring in and out of him, through the damp red passages of his skull. Swain is dizzy, stunned...the force of it coursing through him. The last vowel, the "i" of "is," lies quivering on the air like a note struck on a wineglass.

Then it stops. In the slow way that fireworks die, the knowledge fades. He is left again with his surfaces and the usual vague darkness within. He sinks back toward what he has always known. Then he takes a breath, blinks his eyes, runs a hand down his chest, down one leg. All the same, still there. He turns back around to see if Julie has heard.

But her back is turned, she's serving the two plates that he has set on the patio table. He put them there himself. A breeze is moving the edge of the outdoor tablecloth. She turns back around toward him, looking up the hill at him. It's as if he's watching her in a TV commercial. She's pretty; he doesn't know her; she doesn't know he's there. She's looking into a TV camera, about to hold up a product. "Soup's on," she says, smiling. "Come eat." She stands and waits for him, as he walks, almost runs, barefooted, stepping on rocks and sticks and pine cones, back down to her. He has to reach her, break through whatever is suddenly between them and get to her. He rushes straight for her—seeing her eyes widen, her smile waver—he grabs her with both arms, ignoring her surprise and the half second of her resistance, pulling her close, tight against him, one hand in her hair, one arm down the length of her back. He's as close as he can get.

"Swain," she says, trying to pull back so she can see him.

He holds her tighter. He starts to speak and nothing comes out. He feels the force of his own heartbeat in her body. "Something happened," he says.

She waits for more, but he doesn't say anything. What is going on? "Swain, this is scaring me. Please say something." Still nothing. She feels him take a breath to speak and then stop. "What happened?" she says. She wants to shake him. Why won't he say? "Are you okay?" She runs her hands up and down his back, looking for something wrong. His shirt is wet. "Swain, what is it?"

He tries to say it: "Julie, I heard God." But it won't come out. Then a wave of fatigue washes through him. He lets his arms loosen. "I don't know how to tell you. You'll think I'm crazy."

She shakes her head. "I won't."

But he still can't say it.

She glances at the table. Swain looks where she looks; there is food on the plates.

"Let's sit down," she says. "Then we can talk. . . ." Did he have a stroke? If he did, could he still be standing up? She sees the shelves at the library where she files the books on circulatory diseases. Swain doesn't act like this.

He continues to stare at the table. The fork looks so foreign, so strange. The meat, shining in the patio light. It looks terrible. He shivers. The sweat that soaked his shirt is starting to chill him.

"I'm going to get a jacket," he says. "I'm cold." She nods. He can feel her eyes on his back as he walks into the house.

There are no lights on inside, only the yellowish glow of the patio light through the window, shining on one patch of floor. He can feel the hair standing up on his arms. This is insane, he thinks—I'm not afraid of the dark. He doesn't touch the switch— he forces himself to wait—until he gets to the closet at the end of the hall. There it is. His jacket. He has his hand in the closet, reaching for it, when he hears the voice again. One syllable. "Son." The sound unfurls down the long hall toward him. The word and its thousand echoes hit him all at once. He holds on to the wooden bar where the coat hangs, while the shock washes over his back.

He stays where he is, his back and neck bent, his hand bracing him, waiting. Nothing else happens. Again, it is over. He straightens painfully, as if he had held the position for hours. He walks out onto the patio. Julie, at the table, strains to see his face against the light beside the door.

"Are you all right?" she says.

He sits, looks down at his plate. She thinks, He is not all right.

Swain holds the jacket, lays it across his lap like a napkin. He shakes his head. A sob is starting low in his chest, dry like a cough. He feels it coming. He's crying, his own voice tearing and breaking through him. He hears his father's voice saying, "Swain, I cannot have noise. Not in this house." But he can't stop. Inside him, walls are falling. Interior walls cave in like old plaster, fall away to dust. He feels it like the breaking of living bones. In the last cool retreat of his reason, he thinks, I am seeing my own destruction. Then that cool place is invaded too. He feels the violent tide of whatever is in him flooding his last safe ground. He holds himself with both arms; Julie, on her knees beside his chair, holds him. God has done this to him. This is God. Tears drip from his face and trickle down his neck.

An hour later, he lies quietly beside her in bed. He has let himself be put to bed like a sick child. She finally believed him that he didn't need a doctor and crawled in beside him. The sheets feel cool, making a little tent over him. He keeps his arms close to his sides under the covers. He says, "Out there in the yard, I heard something. A voice."

"Yes? A voice?"

"God," he says. His mouth is dry. His eyes follow the patterns of swirls in the plaster of the ceiling.

She turns her head toward him, the light is shining on his face. She looks at him carefully now, her eyes scanning his eyes. He is going to tell me. She feels her heart thumping.

"Standing up there on the hill," he says. "I heard God."

She hesitates. "So...what did it—what did the voice sound like?"

Swain repeats the words he heard. He still cannot say what happened: that hearing the voice, he felt the living hum of his every cell. That he is as weak now as a child who has had a terrible fever.

She reaches over and touches his hair, strokes it. So this is what it's about. The voice of God. All the air goes out of her. What a relief. Her whole body lets go worrying and sinks right down into the mattress. When all this time I was thinking he was sick, or that it was something awful. She says, "I don't think you're crazy. It's all right."

If one of us was to hear God, it should have been her, he thinks. But a different God, not this...She deserves the one he has believed in until now.

"For you it would be all right," he says. He means it as a compliment. He has envied her her imaginings, felt left behind sometimes by the unfocused look of her eyes. Though she'll always tell him where she is, if he asks: that she goes back, years back, to particular days with particular weathers. That she plays in the backyard of her grandparents' house, shirtless, in seersucker shorts, breathing the heavy summer air, near the blue hydrangeas. Swain wants to be with her then. He wants to go with her: "Except ye become as little children, ye shall not enter..." He wants to, and yet he doesn't. Certainly, he doesn't want to go without her. That was never what he had in mind.

He gets up and goes to the church in the morning as usual. He says nothing about it to anyone, that day or the next or the next. Maybe silence will make the whole thing go away.

Thursday night after supper he is lying on the living room floor. Julie is in the armchair reading, her feet in old white sneakers, her ankles crossed near his head. What is she reading? He twists his head around so he can see. P. D. James. She could try staying in the real world for a while for a change, he thinks. All she ever does is read. He watches her feet move, tapping in a rhythm, as if she were listening to music in her head. Maybe she's hearing Smetana's *Moldau*—which she's played so many times he's sick of it. She could be imagining the whole thing, close enough to the orchestra to hear in a pause the creaking of musicians' chairs. She could do this and think nothing of it. She lives in a daze half the time anyway, daydreaming. It's as if she doesn't really take anything seriously. At least she could quit tapping her feet.

Finally he has had the big religious revelation he always wanted, and there's no joy in it. None at all. He has never felt so cheated. As a kid, he wanted something like this to happen. He did think though that it would bring with it some pleasure—great happiness, in fact. He had a daydream of how it would be, set in the halls and classrooms of his elementary school, where he first imagined it. A column of warm pink light would pour over him, overpowering him with a sensation so intensely sweet it was unimaginable. He tried and tried to feel how it would feel. The warmth would wrap around his heart inside his chest, like two hands cradling him there. He would be full of happiness, completely at peace. The notion stayed with him past childhood, though certainly in his teenage years, he didn't talk about it.

But he did what he could to make it happen. Divine revelation. He wanted it. He was so hungry, so eager for some sign. He lay on the floor of his room at home, and he waited. Sometimes he got his mother's car and drove out to a state park, where he'd find a bend in a creek to stare at. He stared until his mind was lulled into receptive quiet. In classes he lost himself in the deep chalky green of blackboards, as beckoning as a limestone quarry pond. But nothing happened. The quiet always passed, without interruption, at least by anything divine.

The search must have ended finally, at least the purposeful part of it. He realizes that now, lying here with the front door standing open and moths batting against the screen. When did I give it up? He doesn't recall any such preoccupation during divinity school, though there was that one thing that happened in his last year.

He was sitting out on the outdoor stair landing of his apartment that was the second floor of an old house. He and Julie, not married then, were in one of their off times. He was feeling bad. His roommate was out somewhere. The concordance and the notepad had slid off his lap. His legs were sprawled, completely motionless, in front of him, hanging off the end of the butt-sagged recliner. He had lost Julie; he was bone-tired of school; he wouldn't have cared if he died.

He was staring at the dark trunks of the trees at the back of the yard, at the mud ruts of the makeshift parking lot, at the falling-down shed. Nothing mattered at all. Then while he watched, everything—without motion or shift of light—everything he saw changed. He stared at the peeling boards of the shed, at the water standing in the tire tracks. It was all alive and sharing one life. The trees, the bare ground, his own being and the porch around him had become the varied skin, the hide of one living being. In the stillness, he waited for the huge creature to move. Nothing stirred. Yet he felt the benevolence of the animal, its power, rising off the surface before him like waves of heat.

What he felt then was a lightness, a sort of happiness. A touch of that power stayed behind with him, fading slowly until he was back to his usual pale, forgettable self. But briefly, it was at least a hint of what he had always imagined—something he could be part of.

That afternoon, he was buoyed. He finished the work he had sat with for hours. He fried himself a hamburger and ate it and was still hungry. He watched a few minutes of the news on his little portable black and white TV. He did not die nor had he thought further of dying since that day, other than for the purposes of sermons, counseling, and facing the inevitable facts.

Facts. He is lying on the floor of his living room, the warm damp air coming in through the screen. Julie is reading in the chair. God has spoken to him, in English, clearly, in an unmistakable voice. And he is miserable. He wants to grab the rocker of Julie's chair, her tapping feet, and say "Stop that noise, goddamnit." He wants to get up and break something, that pink and white vase that he hates. Instead he lies here quietly and does nothing, the way he has all his life.

"What would you do, Julie?" he says. He's looking at the ceiling, he doesn't turn his head. "Would you stand up in the pulpit and tell them, 'I have heard the voice of God'? Would you do it?" He rolls over on his side and looks at her. Her foot has stopped moving. She has put her book down.

"I've been thinking about it," she says. As if I could think about one other thing, when he's lying here in a funk every night since it happened.

"What did you decide?"

"Yes," she says. "I would."

"Oh?" There's an edge in his voice. "What else would you say? How would you explain it? Explain to me, if you understand so well."

"Say as much as you know," she says.

"What is that? One piece of a sentence? I've got nothing to say."

"It's the whole point of your job, isn't it?" she says. "To tell them. Isn't it?"

"Yes," he says, slowly and carefully, "it is. But if you'll remember, Presbyterians do not make a habit of getting up in the pulpit and talking about their personal lives. I'm supposed to be talking about Scripture—"

"Swain, you can't go over there and talk about some Bible verse when this has happened."

If she had to get up there and do it herself, he thinks, she wouldn't be such a know-it-all. "Of course," he says, forcing his voice to stay level, "when I have a little better understanding of what is going on, I will have something to say—"

"Now is when you have something to say. I can't see the point in waiting until you've written a dissertation on a bunch of other people who have been through the same thing."

"And what if I don't do it?" he says, the anger rising in his voice. "What if I never say a word and you spend the rest of your life thinking I don't have the balls to get up and say it? What happens to us then?"

She shakes her head. "That's not going to happen."

Swain gets to his feet, straightens his pants leg. Then he looks at her, making sure she sees the coldness in his eyes.

She stares back at him, just as hard as he's looking at her, then goes back to her book, or at least pretends to. She hasn't read three pages in an hour. What did he expect me to say? she wonders. It's perfectly plain what he should do. She stares at the book. Not that it mattered in the least what I said, he was going to be mad anyway. You'd think if God spoke to you, there'd be something good about it.

He leaves the room, goes into the kitchen, gets out a small tub of Häagen Dazs and a spoon. Standing near the fridge, he eats from the container. There is no sound, total silence from the other room. Pink light—what a joke . . . childish sentimental crap. "Suppose ye that I am come to give peace on earth? I tell you, Nay; but rather division." The voice didn't warn him, didn't remind him. He shakes his head. This whole thing has done nothing but piss him off, that's all it has done. He digs and scrapes at the ice cream.

The following morning, he sits alone in his office. How is he supposed to tell this congregation about anything so bizarre as this? His notepad is blank. He tosses his pen away, onto his desk.

What am I going to do—get up and say that I heard the voice of God and the whole thing was a rip-off? "Know that truth is"—what a piece of shit.

He props his elbows on his knees and stares at the floor of his office. His eyes follow one of the cracks over to the wall, follow another one back. The afternoon is like a night when you can't get to sleep: hot, itchy, restless, it's never going to end. He has to write a sermon. There's no way to avoid it. The topic is already out front in the yard on the sign. The secretary is holding his calls—it's a rare moment of quiet. How often does he have such a luxury? He hates it, he wants out of here. He has already gotten up and opened the window behind his desk. Now he stares out into the shimmering heat and listens to the churning of a lawnmower. I'd feel better pushing a lawnmower. Maybe I can do yards for a living after this is over.

"Son." He keeps coming back to that one word in his mind. But it wasn't his dad. His father would never in any of Swain's wildest fantasies have blasted out like that. He would have simply appeared there on the hill, standing quietly, looking at Swain, distant and disappointed. He pictures the old guy standing in shirtsleeves on the side porch of their house, which, up until it was sold and torn down, was only three miles from the church. His father could walk to the campus to teach his classes. At home, he would step out the door of his study onto the open porch for air. He did it a dozen times in a day, no matter what the weather. When Swain was little, it seemed to be one more proof that his father was very special, that he could stand out there in the cold and not even seem to notice it. Snow on the ground and there he was in his white shirtsleeves and his big baggy pleated pants, staring off somewhere, his breath smoking up the air.

If he closes his eyes, he can hear the clock ticking in his father's study. He's sitting on the edge of a chair, his feet dangling halfway to the floor, his father saying, "Swain, I cannot have noise. Not in this house. I have work to do. Please exercise some consideration, if you will."

Swain saying, "I was coloring in my coloring book. I was being quiet."

"You have not been a problem today. But at other times I've heard too much running in the house, bouncing balls . . . I don't want any more of it. I wanted to mention this while I was thinking of it."

"Yes, sir." Swain slid off the chair. He was going out the door when his father said, "I'm sorry but I can only tolerate so much." Swain went back upstairs to his coloring book—*Roadrunner and Wile E. Coyote*. All the time he was coloring then, he was careful not to bang his foot against the leg of the chair. For a long time after that, he tried to be so quiet that nobody could even tell he was there. He wanted to be the quietest person in the world. At the table, he would put his fork down in slow motion so nobody could hear it.

Swain twists in his office chair, resettles his legs. He sees again the reddish-gold light of the late sun in the backyard. He feels the electrifying surge that he could almost see pushing the air in front of it. A tidal wave of sound rushing over him and drowning him. Then his memory stops, as if he'd ripped a cassette out of the deck, pulled out the tape and destroyed it. He doesn't want to feel it again. Ever. Do you hear that? Not ever. I've spent thirty-eight years, my whole life, waiting for something that turns out to be this.

What am I going to tell them? He imagines himself in the pulpit, staring out at the congregation. He sees the horror waking on their faces, as they understand him. He sees them glancing at each other diagonally across the pews. I'd be out. It would cost me the church. They'd gradually, delicately ease me out, help me make "other arrangements." I'd get shipped off to some church with a sign out front that tallies up the number saved on a Sunday, the kind of church that has buses and an all-white congregation. Better to mow lawns.

Why go through with it anyway? Nobody in the church is going to believe me. Unless maybe Bernie, as far back as we go.

Bernie will listen at least. And Patrice. He smiles. She'll listen to me. And Julie . . . But most of the rest of them—coming here and saying they believe in something. I'd like to slam a few of them against a wall. Get their attention, for once.

He turns his chair away from the window, back to his desk. I have nothing to say. Know what truth is? A half sentence? Absurd. I could get up there and tell them that God is the biggest letdown a man could ever imagine. Swain stops. Then the longing that he has felt so often sweeps over him again. He wanted there to be something . . . He can't think about that now. The congregation is what he has to deal with. He'll have to tell them. I have to stand up in front of them and make an ass of myself. That's what will happen. I might start to cry—like I did that night. Swain reconsiders. He despises the kind of minister who gets up and makes a display of himself.

He rubs his face in his hands. He wants to be left alone. With Julie. With God, but not with the God that is doing this. The last thing in the world he wants is to get up and talk about this. But, Swain thinks, a man couldn't remain a minister with such a secret.

Swain Hammond's picture, like that of every other member of Westside, is in the church directory. The congregation compiled this book two years ago, after a brainstorming session on a weekend retreat to the beach. This was one of the ideas for bringing people together and helping to make Westside more of a community. The picture of Swain and Julie, seated side by side on a sofa in the church parlor, is listed under "H." Swain modestly objected to the idea of putting himself at the front of the book. So there they are, the same size as everybody else, in black and white, sharing the page with Mike and Sally Griffin and Mary Ellen Highstaff.

Swain is tall. You notice that even when he's sitting. His big bony knees and his long legs make sharp angles in the foreground of the picture. One arm drapes along the back of the couch, lightly encircling Julie. He's a good-looking man, but you can see from the way he's sitting and the expression on his face that he still doesn't believe it. He looks as if he might spring off the couch in a second if anyone questioned his right to be there. And there's something about his smile that's a little tentative too. His face looks as if it stopped halfway between two clear-cut expressions. There's a slight curve to his lips, but it doesn't tell you a thing.

What's obvious and unequivocal about him is dark eyes and a lot of brown hair. His hair falls forward on his forehead, a thick pile of it. Just looking at the picture, without knowing him, you could almost see him reaching to push it back, as he constantly does. Then you notice his eyes, how carefully they watch, the way people watch the needle on a scale, waiting for it to come to a stop. Though it's hard to see in this picture, one eye is slightly different from the other. There's a notch in the oval of his lower right lid, a little break in the circle. When he was a kid, about six, he climbed up on the roof of the backyard garage, using the wisteria vines to get up there. Then, somehow, he fell. On the way down, one of those same vines he used for climbing raked across his face. The only mark that stayed on him was that slight irregularity. Sometimes Swain thinks he notices people staring at it, and it's true, he's not imagining it. For most of the people who know him as an adult, it's the only thing about him that has ever been a little out of line. Swain, as even Julie would say, has until recently been a very deliberate and careful kind of man.

Julie sits on the sofa next to him, slightly inclined into the curve beneath his arm, smiling easily for the camera. Her body looks as if it has taken this position naturally, not been placed and arranged by a photographer. Her hands lie open in the folds of her loose sleeveless dress, her shoulders, arms, neck as strong as a swimmer's. She is short, large-breasted, and it's easy to imagine her sunburned from working outdoors. Looking at her calls up a certain sort of imagery: a white pitcher of milk in a patch of sunlight on a table, or a yellow bowl of daisies. Of course, she is not as simple as all that. And it's that very complacency and ease before the camera that's the clue. But at first blush, there she is: freckled, full-bodied, wide-eyed, disarming. A preacher's wife who has until recently seemed to treat that demanding role as something she hardly noticed. She has given her warmth and her presence, and if the church has expected anything else of her, they've never let her know.

What was portrayed in this picture of the two of them—if a picture can portray a marriage—was Swain's only real success in human relations. Then as now, and this was taken about two years ago, they were happy. Swain and Julie, married thirteen years, are very close. And though they have endured the usual difficulties, from the start this marriage seemed like a pretty sure thing.

Swain's personal ministry has been a different matter. He has always privately considered the counseling part of his work a disaster. Although he got by very respectably—no one seemed to notice his discomfort. At worst he seemed a little distant, stilted, aloof. And at Westside, a reserved, perhaps too intellectual sort of person is, at the least, easily tolerated.

Swain, pulling up into the driveway, stops to watch what's happening in the yard next door. A mob of kids running around yelling. The Gustafsons and some of their buddies out playing under the sprinkler. He slowed the car when he first saw them jumping around in the spray and running from it, pushing each other into it. Now he sits in his own driveway, watching. He always thought somehow that if he found what he was looking for—from God—he would be able to run around and have fun like that. God was supposed to unlock whatever it is that keeps Swain Hammond so tied up. Sometimes he feels as if his arms are tied to his chest with barbed wire, and all around him, everywhere he goes, people are reaching over and touching each other, as if that were an easy, ordinary thing to do. If I went around telling people that God had picked me to talk to, they would all know why: the last shall go first. So it is written. Swain Hammond, tight-ass. Who could be more last?

Water splats against the back of the oldest boy, then comes the softer sound against the grass as the spray swizzles away. His own skin feels dry and dirty. Julie isn't home yet, her car isn't here. I could go over there and try it, act like a kid for once. Wash the dust off me. Now. Fast, before I can change my mind—go over there and act like a happy kid. Run around yelling and getting wet like the rest of them and having fun.

He gets out of the car, slams the door, goes into the house, straight to the bedroom. He doesn't pause. He puts on his bathing suit, then looks at himself in the mirror. He is so long and white, just a touch of softness at the sides of his waist. But so white. He puts his undershirt back on and inspects himself again. Better. I can take it off as soon as I get over there and throw it aside on the grass.

Now, Swain, go, he tells himself. Out the front door, passing his briefcase, where he dropped it, with the new book on bereavement. He picks his way, barefooted, across the concrete driveway and the Gustafsons' gravel path.

"Hi, Dr. Hammond," the biggest boy says. Swain can't keep up with their names. The kid has a stretchy red striped bathing suit that looks as if it was rolled down onto his skinny frame, the way you put a sweat band around your wrist to play tennis.

"Dad's not home," the kid says. The boy stands there and waits for him to say something and then go away. They all do, all five of them. The sprinkler swishes back and forth over them and they don't even notice. The littlest one puts two fingers in her mouth and continues to stare. Their scruffy dog stands with the water dripping off him, looking from one kid to the other.

"I wasn't looking for your dad. I wanted to come play under the sprinkler with you."

"Oh...uh, okay," the kid says, shrugging, looking down the street, as if he'd sent somebody to call for help and the police ought to be on the way. "Sure," he says. They all continue to stand there. Swain has succeeded in turning the whole crew of them into a statuary garden, with all the alabaster eyes on him. They wait for him, then, to go play under the sprinkler while they stand and watch.

All right, then. The little bastards. He pulls his T-shirt off and throws it over onto the sidewalk. He walks deliberately onto the circle of dripping grass. And he stands there until the stream of water spatters and jerks its way around to him, and for three beats of its trip—he stands motionless with his eyes closed—the needles of water drill against his chest. Then it swishes away, hitting grass, circling with the same inevitable rhythm.

He opens his eyes. The kids are still staring, pretending that they didn't exchange glances and that nothing happened while he stood blind under the shower. But now they are standing farther apart. He has dispersed them a little more, like a game of billiards. They are each a little more distant from him and a little farther from each other. He has done that, and it was so easy. It is all exactly the way it has always been. Nothing is any different.

When he tells the congregation that he heard the voice of God, they're going to stare at him just like this. Like these kids and their damn dog. As if he's some kind of alien, which he is, but now they'll all know it.

He waits until Saturday night to decide that he will definitely do it this Sunday—so he won't spend the whole week dreading it. He has scrapped the sermon that he was supposed to give, that he had finally forced himself to write. He is going to tell them, and he's doing it at the first possible opportunity, the first Sunday after it happened.

He is still in the safety of his bench behind the pulpit. The last notes of the organ have died away into a vibration. They're all out there, waiting for him. This is it. He swallows and makes himself start to move, walk forward into the pulpit, stand with his hands on the wooden rail. His fingers seek out their familiar places along the tiered wóod.

Sam Bagdikian settles back in his pew, rests his hands on his stomach. Time to lie back for a little snooze. Swain can say some interesting stuff. But his voice has such a rhythm to it, kind of lulls you. You're supposed to be able to learn languages if you listen to the tapes in your sleep.

"Friends," Swain says, his eyes moving back and forth across them. "I have struggled with what I must tell you today.

"I have come before you this morning to say that I have heard the voice of God."

He looks past the faces, stares just beyond the last row at the back wall, and waits for the explosion or at least a sudden freezing silence. Nothing happens. His eyes sweep forward again, from the window back across the three hundred faces. They're blank, waiting, mildly interested. No one is alarmed. They can't have understood.

He starts again. "I think you know that I believe in an immanent God. I think you know that I believe in the presence and power of God in all our lives. I have come to tell you today that something has happened to me in recent days which I do not understand.

"A voice has spoken to me. I know that it is the voice of God." He pauses. He looks at them: no reaction. He can't believe it.

Halfway back, Bill Bartholomew recrosses his legs, twists his wrists inside his cuffs. Get to the point. We've all heard God. Everybody that got out of Korea knew what God was. Operating in a tent with the shelling going on night and day. He drums the tips of his fingers against the hymnbook, then rakes a hand through his stiff gray hair.

Swain continues, "My wife, Julie, and I were cooking dinner on the grill of our back patio...."

Now the rustlings of movement stop. Face after face grows taut with attention. Joe Miles slowly pulls his gaze away from the long blond hair of the girl in front of him. What's he saying? The voice of God on his patio? Patrice picked a good day to lean on me to come. He looks over Jakey's head at her. She's staring up at Hammond as though he's the one who's God. He watches her, just the way she sits there... elegant. The woman is a Rolls, a 500 Benz. And sitting there staring at Hammond, of all people. It's a hell of a line, hearing God. He looks back at the girl in the pew in front of him. How can anything that looks like that be Bruce Hoggard's child?

DeWitt Chambers, seated alone in the same corner of a pew where he has sat for more than forty years, looks over at Julie, who's as white as milk, just as nervous as she can be. What in the world are she and Swain up to? He looks back at the arrangements of flowers he brought in this morning. What a burst of glory those gladiolas are. The nicest ones he has seen this whole season.

Swain feels a stillness fall over the church all the way up to the back pews of the balcony. They know now this is not a metaphor, not a parable he is telling. His wife, Julie, the back patio—they are listening, staring at him and waiting. Swain feels a trembling deep in his gut. He begins with the lady's slipper and the voice that came over the hill.

He tells them about the word "son" and the windbreaker and his own tears. "I asked myself whether I should bring this to you on a Sunday morning," he says. He looks from face to face in the rows in front of him. What are they thinking? He can't look at any one face long enough to tell. The shaking inside him has moved outward to his hands, damp against the wood of the pulpit rail. He doesn't trust his voice.

"When I first heard what I heard, I began to ask myself what I could say to you."

Now Swain looks at Julie. He can see her wrists, before the back of the pew breaks his vision. He knows her hands, out of the range of his sight, are knotted together, moving one against the other.

Out of the corner of her eye, she can catch a glimpse of a few of them. She's almost scared to look around. Bill Bartholomew—

her heart sinks—looks as if he just ate the bitter part of a pecan; sitting there in his gray suit and his shiny glasses, he could be made out of nothing but gray metal. DeWitt Chambers, with his finger pressed against his pursed-up lips. He probably watches soap operas all day while he polishes his silver. He doesn't care what happens as long as it's juicy gossip. If they can't listen to anything about God, what are they doing coming to church? What are they here for? She's disgusted with all of them. They don't deserve to hear Swain talk, or God either.

Swain says, "I asked myself whether you would want a pastor who hears voices. Whether you'd think I'd completely taken leave of my senses. Or even whether some of you might come to expect wisdom from me that I don't have."

Bernie Morris rolls his bulletin into a tube and hits it against the pew ahead. What is all this coming out of the blue?

Did he come to me and say, "Bernie, old buddy, I got to tell you what happened to me. Bernie, what do you think, what do I do?"

No, not Swain. No, he gets up there and mouths off and looks like an idiot doing it. Voice of God. What am I doing here anyway? Sitting an hour every Sunday, mainly because of him, I'm up to my eyebrows in this church and I've hardly gotten a nickel's worth of business out of the lot of them, and now he gets up and does this. I should have taken Lynne and the girls to the beach. Bernie beats a fast staccato with his ring against the back of the pew.

Patrice Miles is leaning forward, her hands gripping the edge of the seat. Did he say what I think? She looks over at Joe, but he's obviously paying no attention. When we get in the car, he probably won't know anything happened.

I must have heard wrong. Straight reliable old Swain? She has always wanted to pull his tie loose, or mess up his hair. She smiles. Jakey elbows her. She looks down at him. He whispers, "What's so funny?"

"Nothing."

"You were laughing."

She whispers back, "I wasn't."

"You were too."

She rumples his hair. Nine years old and he's in charge of everything.

He pats his hair down and looks around to see if anybody saw. She acts like I'm a baby, he thinks. What's so funny about God talking to somebody? I bet she wouldn't laugh if God started doing stuff in our yard.

Swain is saying, "I don't know what to expect from you. Neither do I know what to expect from God. What I heard is not what I ever would have hoped or expected to hear. It hasn't given me any wisdom or any peace. But I will listen and pray to understand more." He steps back, hearing as he does so the first note of the organ.

Gladys Henby is still sitting with her hands clasped on her purse just as they were when this sermon began. She is so startled she hasn't even moved. Now she pats one gloved hand gently against the other. This quiet sensible young man is saying that God has spoken out loud to him in his own backyard? She wants to turn and find Walter beside her and see whatever to think about such a thing. She does the math again: eleven years and three months since he died. If Dr. Hammond can hear God, then maybe it's all true. The life everlasting. The tears well up in her eyes.

Around her people are rising, hymnbooks in hand.

Swain looks out at them, standing, now singing the closing hymn, as if nothing has happened. No one has leaped up from a pew to challenge him. It's as if he had never spoken at all.

He takes his place as usual on the front steps to shake hands and greet people. Going on as if it's all ordinary, the sun heating up his black robe. People filing past him and shaking his hand. It's stunning...weird. How can they do this? How can I...? Three out of all of them tell him that the Lord works in wondrous ways, or something to that effect. Mrs. Frances Eastwood squeezes his elbow and tells him to trust. Ed Fitzgerald lays one hand on his shoulder, close to his collar, and says, "I like what you did here today." Bill Bartholomew shakes his hand and nods curtly, hurries past. He's the one who'll call the elders into session to talk about it. He's the ticking bomb. Gladys Henby peers up at him as if she has cataracts and can't quite see. Maybe she does and hasn't told him. She stares at his face as if she's trying to memorize it, but she doesn't say a word about the sermon. Not a word. DeWitt stops and stares at him as if he's slightly amused. "My, my," he says, shakes Swain's hand and goes on.

On the way home, Swain is quiet in the car. Julie sits closer to him than usual, with her hand first resting on his shoulder, then his leg. "They just sat there like zombies," Swain says.

He wriggles his foot inside his shoe. He itches all over. His feet itch, his scalp feels as if he needs to stop the car and scratch every inch of it with both hands. "They give me the creeps," he says. "I get up there and I tell them, and all they can do is stare at me. I can't believe it."

"They need time to think about it," Julie says.

During the afternoon at home, the phone rings twice. One man calls to congratulate him for speaking out. But the guy was just a visitor, not even a member. Swain doesn't recognize his name. He hears nothing from Bernie. Nothing from Patrice or Joe Miles. Nothing from Ed Fitzgerald, or any of the ones who mean the most to him.

Coming back into the kitchen, where Julie is cleaning out drawers to keep busy, he says, "It's the ones who don't call... They're not calling me, they're calling each other...."

TWO

The fact that Julie and Swain ever got together in the first place is surprising to a lot of people. Julie comes off as such an easy kind of person. Swain doesn't, though as smooth as he has always seemed in working with people, adults anyway, it can be hard to put your finger on just why.

The two of them met in Chapel Hill as undergrads. Swain was walking through the parking lot behind the dorm where he was going to borrow notes from a girl in his British History class. He was mildly interested in the girl and he did need the notes. He was walking along, still far from the porch of the dorm, plotting the upcoming conversation. A tennis ball sailed over the tall link fence around the courts next to the parked cars and dropped a hundred feet in front of him. He watched it take one long bounce and then make a hollow thud on the top of a blue Mustang and roll off onto the grass. At the same moment, from the far corner of the tennis courts a girl in cutoffs and a Mozart T-shirt started out of the metal door, jogging, carrying her racket by the throat. Swain watched her breasts shift heavily to the left and then the right under the T-shirt as she trotted across the lot toward him. He looked at her, and then he stepped over the low brick wall into the grass and found the ball.

She was looking under cars, one after the other. He saw her head bob up and then she'd disappear again. "Over here," he said. "Here it is. I've got it."

She looked up and smiled, her hand on the hood of a car.

"Thanks," she said, and met him at the wall. She was still out of breath. The circle of his focus was on her face, a head below his own, but he could feel the rising and falling of her chest like a background rhythm. Dampness had beaded on her upper lip. She squinted against the sun and looked up at him. He wanted to touch that sweat on her lip with his tongue. He put the ball in her hand.

"I'm Julie Kerner," she said.

"Swain Hammond."

"You play tennis?" she asked.

"Sure. I mean, a little."

"If you can keep it out of the parking lot, you're doing better than we are." She took a diagonal step backward, moving toward the pavement, away from Swain. "Got a doubles waiting," she said. "Thanks for the ball." And then she did the extraordinary thing that has become part of the story they repeat to each other about how they met. She reached out with her racket and gave him a light pat on the ass. Almost the way a coach might do it. But not quite. Swain stood on the grass dumbfounded, watching her pause for a slow-moving car and then trot back across the lot. When she got inside the court enclosure, she looked back at him, and waved once with her racket.

"What did you see in me?" he asked her weeks ago, the last time they lay in bed on a Saturday morning and talked about it. It was late enough for the sunlight on the sheets to be hard and yellow and for the rusty chains on the next-door swing set to be shrieking.

"The Marlboro man," Julie said. "Without his hat."

"What else?"

"I don't know how to tell you," she said. "You seemed not simple, even that day. Your eyes were like looking down a well that has smoke in it. Maybe I just like murkiness." She ran a finger down the length of his chest, trailing across a nipple. She said, "I don't know. Maybe I like potential."

Eight days after he first heard "the voice," in the week following his sermon, Swain is turning his car into the church driveway and it happens again: he hears God. His window is open. The car is lurched upward onto the incline of the pavement. The radio is on, but low. The smooth-voiced announcer is reading the Arts Activities, as Swain is easing the car up over the bump into the lot.

Then from the hedge, a few feet from his elbow on the ledge of the car window, the sound emerges. It comes from a specific place deep in the dense greenery that is close enough to touch: a burst, a jumble of phrases, pieces of Scripture. "He that heareth and doeth not...for there is nothing hid...the word is sown on stony ground...why reason ye...seeketh his own glory...he that hath ears...he that hath..." Coming at him like something thrown. It's a nightmare. A horror. A barrage of accusation. Swain stares straight ahead. A hot weight presses into him, just beneath the joining of his ribs. It hurts, pins him to the seat, holds him. He's going to die right here. He puts both hands over the spot where it burns and waits, braced against the floor of the car and the back of the seat, while it eases off, gradually, the way a muscle cramp lets go.

Another car is waiting behind him, easing toward his fender. He has to move...get out of the way. His hands and feet make the car do whatever it does. On the other side of the parking lot, he shuts off the engine. His face is as hot as the plastic car seat. He sits behind the steering wheel and looks across the hoods of cars at the hedge, between the sidewalk and the street. Tear out the hedge—that's what he wants to do. Pull it up with his hands. He wants to kill something.

I don't believe in gods that quote the King James version out of bushes and trees. I *don't* believe in any of this shit that's coming

out of nowhere. I've waited all my life for this? What a fool...
how could I have been such a fool?

He avoids the back parking lot for the rest of the week, leaving
the car around the corner and going in the front entrance. Super-
stition, he tells himself. But then, he thinks, maybe that's what
religion turns out to be anyway.

On Saturday, he arms himself with a big pair of clippers and
goes back to the spot where it happened. It is Clean-Up Day. The
yard is full of people. Swain is trimming the hedge. Each slice
makes a flat clacking sound. The tall sprigs are disappearing, he's
mowing them down. Everywhere he's already been—about eight
feet of hedge—is as level as pavement. Neat as a column of figures. It's the only good thing about being here today. He wanted
to stay home in the air-conditioning and read. Instead, he has to
come back over here and help clean up. He slaps the back of his
leg where a tall weed is tickling him.

Becky Johnstone and one of the little boys are arguing. "You're
not doing your part," she says. "You're just playing. We're supposed to be getting all the trash." She stands, in white sandals and
pink shorts, with her stomach stuck out, her back arched. She's the
oldest. A whiny little tyrant.

Something—small, thrown hard—flies at her. It bounces off
her stomach, hits the ground. "I'm going to tell," she says.

"You do that."

Kids are obnoxious. Probably once a week some jerk asks him
when they're going to have one. He'd have asked for an all-adult
congregation if there were any place in the world he could have
found such a thing.

"Swain." Burton Echols is crossing the grass toward him. Swain
stops, both hands on the clippers. Burton should be plenty cool,
he's wearing almost nothing. Running shorts and flip-flops. He's
carrying a can. "Have you ever used Rustoleum, Swain?"

"Never have." He smells like coconut oil.

"I was just starting to redo the railings on the stairs. I don't
know how much—"

"All I know to tell you is, read the can."

"I tried that."

"I don't know any more than you do."

Burton looks back at the block of instructions on the back of the can, and stands there, reading. Finally, he leaves, walks away, still studying the can.

Swain bends and wipes his forehead with the bottom of his shirt. And a sound starts—like a police whistle, a shrill sound getting wider and wider. He lifts his head and listens for one-half second, the way an animal does at night, and there is silence, and then the sound reaches him again, full force. My God—

He drops the clippers, runs, jumping over the chains across the walkway, ducking under the low limbs of the fir. The brick side of the building moves past him in slow motion. He isn't going to get there. He'll never get there.

They're huddled, bending over. On the ground, emerging from the circle of adult legs, are two small bare legs, feet in checkered tennis shoes. Other children stand back, crying, staring, one with her clenched fists pressed against her face. All of them lit with stage lights. Brilliant lights. Everything is so clear. The feet in tennis shoes don't move.

Now Sam Bagdikian is lifting the child. The circle breaks to let Sam walk, carrying him. Jakey Miles. Patrice's boy. Joe's boy. Swain's stomach rolls inside him. Blood is coming out of Jakey's eyes, pouring out of one of them.

Blood running down the side of his face, blood in his ear, in his hair. It's dripping onto the grass and leaving a trail. Swain's mouth waters hot and it tastes like blood.

"Call an ambulance," he says to a spot where nobody is. He imagines the conversation. Come to 569 Redfern Drive. Westside Presbyterian. Which way is the phone?

"Help me get him in," Sam says. A car is pulling up toward the curb. Fred Ritchie, his face white. Swain takes two long steps ahead of Sam and the boy, and flings open the back door, pulls it back hard against its hinges. Sam lowers himself backward into the seat, edging in the child's head and then his dangling legs. Swain puts his arms under Sam's arms. Everything he sees trembles. Like a projector wavering. He's underwater. It can't be happening.

He looks at the child, his other eye, the one that didn't really bleed, closed now except for a rim of blood-reddened white. Everything goes out of focus except that eye. Long straight black eyelashes. "Okay," Sam says. He's in the car, gripping the boy. Dear God. Sam is staring straight ahead. "Come on," he says. "For Christ's sake, shut the door."

Swain shuts it, runs to the front and gets in.

"Six blocks," Fred says. The light is with them on the first intersection. Fred is breathing with his mouth open. Swain turns back to Sam.

"What happened?"

"Gravel hit him," Sam says. The car goes over a bump. Sam cushions Jakey against the jolt with his arms. Sam is bent over Jakey's face, which Swain doesn't want to see. The light is shining on the side of Sam's head and he's rocking the boy, back and forth, back and forth. A low crying sound is going to start coming out of them. Before it even happens, Swain can hear it in the car engine. A beating drum. Oh God. Not this. Oh God. Not this.

"Gravel flew off the back of a truck. Rocks hit the sidewalk near me. The truck was going way too fast." Sam's voice shakes. "I was supposed to be watching him. I brought him over here with my two."

He talks toward the side of Jakey's head. Swain looks once at the brown crust of blood on Jakey's ear and turns away. Sam stays bent over him. He keeps looking and looking. How can he do it? Why wasn't he watching the kid anyway? . . . letting this happen.

The car is turning. Pink crape myrtles. Petals mashed in the street. Sam's breath squeaks. Every breath as it comes out. There's a lightness in Swain's head just behind his forehead. He's going to vomit. When his parents were killed, he stared at their faces. He walked from one casket to the other, until Julie made him stop. She pulled him away.

The car pulls into the emergency entrance. It's still rolling. He gets out. Through the swinging glass doors, into the blast of air-conditioning. "Stretcher," he yells. People waiting in the rows of plastic seats look up. A little boy crawling across two seats turns his head toward Swain. "We need a doctor. A child is hurt bad." The nurse at the desk leans to speak into the intercom. He wants to go back there in the back himself and find somebody and get them out here. Swain looks behind her at the dark green curtain that hides the corridor, where they'll take Jakey. Someone has just gone through it. It's still waving.

Jakey is wheeled in and away. Swain stands, dazed, in the doorway, then sees a pay phone: has anybody called them?

Sam finds him where he stands at the phone, his hand still gripping the receiver in its cradle. They've already left. He could squeeze it into two pieces, the receiver, without even noticing it.

"Did you get them?" Sam says.

"They're on the way."

Swain touches the dried blood that has stiffened on Sam's shirt. Jakey. Eating a charred-black hotdog at the Memorial Day picnic, stuffing his mouth too full, Patrice saying, "Wipe the mustard off your chin." Nine years old, or maybe ten.

"Any word from the back about the boy?"

"Nothing. They've only had him back there five minutes, Swain." He adds, "Fred went back to the church to look after my kids." Sam looks at the row of orange chairs, at the tiles on the floor. Without looking up, he leans slowly toward Swain. Their two chests meet. Their arms descend around each other. Swain leans the side of his face against Sam's hard bald head. Sam is crying, leaning against him. His shoulders and back shake without any sound at all. Swain watches himself and Sam from somewhere else—two tiny little figures so far away you can't even tell who they are.

Sam pulls away, rubs both hands across his face. "What am I going to say to them? What am I going to do? I'm responsible for this. I let it happen." His face contorts as if somebody else is twisting it. "I can't stand it. If that boy—"

"I'm going to say a prayer," Swain says. When he speaks it feels as though somebody is pressing down on his throat. "Sam, will you pray with me?"

Sam's eyes shut. He steadies himself against the wall. "Keep his eye," Sam says. Tears are rolling into the lines of his face. "Let that boy have his eye."

"Father," Swain says, staring past Sam . . . people waiting in the chairs. "Father, help us. Give us the strength we need now, that we will need in the days to come." Like a recording. "Help Jakey Miles and the doctors who attend him. Guide their hands. Keep us from wounding ourselves with guilt. Help us to live with what is happening, now and—"

Beyond Sam's shoulder, coming in the door, there they are. Of all the people in the world for this to happen to . . . Patrice in a bathing suit, a shirt, running now, crying . . . he wants to pick her up and carry her straight out of here, so she won't have to see it. He glances at Joe and feels the fear start to loosen his gut. He needs to find a bathroom . . . Joe could do anything . . . if the boy . . . Joe'll tear the hospital down, he'll kill everybody in sight.

"Amen," he says.

Sam says, "Amen."

"Patrice." She sees him. He steps around Sam, who slowly turns.

"Where is he?" she says. "Where have they got him?" Joe, beside her, holds on to her upper arm with a grip that has turned his hand, her arm white.

"How bad?" Joe says. His eyes are shiny black, his face is narrowed down around them.

Sam is shaking his head back and forth slowly, looking at Patrice, then at Joe. "I'm as sorry as a man can be." Swain's voice is trying to get started, to say he doesn't know.

Patrice has spotted the desk, the nurse. She runs, Joe behind her, her sandals slapping at her heels. "Where is Jake Miles? I am his mother. Where is he?" Swain hears the words across the room: I am his mother. Her child lying in there with the blood all over him.

"Come with me." The nurse leads them through the green curtain. They are gone for seconds. The nurse reappears.

"Should we go?" Sam says.

Swain walks over to the desk. The nurse's tag says Hinton. "Mrs. Hinton, I am the Mileses' pastor."

"Yes," she says, and stands again. "I'll take you to one of the family rooms. You'll have more privacy there." A telephone line is blinking on the panel on her desk. "If you will wait just a moment..." she says.

Privacy. He's dead. She's telling them the boy is dead. He looks back at Sam. They stand and wait. Sam drifts toward the chairs, sinks down into one, puts his head in his hands. Swain starts to pace. Waiting for God to talk. To say something—anything. Now, for Christ's sake.

Swain rubs his eyes. First God and now this. Only two weeks ago everything was normal. He walks along the wall, hitting it with the back of his fist. What's keeping the nurse? She said just a moment. She must know—

She puts the phone down. "Come on," she says, motioning to him. Swain puts his hand on Sam's shoulder. Sam gets slowly to his feet. She leads them down a corridor, down another corridor, past a bare white-sheeted gurney with straps lying loose on the top, past a canteen. People are in their talking, getting drinks from a machine. Swain hears the clunk of a drink can falling down the chute. The nurse's feet are silent. Those thick-soled white shoes. She doesn't make a sound. They go deeper and deeper into this labyrinth. The loudspeaker calls doctors from a box high on the wall. The box is ahead of him, now it's behind him, still calling. They keep walking. The nurse is leading them in circles. She's never going to get them there.

She pauses then, puts her ear close to the crack of a closed door.

As she slowly turns the knob, he hears Patrice's voice. The nurse steps back to let them enter. Patrice is on the sofa, holding her elbows, hugging herself. Joe is standing.

"Is he—how is he?" Swain says.

Joe turns to face him. "Nobody told you?" he said. His face is like that of a criminal who's just been caught, just being led to the patrol car. The handcuffs are still cold on his wrists. Joe's nostrils flare; his beard is a dark stubble. "He's blind."

Sam's breath makes a noise like the sharp cut of a saw. Swain reaches a hand toward him, without looking away from Joe's eyes. They look yellow in the whites, the skin under his eyes has turned yellow.

"Blind? Both eyes?"

"It's not true," Sam says.

"Yes," Joe says, looking now at Sam. "Pieces of gravel hit both his eyes. One big one. Lots of little ones. Like sharp little pieces of pepper, that's what the doctor said. The damage is so bad that they already know. There's no question."

Patrice is crying. Her head is bent over, her shoulder blades draw together and let go. She rocks back and forth. Swain gets on his knees in front of her, puts his hands around the twisting knot of her hands. He feels the stiff carpet against his bare knees. His eyes blur with tears. Oh, Christ, Patrice...He holds on to her hands and steadies himself.

She looks at him: Swain, his face so close. He smells. They were working out there. If Jakey had gone with us to the pool...She lets herself fall slowly toward Swain, presses her face against his T-shirt. They won't even let me be with my child. She wants to say something: "make it stop." Nothing will come out. Her mouth opens wider and wider as if she's going to scream, but there's no sound. They are taking Jakey's eyes.

Swain puts a hand on her hair. He can't say anything that will help this. An ache has spread through all his bones.

She feels the hand softly brushing back her hair.

Swain hears Sam's voice behind him. "Are you sure?"

Joe says, "We had to sign. He's going to lose his eyes."

"Jesus."

"What happened?" Joe's voice is hoarse. "How did this happen?"

Swain gets to his feet. Sam moves away from the door and walks over to stand in front of Joe. His hands hang loose by his sides. "We were picking up trash from the front yard. Litter from people passing by. The last time I saw, Jakey was trying to get something out of the curb gutter. He was on his knees, leaning over poking in there with a stick. He was right on the street." His voice quavers, gets high and breaks. "I should have stopped him. I swear to God, Joe, I wish it had been me."

"So do I."

Patrice is looking up now. "Who told him he could go put his face down in the street?" she says. "What were you thinking?" Her face was wet. Each breath she takes is a sharp rise and fall. "Who let him do such a crazy dangerous thing as that?" She looks at Swain, then at Sam. "Did you tell him he could?"

"I told them all to pick up whatever trash they saw," Sam says. "I looked over there once and saw he was doing that, but I didn't stop him. It's the wrongest thing I ever did in my life. Not to stop him. I don't know how to tell you . . ."

Joe turns away from him, to Swain. He walks over to stand close. Joe says, "Where were you?"

"In the back. I was working in the backyard. I heard . . . and I ran to the front."

Joe's eyes are glinting, inches from Swain's. "You're just as responsible. You got those kids out there to pick up trash. I hope your yard is goddamn clean." He hits Swain's chest with the flats of his open hands, pushing him. "You did this."

Swain braces himself, one foot behind him.

"It was you, Hammond." He's coming too close. "It was you."

Swain stands his ground, watching him. "Joe," he says, "don't do this. Joe, Patrice needs you."

"You don't know what my wife needs. You don't know shit." He slams both hands into Swain's chest.

Swain stumbles back against the wall.

Joe is saying, "Pray for my boy, why don't you do that, now that you've destroyed his whole life." He folds his hands. In a simpering voice, he mimics Swain: "Dear Father Almighty in Heaven..."

Swain lunges, his fist out, his arm straight. His knuckles against the side of Joe's face. One hard crack like a bat. Yeah, this is how it feels: his fist smashing down into that face. Joe's head turning, his body arcing back.

Then everything freezes. My God. All the sound is gone. Swain stands motionless. If I don't move, everything will stay stopped. We'll stand here exactly where we are forever.

A nurse flings open the door. The motion starts again, the noise. Sam shouting something. Now Sam is grabbing his arms. Patrice reaching for Joe, Joe starting to sit up.

Patrice looks up once at Swain. Did he do that? Swain?

Then she understands: the whole world has gone crazy. Nothing will ever be right again.

Swain, with Sam hanging on to him, looks at Joe. I hit him....
He shakes himself loose from Sam and looks around the room—ashtray, sofa, cold blue light. Patrice, staring at me. Joe staring. Like I'm some kind of wild man. He pulls away from Sam. He rubs his knuckles. He sees himself in huge heavy boxing gloves, the fight over, his arms raised in victory, the crowd coming up into the ring. I hit Joe Miles. He cradles his balled-up fist against his chest.

THREE

Swain is sitting on the closed top of the toilet. It was 4:11 on the digital clock when he got out of bed. He sat up in the dark and looked at the green lights on the dial and thought, He has been blind for twelve hours.

Julie, wrapped in a cotton robe, balances on the edge of the bathtub, her knees almost touching his. She rubs her forehead with the tips of her fingers.

"I think you need to get some sleep," she says.

"I can't. I can't stand to lie there anymore. My legs twitch, they won't lie still." The toilet cover feels fuzzy and itchy against his balls and the backs of his thighs. The maddening tingle is running through his legs again, like something electric. He shakes them. Stop it, he tells them. He stares at his own legs as though he has never seen them before, long and skinny, calf bones like pieces of split wood. My toenails need cutting, he thinks.

"When I lie down, I hear the kid. Screaming. I never could have believed there was a sound like that. You can't imagine it." He lets his head hang. He stares at the floor between his feet. His stomach is queasy. "Sam's probably drunk by now."

Julie nods. "Probably."

One of the faucets drips. One drip. "Julie, I hit Joe Miles."

"So you've told me." She sighs. Her eyes are bloodshot. She looks terrible.

"You don't believe me?"

"Of course I believe you."

"Why did I do that?"

"Swain, I have no idea." He acts like I have the answers for everything, she thinks. But there's no answer for this. She can't even picture it in her mind: Swain actually hitting a man.

Swain puts his head down in his hands.

"I'm surprised he didn't hit you back."

"When he finally stood up, I thought he would. He stared at me and then he grabbed my wrist and squeezed it until I thought the bones were going to break, and he said, 'Hammond, get out of here.' His voice was so hoarse. Sam came out with me. Then I called you. Julie, what am I going to do?"

"I don't know, Swain. I used to always know what you were going to do, but I don't anymore."

He rubs his eyes. He thinks, I've wrecked my whole life. In one instant. He says, "I can't make any sense. I have to go to bed. I have to preach in the morning." He can picture what it's going to be like. People are probably gathering at the church this very minute, to bar the way, keep him from even getting in the door. He slowly gets to his feet. Julie doesn't move.

"I'll be in in a minute," she says.

When he's gone, she slides off the edge of the bathtub onto the floor. She leans back against the cold side of the tub. He doesn't seem crazy, he seems like his regular worried self, not somebody who's losing his mind. She keeps trying to picture it, him hitting somebody—what did his face look like? She's never seen a look on his face that would go with doing something like that.

What am I going to say to people when they come up to me after the service tomorrow? Janet Epworth or maybe DeWitt Chambers, smiling and friendly, pumping me to find out if it's true. Did Swain really do it? Did the voice of God tell Swain to do it? Hiding a snicker. Church people do seem to love trouble.

This may be the end of church for us. But what is Swain going to do? He has to be a minister, there's nothing else he was ever meant to do. What was he thinking? She lies down on the floor next to the tub.

From the bedroom, Swain calls, "Julie, are you coming back to bed?"

She stares at the ceiling. Lying in there calling me, like it's something I can come in there and fix. I can't fix this. You've gotten yourself into something now that's way beyond me. She gets up from the floor slowly and goes back in and gets into bed.

There was another time in Swain Hammond's life when two enormous events happened at once: when he lost both his parents at the same time. It was in the fall of his second year at Yale. Paul and Vivian Hammond were killed in the crash of a small private plane. They were flying with friends to the Coast for a seafood dinner, just for the evening, so Swain was later told. It was his mother's birthday, the sort of occasion on which the two of them behaved for all the world like a happy couple, which they were not.

A half hour before he tried the number for the last time, the plane went down over Bogue Sound. Swain has an image in his head, like a piece of video, of an airplane upended, spiraling down through the dark toward the water. The film stops there. It picks up again with the Coast Guard cutter, points of light on its bow and its stern, as it heads out toward the X on the water where the plane hit. The pilot and the four passengers were drowned. Their bodies were taken from the plane that night. Swain flew home in the morning on a commercial flight. He sat in a window seat and saw the Chesapeake sliding slowly past below him, under the wing of the jet. So incredible that they died together...

There were a lot of people there by the time he got home. Aunts and cousins he hardly knew. People from the faculty. Even Walt Emrich, his mother's lover, who shook Swain's hand and left quickly. But it was as if they were all separated from him by glass. He was in a glass box, a recording studio, maybe. Julie was there too. But he couldn't quite hear what any of the rest of them were saying. And there were so many. People kept coming.

He remembers sitting in an armchair in the living room, near the piano. He would stand up when people came in, he would stand again when they left. Otherwise, it was as if he sat apart from them, while images of his father, then his mother assailed him. He pictured them in academic processions—that was the memory that kept coming back—graduations, when he was very young. His mother's department would come in first. He would watch her in that long line of people walking slowly in their black gowns with the colors that showed what school they represented. They looked important. He would follow his mother with his eyes until she was in her chair and all he could see was the black square of her mortarboard. Then his father started the slow trip down the aisle. . . . He wanted to tell the people sitting near him that those two down there were his. He was proud. Sitting high up in the bleachers, he could see them both and they didn't see him.

If it had only been one of them, there would have been some relenting of his grief. But this way, with both gone, when the loss of one drifted from his mind, the loss of the other would hit him harder. As if two people were beating him—while one landed a blow, the other was drawing back to strike again.

In his first few months back at school, he didn't sleep well. But in less than a year, it had all washed away. It was like a place on his skin with no sensation, a small irregular patch at a spot where it didn't really matter. He had never in his life been the kind of person who would dwell on the past.

And now he is hearing voices. Each time another one of those episodes has occurred, his own being and everything around him has become less reliable, less familiar. It's almost as if a knife were to come unexpectedly through a painted panel of a stage set. Straight out of a puff of cloud or a bowl of flowers or the tieback of a drape. Worse, he cannot trust himself. He hit Joe Miles. And he liked it . . . it felt good; that is the worst of it. And then there is Jakey . . . dear God . . .

Hymn 364. "Come, Ye Disconsolate." From his pew behind the pulpit, he hears the rumble of the congregation rising to its feet. The organ notes buzz in his empty stomach. Swain stands with his hymnbook in front of him. Then the singing comes toward him like wind. If they would keep on singing...I have to first get through this, then find Miles and apologize.

Four stanzas. They sink back into the pews. He steps forward to the steps of the chancel, stands in the center before them. "Many of you have probably heard about the accident in our front yard here yesterday afternoon. I must tell you, those who do not know, that Jakey Miles, the son of Joe and Patrice Miles, was hit yesterday by pebbles that fell from a passing truck. Jakey is blind."

The whispered "oh" from row after row of them falls on Swain. It's like standing in front of the ocean. One sound piles on another, it's one deep constant moan.

"I tell you this with grief heavy in my own heart. The Miles family, everyone touched by this tragedy, needs our prayers. They need the strength to face this loss. Jakey will need your acceptance and your love." How can I stand up here and say this after what I did?

Near the front, old Mrs. Eastwood is crying, little muffled gasps into a handkerchief. Swain's lips are dry and hot. There's no rail to hold onto here. Ghosts of Jakey are in the air. The sanctuary is filling with a fog that is nothing but moments of Jakey. Running through the hall of the Sunday school, knocking into people, chasing another kid. Doing cannonballs off the end of the boat dock. Balancing hymnbooks on the balcony rail.

"I would like to ask the children of the congregation to come forward and sit with me here. Today we're going to begin with Children's Church."

Near the front, Melissa Haddonsfield is eyeing him from behind her mother's arm. A boy he always confuses with another boy is coming slowly forward, dragging one hand against the side of each pew. A few more follow tentatively. Their parents are making them. Maybe this was not a good idea.

"No way." From the middle of the center aisle, a boy shouts. Swain's heart races. "What do you mean—blind?" It's Bryan—Jakey's friend. Yelling down the long aisle at Swain. "I don't believe you. It isn't true." He clenches his fists at his sides and he leans forward to scream at Swain: "He isn't either blind. You're lying. It isn't true." The other children are stopped wherever they stand, stepping to the side to get out of the way.

Swain starts down the chancel steps toward Bryan. Bryan's mother is struggling to get out of the pew to get to him. Maybe it will be over when he gets there. "Bryan," she says. "Bryan." She runs toward him and reaches him just as Swain does. Bryan turns on his mother. "You didn't tell me."

"Bryan, I didn't know." She looks up at Swain, holding Bryan against her. He breaks away, turns to Swain.

"How do you know?" Bryan says. "Are you sure?"

"I was there when it happened, Bryan. I'm sure."

"I'm going over to his house."

"Bryan," Swain says, to the boy's turned back, to the whole congregation. "Bryan, Jakey will want to be with you as soon as he can. He'll want to talk with you and be friends like always. But he won't be feeling good enough to have company today." If I can just keep moving, keep talking. Not stop here in front of all of them at the mercy of this kid . . .

He reaches over and touches Bryan's shoulder. "Come on," he says. "All of the children," looking at one and then another standing frozen, dispersed along the aisle. "Come sit with me." He leads them back to the chancel steps, where they sit as they always do for the children's sermon.

"Let's talk about things we can do to help Jakey. To show him our love and help him cheer up." Bryan has moved a little away from the group, thrown himself down across the three steps. Propped on one arm, he is pulling at the stiff red bristle of the carpet, scraping it with his fingers as if he's trying to pick it bare.

Silence. Nobody says anything. "I'm sure some of you have some ideas."

More silence. Melissa says, "We could make a huge card for him and everybody write their name on it."

Bryan lets out a contemptuous hiss.

"I made a wooden belt buckle in Brownies," says a long-legged girl too tall to be up there.

"I made a potholder out of three colors," says another one.

"We could draw a big picture on the card," Melissa says. "A picture of—" She drags it out while she tries to think of something.

"He can't see pictures," Bryan says, sitting up and leaning toward her. "He can't see anything. Get that through your dumb head, if you can."

"Bryan," his mother's voice comes from the back.

Bryan's face is scarlet. Swain says, "This is a very hard time for everybody who loves Jakey. Bryan, maybe I made a mistake in asking that you stay here. Maybe you'd like to be alone with your mom and dad now." The kid's face is mashed into wrinkles, but he doesn't cry, there are no tears, he's not making a sound. He nods and gets up. Swain reaches toward him to put a hand on his shoulder, but Bryan is gone. Swain waves his black-robed arm through the air instead, as if he were shooing Bryan away. Should I get up and walk with him? But he's almost back to his mother— she's gathering up her pocketbook, coming to meet him. There's a ripple of whispers around the two of them, the rest wait in silence for them to be gone.

Swain is down to half a dozen kids who want to talk about what they made in Brownies. He wanted to look at Julie. At least she came. She hasn't left me yet. The kids are looking at him, except for the ones that are picking at their fingers or staring at their shoes. Pradeesh is sitting at the edge of the circle, a little apart. He's wearing shorts and his skinny brown knees are collapsed against each other the way he's huddled on the step. He sits as if

he wishes he didn't exist. Swain looks at the dull gloss of his black eyes.

"Pradeesh, do you have any ideas about things we can do to help Jakey?"

The kid shrugs, doesn't answer. A hand is waving frantically at the edge of his vision on his other side. He hears: "I know. I know," and ignores it. "Pradeesh," he says. Silence.

"Maybe you don't know him very well. He's a little older than you."

Pradeesh looks back in the direction of his parents who forced him to come up here. He looks at Swain as if there's no reprieve, he may as well say it. "He chased me. He pushed me off the steps."

Swain hesitates. "You were probably very mad at him," he says. "But that didn't make this happen to him. It was an accident. It had nothing to do with anything you thought or did."

Pradeesh stares at Swain with the same dull stare. Then he folds himself into a little knot, his elbows pulled up close to his sides, his head bent over his crouched knees. Closed for business. Try something else, Dr. Hammond.

Swain looks around at the rest of them. The hand that was waving has stopped. They watch him, all their big eyes, waiting. I hate these kids, I never knew until this minute how much. If I sit here any longer, I'm going to explode.

Then Melissa looks back at her mother. Jimmy McDougall starts to slide slowly, an inch at the time along the carpet, down one step, while Swain watches. The rush is starting. They're going to leave me sitting here by myself.

Swain speaks to the congregation: "We are all suffering today, thinking of our own times with Jakey Miles. Bryan and Pradeesh are not alone. We are all of us joined in our different ways of being sad, in our struggles to understand how such a thing can happen." Jimmy has made it down the stairs, sliding his butt along the carpet. "Boys and girls, as you go back to your seats now"— five kids light out from the steps, trooping down the center aisle, down the side aisle, a stream of refugees—"remember that you can help make it easier for Jakey, by being his friends as you have always been." Swain stands and looks out at the rows of faces in front of him, the adult faces. His eyes slide over the spaces in the pews where just a top of a head is showing. The little shits. They'd better hide.

"Keep with you the words of Jesus: 'I will not leave you comfortless; I will come to you.' So much of God's comfort is that which we give each other." I hauled off and hit the man. How many of them sitting here already know that? He looks around for Miss Bateman. Can't she tell to start? A few seconds pass. Here it comes, saving him once again, the first clang and moan of the organ.

W hen Swain and Julie came to visit the church, at the last round of talks before he was invited to take the pastorate, he had one long session with Scott Friedman. Scott is dead now, has been for some years, but he's one of those people that everybody in the church goes on talking about and quoting. "You know what old Mr. Scott would have to say about that. . . ." That sort of thing.

Scott and Swain sat back in the church parlor in a couple of the big wing chairs. Swain had on a dark suit and his most preacherly-looking lace-up shoes. He was about five pounds thinner then, but otherwise the same.

Scott, who was pushing seventy at the time, said, "Son, did you ever try to figure out exactly what it was that made you choose the ministry?"

Where to start? In the small damp chapel where his mother first took him to services? "All my life," Swain said, "something has kept me company when I'm alone. I've spent a lot of time alone. I was a pretty lonesome little boy." He hesitated. "I can't sit here and tell you that I have a mission to fulfill. I wish I could. All I know is that my earliest longings led me to look for something big and magical. Over the years, my search, my beliefs have grown more sophisticated, but still—loneliness and magic, Mr. Friedman. That's all I can tell you."

Scott looked at him carefully. "And do you plan to have a family yourself?" Moving down his mental list of questions.

"That's something I haven't decided. My wife and I have certainly done a lot of talking and a lot of praying about it. . . ." He paused. "It's not an easy decision for me. I don't want to, and yet I do." He smiled an apology.

Scott kept looking at him and didn't say anything. He sat with his stiff hands on his knees and a hard, measuring look in his eyes. He could turn off his famous warmth in a second.

"I was an only child," Swain said. "I have always been more comfortable with adults."

"Kids can be a handful. They sure can." Scott rubbed his fingers across his chin. "You'd be a good model for the young people here. In a lot of ways. Looking like a basketball player the way you do. They'd pay attention to you."

Once again the way he looks is all Swain can offer. . . .

"How do you feel about working with young people?"

"It's not my strong point. I do reasonably well, with a lot of support from others. My philosophy is, in any of the facets of my ministry, to involve others as much as possible." He smiled. "That's the one where I need help the most."

"It's ironic," Scott said. "I've decided to put in my two cents' worth that we ask you to come here. Even though you worry me a little. You seem a trifle cold, you know. Forgive me if I go too far—but oddly enough, that may serve you well with this congregation." He stopped and stared at Swain's face until Swain shifted in his chair and recrossed his legs. "I didn't used to think that way. I thought the next one we brought in ought to be the sort that would stir these people up, come at them from a new direction. I don't mean guitars in the chancel at eleven o'clock, you understand. We do enough of that kind of novelty—I'm sure we're the world's only Presbyterian congregation that goes to the altar for

Communion. But I'm not talking about that kind of 'new.' I'm talking about someone taking hold here who's not quite so careful, not such a thinker.

"The thing is, you'll fit right in at Westside. Most of these people are a lot like you. Not every one of course, and as soon as I say what's typical, I can't think of a thing but exceptions. But on the whole, you're like them, and yet you've got something of your own to bring here. I can see that. So, both those things considered, I think you'll turn out well."

"You say I'm like them," Swain said, "as if you were not. And yet you've been a member of this church for many many years."

"And you're asking me why," Scott said. "Is that it?"

He waits. Swain nods.

"Well," Scott said, "I started coming here by chance, and out of convenience, I suppose, and I stuck. That's all I can tell you. I've got a sister I don't see eye to eye with either, but we keep on arguing." He slid forward in his chair and Swain moved to the edge of his. Scott paused for one more thing. "It crosses my mind," he said, "that if you went to another church, where they might shake you up a little—in the long run, that might be a lot better for you. Of course, that's not up to me to decide."

Swain pulls into the hospital visitors lot, reaches for the ticket that the machine spits out. The board lifts in front of him and he drives in. This place is like his own driveway, he comes here so much. The windsock on the helicopter landing pad rises and wavers. Yesterday, bringing Jakey here, he didn't look to see if anything had landed.

This happening to Joe and Patrice's child—it has made him an amateur. Last week, sitting beside Madge Newsome's bed, he knew what he was doing. He sat there holding her hand, feeling the huge soft veins beneath the tips of his fingers. Her bony cancer-starved hand. While her daughter Billie hovered nearby, helping Mama talk, reminding her what she wanted to say. Mama was on a lot of drugs. Still he felt the connection when his eyes met hers. I'm not always the disaster I was yesterday, and this morning. I'm not always this bad. But he can't understand what is happening.

He takes the elevator and gets out on the eighth floor. The hall ahead of him is empty except for a nurse. It doesn't feel like Sunday. On this floor it never feels like any day at all. He tiptoes, leaning to check the numbers of the rooms.

He stops in front of one of the unlighted alcoves with sofas. Somebody's asleep. He looks closer. It's her, wrapped in a raincoat, propped so she's facing across the hall toward the door. Her feet lie bare on the cushion nearest him. She came in a bathing suit. Surely someone brought her something. He would have, if he'd known.

Once when he dreamed about her, he told Julie about it at breakfast. Julie never seemed to feel jealous about such things. He had dreamed that night that Patrice Miles was watching him from the car up ahead of him in her rearview mirror. Everywhere he went, there she was, not following him, always ahead. Brown eyes and black eyebrows leading him. "It's true she's always had her eye on you," Julie said. Swain didn't think so. "No," he said. "I'm the one with the heavy crush." Julie shook her head. "Not just you," she said. "Patrice is interested."

Asleep, exhausted, she looks like a kid. It doesn't show on her face, what has happened. He wants to tuck something around her bare legs and her feet. He wants to put his hand close to her lips and feel it covered and warmed by her breath. Since they were in high school, he has lusted for her, and always she has been out of reach. He watches her shoulder rise and fall with her breath. He takes his coat off and lays it gently over her. Quietly, he steps back from the opening of the alcove. She needs to sleep. Her waking, whenever it happens, will be the worst one in her life.

Now he has to find Joe. He turns back toward the boy's room, tiptoes across the hall, puts his head into the open crack of the door. There. The boy. Unconscious, his face cut in half by the eye patches. Nothing showing but the tip of his nose and the familiar recognizable shape of his mouth. That's Jakey's mouth, his dark full lips that look smooth the way a kid's do. He was always yelling, mouthing off at somebody. He lies so still. Swain feels his own heartbeat through his whole body. There's no turning away from it. This is Jakey.

His eyes cross the white room—so full of light...not Joe... Bryan. Standing against the side wall with his back turned, still in his Sunday church clothes, his shirttail hanging loose. His face is turned so Swain can see his profile. He has no idea that Swain is here. He is as motionless as the chair, he doesn't blink, his face as still as Jakey's.

Bryan stares at the boy in the bed, thinks, They put all those tubes in him. Why did they do that? I'm going to get sick at my stomach. He better never wake up. He might as well be dead. My only best friend I ever had. He can forget ever doing anything in his whole life. Ever again. Those bandages they put on him and nothing underneath but holes.

I've got to get out of here.

He turns toward the door, ready to run as fast as he can. He forces himself to tiptoe, being very very quiet. He looks up, and jumps. Dr. Hammond. Standing there staring at him. Oh no.

Dr. Hammond is blocking the whole door. Bryan looks back at the window, the bathroom door. Jakey is going to wake up for sure. What am I supposed to do now?

Swain backs into the hall to let him slip out. The kid tiptoes across the room, shutting the door softly behind him. The two of them walk down the hall, Bryan as if he's in some kind of danger.

In front of the nursing station, near the elevator, Swain turns to face him. Bryan stops, but he doesn't meet Swain's eyes. He keeps his gaze at the level of Swain's belt buckle. The boy looks as though he's waiting to be hit. Maybe he heard about Joe. Maybe the word has already spread.

"How did you get here, Bryan? Who brought you?"

"Rode my bike."

"Where is it?"

"Out front, next to one of those benches."

"Let's go get it and put it in the back of my car and go somewhere. There's a place I want to show you. It will give us a chance to talk. If you want to."

Bryan lifts his shoulders, lets them fall. "Okay," he says, turning to walk next to Swain like a resigned prisoner.

"Good," Swain says, putting his hand for a moment on the boy's back. He pauses to leave a note for the Mileses at the nursing station. He turns back to Bryan and says, "I need somebody to be with this afternoon myself." The last thing I expected was this, Swain thinks. But I can't leave the boy here. I have to at least get him home.

They wait in front of the elevator, neither of them speaking. Bryan shifts from one foot to the other. Swain's head feels light, he needs to go home and sleep. Still no Joe.

An old couple comes up beside them, the man in a robe and soft-bottomed slippers that shuffle. Jakey was old enough not to have to be watched every minute. There's no way Patrice or Joe, or Sam either, could have known. . . .

Swain's parents used to argue over who was going to look after him.

". . . Absolutely impossible, Vivian." They were standing in the kitchen. His dad was wrapping his muffler around his neck and buttoning his big overcoat.

"Then take him with you."

"You must be joking."

"Paul, you figure out something, whatever suits you. I'm leaving here at seven-thirty. You said you would be here tonight. I'm tired of being the one to find somebody to sit."

He didn't say anything. He looked at her hard while he finished buttoning his coat. Swain was standing near the door to the kitchen—he had just come down the stairs.

"I can stay by myself."

She turned away from them both. "You're too young, Swain," she said, with her back still turned. His father didn't seem to have noticed him.

"All right," his dad said. "Very well then." He turned to Swain. "Get your coat on."

He got his jacket and they drove over to the campus and went to a conference room, where seven or eight people were waiting for his dad. "My son, Swain," he said to them when he came in. "I apologize for this."

"Hi there, Swain," one of them said to him. "You going to help us find a new department head?"

Swain looked at the man and then up at his father.

"He's growing fast," the man said. "You're going to have a grown-up boy in no time."

"One wonders," his father said, sitting down at the table. He motioned Swain over to a chair near the wall. Swain went over and sat down, stared at a picture on the wall across from him. If he didn't look at them, they might not notice him.

"He could go play in my office next door," somebody said.

His dad shook his head. He smiled, as if he'd found the perfect revenge. "I promised his mother I would keep an eye on him."

"Dr. Hammond," Bryan says.

"Yes. Okay. Fine." The man in the robe is holding the elevator. Swain makes himself wake up and pay attention. He punches the elevator button for the lobby. He gets the car out of the parking lot. He drives slowly, looking for a turnoff that's hard to see.

It's a small creek, a branch. If it has a name, Swain doesn't know it. He found it one afternoon when he turned off onto a gravel road that he'd noticed but never taken. He was trying to get out of sight of the hospital that day. Just a few minutes by himself, after Millie Freeman's wreck.

The gravel road turns into two yellow ruts that bounce them every few feet. The car lurches. Swain's head brushes the ceiling.

"Jeez," Bryan says. "Where are we?"

"I don't know. A piece of woods. Do you like to play in the

woods? You and Jakey, is that something you like to do?"

Bryan shrugs. "Not much," he says.

"What do you like to do?"

"You know. Hack around with his mom's computer. Stuff like that."

"And riding bikes?"

"I guess."

The car pulls into an open space, next to the creek. Swain pauses and looks at it for a moment before he gets out. There's a place you could drag a little flat-bottomed boat across to the narrow strip of water. Get in a boat and float away from here, this could be the back door to the world, where I make my escape. Bryan and me, if Bryan would go. What a joke: me running off with a kid.

He looks again. Nobody has dragged any boats across here in a while. The weeds are tall. The way is blocked by the split-off half of a tree.

The two of them get out of the car, and the slam of the car doors keeps on ringing in the open air. Bryan goes ahead, wading through the tall grass toward the fallen tree.

He grabs hold of the first branch, walks his legs up the trunk, and flips over onto the limb.

"Don't go much farther," Swain says. "I'm afraid it won't hold you. It's dead. It could break."

He watches Bryan walking higher on the slanting trunk, steadying himself on one branch after another. A quiver runs through his gut, like an elevator dropping. The kid's going to fall and break his neck. "Come down. Now." Bryan hears the change of tone and looks back. He stops, but he doesn't start down. "Move," Swain says.

Slowly, Bryan starts to pick his way backward. He drops the last few feet, and stands in front of Swain, his hands on his hips, sullen. His eyes are squinted a little against the sun that is behind Swain's head. He looks disgusted. "This is about what I figured you'd do," is what that look says.

"I got worried all of a sudden," Swain says. "I'm just jumpy after all that has happened."

Bryan sighs heavily. "Okay," he says. He looks around. "Can we walk out on those rocks? I'll be careful."

"Good idea." They break through the brush and get down to the edge of the creek, where rocks are scattered in an uneven bridge. Swain takes two long steps out to the biggest one, a flat shelf with puddles standing in the sun. The rock looks dark, it's not really dry anywhere. He picks a place and sits, and feels the dampness seeping through the seat of his pants. Bryan keeps going, stepping from rock to rock. He stops, straddling the two-foot break where the water runs fastest. Swain stares into the creek, watches the steady pulling of the stream against the underwater grass.

"There," Bryan says, pointing. "A fish." He teeters and catches himself. "Smallmouth bass. That's what it was. Couldn't be anything else."

"Missed him," Swain says.

"You have to look fast." He jumps to another bigger rock and sits down, takes off his shoes and puts his feet down in the water, swishes them back and forth. Swain watches as the memory of Jakey comes back over him. His face, so much in motion a minute ago, becomes a mask. Bryan sees he's being watched and looks away.

They sit in silence. Bryan pulls at a blue patch of lichen on the rock, tears it loose and throws it onto the water. It floats away. Swain closes his eyes.

"I already tried that," Bryan says.

"What?"

"Shutting my eyes so I couldn't see anything, to see what it was like. I did it in church this morning, while you were talking, sitting up there with that bunch of doodoos."

"What was it like?"

"Jakey's not going to be able to do anything. Nothing. I mean, for him, there is zero."

"His life will be very very different. There are things he won't be able to do. There will be a lot of things he still can."

"Like sit in a chair. That's about all. He can't go back to school. Not even go to school. How can he, if he can't see? I can tell you right now what's going to happen. He's going to be a zero, and nobody will even know what to say when they're around him. As soon as I saw him lying there, I knew that. It was scary. I didn't want to move, he might wake up and I would have to say something."

"What would you want somebody to say to you?"

"Nothing. I'd wish I was dead." He kicks one foot down in the water, sending a splash raining back down on himself. "It's not fair."

"It's not fair, Bryan. It's terribly unfair."

"Then do something."

"There's nothing—"

"I thought you were supposed to know something. I thought you were supposed to understand things. You're just full of bull. All you ever do is say a bunch of stuff and then stand around and stare at everybody."

He slides off the rock into the waist-deep water, swinging his arms, splashing handfuls of water at Swain and lunging against the current toward him. "All the stuff you get up there and say is nothing but a bunch of made-up bull."

Swain ducks his head. The water is coming in sheets, in cupfuls, soaking through his shirt, running cold down his chest. He sits still, propped on his elbows, his head bowed, his eyes shut tight, and lets it drench him. This time he doesn't hit back. Big drops of water pelt across the whole length of him. "I baptize you with water unto repentance." This is what it feels like.

He's stopped splashing. Wherever he is, he's quiet.

Swain doesn't move. A drop of water is rolling from the crown of his scalp toward his face. His whole attention follows its slow path. Behind his closed eyelids, he sees a waterfall pouring through reddish light. A flicker of an image in the dark, barely there, a white stream. Inside the rushing sound of the stream, he hears a whisper. "If ye continue in my word, then are ye my disciples." The skin on his arms prickles. It could wash that whole day away ... everything that happened. It has that much force.

"Dr. Hammond?"

Swain opens his eyes. Bryan is standing in front of him in the water. "I'm sorry," he says. "I didn't mean to. I'm sorry."

Swain listens to the water breaking around the rock under him. "Then are ye my disciples." A child is blind, people are going to pieces—I never expected miracles, or even help. But this—this teasing. "Continue in my word." He looks at Bryan, makes himself pay attention to him.

"I didn't mean to," Bryan says again.

Swain nods. "It's okay."

Bryan is still waiting for something to happen to him. "Nothing's going to happen. You're upset, we're both upset. It was nothing but water. I promise you, it's okay."

He drops the kid off at his house and waits until he has put up his bike and gone into his house. He drives home, into his own driveway, turns off the motor and sits. He stares at the garage door, lets his hands slide off the wheel. His clothes are still damp, wet in places. He's home. Still hasn't seen Joe. He has never been tireder in his life.

"Sam called," Julie says, as he walks in. She's in the hall, putting something up in the hall closet. Her voice is muffled in the closet. He goes where she is.

"Anything from the Mileses?"

"Nothing. I thought you were with them."

He shakes his head.

"You look terrible."

"Come lie down with me."

He pulls off his damp shirt, throws his clothes to the floor against the wall.

"What happened?" she says. He lies down on his back on the bed.

"Patrice was asleep. Jakey was asleep. I talked to Bryan." The light from the window glows through his closed eyelids. "I'm tired," he says.

"You didn't sleep much yourself last night." Her head is turned away from him. She must be looking out the window. This is what Bryan did when he closed his eyes.

Try to remember what she looks like. She has on—what? Did he look? Her hair was tied back. It was coming loose a little, where it's short around the edges. Yellow—that's what she had on. He hears her breathing, the bed shifts as she turns over. She's facing him now. Her breath near his face. A loose yellow sundress that she wears without a bra. That's what it was.

I did see. If you don't know you're going to be asked, it's hard to remember. Wonder how much Jakey will remember. A kid that age, how much has he seen? Wonder if he ever saw a woman. Maybe he walked into the bathroom without knocking, and there she was getting out of the shower—Patrice. He imagines small dark nipples. Water running down her legs. Black hair in her crotch, shining in the white bathroom light. Moving over her, those long hands and a yellow towel.

He reaches a hand over in the direction of Julie. His fingers graze skin. Her arm? His hand crosses cloth, a narrow strip, the strap of her dress. Her shoulder.

"What are you doing, Swain?"

"Taking off your dress."

"I mean, with your eyes squinched shut."

"You know what I'm doing."

"Tormenting yourself."

"Why not?"

He slides over next to her. The bed shifts again. She has twisted around and taken the dress off. "Are you going to keep your eyes closed the whole time?"

"Maybe forever."

"Great. You'll always remember me as young."

Her hand is riffling through his chest hair, as though she's looking for something. Five fingers searching. Now she's gone. Nothing touches him. Now she's back again, cupping his balls, rolling him in her hand. Now wetness on his chest—the first touch shocks him—her lips, her tongue moving down his body. Not seeing her start toward him, not knowing. His hand slides down her stomach, he reaches between her legs. Slick wet cunt. He runs a finger into her, slides it out slow, pushes it in again. She moves toward it, humping his hand.

He rolls her over, falls onto her in the darkness, presses his face down into the pillow. Now she's grabbing him with her twat, wringing it out of him. Jesus. "Julie." The breath shudders out of him.

So fast. "Sorry," he says into the pillow. He lies on her like something toppled. Her ass makes circles under him, slower and slower. He can't move. In front of him is the bedside table: a box of blue tissues, the lamp, the clock radio. Shit. He forgot and opened his eyes.

Swain was thirteen years old on the afternoon when he and both his parents ran into his mother's boyfriend. He was eating ice cream, and he kept on eating, steadily and quietly, ignoring the headache rising in his temples. He ate until his jaws felt light and numb. It was soft ice cream, homemade peach and vanilla and strawberry. They were at a fund-raiser for new lighting for the University Theatre. It turned out when they got there that he was the only kid. It turned out, too—and this was the only time Swain was ever forced to witness the three of them together—that his mother's lover was there.

Swain had found out about Walt the previous year. Eddie, the seventeen-year-old from down the block who gave him a ride to school, told him. That morning in Eddie's father's car, Swain had fixed his eyes on the glove compartment, at the barrel lock of it, at the tiny black shape of the keyhole.

"I don't believe you," Swain said. "That's shit and you know it. I'll tell your parents you said it."

But he did believe it, and it was true. As soon as Eddie said it—"that guy that hangs around with your mom"—Swain knew he'd had a slow-growing idea.

He wanted to throw up. He could open the door and jump out. He stared at the rubber mat on the floor in front of him. The car turned a corner. He couldn't get sick in Eddie's car, Eddie would tell everybody.

It's his father's fault anyway. If he were around...

It's both of their faults. They never even think about what they're doing, they don't care, either one of them.

He didn't make a scene. He didn't throw up until he got out of Eddie's sight. And he didn't tell on Eddie to his parents. Since they probably already knew too. He didn't say anything to anyone.

Then that afternoon a year later—peach ice cream in a tiny little bowl that would hardly hold anything, and here comes Walt Emrich. Swain watched him come across the room toward the three of them and it seemed like slow motion. Like watching an avalanche or a falling tree, played back in slow motion.

"Paul, you've heard me talk about my friend Walt," his mother said. A flush climbed high in her cheeks, like the colors that were beginning to melt in his bowl. She looked beautiful. He hated her. He actually could see her pulse moving in her neck.

"Grand to meet you," Paul said. "Certainly I've heard of you, and wondered if we ever would get the chance to meet. You know my son." He turned his body slightly toward Swain, but kept his eyes on Walt.

"I believe we have met, haven't we, young fellow?" Walt said.

Once, when he was about ten, when he was first allowed to walk by himself in the afternoon down to Franklin Street at the edge of the campus, he saw them. He had been in Danziger's, picking out some candy to buy out of the glass cases they had there. He came out with a sack of vanilla-covered pretzels and there they were, half a block away, standing in the crowd of students milling at the crosswalk, waiting for the light to change. She didn't even look like anybody's mother, she looked more like one of the students. She was tall, even taller than his dad. Then, as he watched, they changed their minds and didn't cross, kept on walking up the broad sidewalk toward the movie theater. Maybe they were going to sit there in the dark and rub up against each other. He didn't think of that then. He just saw his mother, and ran after her, losing her and then catching sight of her again. She had on a blue skirt with a red scarf tied around it for a belt. He followed the spot of red, caught sight of the skirt, like trying to follow one sail in a crowded race of sailboats. He caught up to them, so out of breath he could only stand and let his arms hang loose while his wind caught up with him, and they waited. When he calmed down and looked at them, his mother looked the same way she looked as she presented Walt once again, this time to Paul. If she tried to touch an ice cream bowl with a spoon, her hand would shake and the metal would ring against the glass and everybody in the room would stare.

While his dad watched, Walt stuck out his hand to shake hands with Swain. Swain shook his hand, keeping his eyes on their two hands. "Yeah, I guess so," he said to Walt. Sure they had met. Two other times. It seemed as though his mother wasn't very careful.

"I got to get some ice cream," he said, when Walt let go his hand.

"Get me a little more too, son," his father said. "Vivian? Walt?" He raised his eyebrows at each of them, in offer of Swain's services. They both shook their heads very fast, as if it were something they would never consider and how could he even ask.

Swain went back to the table, where the big cans of ice cream were being scooped. This time it was strawberry, faintly pink. A bunch of people were standing around the table, talking loud and laughing. He had to stand in line. At first, as he waited, he wouldn't look back in the direction of the three of them. Then finally, he did. There they were. His mother standing up very straight like a ballet dancer, listening to his father, who was talking on and on about something. He was standing the same way he always did when he was doing a lecture and he knew what he was saying was good. He would lean slightly from the middle of his body when he was getting to the point, as if he were taking a bow. He looked as if he were talking to a bunch of kids. How could he just stand there and talk? How could he let any of this happen to him? Disgusting. All three of them—a bunch of idiots that nobody could ever trust.

Swain could only see Walt's back and his bushy curly hair, and when he turned his head a little, the edge of his stupid bow tie. Walt had on a suit. So maybe he knew this was going to happen, and he got all dressed up. Probably, Swain thought, the three of them planned the whole thing, and he was the only one who was surprised.

FOUR

The door to Jakey's room is shut. Swain knocks softly, Julie behind him. He waits, pushes it open. Patrice is beside his bed, her two hands on his shoulder and his arm. Jakey's awake. His face, the part that shows, is flushed dark pink, so bright against the eye patches that it looks as if he'd been slapped. Joe is not here.

From across the room, Swain hears Jakey's breathing. A sharp intake, a pause, then it rushes out. Patrice doesn't turn away from the bed, she stays bent over him, her hand rubbing Jakey's arm, his chest, saying to him softly, Swain can just hear it, "My little boy." Her voice so full of pain, it hurts him, he has to stop a second, take a breath and compose himself.

Then he steps over to the bed, touches her shoulder. She doesn't move away from the child in the bed. She glances up at Swain, looks back at the boy. There is nothing in the world but her child, two days blind, lying in this bed. She says, "Jakey, Dr. Hammond is here. And Mrs. Hammond. You remember." He turns to see Julie and Patrice reach for each other, both of them with tears starting to brim, neither of them making a sound, keeping it a secret from the boy.

"Who's in here?" His fists come off the bedsheet, raised aimlessly.

"It's Swain, Jakey. And Julie. From church. We came to see how you're doing, fellow."

He doesn't say anything. Swain starts to speak again, but stops as Jakey says slowly: "Not so good." His voice is thick. His lips hold the shape of "good."

He reaches to touch the boy's hand. Which looks too clean. Boiled and antiseptic. Jakey's hand can't look like this. "I'm sorry, Jakey," he says, almost in a whisper.

Jakey's lips tremble. His chin wrinkles. "I'm going to take this stuff off of me."

"Son, you must not touch—" Patrice stops. She looks toward Swain and shakes her head. Jakey's fists have let go. His breath has smoothed out. He's out again, drifting back into sleep.

Swain's fingers ease away from the hand that's limp now and damp, and so small, curled up at his side. He's so little he hardly takes up any space in the bed. Swain wants to pick him up and hold him. Now, God. Now's the time. Do something. "Will you join me in a prayer?" Patrice makes some kind of murmur. He feels Julie beside him, as though she's part of him, backing him up.

"Our Father in Heaven," he says. "Help this boy." His chest feels stuffed tight, it's too hot in here, there's no air. He steadies himself against the side of the bed and closes his eyes. He feels the boy stir.

"Fill him with your strength. Be with us all now . . . in this time of . . . loss and sorrow.

"Lord. This boy needs your healing power." He hears his own words like an echo. And something starts to beat inside his head. Like a fist on a door. Harder than that. He grips the boy's arm.

Jakey twists his arm in Swain's grasp. What is he doing? All these bandages squashing down on my face. It hurts. I can see as good as anybody. Everything going up and down, makes me sick. Let go.

Swain hears his own words slow, in a rhythm: "hea-ling pow-er." Then other words: "Child, arise."

Julie's arm is against him, nudging him. They're waiting. It keeps on happening: the pulse in his brain turned into a pump, throbbing, each surge bringing something liquid, flammable into him. The level goes higher. His head is filling like a gas tank, a dam-breaking reservoir. He's going to explode. His hand is on Jakey's bare arm.

"Heal him, Lord."

He said it.

"God of all the universe, heal this boy." All the force that was pushing against him is running through him, taking him with it. I want to go. Let it happen. Make the boy open his eyes and look at me. This one thing out of everything I ever asked for.

Jakey tries to slide away, toward the wall. He's hurting my arm. Why does he keep saying that? His hand is so hot. What's happening? Where are they taking me? I'm going, flying backward, I'm getting out of here. My arm is like fire spreading everywhere. Wow, look, Mom! Ocean! I'm going to ride a wave, go a million miles an hour, way up high, faster and faster. I can see everything.

Swain feels the tears start to roll down his face, his eyes shut tight. Just let it all pour through me. I am a pipe... nothing but a pipe. O God, please. "Let the boy see. Let him open his eyes and sit up and see. Now." He grips the child tighter by the arm. It has to happen. God is going to make it happen. I heard that voice.

Swain hears a chair scrape, people moving around him, a hand on his back. He puts his hand up to his forehead. A wave of dizziness pours over him. His own skin feels like ice.

It's gone, stopped. What happened? He steadies himself against the bed. It's over. Somebody turned it off... He's empty. Dry as a shell.

"Swain." Julie's talking. To him. He doesn't answer or raise his head.

He opens his eyes. He's still holding onto Jakey's arm. He can't even tell if the boy is awake, lying so still. Heal. I tried to make him heal. Did I think that could happen? Yes.

Yes, I believed it. He wants it back, that power pouring through him, knowing that at any minute...

"Swain." Julie is pulling him, steering him into the corridor, Patrice behind her. "He's terribly upset about the accident, Patrice," Swain hears her saying, making excuses for him. No need to make excuses. If she knew what it was ... and that boy lying there ...

He turns to Patrice. "I tried to let it happen, not be in the way." They look at him as though he were drunk, Julie pulling on him to leave. He remembers that there was something else he came over to do. He says, "I need to talk to Joe. To apologize."

"Not now, Swain," Patrice says. "He wouldn't hear it. It's not important anyway—"

"Where is he?"

"Down the hall in the waiting room. Staring out the window, not saying anything. Forget about it, Swain, or talk to him later. ..."

"I have to see him."

He pulls away from Julie—she's hanging on to his arm—and heads down the hall to the open door at the end. A TV is going, nobody watching. A golf tournament, the announcer quiet, as though somebody had died. There he is, his shoulders low in the chair. "Joe."

Joe doesn't move. Swain walks around to stand in front of him. Joe is staring out the window, his hands lying lifeless on his legs. Swain says, "I've come to apologize. For hitting you. I was crazy ... because of what's happened." Joe still doesn't move. Swain waits. The TV man whispers about a three-iron. Joe moves only his eyes to look at Swain, the rest of him limp and asleep. He stares, until Swain thinks Joe has forgotten he's there.

Then he says, "Just stay away, Hammond. We don't need you. I don't give a fuck about you ... anything you ever did. You don't matter."

On the night four days later when the elders are meeting without him, Swain and Julie stay home and play Scrabble. Another minister is presiding over the session so the elders can talk freely about crazy Swain Hammond, who actually thinks he heard God. It seems strange that they're talking about that now, with all that has happened. They acted as though it was nothing then. Swain rubs his eyes, counts the days backward. It was only two weeks ago, not even that, that he got up there and told them. How can that be? It seems like a year.

Playing Scrabble was Julie's idea. Swain can't concentrate, he makes himself keep sitting in the chair, staring at the board. All they know is, I hear voices. If they've got a problem with me now, wait until they hear about me hitting Joe . . . and trying to do a miracle with Jakey. He flips a wooden tile over again and again, clicking it against the yellow Formica of the kitchen table. "You're showing me your letters," Julie says. "Play for blood. That way the time will pass faster." Blood, she says, as if it's a word that doesn't mean anything. She puts down JUICE with the J on a triple letter, the whole thing a double score.

The call comes at eleven-fifteen. It's Bernie. I should have told Bernie myself. Not left him out there in the congregation to hear the biggest thing that ever happened to me in my life.

"Okay," Bernie says, fast, as though he's borrowing somebody's phone, he's in a hurry. "Keep in mind this is off the record and unofficial." The upshot of it is that the session voted five to three to privately recommend that Swain get professional help.

Swain stands at the telephone table in the hall. "I see," he says. He wants to say "It's me, Bernie, from high school, from kindergarten, for Christ's sake." Bernie was one of them, he had a vote.

"I appreciate your letting me know what they did." His voice is very carefully level. Julie's standing now in the doorway behind him. He still has the Scrabble tile in his hand, he rubs it across his lips, which are pressed together hard in a line. He can imagine what the discussion was like, as they voted on whether or not he was crazy, in front of a preacher from another church. Whichever one they brought in to take his place. The small bits of behavior and things he has said thrown out for examination and evaluation. As symptoms. And Bernie in on it. And Charlie March. And who else? He sees them sitting around the table there in the church library.

"How did they come to this conclusion, Bernie? I mean, what was said?"

Bernie hesitates. Swain's voice at the other end is so formal. As if the two of them have never met. Maybe he's forgotten everything else, now that God talks to him. He doesn't need anybody else. "We did meet for a while on this, you know, Swain. It's hard to put it all together."

He stops. Swain is waiting at the other end. Bernie feels Lynne step up behind him, put a hand on his back. She acts as though this is some kind of major trauma, me having to call up Swain. He's still waiting for me to say something. "Look, Swain, what it is, I'd have to say that, well, people were...concerned for you. That's all. You've always had everything under control, very well organized, had your head on straight is what I'm trying to say. Everybody's always admired that. So it's a surprise—all this. That's what people were saying. That's all I know to tell you." He needs to wind this thing up fast, Swain would know exactly how to do it. Bernie clears his throat. He says, "This is an awkward... uh, painful situation for all of us, I'm sure you understand."

Bernie? This is Bernie talking? He can't believe it. Jesus. "I hope you don't mind if I ask," Swain says, holding his breath for a second, trying to force some lightness into his voice. "Bernie, which way did you vote?"

He hesitates, makes himself say it the way Swain would, "My thinking was that it would be a help to you to have somebody you could talk to about this..."

"I see. Yes. Well. Thank you, Bernie." Swain hangs up, brings his fist down slowly against the jamb of the door.

The official word arrives in Swain's office at eight forty-five the next morning. Bill Bartholomew is the one who comes to tell him to get help. "Of course," Bill says, "this is something which is not easy to say. But we all go through times when we need the support and guidance of others. You and I both know that." Bill is a urologist. He has neat surgical hands. He smiles politely at Swain and puts the tips of all his fingers together. Like a church, Swain thinks, staring at those hands. Here's the church. Here's the steeple. Open the doors and here are the people. Wonder if Bill ever made a church full of people with his fingers when he was a kid. Maybe he would like Swain to show him how. The committee would love that.

"I appreciate all your prayers and concern," Swain says. He rocks his chair back on its pedestal. His feet leave the ground. It always makes him feel like the sheriff in westerns when he does that. Bill is the bad guy he's putting in jail. "Take him away," he says to the dusty-looking deputies who have dragged the sorry bastard in. Bill is waiting for more—something along the lines of "Certainly I will have my head examined. I'm sorry I put you to the trouble of mentioning it."

"Are you so sure I'm crazy, Bill?" he says. When he stood next to that boy's bed and felt all the power in the universe run through him was when he quit worrying about whether he was crazy. "Doesn't it seem contradictory?"

Bill is watching him carefully, no longer trying to smile. Bill would be a good hit man for the IRS.

"It's okay to believe in God," Swain says, "but only if God is distant. A presence in history. Is that the idea?"

"I'm sure I don't want to debate this with you," Bill says. "It is the will of the session—"

"I understand your position," Swain says.

"Very frankly, I don't think you do, Swain. This entire situation is extremely painful for me. I have always admired your reasonable and pragmatic way of dealing with matters. In fact, I have sensed that you were a person who thinks very much like myself. Unsentimental, I would say. Now I find that I was wrong about that. Unless, of course, this is a temporary condition, in which case, I am sure we all offer our forbearance."

Swain tips his chair forward again. Like himself indeed. He makes his eyes as cold as Bill's. They have that much in common.

"Thank you for coming by to talk to me, Bill," Swain says as he stands. "I know that such a call can be difficult to make." Bill gets to his feet. He's starting to figure out that he came for nothing; Swain has said nothing about getting professional help.

Swain smiles warmly and touches Bill's elbow as they walk together toward the door. Calculated to annoy Bill, which it does. He quickly manages to pull away.

At the door, he says, "Swain, don't persist in this. Stop and think."

"That's all I've ever done. For years and years. There comes a time for not thinking."

"I regret hearing you say that. We can only hope for all our best interests that you will return to your senses."

"Bill, I am trying to tell you—I tried to tell the congregation. I have come to my senses. I heard what I heard. With my ears."

Bill shakes his head. "I see no point in pursuing this further now. There's nothing to be gained."

"I'm sorry you feel that way, Bill. But I'm sure we'll continue our conversation at another time." They shake hands. It's over with. Swain shuts the door and leans back against it; he can still hear for half a minute Bill's heels ringing against the hall's floor tile. If anybody needs help, it's that tight-ass. Alike, indeed.

When news of the elders' action leaks, copies of a petition start to circulate through the congregation. This is a church where signing petitions is not unusual. The Westside congregation has in recent years petitioned against military aid to half a dozen countries, against the death penalty, against prayer in the schools. They have petitioned in favor of public funding of abortions and passage of the ERA.

This time it's different. The card tables don't go up at each entrance to the church. This time it's a covert operation, although by the second day, Swain has been informed. One week after Bartholomew has conveyed the elders' recommendation, Swain is sitting with a copy of it on his desk, patting smooth the two creases in it, as if it were the crumpled map that shows the location of buried treasure.

What the petition says is this: "We the undersigned members of Westside Presbyterian Church support the right of free speech for all people. We admire the honesty of Rev. Swain Hammond in speaking in public about matters that may not be popular or easily received by many of our membership. We support his right to hold whatever views he feels advisable and to express them in appropriate ways as he has recently undertaken. To that end, we offer our support to Dr. Hammond as our pastor."

That's all. There are no names on this copy. It's a Xerox of the unsigned original. Mary Elgar, who brought it, leans toward him, propped on the arm of the sofa nearest his desk. She's tough, built like a tree stump, a squatty little bulldog of a woman. "This is what we're up to," she says. Her sleeves are rolled up to her elbows, as if she expected to be assigned some dirty job in the interests of protecting Swain—or freedom of speech, whichever.

"I promise you, you don't have to worry about a thing," she says. With Mary leading his defense, it's hard to be sure. She teaches in the Slavic languages department. Campus politics and church politics are the two live spots in her life.

"About twenty copies are circulating," she says. "We've formed an action group to make calls on homes to explain to people why it's important that we support you in this."

"Why is it important, Mary?"

"We can't let you be run out just for being controversial. That's McCarthyism. You know what can happen when something like that gets started. Witch-hunts. And you know exactly what I'm talking about. I was lecturing at this university when your father was alive." She looks hard at Swain. The voice of God indeed. Well, the boy has every right to be a little loony. His mother and daddy, intriguing pair that they were, probably wouldn't have recognized him in a crowd.

Swain frowns. He'd forgotten she was one of the ones who

really knew his father, not just knew of him, which everyone did. Once when he was an undergrad, he went to a noon campus lecture his dad gave on his poet Majkov. The auditorium was full, a lot of them kids with sandwiches or packs of Nabs that crackled as they tried to open them quietly. Dad could talk and people would come even if it was at lunch. The way he talked that day made Swain hear balalaikas and want the icy vodka that his father always served when the Department came to the house. Swain watched his dad through the frame of his tennis shoes propped on the back of the chair in front of him. He had thought about not going to his father's lecture. Why should he go? When had Paul Hammond ever listened to him? But he went.

He refolds the petition.

"Of course, there are a few people who won't sign," Mary is saying. "But you don't need to worry about them. They're going to keep an eye out and see if you do anything else they think is crazy."

She focuses a gaze on him that is weighted with meaning. "So of course," she says, "it wouldn't hurt for you to play some of your cards a little closer to your chest. For a while."

Within another long week, the vote is in. Swain wins the round. About 70 percent of the adult congregation signed, Mary proudly reports to him. There was no place for a no vote, but even so, it's a victory. So it looks as if he won't lose the church . . . not immediately anyway. When he looks at the lists of names, he forgets for a second how mad he is at all of them. He reads the names. Ed Fitzgerald. Fred Ritchie. Mr. and Mrs. Frank Dannenford. Jill Ferrando. This is what it would be like to be elected by roll-call vote and hear each familiar voice say "yes." Again and again, "yes."

The following Sunday Swain mentions the petition from the pulpit, but only as a brief comment among the day's other announcements. "Thank you for your love and support," he says. Unexpectedly, as he says it, he feels a tightness in his throat. He looks from face to face.

Bernie looks at his feet, taps one cordovan loafer against the other. Of course I signed the damn petition. What else was I going to do? But somebody has got to set him straight. He can't pull another trick like this.

Somebody should say something to Julie. No, God probably talks to her too. Through her is probably how God got Swain's address. She's always been a flake, had her head in the clouds. They'll both wind up with their feet on the ground if the session has to go to the presbytery for another preacher. Swain's got more sense than to go around acting like this.

Swain lets his eyes travel to the back of the room. Up one side and down the other. They're still mine. My congregation. I won't have to leave. Not today anyway. They're not going to run me out.

I have to stop staring at them, thinking like this. If I keep on, I'll lose my composure. He thinks about the petition instead— they weren't interested in God or Swain Hammond, either one. They voted for freedom of speech—that's all. Nothing more than that. His strategy works. He manages to keep the wave of love at bay.

Then he moves mechanically through the rest of the service, distant from all of them, glad to have it done.

When the car is safely blocks from the church, when nobody can hear him but Julie, he says, "Guess I squeaked by that time. It isn't over though, you know."

"How well I know."

"I don't think the word has gotten around about the other stuff yet, which surprises me. It has been three weeks since I hit Joe. They've had more than enough time. . . ."

"Joe and Patrice have other things on their mind. More important than fist fights or miracles." She pauses. "Explain to me one more time, Swain. What were you thinking? . . . trying like that to make him see."

"Okay." He gets his words together, as if somebody had asked him a question from out in the congregation. He keeps his eyes on the traffic. "For one moment," he says, "I knew there was something more important than blindness, and it was right there in the room. I couldn't turn away from it." He looks over at her. "How could I have turned away from any chance to let the boy see?"

"You say you hate children. You completely lose your head trying to help Jakey. And then you go out and play in a creek with Bryan. I don't understand it."

FIVE

Sam opens his eyes. His mouth tastes bad. He squeezes his eyes tight shut. Still too much light. He reaches for the pillow to put over his head. No pillow. Where's the pillow? He opens his eyes a little crack and looks around him. Carpet. How did I get on the floor?

He twists around so he can see the clock. Eleven o'clock. It's eleven o'clock in the morning. I didn't sleep this late. I took a nap. I already got up. Got out ice, I remember. The paper boy threw the paper up against the door. Like somebody threw a stick, a mob out there with sticks and rocks: kill him, gouge out his eyes. The paper boy. That proves it: I did get up today.

He rolls out flat on his back. It makes him dizzy. My shoulder hurts, must have slept on it. The carpet stinks. Carpet is brown, ceiling is white. Sounds like a song. Things should have the color of them written on them for people that can't see. And the name of what it is. In big letters. Ceiling: white. Ellen liked liquor that was poured into milk. White Russians. How could she stand it? I couldn't stand to look at it.

Could put some vodka in Jakey's milk. Make it not hit him so hard. Make him feel so good nothing else matters. Forget seeing what everything in the world looks like. Forget seeing. Let the liquor roll you backward into your head.

My head has an ax stuck in it. If I move, it's going to fall in two pieces, two halves lying on the floor. I need to just pick up my head and find out what I did with the bottle. It's somewhere close, has to be.

He opens his eyes. He doesn't see it. Up there on the bureau. On the floor. Nowhere. I have to go to the kitchen. Get another bottle. When the kids were babies and Ellen was heating up their bottles, she shook out a drop onto her wrist to see if it was hot enough. All I have to do is get up and go in there. He sits up, pulling from one side first, the other side dragging behind him. One side of him is dead. He is half dead. Half crazy. Half drunk. He wants to be completely drunk soon. One hundred percent drunk. The room wavers, comes back into focus. He eases up to standing, and makes his way down the hall.

He sits at the kitchen table, in front of his glass. Feeling better now. It smells good. I could pour some on me. Smell like a fraternity party, everybody jammed together, you have to hold your drink up in the air over your head to get through the crowd. Everybody spilling drinks on everybody and yelling. Jakey isn't going to do anything like that now. Somebody helping him across streets.

I'm going to do something for that boy. Got to think about how to do it. First thing, I'll donate my eyes. They could take 'em now, give 'em to Jakey, or throw 'em away. I'll put it in my will, who do I have to call?

He sees a drop hit the table. Crying again. Crying the rest of my life. The water falls on his hand. It's cold. He frowns, then wipes off the bottom of his glass on his sleeve. Wonder if the boy can even cry, did they leave him that?

I know what I'm going to do. I'll go over there, I'll tell him: I can't make it up to you, but I'm going to try. He sees himself standing by the boy's bed saying it. He sits up straight in the kitchen chair. He says out loud: "I'll get you anything, whatever you need." The boy'll be a great musician. I'll help him. He could be a doctor. Anything. I'll be right there beside him helping him. I'll put him through college, buy him all the books, drive him to class. He'll be a scientist and discover a cure for something.

He stands up. It's all settled. Find my will and put the boy in it. Right now. Somewhere in a drawer in the back room. I'll make sure he's taken care of. Call up where you give eyes, tell them where I am. He picks up his glass, steadies himself against the wall, and goes back down the hall.

Sam's blue Toyota in the driveway in the middle of a business day is a dead giveaway. He can't hide that he's in there. Swain walks up the drive into the garage and knocks at the back door. The air inside the garage is heavy with the muggy August heat. He waits. Nothing. He knocks again, and waits. The kitchen is dim behind the glass of the door. The light looks dingy. Maybe it's the angle of the window, the time of day. I should have been back over here days ago. He hasn't answered his phone in a week. I tried to call him. I should have called his boss . . . done something . . . gone out and found him. He's probably lying in there dead. A box is turned on its side on the counter. Swain reads the letters one at a time. Ritz crackers. Sam will have to come back into the kitchen sometime. He looks back down the driveway. A kid is passing on a bike, pumping hard up the hill of the street, the front wheel wobbles to the left, to the right. The doorknob rattles and clicks. Swain jumps. "Sam."

Sam doesn't look at him. He focuses intently on the door, getting it open. Very drunk. You could tell it just from the way he holds his lips together. As if he has to concentrate to do it. He pulls open the door, steps back, steadying himself with his weight leaned against the hand on the knob.

Swain steps inside. "You're not in this by yourself, Sam."

"Yeah, I remember you saying that." Sam turns and walks around the end of the counter into the den on the other side of the kitchen. A bottle of Canadian Club is sitting on the counter. "You were wrong."

Swain sits down in a chair across from him. "Where are Joanne and David?" he says.

"I sent them home to their mother. They don't need to see this."

"They don't need to be without you."

"It was time for them to go back anyway. She has them most of the time. They're better off with her. Safer." Sam takes a laborious swallow of his drink. He looks up at Swain. "Come here to cheer me up?" He laughs. It's a dragged-out slowed-down kind of laugh, like something big falling downstairs end over end.

"To cheer us both up."

"You're not the one that did it to him. You don't know anything about it."

"Joe's not so sure about that."

"If you wake up in the middle of the night, you can say to yourself, 'I'm clean. I don't have to worry. It was Sam. Poor schmuck Sam.'"

In the emergency room, they held each other. Swain can feel the prickle of Sam's hair against his cheek. "I hate to see you doing this to yourself," he says.

"You know what you'd do, Swain, if it was you? I'll tell you. You would hate your own goddamn guts all day long for the rest of your days. Same as me."

"It's hard to resist," Swain says. He wouldn't mind about a half inch of that stuff in the bottom of a glass.

"How come you haven't told me that God will forgive me? Or—I know, wait, this is better—God has already forgiven me. Why haven't you told me that?"

"Sam, it wasn't your fault, you're a victim, like the kid. If you could look at it like that..." He stops for a second. "I'm not supposed to say this, but try putting up the bottle, Sam. For the rest of today."

"If I faced it sober, I would die." Sam looks out the sliding glass door, then narrows his eyes and looks back at Swain. "Anyway, I haven't had that much."

"Have you had anything to eat lately?"

"Crackers and cheese." Sam pats the rolls of his stomach. His shirt looks rumpled and slept in. That other shirt with blood on it. Probably still in a wastebasket somewhere in this house. Three weeks and three days the boy has been blind. It's already the middle of August. Swain stands up. "Come on, Sam. Let's turn on some lights. Let's fix something to eat. Come on."

Sam gets to his feet slowly, moves with the bottle and his glass to the kitchen table. Swain looks in the refrigerator. "How about scrambled eggs?"

"No."

"A sandwich then."

He shrugs. "I give up. Whatever you say."

"Where's the bread?"

"Over there. In the box on the counter. Look, Swain, don't think you can stop me. You can't."

"I know," Swain says. He's back in the fridge, searching. "Doesn't keep me from trying." Bologna. Velveeta. Kid crap.

Sam says, "It's good for me. The alcohol. I don't ask you to believe that. But it's true, it does something... gets me to feeling like there's some point to it all. You know. Like what the God business does for you. Makes you feel warm in your gut." He looks at Swain, who has his back turned. "Makes you crazy too. God or booze, either one." Sam laughs. "Least that's the way it hits you and me."

Swain is rummaging in the pantry. Peanut butter. He takes out the jar, grape jelly swirled through it in dark streaks.

"Looks like it's going to be a PBJ." Swain makes them both a sandwich, pours them each a glass of milk, sets it all on the table. Sam turns to the side so he doesn't have to look.

Swain takes a bite of his sandwich and watches Sam and chews. Sam says, "I guess you've seen him. Jakey."

"Yes. Have you?"

Sam shakes his head. "They don't want me there. I can't yet." He pauses. "How is he? He knows?"

Swain nods. "He doesn't believe it." Swain tries to stop the sound of Jakey's voice from coming back into his head. If he just keeps talking... He puts the sandwich down. "I'll tell you something," he says. "I stood next to his bed, and something came over me. I was saying a prayer. Patrice and Julie were there. What I did—I started praying for the kid to heal. I mean, to see—that kind of healing—right that minute. Sit up in the bed and see. I said it out loud."

"Think you're the only man that ever prayed and meant it?"

"I thought it would work, Sam. I swear I did."

"Real blood," Sam says. "Being there having to look at it. Makes a difference." He watches Swain, looks at the sandwich that Swain's not eating either. "One time, I was thinking . . . I started wondering, did Dr. Swain Hammond ever in his life do anything wrong, something totally permanently wrong? It would be a lot easier for you to sell us sinners on the forgiveness routine if you had. Then I saw you haul off and lay out Joe, when he's just gotten hit with all this. And I thought to myself, 'Now, he's going to find out what it's like. Time to welcome young Dr. Hammond to the human race.'"

Sam reaches slowly over to a counter and gets another glass . . . dirty, maybe it had orange juice in it three days ago. He pours it half full of Canadian Club and pushes it across the table. "Swain, old buddy, you deserve to have a drink."

Swain takes the glass. The straight liquor has burned out whatever else was ever in here. He takes a sip, then a swallow. It burns all the way to his stomach. He looks at Sam, raises his drink and nods. "Thanks, Sam. I've been waiting a long time for an invitation."

"You've quit waiting, boy. You've crashed the party."

Swain smiles, settles down into his chair. I don't have to go to the nursing home today. No way. Sam and I are going to sit here and have a pastoral drink. A little communion. The wine and the bread.

An hour later, he is still sitting in the same chair. Sam looks at him from the other end of the table. "You are a wreck, boy," he says. "You are drunker than I am and I've been working on it a week. I have never seen anybody so wrecked."

"I'm just fine, Sam." Swain grins.

Sam stares at him, way down there at the end of the table. So this is what Swain Hammond looks like drunk. Sitting there smiling like a fool. Hardly ever saw the boy smile. Except maybe for a half a second after he decked Joe Miles. Now look at him with a dumb-shit smile all over his face. He's in much worse shape than me.

Sam says, "Isn't this more fun than God?"

"'Bout the same."

"What's your wife going to say when you come home in this shape?"

Swain thinks a minute. What is my wife going to say? "My wife is very tolerant. She accepts me like I am." He laughs. It isn't funny. What does Sam want to do? Ruin a nice afternoon? I'd just like to have one afternoon when I don't have to worry. Julie is never going to leave me: he says it to himself loud so it will sink in.

"Yeah, well, don't push your luck."

"I already did. Too late now." He looks for the bottle. It's just out of his arm's reach. How did it get so far away? He rises up in his chair. Not quite. He lies down across the table on his stomach and slides toward it. If you lie down, short things looks tall. If I don't look at anything else—okay, don't look at anything. Now. See?—it's the Empire State Building. This is what a mouse would see if it looked up at a bottle. He keeps his eyes on the bottle, he's got his hand on it now. "Sam, it's all relative. Just keep that in mind." He rests his cheek against his arm. Then he slides back off the table, his butt lands right back in the chair. Good shot, Swain. Nine lives. Cats have nine lives. He looks up at Sam. "What are you looking at?" Then he remembers.... "Wait a minute. Just hang on for one second, is it Tuesday?"

"How do I know what day it is? Who do you think you're talking to?"

"It is. It's Tuesday. Julie has a meeting at the radio station. She's one of those volunteer announcers." Sam shrugs, he doesn't know anything about it. "You don't listen to her show? Sam, you should listen. She is terrific. She is so wonderful, I'm telling you..."

Sam says, "Maybe it wasn't God you heard. Maybe it was your

wife on the radio." Sam starts laughing and wheezing, rocking back in his chair. He laughs until it turns into coughing. Then he sits still again, pours himself a little more. He keeps his eyes steady on his hands and the bottle and the liquid pouring into the glass. He says, "I'll tell you the truth, Swain Hammond. I hope it was God. I don't for a minute think it was. But I hope to hell I'm wrong."

Swain is pouring a bag of cracked ice into a cooler, around big plastic bottles of Diet Sprite and caffeine-free Coke. He stands and straightens his back.

"Aren't the desserts incredible?" Eva Swansdorf says. "I'm embarrassed to show up with an ordinary chocolate cake."

Swain rips open another bag of ice. "No Jell-O puddings out of this crowd."

"I wouldn't miss this for anything in the world," Eva says. "We make sure not to be at the beach on this weekend every year." Janie Haddonsfield is approaching with a tray, with the wax paper blowing away from an enormous sheet cake. "Will you look at that?" Eva says. "It's the stained-glass window, the round one. Janie, how did you do it?"

Swain lifts the wax paper that still hovers over the cake. "Beautiful," he says. "Really. You got every detail. Even the colors seem exactly right."

Janie laughs. "You're the best judge of that. You're the one who faces this window."

"It's a perfect likeness," he says.

Eva says, "Such a lovely idea."

People are starting to edge toward the end of the table where the paper plates are stacked. Julie is still standing at a little distance, cornered by Mary Elgar.

Over where Mary has hauled her out of earshot of the crowd, Julie is saying, "Thank you. But everything's fine."

"You know you can come talk to me, that's all I'm saying."

"I'll remember that."

"I've always liked that husband of yours. And I felt like I never really knew what was going on here recently. I was thinking—"

"He's very fond of you."

Silence. Mary hesitates.

I shouldn't have cut her off. She means well.

"Mary, ask Swain about it. I think he'd really like to talk about it."

"I've already heard Swain talk about it. What I want to know is, is he all right? I *know* what he'll tell me."

Julie sighs. So much for that. She says, "Swain is okay, he's doing fine."

Standing next to the table, Swain says, "Guess we ought to get this thing rolling." Time to pray. He nods toward Elton Snipes. Elton loves to pray. A quiet falls on the crowd. You can hear the traffic on the other side of the church.

"Our Heavenly Father," Elton says in that authoritative voice, "we thank Thee for the bounty of this laden table. We give thanks for the loving hands that prepared this meal. Thy glory is magnified in the harvest of this rich earth we inhabit..." Swain turns a key over and over in his pocket. Sometimes, especially here at the tail end of the summer, Elton will start praying for a good football season. "...To the nourishment of our bodies, and ourselves to Thy service. In Jesus' Name we pray. Amen."

The talking and laughing resume, the line starts to move down the table. "One piece of chicken. You can come back if you want more," someone says to a child. A serving spoon scrapes against the Pyrex bottom of a broccoli casserole. Swain looks beyond the edge of the crowd, around the yard. Someone—he doesn't know who—finished clipping the hedge.

"Get in there and get yourself a plate, Swain." It's Mary.

"It's not going to run out before I get there," he says. He continues to stand and watch. Like a mother hen. Probably the closest I'll ever come to being a parent.

Hawk Epworth comes up beside him, his mouth full, his fork poised over his plate for the next bite. Bryan's father. A big paunchy guy. He waits for Hawk to swallow and say something. "That sure looks good," Swain says.

Hawk says, "I'm glad you had a talk with my boy. I can't get through to him at all."

"What's going on?"

"He's lying around the house in a funk. Doesn't even bother to turn on the TV. Won't watch shows he's not supposed to watch. School starts in a week and he says he isn't going."

"I'll talk to him. I'm sorry, Hawk. This thing has hit everybody."

"I heard about Bagdikian."

"What did you hear?"

"That he went to the hospital drunk and they stopped him in the front lobby. It was just a few days ago, the boy had long since been taken home. That guy." He shakes his head. "Good engineer, they tell me. Decent sort. What a waste."

Swain turns away. Sam . . . hustled out of the hospital. "I hate that," he says.

"Not much anybody can do."

"There's been a lot of that lately—I'd like to run across something somebody could do something about." He looks at the tables of half-empty platters. The one with the spoon-shaped dips in it, two of them still holding deviled eggs. He's not hungry, he doesn't want anything. Except one thing—which is to huddle everybody here, this whole crowd, into a tight little circle, snug up next to him, where everybody will stay safe until all the accidents and all the disasters are over. Nobody here but Julie would believe he could have such a thought in his head.

So much of the time he was growing up he wished somebody would touch him. He could remember when he was small his father walking behind him with both hands on his two shoulders and steering him, the way you would push a table or chair on wheels. And his mother would kiss him good night, hold him for a second, one arm around him, after he had taken his bath. But the time came pretty quickly when he wished she wouldn't do any of that. It was as if he gave up. Sometimes he wondered if maybe he was really ugly and awful-looking and just didn't know it and that was why they stayed away.

Then when he was in third grade, he fell in love with the nurse at the doctor's office where he went to get shots. He lay in bed at night for weeks after he had been to the doctor and imagined her watching while he did fantastic flips off a high diving board. She was so amazed by him that she didn't even care how young he was. He went to sleep feeling her cool hands on his chest and his arms. She had seen how brave he was, she thought he was special.

By his mid-teens, he was finally old enough to find somebody for himself. From about ninth grade on, no matter how unpopular he felt, there would always be some girl. Even if it didn't go very far, which it didn't for a long time, sex—or if not that, then simply somebody to touch him—was what he wanted with a force and a preoccupation that was beyond the usual.

Once on a beach weekend down at Morehead during high school, he and Betsy McCullough took a blanket out on the beach at night. They were lying up where the sand is soft and still warm from the afternoon, making out. He was a little drunk. Everybody had been drinking a lot of beer. She kept moving his hand away from her breasts, away from her ass. Everything he tried to touch, she grabbed his hand. Then before he knew he'd done it, he'd rolled over on her and pushed up against her between her legs. It was as if he was thinking about something else and did it accidentally. He didn't mean to.

She rolled him off and got up. "I'm going back to the house." She was really mad. He got up slow, dazed.

"Wait." But she acted as though she didn't hear him. He watched her dark shape moving away from him up the beach. Was she running? Jesus...all he did...He wanted to yell for her to come back, but somebody might hear him. Down the beach were other dark shapes huddled together on blankets. Before he could make his legs move to go after her, she was over the ridge of dunes. If she would just stay, he wouldn't do it anymore. That's what he wanted to say.

Julie is standing over there talking, laughing at something somebody said. She would put her plate down and put her arms around me now if I asked her. I wish we could go home. Still a wedding to do, then one call I have to make. After that, it's over for today.

People are still cleaning up and taking down the tables outside when he goes in early, to get ready for the ceremony. Sitting at his desk, he picks up another letter that Mildred left in his box, and signs it, pushing back the black arm of his robe. He likes marrying couples, if it just weren't one more thing to crowd in. Weddings feel important, he's really doing something. Especially when they get together within the church, then it's almost a personal victory. Every one of those weddings—all the ones that feel right—win him another round in an endless battle with his parents. "See, it can work out, people can be happy together." His marriage to Julie is the major victory in that fight.

The pair this afternoon is special. Louise, thirty-eight, his age, is pregnant. She and Miguel, a Colombian, have lived together about a year. She isn't showing, and they're going ahead with a traditional ceremony. He remembers her when she was alone. He could see her on Sunday mornings canvassing the congregation with her eyes, picking out the occasional male visitor holding his hymnbook alone. Watching her in those years, he wondered what his own life would be like without Julie. Whether he would show that same hunger so plainly on his face. He's glad for Louise, pregnant as she is. He caps his pen and stands. The ceremony, pronouncing them married, that's something he can do.

The afternoon light in the sanctuary feels so different from the light in the morning. Different colors come through the stained glass. Maybe it's all the flowers, yellow and white, that stand at both sides of the chancel. The people are seated and waiting. He moves toward the chancel steps. Miguel comes to stand beside him, and they both face the aisle. Louise is about to enter on the arm of her sister's husband. Swain runs through their names in his head—Louise Elizabeth Berryman, Miguel Martinez Vasconcellos. The accent of the Spanish—he's going to get it right, not anglicize. He runs through it again—and a scene unwinds like a scroll inside him. Gerona.

He is twenty years old, standing in a stone-walled room in Spain. The straps of his backpack pull at his shoulders. It's quiet, blocks away from the narrow river and the arched bridges. In this room—he read it in his guidebook—there was a revelation. He stands, with his two friends, in a medieval landmark of the Kabbalah. It is the moment, unplanned, when all three have become quiet, when all he hears is the muted traffic from the street. He's looking for something in this room.

Now Louise is coming down the aisle slowly, slowly. Moving in her long pale dress like a shadow behind the scene of Gerona... where he still stands. What is he looking for? He lays his hand on the grainy stone of the wall of that room. The feel of it sticks. Louise is before him, Miguel turns. It's beginning. Yet he still feels the damp grit of rock against the flat of his palm. He rubs his hand against the folds of his robe, it doesn't rub off. He wears the tingling pressure like a glove. They're waiting. The memory of Gerona drops away from him. He looks at their two faces. He wants them to be happy and not ever hate each other. He wants it to go well for them. For himself, he wants to find whatever he was waiting for in that room, for God to tell him something that is clear and sure. He wants to do something, find something... anything that will help. "Dearly beloved," he hears himself say. Faces stretch in a blur to the back of the church. He hears his voice float out to them, saying, "We are gathered together here..."

Three days later, he's camping in the mountains with the junior highs. Only writing the budget is worse. He can't go to bed until they're all packed away in their sleeping bags. One kid to a bag.

"Okay, guys," he calls out to a pair he knows is lying behind a rock in the dark. "Time for everybody to call it a night." Silence.

"You've got five minutes, guys," he says. It's Hank and Marisa. They're the ones who are still missing. "I'm going to finish cleaning up the fire. When I count heads again, everybody better be front and center."

He follows the oval of his flashlight beam back into the center of the camp.

"Dr. Hammond, somebody knocked over that thing we built for a seat over the hole. You know, for a bathroom?"

Swain shines his flashlight at the voice. It's Woody. "Can't you set it back up?"

"It's really disgusting, Dr. Hammond."

"Wait a minute, let me do something about the fire. Where are the other chaperones?"

"Who? Mr. Edgerton? He's helping Belinda. She dropped one of her contacts."

"Okay, enough of this. We're all going to bed. That's what's happening next. You. Right now. Get in your sleeping bag."

"I have to brush my teeth. I can't—"

"Fine, brush your teeth. You've got five minutes and that's it." He raises his head and yells. To every one of them, brushing their teeth, making out on the ground, whatever. "Five minutes, everybody. Today is over in five minutes."

Finally they're all sacked out. He looks at the glowing face of his watch in the dark . . . 1:12, and he can't get to sleep. George Edgerton is lying beside him snoring. Under him the ground stays level to just below his shoulders. Then there's a wallowed-out place along his right side. He keeps rolling into it. We walked nine miles today, uphill. You'd think I'd be tired.

He turns over again. The side of the tent is up against his face. It smells like dirty socks. This isn't going to work. There's no point in lying here. He slides the sleeping bag off of him and scoots his way out of the tent.

There's no moon up at all. It's so dark he can barely see the trunks of the nearest trees. Two birds are calling back and forth to each other. One close by, the other far away. Fuzzy muffled calls. He crouches and laces his boots. The flashlight—in his pack inside the tent. He'll do without.

He crosses the campsite. He can hear breathing. Between the tents, a few dark shapes are lying around on the ground. He steps carefully, quietly to the path that leads to the trail. There's some break in the trees here. He'll walk up just a little way.

He starts up, on the route they'll take tomorrow, placing each foot carefully in front of him. The trail is nothing but rocks, like the bed of a creek.

The air feels terrific. Up here, you can feel the first edge of cold weather. You can already smell fall coming. The leaves will be starting to turn in no time. What a summer this has been...a whole lifetime.

His legs, his chest are bare. He feels so light. Why would anybody want to sleep anyway? He hardly needs sleep anymore. Sometimes in the middle of the night at home, he sits in the dark with his eyes wide open and remembers that a miracle almost happened. Tonight, if it happened again, he could do it, let it happen. He could do anything.

The night is damp and cool against him, the hair on him stands up against the chill. He leans forward and feels ahead with his hands. The trail is getting steeper. He gets his balance and gets a good hold, and pulls himself up. Then he searches around again and goes another few feet. In the daytime this would be easy. It'll look like nothing tomorrow. In the dark, it's an adventure. Everything is an adventure.

He creeps, rock by rock. In the rhythm of a tune: "We are... climbing...Jacob's ladder..." He sings it out loud, then louder. So what if they wake up? What are they doing rolled up in their bags asleep on a night like this? He's starting to get warm. He's getting the hang of this, picking up some speed. A thin branch scrapes against his leg.

The slope begins to ease off, level out. Cautiously he stands, feeling his way forward with short steps. It's lighter up ahead. It looks like an opening. The trail zags left. He follows it, his hands on one tree trunk, then another. An opening in the trees.

He walks into the small clearing and looks out and takes a deep breath. Darkness. But thinner, less like a blanket. Something huge is out there and he can almost see it. It's like standing at a window at night and looking out at the ocean. Rows of mountains. They're there. He can't see them, but he knows they're there.

A few tiny lights are sprinkled across the miles of darkness. Here and there a twinkle, a cluster. He imagines lines for the roads to connect them. The breeze is cooling him. The lights are so hazy, if his eyes weren't focused, he wouldn't even be able to tell. It makes him dizzy. He steadies himself, one hand on the smooth hide of a tree, and stares out. There's nowhere for your eyes to stop, you don't even know when you've stopped seeing. I could push off from here like a swimmer and float out over it all. If I jumped, I wouldn't fall. It's tempting. If I had the faith, I could do it. . . .

Tomorrow he'll come up here and look at the view. Round green mountains. Long sloping valleys. Sky. Now he can't see a thing, and he stands here in the dark and knows it's all out there —or something is. He can feel it like the presence of another person in a room. Which is so incredible, so amazing, suddenly so exciting, he could run down this mountain and up the next one, yelling, waking up everybody in a sleeping bag in the whole Appalachian chain.

He stays where he is, the gravel under his feet makes a hollow sound as rocks rub against rocks. The lights out there don't change at all, a few here, a few there, it's so quiet. Then the breeze rustles toward him again through the trees.

The gut feeling that it's all there—if I could explain that . . .

show Jakey how much is still left. . . . He lifts his hands to his head. God, if I could just do something . . . not forever be standing useless and helpless beside the hospital bed.

In the morning, they pack up their garbage and cover up the cinders and ashes. Then they hike. Swain wants to press on and on, never taking any breaks, not stopping at the overlooks. He wants to cover ground, eat up miles. He wants to move.

On Sunday, he's back at the front, still with the feel of the climbing in the calves of his legs. The sanctuary is almost full, unusually crowded for Labor Day Sunday. The anthem—the soloist from First Presbyterian—goes on and on. Swain looks across the pews, the summer colors are fading. Dark plaids, rust and burned leaves. People breaking out their fall clothes. Maybe a good freeze will put the summer out of everybody's memory. Certainly most of them would like to forget that "unfortunate" business about the voice of God. The singer, standing in the middle of the choir loft, finishes and sinks back into her seat. He rises and steps into the pulpit. "Will you join me in an affirmation of faith," he says.

"I believe," he begins. The deep whisper of the whole congregation rises to the top of the room. "In God the Father Almighty. Maker of Heaven and Earth, and of all things visible and invisible. And in one Lord Jesus Christ"—there's Patrice, by herself . . . the Bartholomews, and snippy old DeWitt Chambers—"the only-begotten Son of God, begotten of His Father before all worlds"—the rhythm of it, the repetition, the part he loves: "God of God; Light of Light; Very God of Very God." An incantation. If I were a god, I would answer, I would come running. They finish, the "amen" like two notes of music. With a great shuffling and rustling, they sit back down.

He waits. Then, switching into the less reverent tone he uses for his own words, he says, "Most of us have seen those signs on mountain roads that say we are approaching an overlook. Probably we have all pulled off at one of those paved areas, stopped the car, gotten out to have a look."

He looks around, catches the eye of Bernie Morris, his littlest girl leaning her head against his shoulder. Bernie looks away, looks down at his daughter. "There before us"—sweeping one robed arm in a wide arc—"is a great open expanse of mountains. We can see across mountains lined up four to six deep in the distance. Anybody who ever drove along the Blue Ridge Parkway has marveled at such sights. It doesn't take a prophet to see forever, even on an ordinary slightly hazy day.

"This week, I had the opportunity, on the fine camping retreat with the junior highs, to see the view from an overlook in darkness. Darkness that was so deep I could not tell trees from sky." He tells them about feeling his way up the trail, gets a few chuckles. He tells them how excited, how exhilarated he was. Then he says, "I looked out through the same trees the next morning.

"Standing there in the dark by myself, I had sensed the power of those mountains, without quite seeing their outlines. I knew what was out there, though I didn't know in the usual way. And a sermon started to come to mind, about trusting and faith. But it's not the same sermon that I come into the pulpit with this morning, because I made the mistake of going back to look again in daylight.

"What I found out the next morning was that I was wrong about a lot of what I'd thought was out there. I was wrong about where the highest elevations were, wrong about the direction of the long valley, wrong about all the details.

"Suddenly, what I faced was the problem which we all have in matters of our religious faith. Our eyes and our ears and our everyday knowledge tell us that you can't see in the dark, that death is final, that miracles don't happen. But our religious feelings—the upwelling of belief from our deepest selves—tell us that this is not the whole truth.

"We each of us deal with two kinds of knowledge. One a constant barrage of information. The other, which we search and hope for, ever elusive and inexplicable. Two ways of knowing that sometimes seem contradictory. Forcing us to live with the daily awareness that all of our knowledge is incomplete.

"It would be so much easier if our daylight senses would confirm the things we learn in extrasensory ways—" A rustling, a stirring starts. A fire crackling across the sanctuary. That one word—that's all it took. They wouldn't have even noticed if it weren't for what's already happened. Hawk Epworth twists around to look at his wife. DeWitt purses his lips. Ed Fitzgerald looks as if he has a gas pain. "Did you hear that? Here he goes again!" He can hear them saying it. He doesn't look at Bernie.

Bernie gazes up into the rafters and slowly rubs his neck. Talking about his mountain climbing. It probably near killed him to spend two days in the woods with a bunch of kids. But the way he says it, it almost makes you want to go find a ledge on some mountain and look for God. The guy can spin out the words, he always could. What he needs is somebody to tell him to stop talking while he's still ahead.

"I haven't come here today," Swain is saying, "to argue for one kind of knowledge against the other. For insight, rather than sight. It would be so wasteful to ignore the gift of our common sense, our ordinary senses.

"But in some way I knew something about those dark mountains without my vision. That unarguable certainty, though it be wrong in the details, is an equally crucial kind of knowledge that, for the sake of our spirits, we must not abandon."

Three times now, God has appeared to me. As absolute and undeniable as what has happened to Jakey.

"Let us pray," he says. Heads bow.

In the third row, Bill Bartholomew pops the stem of his watch in and out. This is the limit. Some changes have to be made. Hammond can hide it in all the pretty stories he wants to, but he's saying the same thing over and over and I don't want to hear it. I don't come to church to listen to ghost stories. Next thing we know, he's going to fire the organist and have us all waiting here in silence to hear from God. I'm not going to sit back and let this go any farther.

Swain braces himself against his arms, pushes forward, his own head bowed. "God, give us the grace to live with our partial knowledge, our conflicting learnings. Give us both sight and insight. Give us the wisdom to know that in both of these we are limited. That on the sunniest days with the best of eyes, it's hard to see past the fourth row of mountains."

Seated over in the shadows on one of the side pews, Gladys Henby is thinking how long it has been since she and Walter used to go to the mountains. All she sees now is her kitchen, and her mother-in-law lying up in the bed that used to be theirs, yelling to be waited on. She remembers an overlook they stopped at once on the Blue Ridge Parkway. . . .

"Keep us from discarding, in our frustration, the things that don't fit. The miraculous." He pauses. "The illogical. The extraordinary. Give us the courage to believe in things visible and invisible. Amen."

I t's not easy—in fact, it's probably somewhat unusual to come back to take a pastorate in your hometown. Inevitably there's going to be somebody in the congregation who remembers you drunk on your ass in high school, at the very least. All of that was carefully considered—by both Swain and the elders—before he came to Westside.

But Swain was so well behaved as a kid that there wasn't much of that sort of thing to remember. Now he wishes there were more.

Bernie Morris is one person in the church who does remember him from school, all the way back. Swain is still reeling from Bernie's voting to send him to a shrink. Ever since that night on the phone, Swain has had their most daring early adventure on his mind. It was so much fun that now it hurts him to think about. When they were sixteen, they took Swain's mother's car and drove the ten hours to New York and spent a Saturday night. Swain's parents were out of town, Bernie told his that he had an out-of-town band trip for a football game. He played the clarinet.

"We could do this any time, you realize," Bernie said, when they were fifteen minutes outside of Chapel Hill. "I mean, it's not all that hard to do. As long as your mother doesn't check her mileage, which she'll never do."

If she did, she probably wouldn't even believe that Swain would do such a thing. He thinks, She probably considers me too much of a wimp. I hope she finds out.

Bernie leaned his head back against the headrest. Then he sat up quickly and smoothed the back of his hair.

Swain was wearing his herringbone sport coat. He'd brought a tie in his pocket in case he needed one, but when he had looked at himself in the bathroom mirror in the jacket the night before he thought an open collar would probably be the best. Not to look too dressed up as if you were from out of town. He called up Bernie and Bernie agreed.

"When we get back from this trip, we are going to be completely different people, I guarantee you," Bernie said.

"You think?" Swain looked out the window at the fields of tobacco. I wouldn't mind being different. That would be fine with me.

"Oh yeah. We'll probably get hooked up with some girls that are twenty or twenty-one. In a place like New York, it can happen. Then after an experience like that, you're ready for anything. No more sweating the small stuff." He snorted. "Chapel Hill...I don't know why we've hung around there so long. I promise you, we're going to see some action."

"I could go for it." Swain could see the top of his face in the mirror on the visor. His hair covered the pimples on his forehead. He had to keep remembering to brush it down. He looked okay— pretty good, in fact. He could hardly even go to sleep the night before, thinking about it, meeting some girl who didn't know what anybody else already thought of him. First they would take one of those boat rides around the whole city and she would stand next to him at the rail and her hair would be blowing against his face and he would have his arm around her. . . .

"Probably you'll meet somebody and I won't," Swain said. "That's what will happen. I'll wind up knocking around by myself."

"No way, man. You'll do fine. You just have to pretend you have confidence, that's all."

Swain thought about that one for a long time, almost all the way to Richmond. He'd been trying to pretend that for years, and it hadn't worked yet.

"We should stop and load up on food," Bernie said. "I'm starving."

By the time they drove through the tunnel, it was almost dark. They had stopped once for hamburgers, and in the car they'd killed a bag of potato chips, a box of doughnuts, a lot of peanut caramel candy, and some really gross little cakes that were on the rack next to the cash register. Swain was feeling sick, and then the white tile of the tunnel, which looked like a bathroom, started roaring past them, and they were there. God, it was incredible. They came out of the tunnel and they were in New York, with all this traffic coming around a corner into a circle.

"No shit, we really did it," Swain said.

"Chapel Hill High School, good-bye," Bernie said, pulling Swain's mother's car across two lanes. "I hope," he said to Swain, "that you remembered to bring rubbers. I probably have some extras, if you didn't."

"Oh sure," Swain said, which was true. Not that he would probably ever need them in his whole life.

A cab swerved around them, honking. The guy gave them the finger. "See what I mean?" Bernie said. "It's all they think about here."

When they finally paused at a stoplight, Bernie said, "I've got it all planned. We have to find a piano bar."

It took hours to get there, but they did find a bar, with a piano. First they had to park the car, which was a shock, because though they'd both brought all the cash they could get together, they hadn't planned on paying more than a few dimes for parking. "Goddamn highway robbery," Bernie said, when they emerged from the lot and were finally on the pavement.

"Maybe we can come back and sleep in it."

"Maybe we'll be invited to somebody's apartment."

But Swain had started to look around. He wasn't at that point thinking about finding girls at all. The city was dazzling. The lights went straight up into a night that wasn't even dark, it looked sort of navy blue. And the streets. It was like watching a huge river, he could have stood there next to the little grocery store with the oranges stacked in pyramids and stared at people passing all night. But he went along to the bar because Bernie swore up and down this was the thing to do. He had the name of it folded up on a page he had torn out of *The New Yorker*. "Winsome elegant pianist Brooke Tate stars in this intimate room. Nightly except Sundays. Nine to midnight."

They did sell them drinks, which was a major victory. Bernie gave Swain a fake ID, but nobody asked. A girl with shaved eyebrows brought them two bourbons and didn't even look at them when she put the drinks down. The piano player was in the corner plinking away. Swain drank his drink and messed with the green straw.

"All right, over there. What do you think?"

Bernie was pointing to a woman who was sitting by herself, having a drink at one of the little tables in front of the bench along the wall. She looked as though she had gone to sleep with her eyes open.

"Are you kidding, man? She's probably thirty." Swain looked again. It was darker in here than it was outside. "Actually, to tell you the truth," he said, "she may be dead. I think that lady just died." Swain started laughing, he bent over the table trying to hide it.

"You are embarrassing the shit out of me," Bernie said. Then he started laughing and he couldn't stop either.

In the second place they went to, they stood up at the bar and drank, figuring that would work better. Bernie asked a girl who had her back turned to them what time it was. He almost touched her back to get her attention. It was bare, she had on a shirt with a low top. Bernie decided he better not and sort of stuck his head around her shoulder. He said, "Excuse me, do you have the time?"

"Almost bedtime," she said, and touched his chin with her fingers. The other girl she was with laughed.

Bernie turned back around. "Man-hating bitch," he said.

They decided to go get a hotel, a cheap one that Bernie knew about, and check in before it got any later. Then they'd go back out.

Bernie was at the desk getting them a room and there was a mob of people standing around next to their suitcases, or flopped on the sofas. They looked exhausted. "Tour groups," Bernie said. "I would hate to have to travel like that."

Swain walked around and stared at them. He was a little woozy from the bourbon, even after walking blocks and blocks.

He sat down on one of the grungy-looking sofas. It wasn't even two seconds before a girl came and sat down on the other end. She kept looking at a bunch of kids sitting about fifty feet away that she was supposed to be with, but there wasn't any more room over there. Then she started hunting around for something in her pocketbook.

"Hi," Swain said. It was so loud everybody in the room could hear.

"Oh, hello." She had a British accent.

"Did you just come here from England?"

"Yes, we've only now driven in from the plane. My first visit to the States. Are you American?"

"Yes. Although, actually, of course, I was born in Finland."

She frowned. "Oh dear. I had so hoped to meet some nice Americans."

"No, wait, I'm American—I was only over there for a year, and then my parents came home. My father was doing research. Really, I promise, I live in North Carolina. It's true." Her face looked kind of average, but she had definitely above-average tits. Definitely.

"How long will you be here?" he said. "In America."

"Two weeks altogether. We're scheduled for Grand Canyon and Disneyland and a movie studio. I'm quite excited. I'm afraid we shan't go to North Carolina. Pity." She wrinkled up her nose.

Out of the corner of his eye, he saw Bernie look around for him, then see him and check out the girl. He slapped his forehead with his hand and staggered backward. Swain looked away from him so he wouldn't laugh.

"Are you—I mean, do you have plans for tonight? There's this bar I know about, it's in Greenwich Village, if—"

"Oh, they won't let me. We all have to go straight to our rooms. We have so many rules to follow it's completely silly. As if we were twelve years old, you would think."

"I could help you carry your suitcases up, if that's okay. My name is Swain Hammond."

"Oh yes, do. My name is Edith Potter."

Swain and Edith managed about five minutes of privacy in the hall outside her door, before the chaperones surged back down the hall checking their lists of numbers and knocking on each of the doors. Between the light bulbs in the ceiling, the light would thin out and the hall would be a little bit dark. Swain with one arm around Edith, the other dragging a bag, came to one of the dark places and stopped. "I'm so glad I met you," he said as he leaned toward her lips.

She kissed him back as if he were the Statue of Liberty and the Empire State Building and the whole Grand Canyon. She put her hand on the back of his head and pushed them together even more. Her tits were mashed against him. He slowly eased his way up her side until he had one in his hand. For a half second, he thought about Bernie, who was going to shit bullets. His thumb rubbed across her nipple. His heart was beating so hard it could wake up everybody in the whole place. She pressed up hard against him; she was feeling it against her, she had to be. Then a door opened and they pulled apart. She straightened her blouse. "Good night, Miss Windham," Edith said to the woman who stood in the door. Miss Windham watched until Edith said, "I have to go. I'll talk to you later," and dragged her bag inside.

When he got back downstairs, Bernie was sitting on one of the sofas, waiting. "How was I supposed to know what to do?" he said. "You just walk off and leave. How am I supposed to know if you're going to spend the whole night or something? You expect me to sit and wait all night? Jesus, Swain. So what happened? How come you're back here so fast?"

Swain told him what happened. "I mean, I had my hand right on her boob when this chaperone comes roaring out the door."

Bernie was dull-eyed, slack-jawed with misery. "So is that all? Is she going to sneak out?"

"No," Swain said. He hadn't even thought about it. He was doing well to get as far as he did. Better than Bernie...

Bernie brightened. "Obviously you need me around to tell you what to do."

Bernie and Swain stayed friends all the way through undergrad. Then Bernie went into his family's realty business in Chapel Hill after graduation and Swain went off to divinity school. They didn't see as much of each other for a few years and somehow got used to that. But still Swain had thought of him as a close friend.

There are a lot of people in the church that he has known a long time. But only two of them are very important to him. The other one is Patrice Miles—her name had been Guardino. He didn't know her well at all back then. But she and Bernie are his tenuous link to the years that so far amount to the first half of his life.

In 1966, Swain asked Patrice to sign his yearbook. She wrote, "So tall and so serious." She wrote it next to her picture and her list of honors and activities: "Class play: 2,3,4. Homecoming Court. Thespians." She was an actress. So dark, and so intense. So vivid. But that's not what Swain wrote in her yearbook. His message in the margin next to his picture was: "Have a great time at college. Sincerely, Swain." She had been going steady with Gibbs Elmore as long as he had known her, as far as he knew, since she moved here from Pittsburgh in junior high.

Patrice did have a great time in college. The romance with Gibbs didn't survive her freshman year or her edgy desire to get to center stage. She spent the next several years playing one boyfriend against another. Then, at Christmas in her second year of law school, she married Joe Miles, quite a bit older, a brooding Heathcliff type only she seemed easily able to talk to. Next to him, she was like a red-and-green tropical bird. Though saying that is not to diminish Joe. Years ago, he started his own brick-manufacturing company, and sold it at a very good price, so Swain has heard. After that, for something to do, he came to the business school in Chapel Hill. Joe is not a man that anyone could overlook. He gives off a sense of authority that people always notice. He and Patrice together are an impressive sight. And it was important to her at the time to bring home a prize.

For Swain, Patrice was a high school fantasy who had never faded from his memory, who then reappeared in his life in his new congregation, married, with a difficult husband, a new baby, and a job in Raleigh with a company that exported agricultural products to Japan. He wasn't positive about her married name when he went over the list of the membership; he thought, hoped it might be her. Then he looked out into the congregation that first Sunday morning and saw her. She smiled at him, he could have sworn. He lost his place in what he was saying. She looked exactly the same

...she looked beautiful. The full force of his old longing for her swept over him again...prickling, moving, unsettling every inch of his skin.

The fact that, like Bernie, she knew him before he put on the black robe, makes all of it in some ways easier, and in some ways, harder. The fact that her husband has the kind of rough authority that Swain envies has been the most difficult thing of all.

He walks back to his office after the service, taking his robe off and piling it like a thick towel over his shoulder. All he has done is hint at the touchy subject of miracles and he feels as if he's spent two hours in a gym. He stops midway the length of the hall. She's standing in front of his door, waiting, turning the church bulletin around and around in her hands.

"Swain," Patrice says, when he is still ten feet away. "Can you stay a few more minutes? I need to talk."

"Sure." He holds the door for her. "I'm glad you've come," he says. Then he concentrates on putting his robe on its hanger, hanging it on the hook on the back of the door. Suddenly, his hands are shaking. *Her child is blind, she needs to talk, and all I can think about is that the two of us are here alone.* "Sit down," he says. He sinks into the armchair. She sits across from him, on the edge of the sofa.

She starts to speak, stops, starts again. "Swain...what I'm worried about is Joe. I think he's gone completely crazy. He's getting worse instead of better."

"What's going on?"

"He keeps saying again and again—Swain, it's so scary—that he wants to kill you and Sam. That he ought to."

"I'm surprised he hasn't...me, anyway...after what I did."

"But he's not actually doing anything at all. He just sits. Sometimes he goes into Jakey's bedroom and sits and stares at him, not saying anything. It's terrible for Jakey. He can't tell what's going on. He isn't even sure sometimes if his father's still sitting there. But what can I say? 'Don't sit with your son'?

"Sometimes he acts like he blames Jakey. For being in the

street, letting it happen. If Jakey even spills something, he gets furious, he explodes in a rage. Once, after he did that, it came over him what he was doing. He sat at the dinner table and cried, without making a sound, and Jakey never even knew. Joe sat there and stared at him with the tears running down his face, but he didn't say 'I'm sorry,' he didn't say anything. At first, I felt so sorry for him, for all of us. But now he's starting to scare me." She pauses. "Then later on, in the middle of the night sometimes, he'll start saying all that stuff about what he's going to do to you and Sam. Jakey's doing fine compared to how Joe's handling it."

She goes on: "I'm so proud of Jakey, how he's trying. It's like he has to start over, in every way. It's awful. You wouldn't even believe it," she stops, blinks back tears. "It's like he's an infant again. But he's not crazy. Not like Joe."

She looks away, the light from the window throws white patches of glare on her face. "I wish he would go away for a while and let us get through this, get used to it."

"Patrice, it's only been a few weeks since it happened. You can't expect . . . It's too soon for any of you to even start getting over it. It's going to hit all of you differently."

"So I tell myself. But he's making it so much harder for Jakey, and for me." She fiddles with a button on her blouse, stares off into space. He can't take his eyes off her hand there.

He makes himself say something: "Are you both back at work?"

"I go back this week. I took a leave. Joe—officially he's working. I don't know what he's doing really. I was supposed to be in Kyoto this week. Now everything's stopped. There's nothing but this. I still can't believe it has happened. I look at him and I'm numb."

He shakes his head. "I'm so sorry, Patrice." The words sound as if they're made out of Styrofoam. I'm not going to be able to help, sitting here lusting after her. "How about Jakey?" he says. As if my asking for more and more facts would comfort her, do her any good. "What does he do all day?"

"He's feeding himself. He's getting pretty good at the daily routine. Things I would never even think about. Going to the bathroom. But he's not really doing anything all day, nothing that might interest him or distract him, I think that's making him even more depressed."

Swain thinks, I should have been over there talking, playing games, singing songs . . . anything. It's been a week . . . more, since I've seen the kid. What have I been thinking of? "Patrice, look I'll start coming by—"

"He isn't going to be at the house much longer, Swain. I've made up my mind about this. It's the best thing for him. I want him to go down to Mill Ridge to the school for the blind. I know you're going to say it's too soon. But he needs to be somewhere doing something. Now. School's just starting. He could be a little late. It's only seventy-five miles—we could see him anytime, and he could come home on weekends." She pauses. "I can't mention it to Joe without him yelling or getting up and walking out. He won't talk about it. I followed him out into the backyard. I said, 'Joe, he can't just sit here. What is he going to do—listen to the radio?' Joe didn't answer at all. He started throwing firewood from one stack to another on the pile, slamming it against the back wall of the shed."

"I'm not going to say it's too early, Patrice, I don't know. How does Jakey feel about it?"

"He doesn't really want to do anything. Sometimes all he'll do is cry and say he wants to stay home. I don't know what to do. Maybe it is too soon. I don't know. But he's memorized where everything is in the house. He's getting himself around. All he has to do now—" Her eyes fill up and tears spill down her face. She rummages in her pocketbook for a tissue. "All he has to do is memorize everything else in the world and hope it doesn't change."

Swain stands up, then sits down. He gets up again and gets the tissue box from the end table and hands it to her. He backs off and stands in the middle of the room, then takes a long step forward again and drops down beside her on the couch. He puts both arms around her. "Patrice," he says. Now she's really crying ...too hard to feel how his heart is beating. "Patrice." Her arms all bunched up against his chest, like a kid almost. Then that notion vanishes and his lust for her pushes past everything else. He wants to touch all of her in one motion, all at once. I have to stop this. He doesn't move. He makes himself breathe slowly. Julie...he thinks...Julie Julie Julie. Slowly, carefully, he strokes her hair.

She sits very still in his arms, her crying stopped. Swain Hammond is sitting here with his arms around me. All these years of watching him from a distance, his wide skinny shoulders. Now his hand...

He has always liked me. Is this where it's going? Are we going to do it right here on the couch? He couldn't have changed that much. She holds her breath and waits. She feels his leg where it touches her leg, her face against his chest.

She is so still, he thinks. She's sending me my cue to let go. If I drag it out now, she'll know. Slowly he sits back from her, gives her arm a pat and pulls away, not looking at her. If I look at her eyes, I'm in trouble. If I look at her lips...

She turns away, reaches for another tissue, sits and stares at the floor. Swain slides away onto the other cushion of the sofa. She thinks, I was wrong. It was sympathy.

He watches her wipe her eyes. Her child has just been blinded, why can't I think of that?

She turns to him, looks at that long solemn face with the hair falling down in his eyes. So much of the time he looks disappointed. Jakey will probably always look like that. Permanently disappointed. It sweeps back over her again, as if it were the first time: Jakey is blind. "Oh, Swain, all this that I've been saying— about Joe—it doesn't matter. Not compared to what has happened to my boy. My baby. You can't imagine...the whole rest of his life." She looks as though she's going to cry again, she forces herself to stop.

"It wasn't Sam's fault. Or yours. I don't want any more trouble, anybody else hurt. If it weren't for that, I'm to the point I wouldn't even care what Joe does. As far as I'm concerned, you can come over to the house and hit him again." She starts to look around for her pocketbook, gathering up the Kleenex. "I've got to go, Swain. I know you're ready to get away from here and get home."

"I'll come over and see Jakey," he says, when they're standing in front of the door. She nods, reaches up and touches his cheek.

She must know what she's doing to me, even now. Surely she always has known.

She says, "Thanks, Swain." She looks back at him once, makes an effort at a smile, as she walks out.

He shuts the door behind her and goes back and sits down in the chair. Her perfume is still in the room. He leans back and closes his eyes.

SIX

"**D**o you realize this is the first time you've ever asked me to do any such thing?"

"I hadn't thought of it." He pulls out onto Woodland. Julie is going with him to visit Jakey, taking her lunch break to do it. "I just wanted you to go."

"How come? Scared you'll hit Joe again?"

"I doubt if he'll be there. I expect it will just be the boy and his mom."

"I'm surprised you want me there, then."

He thinks, I want you there. "I thought you were interested in the kid."

"I am." She looks out her window.

He nods. "So am I."

He takes her hand, not saying anything, driving. She looks over at him. Then her hand settles into his. She sighs and leans her head back against the seat. "I look forward to getting back to ordinary regular life again. Things the way they used to be."

"How did they used to be?"

"I had a general idea of what was going on."

"Pretty boring."

"It wasn't so bad."

"You were always the one who was saying, 'Loosen up, Swain.' That's exactly what you said."

"I was serious at the time. I guess I didn't think there was a chance in hell you'd ever do it."

He pulls into the Mileses' street. "There it is, over there." A bicycle leans against the side of the garage. Why don't they put that somewhere they don't have to look at it every time they come and go? Probably Joe won't let her move it.

Patrice meets them at the door. Backlit by the big den window, she's silhouetted, hard to see at first. "Thank you for coming, both of you." Touching them each on the arm. "Jakey's in the back. He's feeling kind of low this morning. This is the time he'd be going back to school with his friends."

She leads them through the front hall and back into the den. Her hair all tied up like that, she looks as if she just got out of the bath, still that same perfume, strong, as though she just put it on. "Jakey, you've got company," she says.

There he is. Sitting in a big reclining chair. Most of the bandages gone, just the edge of a patch showing around the big silver reflector sunglasses. So skinny and little he has to reach out to rest his arms on the arms of the chair. Those big sunglasses that must be his dad's covering half his face.

Julie says, "Hi, Jakey. It's Julie and Swain."

He lets out a breath in complaint. If he could see, he would turn to Patrice with a look that says "Why do I have to do this?" He shifts in the chair. "Hi," he says.

"How are you doing, fellow?" Swain says.

The kid shrugs, makes a face.

Julie says, "Pretty spiffy shades you picked out."

Jakey says, "I guess."

Silence. Patrice starts to say something, as Julie says, "So, what have you been up to all morning?"

Jakey hesitates. Swain thinks: they're doing him a favor putting him through this? "I was listening to TV," he says. "She tells me what's happening in the parts where they just play music."

"Are we making you miss a good show?" Julie says.

"Naah. I don't care. It was a drag."

Silence settles over them again.

After a moment, Swain says, "I guess pretty much everything might seem like a drag right now."

"Yeah." Now the boy's legs lie so limp on the seat of the chair. You could forget and think that he's paralyzed and that's why they're here.

"Probably it will be like that for a pretty long time and then things will start getting a little better. After a while." Julie looks at him as if she's not sure he should have said that.

"I'd be sad too," Swain says. "It's a pretty awful thing." He sees the kid's throat bob. Tears start down one cheek, just sneaking out from under the sunglasses. Jakey wipes them away quickly, lifting the glasses just enough to do it. The other side of his face is dry.

Patrice says, "Careful, Jakey. Don't touch." Swain feels a tightness in his own throat.

Julie jumps in, takes over. "Have your friends been coming by to visit you?"

Jakey shrugs. "Yeah."

Patrice says, "This Saturday—"

Jakey says, "I wish I was dead."

"Son."

"It's hard," Swain says.

Julie leans over and puts her hand on Jakey's arm. "Mom?" he says.

"It's Julie." The boy stiffens and waits for her to take her hand away.

"Mom, I'm tired."

Sitting there...not even knowing who's touching him. A blind target. How could anything be lonelier than that? Looking at him, Swain can remember being swallowed up by the size of a chair. But he wasn't blind. He didn't have anything to complain about. He was lucky. He had everything. His mother was often gentle and attentive...whenever she was around. She taught art history; sometimes she'd go off for weeks on tours to look at cathedrals. When she was home, he would go find her wherever she was in

the house and she would look up and smile at him and wait for
him to say what he wanted. She was so pretty . . . like some sort of
magic princess; you couldn't just call somebody like that and expect them to come.

Then he found out about the affair. For a long time thinking
about it made him feel tired, made him want to sleep, or just not
do anything. But after a while, he got used to knowing at the back
of his mind that his family wasn't really a family at all. It didn't
matter, it didn't change anything really.

He wondered sometimes if there were somebody else his father
loved, and if maybe she had kids that his father hung around and
played with. But he never really thought so. Once he lay on the
floor of his father's study reading. He was allowed to do that
sometimes, if he promised to be very quiet. Dad was working at
his desk. Swain watched the blue drifts of cigarette smoke float up
beyond the lamplight.

Dad turned around and saw that Swain was looking at him and
he leaned back in this chair, rubbing his shoulder as though it
were tired.

He said, "What are you reading?"

"*Hardy Boys.*"

He laughed. "Is it good?"

Swain nodded.

"I'm glad you like to read, son. It will keep you from ever
having to be lonely." It crossed his mind then for the first time:
that maybe Dad was?

He looks at Jakey. Knowing more about pain than Swain ever
will. It's crazy . . . he has no right to even think it . . . still he knows
in his gut how it feels to sit in that chair.

Julie catches his eye. Time to go.

"Jakey," he says, his voice sounding way too loud. "We'll come
back by to check on you another day soon." The kid doesn't say
anything. His head doesn't move. Julie says, "Good-bye, Jakey."
Jakey says, so you can hardly hear it, "Bye."

Patrice walks them out. "I'm sorry," she says at the door. "I think it helps even if it doesn't seem like it. Thanks.

"Come back again," she says, looking at Swain. She looks as if she wants to get them out the door before she starts to cry.

Julie is waiting in the studio at the radio station, watching the panel of lights and monitors and the slow-turning plastic reels. A taped show is airing now, and in three minutes, two minutes, fifty-seven seconds, she is on. It's not scary at all, being on the air. She didn't have stage fright even the first time. It's so cool and quiet here. An ivory tower, from ten to midnight on Sundays. Being alone, talking into the mike. At the hospital, the library's never quiet. The loudspeaker all the time paging doctors. People coming in and out talking as if they're in a mall. Here you can forget there's anyone out there. Except Swain, lying on the sofa wearing headphones. He's probably already there.

If he goes on the way he's going now, I can just move in here full-time, talk to him from here, keep my sanity. My secret boudoir. Thousands of people, out there half listening. I could whisper something, slip in something so low they don't even know they heard it: something sexy, get them all into bed. Or I could say, "This is God talking. You listen to Swain—he knows."

At the church they all keep looking me over to see if they can get some clue to what's going on. Whatever dark circles will tell them, they're welcome to know. I can't tell them what's happening. I'm not even going to try.

So many times I've heard a voice, or imagined whole scenes spread out in front of me. My river with the castles high up in the mountains looking down on it, a shine on the water way down there, and I can see the whole thing, like I'm drifting down into it. Swain doesn't have to lose his mind over hearing that voice. I wish I could have heard it too, exactly what he heard. If he's going to go crazy, I'd just as soon go crazy too.

A face appears in the studio window, smiling. Andy, passing by.

Such a cutie. All the students who work here...Andy presses his lips up against the heavy glass. She blows him a kiss. Thirty seconds to air. She sits up straight in her chair, takes a deep breath. The light goes on. "Good evening, this is Julie Hammond. Welcome..."

At home, Swain is still on the phone at the moment the show starts. Maria Durden's daughter caught the first week of school with a Ziploc full of dope. At least that's all she had, it could have been worse. He finally gets off the phone, hurries into the living room with his coffee and stretches out on the sofa. He adjusts the earphones. The blue foam rubber part is coming off one side, the metal's cutting into his ear. He resettles his feet on the arm. Ready finally. He makes himself relax and slow down.

The piece that's on sounds like an old music box. He pictures men in tight leggings with powdered wigs. Not what Julie usually picks. Two hours a week she does this. Not the best time slot, but her audience is easier than his. He moves the hot circle of his mug of decaf to a different spot on his chest. He should take the phone off the hook.

Here she comes. Small sounds of her mouth close to the mike, then: "This is listener-supported public radio WCHU-FM. We've been listening to Strauss's *Watercolors March,* performed by the Vienna Philharmonic." She must have picked it for the name.

"Now on our evening concert, we will hear Telemann's..." He hears her voice, but not the words, then she's gone. Her mike is off, he doesn't hear her breath in both his ears. Out of the silence, the deep voice of a horn starts a slow climb. He closes his eyes. The low notes hum inside his stomach, like a faraway ship's horn. Other instruments are starting to come in. It's a slow processional. He can see it, a row of ships, coming up a river, moving to this tune—the orchestra playing on a bluff high above them. Parade music, for white ships that one by one leave the mouth of the river and head out to sea.

The sound of the horn wavers. In his fantasy, he moves the orchestra to a different place. Not on a bluff now—on a cloud, drifting over the whole scene. A whole orchestra, guys in black tuxedoes with shiny brass horns and big fiddles, up to their knees in white cloud smoke. Like a cartoon of Heaven. Julie would love it. Again the music is gone.

"A short work now by Beethoven." He should have a special telephone to her, attached to her headset, so he can talk back. "The Overture to *The Ruins of Athens,* performed by the Berlin Philharmonic, Herbert von Karajan conducting." It starts with an echoing chord. Zooming up to a high pitch. Like movie music for a haunted house. The camera is about to zero in on somebody tiptoeing up to a closed door. Now the wind is sweeping around the dark house. The station needs him to come on with Julie and explain what's really happening.

"Swain."

His feet stop moving.

"Swain." It's not a real voice. It's inside him, in his head.

"Listen. With your heart." He lies so still, the blood stops in his fingers. There's nothing but the washes of color he sees when his eyes are shut. Yellow orange brown—then fine white lines moving like a computer graphic. There's nothing there. His own internal voice says into that silence, "I'm listening."

His words drop into a bottomless space. He is facing into something huge. Something's going to lunge forward at him, he's going to fall. "I'm listening." The sound dissipates into the space.

For one second, he feels again the pressure of the earphones against his ears, the sofa pillow on the back of his neck, his legs. Then he leaves the motionless surface of his body and goes back inside. The music is muffled, he hears it as a diver would.

Then come the words, in silence, carved by a knife on the surface of water. "This is the universe. Which you abandoned." Soundless words fly at him, like satellites, meteorites, out in space where there's no up and no down.

He waits for more, but nothing more comes, and as he waits the sound of the music pours back into his ears. Here are his sprawled legs, the rough weave of the upholstery. It's over.

He stretches, as if he'd slept for hours and he's slowly waking. It has happened again.

"We'll be listening to music by Mozart, a piece that I hope you'll enjoy as much as I do: Piano Quartet in G Minor, Koechel Listing 478. Artur Rubinstein, performing with the Guarneri Quartet."

He's in bed when she gets home. Hiding, not wanting to talk. This time it has left him so stunned, so quieted, he doesn't want the stillness broken.

A cabinet opens and shuts in the kitchen. Fixing her snack, assuming he's asleep. He looks over at the clock—1:03. He ought to be asleep. Tomorrow he has meetings day and evening, Monday, which is supposed to be his day off. The floor creaks in the hall. The line of light shines under the bathroom door. He sees the shadows where her feet pass back and forth. Then the strip of light is a solid line again, the shower goes on.

She's standing there under it, with soap lathered up in her crotch hair, water pouring over her. He works one hand through the tangle of sheets to his prick. It pushes against his hand. Why am I doing this? I wanted to be alone and quiet. He pulls the covers aside and gets up.

The full glare of the bathroom light hurts his eyes. He waits a second until he can see. Steam has clouded the mirror. Water rattles against the shower curtain. Julie's a shadow behind it. "Hey," she says. "I thought you were asleep long ago." He pulls the curtain back a crack and steps in.

"Wasn't sleepy." Water is streaming off one tit, as if she were one of those spouting statues in a fountain. He touches the hard center, the water pours into his hand.

"What were you doing while you were listening?" Her fingers follow the line of hair down the middle of his stomach. Her lips curve, suggestive, almost a smile.

"Not that."

She stands close to him. The spray is fine mist between their faces. He reaches over her shoulders, her whole back, with both arms. He curves over her, reaching into her crotch from behind. He doesn't go in, he rubs a finger along each side, feeling the thick pads of swelling, the crease of her legs, her dripping hair.

Her hands are motionless, pressed against his back, as though she's forgotten herself and him, except for that one pulsing mouth between his fingers. He teases her. Back and forth. Her hips push against him, his cock against her stomach. She wants it. He reaches in, with all his fingers into the first slick lips. He holds her open as though all that dark space inside her could spill and be his. He doesn't go further until she says, "Swain."

It comes from far down in her throat. Her head falls back away from him. Her eyes are shut. Water is hitting her face and neck.

He pushes her back against the tile wall and lifts her. She starts her moaning before he's in. His hands under her ass, he lowers her onto him. He feels the squeeze of her contraction, wrapping around him, as the tip goes in. She falls still, hanging limp and loose in his arms.

He holds her, still inside her. Slowly she starts to move again. He leans his weight against her, holding her against the wet wall. He can't stay like this much longer. Then: slow motion, starting at both ends of him, two tidal waves that meet in his gut. Exploding out of him, leaving him. His forehead leans against the wall, the water beating on his back. He feels it again like an echo. Instant playback. Shooting off inside her. Seeing it as if he's down there, seeing inside her. A slow falling of white fireworks into the huge dark space of her. The universe. His heart makes slow hard beats, like a funeral drum. No—not his universe, this is another kind of darkness. But it's as close as he knows how to get.

Julie's waiting outside the cafeteria at the mall. He kisses her. "I've got half an hour," he says.

They move toward the line. "What's on tonight?"

"The church school committee. They've had a few complaints

again that the kids aren't learning anything about the Bible. One from George Walters, which surprises me a little. I haven't seen the letter, but apparently he said his third-grader had never heard of Moses. Got a little sarcastic about it, so I'm told."

"This always comes up. Same thing, every few years."

Swain sighs. "Yes." The line moves forward. Julie picks up a tray and a napkin of silver. Swain looks at his watch. "Good. We'll be eating in five minutes."

At a table near the door, they take the dishes off the trays, sit down. Relax for a few minutes. He looks over at Julie. She looks tired. There's a shadow under her eyes, her lips look pale. "You didn't get to sleep early enough last night," he says, and watches her to see if she's reminded. She smiles, a tired smile.

He says, "I had a strange kind of day."

She stirs Sweet'n Low into her coffee. "Yeah?"

"All day I've been remembering things. Not exactly remembering. More like—seeing old movies, or being there. I don't know." He watches an old couple moving slowly toward the checkout desk across from them, the man carrying a wide-brimmed light straw hat, the woman with the straps of her pocketbook cutting into her big soft arm.

"I remembered my grandfather," he says. "I was going into a meeting this morning over at Trinity, walking up the alley from the lot next to the church. I guess I wandered into the exhaust from their kitchen in the annex, meat loaf and beans and something frying in oil. All of a sudden, I was walking down a street in Toronto. With Grandy. I must have been about six. He's been dead nearly thirty years.

"It was as if I was there. In early fall on a day like today. I could feel the warmth of the sun off the pavement up to my knees. The rest of me was cold. I had on a navy blue sweater with pockets and big buttons. I kept running ahead and he would tell me to come back."

"So what happened?"

"Nothing. That's what's strange. It just flashed through me. There must have been a restaurant there that had that same smell. If I was ever actually there. I don't remember any such moment. I don't remember that sweater." He takes a swallow of his water. His fish is getting cold, he doesn't have much time. He says, "I've been doing that a lot lately. It's as if everything that ever happened to me is all coming back. All at the same time. It's as if I'm a hundred-story building, and I can vaguely feel what's going on on every floor. Something happened last night while I was listening to you—" Julie's looking past him. He turns. As something crashes behind him.

"So awfully sorry," Sam is saying. Loud and magnanimous. He's just knocked over the empty chair at a table. "... Terribly clumsy ..." He continues to lean over the table where a couple is sitting, one hand on the man's shoulder. "I should look where I'm going."

"No harm. Don't worry," the man says again, and makes a point of returning to his dinner.

Behind Sam is a woman with a stiff black hairdo and a strained smile, looking as if she wants this to be over. Sam's heading their way now, leading her by the hand. He reaches out toward Julie while he's still six feet away. Sam's never been a gracious drunk, not that Swain has seen. Swain gets to his feet. Julie takes Sam's hand. He says, "My dear, you look lovely as always.

"And Swain." A shadow passes over Sam's face. "Ever my friend in need."

"How are you, Sam?"

"Excellent," he says. "I have someone very special I want you to meet." The woman edges closer to the table. Dressed like a hooker. Tight skirt and a low-necked ruffly blouse. The way hookers are supposed to look anyway. But old. She could be sixty. Where did he get her? What is he doing with her in the K&W, of all places?

"This is Velma," Sam says. He takes her hand and holds it in both of his. "Velma Jones."

"Velma, this is my pastor, Swain Hammond. His wife, Julie."

"Oh," Velma says. "Your—Reverend, I'm so pleased to meet you."

Sam winks at Swain. "We could be needing your services pretty soon, old buddy," Sam says. He puts his arm around Velma. His hand presses so tight against her shoulder that his fingernails look white. Dark pink spots, surrounded by white.

"Not smart to rush, of course," Sam says, giving Velma a jiggle with his arm. "But I've got a feeling this time."

Swain clears his throat. "Well, that's—good news, Sam."

Velma cuts her eyes sideways at Sam, who's starting to turn her toward the door. "We need to be going now," he says. "Don't want to be interrupting you folks' dinner. Come to see us."

"It was real nice to meet you," Velma says, looking back over Sam's arm.

They get out on the sidewalk in front of the mall and Sam says to her, "Let's go home. I don't feel like going dancing."

That night, Swain lies in his bed and looks at the ceiling. Then he turns and looks at the wall, then he turns again. It has been so long since he slept through the night, he's forgotten what it's like. There's no point in lying here.

"Where are you going?" Julie's voice is muffled in the covers.

He's trying to find something to put on. "I can't sleep. I'm getting up for a while," he says. He hears her turn back over in bed.

He steps into jeans and a shirt and tiptoes out, down the hall, through the living room, out the front door into the night air.

It's almost cold, he thinks. I should have brought a sweater. Julie said she was going to get out winter clothes this weekend. I could get them out tonight and surprise her. Air them out on the line. I've got energy to burn.

His feet sound too loud on the sidewalk. Maybe somebody will think he's a prowler and shoot him. But he's so wide awake, wired-up, manic...a bullet would bounce off him. Every twig on every tree is clear as day. In the middle of the night, it never matters that he can't sleep. It's only in the daytime that he remembers why people sleep. He's getting more and more tired every day.

All day fragments of his past float up in his face so he can't see what's in front of him. Maybe I should find a job where I can sleep all day. A night watchman.

All the houses are dark. No cars. The street lights are a dead white, bluish.

He turns at the corner to go around the same block again. If I walk and walk around the same block a hundred times, maybe that will make me want to go to sleep. I have to sleep, he thinks. Something has to change. I'm getting crazier and crazier every day.

On his way home after work the next day, he drags himself to the grocery store. He sits in the parking lot out in front of Harris-Teeter. He promised he would do this. It's warm in the car in the sun. Here, I could curl up and go to sleep. Get arrested for vagrancy by some cop shining a light into the back seat in the middle of the night, me lying in the only car left on the lot. Open the door, he tells himself. Get out and move. Walk across the pavement to the curb. Slowly he persuades himself.

Inside, he plops a bunch of bananas, a paper basket of seedless grapes in the part of the cart that the two-year-old is supposed to sit in. He always buys the bananas for the smell, and more often than not they rot before anyone eats them. But he likes them sitting there on the counter at home, turning dark and soft and filling up the room with that rich oily smell. He drops paper napkins, fettuccine noodles, Shredded Wheat, wild rice—lots of light rattly boxes—into his cart. He looks at the list written in two handwritings: mackerel steaks, ginger root, cream cheese. He's waking up a little. It's time for him to wake up, since it's almost night.

Ginger: he searches above the aisles for the Spices sign, backs his cart out of the one he's in and turns it in the other direction. It bangs against another cart. The metal rings.

"Sorry," the guy says, pulling back, jerking his basket free of Swain's.

"Joe," Swain says.

Joe Miles looks up. His eyes widen, then narrow. "Hammond." His face settles in an instant into a wary cardplayer's cool.

"I'm sorry I've missed you the times I've come by," Swain says.

"Patrice is the one you want to see." He stares at Swain across the length of two carts. He's rolling his cart back and forth, a few inches back, a few inches forward. It looks as though he's building momentum to ram into Swain.

"Joe, look—I made a terrible mistake. I tried to tell you at the hospital, but it was the wrong time. I'm sorry. I don't know what got into me, to . . . hit you, and at a time like that."

"I understand you got up there in that church and made a sermon out of my child being blind."

"I didn't think—I'm sorry if that caused you embarrassment, Joe."

"Embarrassment?" Joe says. His voice rises. "Let me tell you something. You are the one who ought to be embarrassed. You have some responsibility for what goes on at that building. I have more important things than you to worry about now. But you keep in mind, you can be held accountable. Then we'll see who's embarrassed." He pulls the cart away, swerves it in the other direc-tion. He turns back to Swain: "Don't come anywhere near my house again. Anything you and Patrice are doing, you better do somewhere else." He wheels the laden basket away.

Swain puts one hand out and braces himself against the nearest shelf. It teeters. He catches it, a rack of hosiery, orange plastic packages of panty hose falling to the floor. He turns back, Joe's gone.

He sits at the table that night after dinner. "What do you think he's going to do?"

"There's no telling," Julie says. "Maybe burn the church down during eleven o'clock. Maybe nothing. He's so unpredictable." She pauses and laughs. She hears herself laugh and thinks, Why am I laughing? She says, "He's the opposite of the way I always used to think of you."

Swain smiles. It surprises him to feel his face move like that. When have I smiled recently... on my own time? "So now I'm like Joe," he says.

"More than you were, that's for sure."

"That's nice."

"You're kidding." He wants to be like Joe? This is what I've got to look forward to?

"No, I'm not kidding. Do you think I want to be a wimp preacher all the time?"

The thought stays with him the rest of the week: he's turning into a slugger. The real Swain Hammond. Every time he thinks of it, it gives him a rush. He would have figured he'd be in a lot of trouble by now. But apparently Joe hasn't told anyone. Maybe he doesn't want to admit he was actually laid out by Swain. Swain almost wishes he would tell. They'd take him seriously then. Wonder how Bernie would vote to treat the minister who slugs a parishioner in his time of need.

Sunday is Communion. He has always loved it. The silver trays of glasses are stacked beneath the thick purple covers. Soft cloth, like for polishing shoes. The little stale cubes of white bread are piled on the platters. Ready to pass. Swain takes his place behind the table, the place he always stood when he was a kid imagining being a preacher. He remembers being in church beside his mother, having to hoist himself up into the pew, and seeing the glasses and platters unveiled. His mother went forward, he was too young. He watched the man up front in the black robe, so murmuring and gentle, as everybody came to him to have a sip of wine. They were all so quiet and different from their ordinary selves. He wanted to be old enough. He wanted to be the one to give them the wine.

He faces the congregation. "Ye who do truly and earnestly repent of your sins"—he loves the sound of it—"and are in love and charity with your neighbors, and intend to lead a new life, following the commandments of God, and walking from henceforth in His holy ways; draw near with reverence, faith, and thanksgiving, and take the Supper of the Lord to your comfort."

He takes the cloth away from the stack of trays, a magician whisking the handkerchief off the top hat. "Will those of you in the first four rows on the right who wish to share in the Lord's Supper, please come forward." Ushers stand at the fourth pew. Mrs. Lampley starts up the side aisle slowly, on her three-legged metal cane. The Helgesens are behind her, taking a step and waiting, taking a step and waiting. Bless her heart, here she comes. Swain steps forward to meet her. She takes his arm and he escorts her the rest of the way. The rest of them follow.

The bench is full, they're kneeling, Swain starts down the row. "This is my body. Take. Eat." Stopping in front of each, to offer the bread, the grape juice. "This is my blood."

The glasses clink. Glass against metal. Glass against wood. The empties multiply in the slots of the bench. Hand after hand takes from the platter of bread. He moves up and down the row again, a quiet shuttle on a loom. People rise and go. More fill the bench again. They whisper, moving along the aisles, back to the pews. "Take," he says again, "eat, in remembrance of Me." The Haddonsfields. Emmy Barwick. Janet Epworth. Miguel and Louise. "For whosoever believeth in Me..." He could do this for all the hours of his life. Moving back and forth, holding the platters before them, talking in a voice that lulls his own mind. Like watching a child on a slow swing. "In love and charity." The soft footsteps on carpet. Like blankets around him, a place to be warm and to hide.

He starts. Julie is kneeling at the bench before him. He didn't see her coming. Her head is slightly bent. She looks up to take the bread. He stands in front of her holding the tray, and watches her hand, freckles, short fingernails, the way her thumb curves back —as familiar as his own. I'm the waiter, she's the one at the table. No, I'm the king, she's my beautiful abject slave.

"This is my body."

She meets his eyes for a half second, feels her own eyes warm, then drifts away. She goes to the place where she always goes when she kneels here. Peaceful. She is swimming in blue-green water, the pond surrounded by trees that keep out every sound. The water holds her, sways her hands and her hair like water grass. All of it curves soft around her. She thinks, I am safe from everything: whatever happens next.

Moving to the next person, Swain still watches her. She should laugh that we're doing this: "This is my body." But her eyes are serious and steady. Mostly she's looking past him—she doesn't even notice him—perhaps listening, with her heart, to whatever voices she hears.

SEVEN

He's wearing a patch on one eye, with a pale purplish scar showing around the edges. The other eye, glass, with the lid half shut, would be seeing the front seat floor. He doesn't say anything unless you force him, doesn't even move.

"Got enough room there, fellow?" Swain says, shifting his long legs toward the door.

"Yeah," Jakey says. He doesn't turn his head.

"Tell me about this new school where you're going," Swain says. "Jakey."

Silence. Patrice stiffens. Her arm looks as if it's holding the steering wheel in place in the car. Somebody needs to stroke that arm until it relaxes and lets go. Tight as he is, he's got a lot of nerve telling anybody else to relax.

"I don't know anything about it," Jakey says. "It's too late to start school anyway. Everybody else has been at my real school for weeks. It's already October. I still know what day it is."

"Jakey," Patrice says.

"So what do you want to know?" he says to Swain. "They're all blind. Everybody at this school." He kicks the toe of one running shoe into the space under the dash. "Half of them are spastic or retarded too."

"Jakey, you know you want to learn to do things on your own," Patrice says. "You always say that—when anybody tries to help you."

"Dad said if I don't like it, I don't have to stay. I don't see why I can't go back to regular school anyway. I know where everything is. I could get around fine."

"Jakey, we've been through all this before."

"Jakey, maybe one of your friends could come to school with you here for a day. Just for a visit. Maybe somebody like Bryan."

"Great. He can see me with a bunch of weirdos." Out Swain's window is a field of pumpkins, the first he's seen this year, so many lying all over the ground there's hardly any room for vines or leaves. The whole field is a blaze of orange. He opens his mouth to say, "Would you look at that color," then stops himself. Jakey says, "Anyway, I don't really like him all that much anymore."

"How come?" Swain says.

"When he comes over, he acts—I don't know, you know—I mean, it's like he doesn't want to come and his parents make him. I wish he would never come over again."

"It's hard for him to know what to do," Swain says. "I think he's probably scared of saying something that might hurt your feelings. He's doing the—"

"His parents are making him," Jakey says. "And you might as well tell them to stop it, Mom, because I don't need it."

"Check the directions, Swain," Patrice says. "We're looking for a turn pretty soon." Jakey kicks the bottom of the tape deck, lets out a snort of disgust. "I'm listening, Jakey. I'm just trying to get us there."

Jakey slides down in the seat, leans his head back. "Don't bother," he says.

"Two more stoplights," Swain says. "Then a right just past a Burger King." He's hardly said a word to her the whole way, or she to him. The whole thing, his being here, feels awkward, a mistake.

They cross a traffic bump and turn down a narrow road, through a brick entrance. Swain sits up straight and looks around. Tall hardwoods with leaves turned to yellow and red and brown, a lot of open grassy space, two-story brick buildings. "I haven't been

here," he says. "I thought I'd visited every institution in the state."
He flinches at the word.

A bunch of kids are coming down the sidewalk. Hard to tell
which ones can see a little, which ones are blind.

"Here's the office," Patrice says. She pulls into a space. "I'll run
in here and find out where we need to go. I'll be right back." She
jumps out and runs up the steps. Since it happened, she's even
more efficient, more hyped-up, speeding. He watches her fast-
moving legs, flashing up the stairs. Gone in a second. She disappears into the front door.

"Dad said he didn't need to see this place, he already knows
what places like this look like," Jakey says.

"He said that to you?"

"I don't know. I heard him."

Jakey's head is bent over, slightly hung forward. As if he's
trying to hear better, or is guarding his hands lying still on
his legs. His jeans look loose around his legs, his shoes even
look too big. He's lost so much weight, he looks frail and de-
feated.

"It might help, Jakey, for you to be able to talk to other kids
that have been through the same thing."

He doesn't say anything, he pulls at his cuff.

"I know it doesn't seem like things are ever going to get any
better—"

"They're not." Jakey raises his head, turns it slightly toward
Swain. He feels the tremble in the boy's shoulder where it touches
his arm. "It's for the rest of my life."

Swain wants to put his arm around him, but he can't. He has
no business thinking he knows. . . .

Jakey sits motionless, rigid, his head bowed. "If I'd been awake,
I wouldn't have let them do this to me."

Swain puts his hand on the kid's shoulder, he makes himself do
it. Tears come to his eyes. Jakey doesn't move. He stays hunched
as if he's waiting for something to hit him.

"I wish it would happen to everybody in the world," he says. "Then everybody would be the same."

Patrice is coming out the door of the building, motioning to him directions before she ever gets to the car. Swain blinks away his tears, clears his throat, straightens. "Your mom is coming."

"Yeah. She can't wait to get rid of me. She says she wants me to learn how to do things. What she really means is she wants to not have to be bothered with me."

Patrice gets back in the car. "Where we need to go is right down here," she says, pulling out, heading them for another building. She thinks, Just get this over with. Keep moving and get it done.

"We're looking for a brick building on the left with columns," she says. If I stop to think about it, I'll drive away from here as fast as I can go. I'll keep him with me and take care of him forever.

Jakey says, "I'll let you know the minute I see it." Sarcastic.

She presses her lips together. I can't stop seeing because he has.

"Over there," Swain says.

A group of kids is walking past in front of them, laughing ... blind, their heads lifted a little toward the sky or held at odd angles. The boy on the end—his head turns one way and then another. It doesn't matter which way he faces. It's all the same.

When she took him to kindergarten on the first day, he cried. He didn't want her to leave. She made herself do it, she told him he'd be fine. His eyes full of tears, looking up at her. How he was ... Her throat locks up tight as if a hand has closed around it. She turns sharply, pulls the car into a parking place.

"Okay, Jakey. Let's go in and find out about this school. Swain and I will be right here with you. We're just going to see what it's like, and you can see what you think of it. Then we're going back home."

"Dad didn't need to come because he already knows I won't like it."

"Jakey, wait and see."

See. Everything I say is "see." The more I try not to, the more it comes out. Patrice grabs her pocketbook out of the back seat. Maybe somebody in this place can tell parents how to act, what they're supposed to do.

She gets out. Swain gets out. Jakey doesn't move.

"Jakey," she says. "Please." Jakey keeps his feet braced against the floor of the front seat.

Swain hesitates, resting his arms on the roof of the car, looking across at Patrice. There's no question in his mind: if Jakey doesn't get out, it's going to be the last straw for her. She's going to fly into a million pieces. She looks once at Swain, then off across the campus.

Swain watches her for a moment, then he slides back into the car. "Jakey," he says, to identify himself. He doesn't touch him. He says, "Jakey, give your mom a break. She's having a hard time. She's trying to do the best thing for you. It's not so easy for her either." He pauses.

Jakey doesn't move.

Swain says, "Jakey, you're not going to be by yourself. We'll stay with you the whole time if you want. Your mom will do whatever you want. Then maybe, after you find out what the place is like and get to know the people, then you might want to come back later." Swain feels the sadness piling up in his chest. The kid is so little, his skinny legs like sticks. He's too young, a thing like this shouldn't happen to a kid.

Jakey says, "Give me the keys."

"What?" Swain looks at the boy and then up at Patrice, who is leaning into the open door on the other side.

Jakey says, "I want the keys to the car, so I know you're not leaving without me."

She leans closer, as if she didn't hear. He wants the keys. It takes the wind out of her. Then she realizes, Why should he trust me? I let this happen to him. She reaches over and puts the keys in his hand.

Swain watches her face, gone dead like someone paralyzed. Except for her eyes. All that sorrow in her eyes, pouring out over the child like light and he doesn't even know it. Swain has to look away. That's how his own mother looked at him. He saw it sometimes, she loved him. But it was so quick, and then it was gone.

Jakey tucks the keys into his jeans pocket, sets his mouth to look tough. He slides out and backs away to leave room for the car door to slam. "Okay," he says and reaches out a hand for someone's arm. Swain steps close and gives him his arm.

They meet with a principal, a counselor, teachers, one after another. "Your son..." one of them says to Swain, discussing Jakey's adjustment. Jakey is at the other end of the room talking with a kid about twelve. Patrice is filling out forms. "I'm the Mileses' pastor," he says.

The woman says, "I know Mrs. Miles was happy that you could come."

Jakey comes back down to where they sit, his hand lightly on the boy's shoulder. He says, "We're going to go wander around. Tom's going to go with me."

Patrice looks up, her face lights. Jakey stands there with his jaw stuck out as if he's daring anybody to say anything nice.

"Fine," Patrice says. "We'll be right here." Swain watches her watch the boys leave. A weight has just lifted off her, but most of it will never be gone.

She looks back at Swain. "Thanks for getting us this far."

He nods. Some life has come back to her face. She is so beautiful. "Sure," he says. "I'm glad I could help."

Out on the sidewalk, Jakey stands still for a moment beside Tom. "Where's the building?" he says.

"Which one?"

"The one we came out of."

"Behind you and to the left."

"Oh. I get confused."

"Yeah, well, you'll start to figure it out. It didn't take me too long. But I probably did it faster than most people. I'm getting good at that kind of stuff."

"Yeah, me too." Tom is leading him along a sidewalk, into shade, back into the sun. He hears some kids pass. "Hey, Rambo," one kid says to Tom.

"Hey," Tom calls back. "Don't mess with me, man."

Jakey waits until the kids are passed. Then he says, "So when did you get blind?"

"When I was six. I got hit by a BB gun and the other eye went blind too, just because the first one did. Sympathetic ophthalmia."

"I never heard of that."

"A lot of kids around here have it. It's a bummer."

"I got hit by some rocks that fell off a truck."

"Yeah?" More kids pass. Tom says to one of them, "You guys don't even need to bother to come to the swim meet. You're going to get killed."

"Don't count on it," a boy's voice says back. A girl says, "Hi, Tom." Then more voices, everybody is talking around him. Finally Tom says, "This is Jakey. He's new."

Jakey says "Hi" to nobody in particular. A couple of voices say "Hi" back. One guy says, "If you can race, tell them to put you in Thompson."

Jakey turns his head to look at Tom to see whether he should ask to be in Thompson. No Tom. Just blank gray that doesn't even stay still. Shit. How could he forget even for one second? How are you ever supposed to know anything if you can't look around and see what anybody else thinks? He shrugs, says, "I can swim, fast. No problem."

He hears another boy say, "Tell them you want to be in Carver."

He grins. "Jeez, I don't know where I'll be—" He feels Tom's arm move against his, like he's getting ready to move on. Tom says, "You guys are too late. C'mon, Jake, we got to get going."

Waiting for Jakey to come back, Patrice sits beside Swain, quiet on the porch bench of the main building. It's as if some kind of deadline has passed, a big effort is finished. They've gotten this far, now she needs to rest a minute. The sound of kids in class comes through a window onto the porch. She feels herself finally slowing down.

Swain, looking off into the trees, beyond the porch, pretends to rest too. But he isn't resting, sitting here listening for her every breath and slightest motion. She is a million miles away from him. He wants to say something that will reach her, bring the two of them together, for just a minute, sitting here. He was so pleased when she asked him if he'd come.

A boy comes out the door of the building. About seven—carrying a yellow toy truck, his fingers thrust through the open windows of the cab. There are dark rings like bruises around his eyes. He takes little careful steps. Patrice watches him. He heads at an angle toward the steps, his hand beginning to feel for the rail that's still four feet away.

Swain gets up, goes over to him. "Can I help you, fellow?" He looks as if he isn't sure anyone is talking to him. "You with the yellow truck." If yellow means anything . . .

"I'm okay," the boy says. "Thanks." He finds the railing with his hand and goes down the steps. Swain sits back down. Patrice is still motionless, following the child's back.

"It's hard not to tremble every time he takes a step," she says. "I feel like I'll die when I think about him trying to cross a street. Standing at the curb while cars whizz back and forth a foot away from him. Somebody else will have to help him learn to do that. I can't do it."

"Does Jakey understand why you want him to come here?"

"I don't know. I've talked with him about it. I don't know if I've gotten through. But he can't go on just sitting in the house doing nothing. He'll go nuts, anybody would. Do you think I'm wrong?"

"I'm not sure. I see it one way, then the other."

"Joe and my mother both think I'm a monster. But they haven't spent the hours I have with Jakey."

"I ran into Joe in the grocery store."

"He told me. Though it's fairly rare that he talks to me now at all. Not that I care. . . ."

She sighs and looks away. He can still feel how it was all those years ago. There she is, walking down the hall of their high school, up ahead of him in the crowd, everybody saying "Hi" to her. She turns into a classroom doorway, and the light from the window across the room hits her face, her skirt whirling out a little as she turns. She's smiling. He'd have killed for her. He turns back to her, and all of it rushes to his head. It hasn't changed at all.

She's looking down the length of the porch out at the trees and the open space of yard. If she knew what goes on in my mind...

She says, "Swain, I have to tell somebody." She turns to him. He's sitting there waiting, trying to guess what she's going to say before she says it. I have to tell *somebody*. She says, "I've been seeing someone."

"A therapist," Swain says.

"A man."

"A man. You mean...?"

She says, "I'm having an affair."

Swain's eyes stop on a dry leaf on the top of the steps.

"I can't deal with what's happened by myself, Swain. And Joe's just making it all worse." And you, she thinks, you had your chance, and you didn't take it.

He watches the leaf rock back and forth in the breeze. I came down here to be with her. Not just Jakey, her.

Finally, he turns, looks at her. He lets his eyes wander over her face slowly. She's so dark, the whites of her eyes so white. Why is she telling me this? She knows how I feel.... "Patrice."

"I know. It's the wrong thing. I shouldn't be doing it. But you have to understand—"

"Who's the guy?"

"Burton Echols."

"Oh, for Christ's sake, Patrice."

"Swain, you don't know him. He's a really good person."

"That's wonderful. I'm glad to hear it."

She doesn't say anything. He looks straight ahead. All right, if that's what she wants.

"Look, Patrice. I don't care if you're running around on Joe. That's your business. Did you think I was going to quote Scripture? Is that what you expected? That's not how it is. I'm much too involved to try to pull that one off. I've wanted you for a hundred years and you know it. Burton Echols..."

She's staring at him. "You never told me that."

"Why do you think I blew a fuse and hauled off and hit your husband?"

"Was that supposed to be my clue to your interest? That you hit my husband? There are better approaches, I'll tell you."

"I wasn't planning on making any approaches."

"That's what I thought. You've always seemed happy with Julie."

"I am."

"So?"

"So that doesn't stop me from being obsessed with you. Lately it has completely gotten loose in my head. I haven't said anything, I never meant to do anything, but I can't stand the thought of you and Echols." Him and his gold chain and his suntan oil... painting the stair rails in his bathing suit. "The guy is a lightweight, that's all."

He looks over at her. She is staring down at her hands, slowly rubbing one against the other. He says, "Why tell me anyway? Did you want me to stop you? Or did you just want to make me jealous?"

"I wanted you to tell me not to feel bad about it, to give myself a break, a time-out."

"You really thought I'd say that?"

"I guess not." She sighs. "But this is sure not what I expected to hear. The way I've thought of you... since you've been back here ... I always felt you had some answers. You never let your emotions get out of hand or push you around. When you hit Joe... I'd wanted to do it so many times. When you did, I thought for a second... okay, Joe has it coming. Because Swain always does the right, the reasonable thing. But I knew there wasn't any reason in that. And then that thing that happened with Jakey in the hospital. You aren't like you were, Swain."

I am not like I was. From that first night of the voice: "Son." And then the sense that a flood was pouring in, and everything rational was gone and nothing would ever be the same again. Back in July. Months ago now.

He nods. "I know."

She says, "I'll tell you something, since we're telling secrets. I thought for a moment there in your office a few weeks ago that you might be seducible. That maybe you had changed that much."

He looks at her face, eyes, lips. Have I changed that much? He looks away.

He wishes he had.

Footsteps. Jakey and the other kid coming up the sidewalk. "Here they come," Swain says. Jakey is walking differently, faster than when he left, keeping up with the other boy. Now they're on the steps. Jakey calls out, "Hey, Mom—"

She says, "Over here, son." Swain thinks, That's that. The book is closed. All she wants is an escape, and she found him.

He looks over at Jakey. Amazing. The kid's out of breath, rosy-cheeked, as if he's been running in the brisk air. Swain feels his own spirits lift, just a little. The boy looks as if he's having a good time.

On the way back to Chapel Hill, Jakey actually talks. Patrice is so delighted that everything else seems to fade from her mind. Swain is driving.

"Tom—that's the guy who was taking me around—he said they have these water fights in the dorm. . . ." His legs move, his shoulders move, little ordinary stirrings you don't even notice unless they're gone. He falls back into silence twenty miles down the road. Still, it's the first good sign.

Swain looks over at Patrice. She doesn't care about anything but that the boy is doing better. He looks back at the road. We came that close, we came within an inch. It could drive him mad if he thinks about it. He's not going to think about that or Burton Echols.

In the back seat, Jakey is talking again. "Next week is a swim meet...." He seems really excited. He's a good little boy. That business with the keys: that was gutsy. If other children were like Jakey, I'd have ten.

They drive back into Chapel Hill. He picks up his car at Patrice's house, tells her good night, seeing only her dark silhouette, the lamp of the streetlight behind her. Just as well, he doesn't want to see her face. He doesn't touch her. He gives Jakey a pat on his shoulder. Then he drives home, thinking about a boy so scared of being left alone that he'd even come up with the idea of demanding the keys.

He lets himself into the house through the back kitchen door. A box of take-out pizza is on the counter. He picks up a cold limp slice with the tips of his fingers. Julie's on the phone. She hangs up and comes into the kitchen. She glances at him and walks past him to the other counter. "Pizza," he says.

"George came by and brought it, wanted to talk about his problems."

"Did you get them all solved?"

"Mmmmh." Her back is turned. She goes over to the table. Still she's keeping her back turned.

"What's on your mind?"

"Nothing. How did today go?"

"The trip to the school?"

"The trip to the school."

"Went fine." He leans over and reaches between his legs to grab the rung of a stool behind him. He pulls it under him and sits there in the middle of the kitchen, an island at low tide. Julie keeps straightening things. She pushes the edges of the row of cookbooks together so they make a straight line.

"I'm glad to hear it," she says.

Pretty cool treatment I'm getting, he thinks. He says, "I had a few minutes by myself with Jakey."

"Oh?"

"He thinks Patrice wants to get rid of him. Although, by the time he'd been around the school and met some kids, things seemed a little better, like it might be okay. Maybe she's right, maybe it's the right thing to do now."

"What about her?"

"I guess she's handling it okay. Seems wired-up pretty tight." He looks at the knob on the cabinet behind Julie's head.

She says, "That's not what I meant."

"What *did* you mean?" He looks at his foot on the rung of the stool.

"You went off and spent the whole day with her." She is mashing the trash down in the garbage bag to close it. She yanks the bag out of the can and sets it next to the door, and faces him. "She's obviously trouble looking for somewhere to happen."

"You think that?"

"She's firing on every man in sight, including you. And you've always had a crush on her."

"Don't worry. She's turned her attentions elsewhere."

Julie raises her eyebrows. "Who?"

"I wish I could tell you."

She shrugs. "I'll hear it from somebody within the week." She laughs. "From three or four somebodies probably."

He watches her for a moment. "You're easily placated. I thought you were ready to divorce me when you first walked into the kitchen."

"I'm uneasy, Swain."

"You couldn't really be worried."

"I wouldn't have been six months ago. But now there's no telling. What do I know?"

"Enough to trust me not to fool around, tempting though the idea might be." I don't have to say exactly how tempting, but I didn't actually do anything, I never even tried.

She looks at him carefully. He looks more like his old self to-night, she thinks. More than he has in months. Maybe it's all smoothing out. His midlife crisis, or whatever it is. Unless this is the calm before an even bigger storm. I don't know anymore. She looks at him, sitting on the stool, his long legs, his big gawky knees stuck out everywhere. Somehow he's still such a baby. If you only look at his eyes, it's like looking at a child.

"Okay," she says. "I'll mark that one thing off my list of worries. You aren't going to run off with Patrice. Nice to have that much settled." She pauses. "So what happened with our boy?"

EIGHT

Being around the church is becoming more like the way it was for Swain back in junior high: a big group of people who all understand each other, and he doesn't fit in. Once he and a bunch of other kids were sitting on a wall between Franklin Street and the campus downtown. Somebody had a radio on and Peter, Paul and Mary came on. "Puff, the Magic Dragon." It was the first time he had heard it.

Roger was lying on the wall with his head in Cindy's lap. She was messing with his hair and he was acting as if he were putting up with her doing it. Some of the other guys were sitting around on the ground. Swain wasn't really with anybody, any girl. He was sitting there sort of by himself next to Cindy, because Rodge had asked how come he never went with them down to the wall to hang out. So he went.

It was boring and stupid just sitting there. Until he heard the song.

"El grasso," Rodge said and yawned. "Weed. You know that's what it's about."

"They are so terrific," Lynda Dudley said. Dick Francesca was playing air guitar.

Watching Dick's fingers moving against imaginary strings, Swain drifted. At home his dad played old recordings of Chaliapin. But you couldn't hear anything much but scratches and how far away and old it was, like a voice trapped in a box. Hearing it was the way he knew for sure that his father was home, he would hear that voice when he was passing his door.

This song was like being inside a cartoon. All the colors were bright and clear, like Popsicles. Like something you would bang out on a xylophone that only had five or six metal keys. "They frolicked in the morning mist in a land called Honalee." He imagined riding on the bent neck of a dinosaur, hanging on as it swayed him toward the ground, then picked him back up.

A few nights before, Swain had borrowed his father's desk in the study to do homework. His father wasn't home. Swain moved his algebra book and his notebook downstairs and turned on the soft gold circle of lamplight. The room smelled like the leather chair and the Silk Cut cigarettes from England that he always smoked. Swain rubbed his long fingers across the patches in front of each earlobe that he'd begun shaving, and he frowned over his notebook paper. Simultaneous equations. They're the worst. His father thinks poetry is hard. He doesn't know anything.

And that's the truth, Swain thought, sitting on the wall. He doesn't know anything. He never did. Mom either. I should have figured that out a hundred years ago. I was wrong about them from the start.

Even thinking about them at all—especially his father—made his eyes feel like a dragon's eyes—hot, with red rims. He stared at the girls crossing the street at the crosswalk. They were ugly. Both of them. They probably couldn't get a date in a million years. Except maybe that guy walking back behind them, who's even worse. So what am I doing sitting here on this wall anyway? I could leave, get up and go somewhere. Where else am I going to go? Home?

A couple was passing in front of him on the sidewalk. Real old, and the lady had a little dog on a leash that was running up ahead of her, pulling the leash tight. Swain wanted a car to jump the curb and run over it. Or maybe all three of them.

The song was still playing. "Little Jackie Paper. . . . One day he came no more."

"I heard they're coming to do a concert at Greensboro Coliseum," Lynda said.

"We've all got to go," Sally said. "I mean, everybody."

"Swain can chaperone," Dick said.

Swain stared across the street at a store window he could barely see into, it was like a sheet of thick cellophane. The best thing is to ignore him. So he smiled. As if nothing Dick ever said in his life could possibly matter at all. "You should be so lucky," he said.

"I mean, you can read maps and talk to the cop if we get stopped for anything," Dick said.

"My brother would drive us, if we would buy gas and then split when we get there," Cindy said.

"So what do you think, Swain? Do you stay out that late?"

"No problem," Swain said. He squinted at the people on the far sidewalk, as if he were looking for somebody he was expecting. He wasn't expecting anybody. He had to act as if it didn't bother him. Otherwise they would hate him even more than they already did.

Once again, on this late October Sunday morning more than twenty years later, Swain has taken up with yet another group that he knows isn't going to put up with someone like him. Here he is anyway, without a hope of fitting in.

A ripple of yeses and murmurings is rolling across a congregation he has never seen before. "And thank you, Lord," Valeria booms out over them, "for the healing and the comfort you have brought to the sick during this week."

A bony-looking woman in the second row is holding her elbows and rocking. "Yes, Jesus," she sings, in a wail that floats apart from the other voices. "Thank you, Jesus." Swain can just see her around the angle of the lectern.

Valeria leans her immense weight into the pulpit, pressing with her hands. "For how you have made our burdens less," she says.

There's a little hum coming from her, even when the words finish. As if she's got an engine in her. "Thank you, Lord," she says. A man near the back is clapping, a slow clap that misses the beat, every time misses the beat.

"We know how you come to us. How you come when we are weary. How you enter our hearts when we are troubled. How you make us so we can bear it." What am I doing here? This is a mistake that's going to get worse before it's over. "Thank you, Jesus," she says. "Thank you, Lord."

Five minutes of praying and she's still going. The walls of the church are probably starting to bulge out from the force. "Put the spirit in our hearts, Lord."

"Yes," the congregation says.

"Put the fire in our hearts."

"Yes."

"Let us know you're here within us."

"Yes, Lord."

"Let us feel it."

A shrill cry rises up behind him. Someone in the choir. Swain doesn't look. No one in the congregation in front of him is watching, except one kid in a bow tie, staring and picking his nose. "The Spirit's on me," the woman says. "Now. O, Lord, now. Yes, Jesus." Swain closes his eyes. The Spirit is on me. When it happened to him, he didn't make a sound.

Valeria again, so quiet now: "Be with us, Lord." She's bringing it down, like a conductor. The room is so peaceful. He can almost feel her hand on his hair. She has pulled the covers up around him. The sound of her is like being rocked in a rocking chair. It makes him sleepy-eyed.

The guy who was clapping has stopped. He's sitting with his big hands clasped together on the pew in front of him, his head bowed. The skinny lady near the front is wiping her eyes. The piano player starts a slow sweet hymn. The music moves across Swain like a light warm breeze.

The congregation shifts, resettles in the pews. These people would listen if he had stood before them that day and told them he had heard a voice. Their own voices would embrace him: yes, tell it, brother, yes. *This* is a congregation that welcomes God.

Valeria is talking like her ordinary self now. "We do thank the Lord for being with us in this hour." She pauses, he watches the hem of her robe sway. "Reverend Hammond," she says. He jumps. Is it time? He straightens, adjusts his face. "Reverend Hammond, come on up here and stand with me. I want all these people to get a good look at you." It's going to be worse than he thought. He stands and walks forward, she puts one arm around his shoulders that are almost even with hers. "This is a man of the Lord," she says to them.

And Lord knows, he needs some company, she thinks. She rubs his shoulder. Standing there in that robe like one big choirboy. I'd hate to have to tell those folks over where he is anything about God. I would. And them all sitting stiff as posts.

"The Lord is good," someone calls out. "Thank you, brother," another voice. A man at the far corner of a pew fixes a cold stare on Swain. He probably wouldn't notice it if he weren't the only white person in the church.

"This man of the Lord has been a friend to me for many many years," Valeria says. Her voice rolls out through the room. He feels the heat of her radiating next to him, through their mingled robes. "He and I have sat through long meetings of the ministerial association together. You can picture in your mind what a meeting of preachers is like." She laughs. The congregation laughs. She says, "I know you can."

"Reverend Hammond and I go sit there to try to keep some good sense in all their goings-on. We do the best we can. We can't do much good. But we do what we can.

"I asked Brother Hammond to bring his message to us today. Bring himself to this pulpit this morning. Himself and his knowing of the Lord.

"Because, brothers and sisters, he knows the Lord. I know it to listen to him. I can feel it." I told her to go easy, and she's not doing it, Swain thinks. He looks toward one of the tall windows along the side of the sanctuary. It's the kind of glass that lets through only a white glow of the cool sunshine outside. She's not doing what I said, but she thinks I know the Lord. He wants to turn around and hug her. He looks out across the congregation staring back at him. They're not going to think I know the Lord, not the way I preach. They're going to hate me.

"He said to me, 'Valeria, they don't want to hear me. You know they don't.' I said to him, 'I know they do.' And I know you're going to get so much from what this pastor brings us. I'm going to sit right down and let him get on."

Do him good, she thinks, going back to her seat. Put the boy here where he belongs. Weren't for that wife of his, he be by himself over at that place. No wonder he thinks he's going crazy.

The murmurings of assent stop as she moves away. She's gone, sunk into a seat behind him. Once he stood and stood at the end of a high diving board, seeing the pale blue bottom of the pool through the smooth surface yards below. They're all of them sitting so still.

He waits until everything that Valeria has said has filtered out of the air. Then he starts: "I'm happy to be with you today. I'm glad to have this opportunity to join you in worship. I'd like us to think today about those people that Jesus knew in his lifetime. The disciples. Those who stood in the crowd and listened as he spoke. Those who came forward to be healed. Those who persecuted him and crucified him. What would each of us have done in those days? What do we do—faced with the fact of Jesus now?"

He looks back at the lectern. "There's a story about all of those who knew Jesus in the Bible: Mark 8:27. 'And Jesus went out, and his disciples, into the towns of Caesarea Philippi, and by the way he asked his disciples, saying unto them'"—he starts to read faster, it's taking too long—"'Whom do men say that I am? And they answered: John the Baptist: but some say, Elias; and others, One of the prophets. And he saith unto them, Whom say ye that I am?'" He looks up—at last. The congregation is motionless.

"Peter said to Jesus, 'Thou art the Christ.'" No one says "Yes, brother." No one says anything.

"I think that most of us, looking back on that, would like to be the one who recognized Jesus, who said to him, 'Thou art the Christ.'" He looks out at stare after stare. They're not buying it. He misses Valeria's voice, he doesn't want to hear himself either.

"We'd like to be the ones who recognized him and did not deny him, the ones who were not ashamed to acknowledge Jesus." It was as if she were singing when she was up here, and now I'm droning on and on. And I've just gotten started.

"God is among us now," he says. "We don't have to imagine what we would have done then. God is here today because we are. God resides in us." That's better. "And we know that God is present in our lives. We sense him as we sense the ocean at night, a massive force that is only partially seen. We hear the crashing waves. We see the glimmer of the foam. We touch the edge of the water." He stops. He wants to do it as they do, as Valeria does.

"I've seen you move this morning with the knowledge of the spirit in you. I've never done that. I've felt the presence of God, and yet I've never done that." He has put his sermon aside. He puts both hands on the sides of the podium. "Standing before you this morning, I know how much I resist the power that is in God. What I have seen here this morning is how the spirit can move the body. How hard I fight to keep it from moving mine."

"Witness, brother." He didn't see who spoke.

"But I feel the power," he says. "Sometimes, we don't know how to find God inside us. We live in cluttered houses. We know where to find the refrigerator. We know how to find the TV"—it's Valeria's rhythm, her voice, taking over—"We all know these things. But do we know how to find God?"

"Tell it." The old guy is starting to clap. "Find Jesus."

"We don't know where to look. We don't know what to do."

"Yes. Yes. Yes."

"Sometimes God makes his presence known and we don't want to know."

"Forgive us, Lord." From behind him in the choir. They're coming to help him from all sides.

"We don't want to look. We don't want to feel what it feels like to know the living presence. It's too much. It asks too much."

"Yes." From behind him. Valeria.

There he goes, she thinks. Come on, boy, that's right. Let it flow.

"But we can find in God the strength that we need. I feel the power." It's like dancing, singing, yelling with a crowd. "I feel it." What's happening to my voice?

"I feel a strength. I don't always know it. But it's with me here." Now he's shouting. "I'm not going to hide from it. Not going to run from it." They're all swaying, moving, the whole church full of them, like a field of grass on fire. He's moving with them, dizzy in his head, the whole church circling, the colors starting to blend. God is coming. Yes.

"I tell you, I'm going to change." The blood pounding in his temples. Bring God now. "I'm going to find the power and use it and glorify—" What is happening? The church slipping slowly sideways, upward, everything in front of him tilts. He hears their shouts. I'm falling.

He catches hold of the pulpit, rights himself. I fell. I lost my balance, that's all, I started to fall.

The congregation sits stone-silent before him, he looks out at the faces, motionless, staring at him. They think I'm crazy too. Where is Valeria? He wants to walk out the side door away from here. Jesus, how awful, how embarrassing.

Suddenly he's tired. He says to the church, "I lost my balance. I'm all right. I'm sorry if I gave you a scare."

The stirrings of movement start up again. Time to finish and get out while he can.

He says. "I want to thank the God in each of you for reaching out to touch the God in me. That is what is meant by brotherhood. We are brethren here today."

He bows his head, leans his weight against his arms, collapses against them like two stiff props. "Let us pray," he says. He says a few words, "Thank you, Lord," "Help us," and he wraps it up. The piano music begins softly just as he says his amen. Amens come back to him from all over the church. The music and the voices float him like rising water. The choir sings, swaying back and forth slowly. Swain backs away from the pulpit, drops into the chair beside Valeria.

He looks at her. He slumps and waits. He's too exhausted to make his face move. Hers looks mean, haughty, drawn up into hard angles. So she thinks I was faking it, making fun of them. Maybe she thinks I'm crazy now too. Well, let her.

Then in one instant, all the angles let go. Her eyes, the color of coffee with cream, are pouring such warmth over him. He closes his own eyes. He's glad, all the way into the middle of his bones, he can feel that warmth, as if he's been waiting for it all his life. At the same time, he's too tired to care.

On Tuesday, for the first time since he was a kid, he goes out to play ball. This is the night the recreation-for-the-blind program offers beepball at the city park. He and Julie started going over and reading to Jakey, playing some board game with him with dice that have bumps instead of dents. They did that until he went to the school. But Swain still needs to do something, whether Jakey's home or not. He walks back and forth to keep warm. It's the wrong season for baseball.

"Hey." Swain turns. A tall skinny guy in a bill cap is loping over to him. He's out of breath, he sticks out his hand. "I'm Martin. You must be Swain. Glad to meet you, glad to have you. Heard you were coming. The guys will be real pleased you're here."

"Thanks." Martin drapes an arm around his shoulders and heads them both over to the bench where bats and gloves are piled up and people are milling around. Martin can see, Swain thinks. He seems to be the only one here besides me who can.

"Know anything about all this?" Martin says.

"Blindness?" Swain says.

"Beepball."

"Not a thing. That's what I want to find out."

"Jimmy, come over here and explain to this man about beep-ball." He grabs a kid maybe thirteen, by the elbow. Jimmy turns toward them. His eyes are angled so he'd be looking up. As if he's trying to see what's on top of a house without raising his head. He has on two hearing aids.

"I'm Swain, Jimmy."

"Hi." Jimmy sticks out his hand. His forearm is thick, maybe he does wrist curls. A blind and deaf jock.

"I'm glad to see you," Swain says.

"Good to meet you."

"Swain doesn't know how to play," Martin says. "How about telling him while I get some things squared away?"

Jimmy shifts his weight back and forth as if he's getting lined up to hit a golf ball. "It's pretty simple. What you do—the ball has this beeper in it. So you stand up there with the bat. The pitcher yells ball as soon as it's coming at you. And you hear the beep and you swing."

"Doesn't sound easy."

"You never played this before? What're you, sighted?"

"Yeah."

"That's okay, man." He waves his arm out toward the field, long white lines chalked on the damp grass. "So you hit it and it goes out there. The ball goes into one of those zones, and there's a guy in each one. He hears it coming and fields it. You try to get to the base before the guy gets the ball."

"How do you know where the base is?"

"The beeper. There's a beeper inside the base."

Night-lights have come on around the whole field. Down at the other end, some guys—sighted guys—are pitching and hitting. The crack of the bat sounds like a dry twig snapping. The ball in midair goes dark against the lights. Swain looks around him at the beepball field. About a hundred feet away from the plate is an orange traffic cone.

"The base—is it one of those rubber things they put out in traffic?"

Jimmy frowns. "It's like"—he makes a swirling gesture with his hands—"like an upside down ice cream cone."

"Gotcha."

Martin is coming back over to them. "Here," he says to Swain. There's a light wisp of a cloud from his breath. He hands Swain something black, dangling. "Here are a pair of goggles." Swain takes them, two black rubber eye cups on a stretchy band.

"Guess I'm going to try this," Swain says to Jimmy.

"Sure," Martin says. "We don't have any bench warmers around here. You want to stay warm, you keep moving."

Swain is on the team that goes out into the field. Young boys, a few men, a couple of girls—people scattering all over the place as if they know where they're going. Some in pairs, one holding on to the other's arm. An albino black girl with thick glasses. Swain comes to a stop in the middle of one of the chalk triangles and puts on the goggles. Darkness. The high-up white lights used for night baseball are gone. There are little airholes in the center of each eyepiece but you can't see them when you have them on. Not at all. Swain opens his eyes very wide and blinks. Nothing there.

"Okay, team." It's Martin. Over near the bench. Footsteps, swishing through the grass, are moving in his direction. One person. The footsteps are going past, the person, whoever it is, making a little throat-clearing sound that's hardly a sound at all. It's eerie, somebody walking past three or four feet away. It might be somebody blind who doesn't even know I'm here.

Voices call back and forth. He's quit thinking about Jakey and started being him. I can't see my own body, I could be ten years old, a prisoner, with something tied around my eyes. "What zone am I in?" He says it loud, at random, to anybody. Jimmy and Martin are the only ones he's met. "What number?" he says.

"You're five," says a voice a little distance away. The sound seems to carry the way it does over water. They're calling back and forth from boat to boat. "I'm next to you in four."

"Who are you? I'm Swain Hammond."

There's a second of silence. Maybe the guy's gone. If he left, he was sure quiet about it.

"How you doing, Swain? I'm Charlie." Charlie laughs. It's a man's voice. "You haven't been out here before."

"First time."

"Wearing goggles?"

"Yeah."

"I thought so."

"How could you tell?"

"Either that or you're a blink."

"A blink?"

"You never heard that? That's somebody blind who goes around acting like they can't take care of themselves. Standing there waiting for somebody to get them across the street. You know what I'm talking about."

"Seems a bit harsh."

"I can say it. You can't." The laugh again. He laughs like a smoker.

Martin is yelling: "Okay, we're ready to go. Pitching to George. Okay, George. You guys in the field get ready for a long one." Which one was George? I'm probably going to get knocked in the head with the ball. Silence. Swain leans forward, tensed like a tennis player. He lets his head hang down, he doesn't want to catch it in the face. "Ball." Nothing. No hit. A wait. It's as if half the game is missing. In place of seeing the pitch fly across in front of the guy, you stand out here and wonder when it's going to drop on your head. I feel like a shooting-gallery target.

"Ball." A thump. That's it. He hit it. Martin's yelling, "Zone four." What was his zone? It's Charlie. Another thump, like a knuckle on a watermelon. It's on the ground, moving, beeping, somewhere over there.

"Come on, Charlie," from the other end of the field. Dry grass tearing, a few feet away. "Okay, got it." A quick burst of breath, from the gut. Charlie heaved it. It's in the air.

"Too late," somebody yells. George is on base.

"Jimmy, you're up." Martin again. Swain imagines Jimmy leaning forward, the bat drawn back. "Okay, Jimbo. Here she goes." A half second. "Ball." Whack. First try, good for—

"Five. Heading for five. Swain, move."

Like a knee in his stomach. Jesus. It hit him.

Where is it? Where did it go? The beeping—like it's going away, rolling. Shit. Martin yelling, "Are you all right?" Where is it? Beep—beep. He runs his hands along the dead grass, the hard ground. Closer. It's here somewhere. Where's it coming from? "Okay, okay," he yells.

He can't tell the direction. It's coming from everywhere. He leans his face into the sound. Beep—beep—beep. Like a siren, an emergency light. On and off. On and off. "I am—" What is he hearing? "I am." In the rhythm of it: "I am the Alpha and the Omega." Beep. "The beginning and the ending." He freezes, blind, in his crouch on the ground. "Which is and which was." Dead machine robot voice. The cold dew soaks through his pants to his knees. "And which is to come." He grabs at the short grass with his fingers, holds his balance. "Almighty." Beep. "Almighty." Beep. "Almighty."

An icy cold climbs from his wet knees, spreads through the pit of his stomach, fills his chest, weighs him to the ground.

"You." Beep. "You." His breath stops. "Are my beloved son. Do my work with labor and patience. You have sought me. You have loved me. You are chosen. The time is at hand."

Swain leans, reaches toward the pulsing sound. The beeping. It's straight ahead. Four feet. Three feet. He walks on his knees, falling onto his elbows onto the grass.

"Close, Swain." It's Martin. "You're almost there. Don't stop now."

He can't stand it. He rips off the goggles, blinking in the bright white light of the field. The grass shines in the light. He squints.

"Hey, no fair looking," Martin says.

"Give him a break. It's his first time." It's Charlie's voice. Swain turns to see him. Rough-looking and wiry, like a jockey. Like somebody hanging out around a bus station. Slowly, dazed, still light-blinded, Swain looks at the ground in front of him. There it is. Beeping. Pinging away. A big gray leather softball.

He picks it up, gets to his feet. He holds it for a second against his face, wanting to remember the feel of it, the sound of it forever. What work? What is at hand? What do I have to do? The ball smells like leather and cold wet ground. It doesn't matter what—it's coming. I'll do it. His heart is beating against the whole inside of his chest. Thank you, he is saying, to the rhythm of the beeping. Thank you. Then he pulls the ball away from his face, draws it far back behind his shoulder and slings it toward Martin, following its high arc.

At last, it has happened. All over the field, men standing waiting in the chill air, as if they knew. He loves every one of them. Jimmy, Charlie, Martin, all of them.

"One–zero," Martin yells. One point for the other team. "Sorry, guys," Swain calls out across the field, everything in him pouring out to them.

He signals to Martin he's ready to go on. "Play ball," he says. He fits the goggles back over his eyes.

When he gets home, Julie has gone to bed early. He walks into the bedroom, flips on the light.

"Julie. Honey."

She rolls over, squinting at the light. "What time is it?"

"Hardly even midnight. Time to wake up. I've got something to tell you."

She stares at him, still blinking. "What?"

"Julie, I got my instructions."

She pulls herself up on her elbows. "What are you talking about?"

"Finally, after all these years . . . I was called. By God."

She looks at him hard. She's awake now. Who could sleep? He's so excited, something carbonated is bubbling through his whole body, fizzing in his veins.

"So . . . what are they," she says, "—your instructions?"

"I don't know."

"I don't understand."

"I'm supposed to do God's work. That's all. I don't know what exactly."

She is looking at him so carefully she could count the dark hollows of every sliced-off whisker in his beard. She could see through his head to the door of the closet behind him. She's looking at him that hard.

"What did you hear, Swain?"

"That I'm chosen."

"Chosen?" It's as if she's turning the word over and over.

He waits.

She falls back on the pillow. "Oh, Swain."

He tells her the whole thing, Alpha to Omega. He stands up, goes through the motions of his search for the ball, scrambling for it with his eyes shut. Then he looks at her again. She just lies there.

"Julie, I'm happy," he says. "I wanted—I want you to be excited too. Before when it happened, it made no sense. This time it's clear."

"I'm glad it's so clear to you. I don't understand it one bit." Is he crazy? Have I been sitting here watching him go really crazy?

"Honey." He hates himself for how he sounds, pleading with her.

"Swain"—she sits back up slowly—"when all this started, I could understand it. It was as if you were turning into a daydreamer type like me. But it has gone on and on. What's happening to you I don't know about. The things I imagine are all me. My voices. Somehow or other." She looks at his face, feature by feature. It has gone so far beyond anything that makes any kind of sense. This is dangerous. Chosen? Next thing he'll be saying he's the Messiah or Napoleon or who knows who. "You're sure," she says, "that it's not just you."

"I'm sure. I'd stake anything on it." The exuberance has gone out of him. Damn her. Sitting there as if terrible news is sinking into her brain. It's like watching a spill soak in. He doesn't know how to stop it. She just sits there. Please, Julie.

She looks up at him still standing where he stood to pretend he was back on the ballfield. She wants to grab him and shake him until he takes it all back. The way he's going, he'll wind up on a street corner, people making fun of him. Then the thought of anybody hurting him sweeps over her. She thinks, I'd stand there with him.

NINE

"Jakey's coming. We've sent somebody to get him."

"Thank you."

She must have put the phone down next to a stereo speaker. What's going on there? Maybe it's the dorm Ping-Pong room, or the canteen. This is going to be impossible.

"Okay. Okay." Jakey is talking away from the mouthpiece to somebody there.

"Hello?"

"Hi, Jakey. This is Swain Hammond. Just thought I'd check in with you and see how it's going."

Pause. "It's going okay."

"Are you liking school?"

"It's mostly boring."

"Same as usual, huh?"

"I guess."

"Your mom says you've been doing great."

Silence.

"I've missed seeing you."

"Unh-hunh."

"Are you making a lot of friends there?"

"I guess. I've only been here a few days."

"Sounds like a lot's going on in the background. Where are you?"

"In the office where the mailboxes are. I can hear you."

"It's pretty quiet here."

Silence.

"I'm in my office at the church."

"I haven't been back there. Dad said I didn't have to."

"I guess that might be pretty hard for you."

"I don't know." Swain hears him take a long breath, like a sleeper turning over. He still sounds awful. Or maybe he's doing much better and I'm the last person in the world he feels like talking to.

"I'd like to come down and see you at school pretty soon. Would that be okay?"

"Yeah. Sure, I mean, if you want to. I have to go now."

"Talk to you soon, Jakey."

"Bye."

Swain settles back in his desk chair. The kid sounded worse than he did last week when Swain stopped by the house. Patrice was packing him up to go. Jakey was helping. Swain watched him handle his stuff and decide what to take with him. "You'll be back here next weekend," Patrice said. "You can take more things with you then." Jakey was so deep in his own world that he didn't even hear her.

Going by to see Jakey, he has gotten used to seeing her in her own house, in jeans and some big baggy shirt. He's seen her . . . he counts, three, four, five times since the afternoon weeks ago at the school . . . the day of their big talk. Now she seems to expect him, or Julie, or both of them, to be around. Seeing her doesn't throw him the way it did. He has forced himself to get used to it. But still he wants her, watches her when she's not looking, knowing Jakey won't see him watching. And the thing with Burton Echols still infuriates him. That's who I should hit next. Lay him out cold on the church steps. Patrice has never mentioned him again. He has decided to assume it's over, a brief mistake. He won't think about it. He looks at her sometimes and imagines lifting the loose hem of that shirt and taking it off her. Then she'd find out if he's seducible. But as much as he still wants her, Jakey has become half, more than half, of the reason that he's kept on going by.

The phone buzzes. Swain picks up.

Mildred says, "Bryan Epworth is here."

"Thanks. Send him on back."

Bryan walks in and makes himself at home. To Swain, it is always a miracle when a kid can do that. Bryan starts off complaining.

"This is completely stupid," Bryan says, as he gets to Swain's desk and makes the turn. He heads back across the ten paces of open floor to the closed door. Swain, sprawled across half the sofa, follows his pacing with his eyes.

"What's stupid?" Swain says.

"My father made me come here."

"What did he make you come here for?"

Bryan's sweater is riding up on his ten-year-old's paunch. Below it, like the stuffing of a toy, his plaid shirttail is spilling out.

"He said I had to come. That was all. To talk to you." He shrugs.

"There must be something we could talk about. Since you're here."

Bryan gives the far wall a shove, the way a swimmer does, making a racing turn. He walks past again, not looking at Swain, not saying anything.

"What are you doing with yourself these days, Bryan?"

"Going to school. Hanging out."

"Do you see much of Jakey Miles?"

Bryan stops, looks at his feet, at the toe of one running shoe. Then he stands the toe against the floor and kicks as if he's trying to raise a divot. "Now and then. He's gone off somewhere to school now." So that's what they made me come here for. Jakey. They've been planning this whole thing, my parents and Dr. Hammond and Jakey's mother too, probably.

"How does it go? Do you still have a good time together?"

"No."

"Why not?"

"It's exactly like I thought. He's gotten freaky."

"You don't like being with him?"

Bryan twists one way and then the other. "I don't know," he says.

"But you call him?"

"My parents make me. They make me do everything."

"What would you do if you did exactly what you want to do?"

"Nothing."

"Nothing?"

Bryan is still now, no pacing or twisting or kicking the floor. "There's nothing to do." He makes a face. "Everything's boring."

"That doesn't sound like much fun."

Bryan, motionless in the center of the room, lets his head droop. He stares in front of him at the bare floor.

He goes to the far end of the sofa and sits down, on the edge. He keeps his eyes on the floor. Something that felt tight loosens up a little inside Swain's chest.

"Bryan, did you and Jakey ever talk about his accident, about him being blind?"

"No. I mean, he said something a couple of times that was sort of about it. But that's all."

"But you were sad and upset when it happened. Jakey might like to know you feel that way."

"I'm not saying any stuff like that."

"It's not as hard as you might think."

"No way."

"What would you say to him if you could say anything?"

"I'd tell him, 'Now everything's ruined.'"

"Do you have other good friends, Bryan?"

"I don't have any friends. Not anymore."

This is what I'd have been like, if I'd been shorter and fatter and had the guts to gripe. He imagines himself touching the kid, putting an arm around him. I'd have to slide way over there to do it. Bryan would probably clam up, or get up and walk out. Later, I'll do it, when we're standing at the door.

"Bryan, what do you think it would take to make you feel better? Just a little better?"

"If everybody at school wanted to hang around with me and then I would just say, 'Who needs you? I've got better things to do.'" Bryan leans back against the back of the sofa, satisfied with his answer, imagining it. That's exactly what is going to happen. He can picture it: everybody would want to hang around and do stuff with me, and all their parents would wish their kids were me.

"If you had a kid," Bryan says, "he would probably be my age."

"Maybe."

"So how come you don't have any?"

Swain slides his eyes across the row of books in the cabinet opposite him. That question. It's like a car I keep passing on the highway. Every time I pull off to get gas, every time I look around, I have to pass the same car again.

"I don't know, Bryan. I think about it."

Bryan lifts one side of his mouth in a grin. "Maybe you and her could get a divorce. First have kids and then get a divorce and you would just have them every other weekend." He laughs. "That's what lots of people do."

Swain smiles, makes a face. "I don't like that idea at all."

"Oh yeah? How come?"

"Because I don't want to be separated from her. Julie—my wife. You know her."

"Most people get a divorce."

"Your parents haven't."

"Yeah, but you never know when that could happen, because most people do. You can ask anybody."

"Are you afraid your parents might do that?"

"No. I wouldn't even care if they did. What I'm saying is, you never know." He props his ankle on his knee, puts his arms behind his head. He looks middle-aged, full of authority.

"You're right, Bryan. You never know. But tell me this, would you like to have kids when you grow up?"

"I'm not getting married."

"You think I should have any?"

"You're too old."

"Besides that."

Bryan frowns, looks at Swain hard. "You'd probably do okay. I guess."

Swain smiles, and feels himself trying not to.

"What makes you not sure?"

"Well, you act so, I don't know—strange, sometimes. Like that day at the creek, way back last summer..." He hesitates.

"When you threw water on me," Swain says.

"You never told my parents."

"Right."

"That's how come you'd be okay for a father."

"I see. I'm not a tattletale. So that's what it takes." He wants this kid to tell him everything. Whether he'll wish they'd had a child. What it means to hear God.

But Bryan is sinking again.

Swain reaches over and touches the boy's hair, lets his hand fall to his shoulder. Then he takes it away. "Bryan," he says. His voice feels soft, coming from a different place in his throat.

"What difference does anything make anyway?" Bryan says. "No matter what your parents do, you could all of a sudden be blind."

Swain opens his mouth, and closes it. He wants to hang on to that feeling, like a lamp coming on inside him. The more he wants it, the more it dwindles.

"There's no way to guarantee that nothing bad will happen. Your parents, nobody can do that. But good stuff happens too. Don't forget that."

"Like Jakey still gets to have a birthday cake? Even if he can't even see where it is to blow out the candles? If it happened to me, I'd kill myself."

"I wouldn't."

"What would you do? Spend the rest of your life lying around listening to TV?" He narrows his eyes, his lips curve. "You'd probably lie around and listen to God." He grins, it moves across his face slowly. Smiling, he crosses his arms on his stomach and waits.

"Maybe," Swain says, a little defiantly. He can't help it, even with a kid. "Sometimes I hear God when I'm doing things. Like playing ball. That happened to me a few days ago."

Bryan is looking at him sideways. "Oh yeah? For real?" He thinks, Wait until I tell my dad.

"God is for real, Bryan."

"God doesn't say anything to anybody else I know. How come you get to be the one?"

"I don't know exactly. I think just wanting God to talk to me, or something—and wanting it so much..." The last shall be first: that's what I ought to say.

Bryan's looking cagey. He's holding good cards and can't hide it. "Are you going to start doing miracles?" Swain is standing again at Jakey's bed. "Are you?" Bryan says. He pushes his outspread hands into the upholstery at his sides.

Swain wants to hold him in place with both hands and make him listen to it all. "I tried to let a miracle happen," he says. "I wanted him to see again. It felt like it was possible."

He sees Bryan's face and stops. Wide-eyed, his mouth actually hanging open a little. "Bryan, what I'm saying is that everybody has the power of God in them. We just don't let ourselves know it, most of the time."

"So what does it feel like?" Bryan stays very still and acts not scared a bit, just like you do with a dog that's growling at you.

"Like a furnace going on inside you."

"Did you do this stuff when you were my age?"

"No. But I wanted to."

"Are you going to make dead people come out of their graves?" A shiver crawls up the back of his neck. "I'll tell you right now, this stuff is giving me the creeps."

"I can't seem to explain without making it seem—"

"Weird."

"Yeah, weird. Which it's not at all."

Bryan is sliding forward to the edge of the sofa. "My mother's coming to get me," he says.

"Wait a minute, Bryan." He has to get the words right fast.

He stands. Bryan, edging toward the door, looks up at him. They both stood in that hospital room, nearly four months ago, looking at the same boy. The patches on his eyes. The feeling is coming back. The roaring heat that filled him, like a tune far off. He can feel between his fingers the plastic band around Jakey's wrist that he held in both of his hands. The scalding force that poured through him. His eyes burn. God has called him. "Bryan," he says. "God is a mystery. All you can do is listen to what you hear inside yourself."

Bryan looks at Swain, at the door, at his own feet.

"Dr. Hammond, I really do have to go now. Honest."

"Okay," Swain says. "Another day." He shakes his head. There's not going to be another day. I can't explain it. I should just give up. "See ya, Bryan," he says.

Bryan says, "Yeah. See ya." He's out the door.

Swain drops into a chair. I sat here and told the kid I tried to do a miracle. Nobody else but Patrice and Julie, and maybe Jakey, knew about that. He plays back what he said in his mind. It wasn't all that much. I didn't go into a lot of detail. The kid will probably forget it. And if he doesn't, if the word about that episode gets around . . . then fine. This congregation got off far too easy, deciding that the voice of God is nothing but an idiosyncrasy of Swain Hammond. I'll give them something else to think about. They might as well know it's not over.

On Sunday, he is sitting in on the Contemporary Issues church school class. The circle of chairs is angled in his direction. These chairs always feel too small for him. His knees stick up. The back hits him at the wrong place.

"The question I keep coming back to is, who's to decide whether the other guy is in the wrong." Honey Robison, wrapped up in one of the shawls she weaves. The tips of her fingers stay the color of some vegetable dye, like somebody who's been eating blueberries.

"But when it's obvious, clear-cut. Say a murderer." Bernie. Things have always been clear for him. "How are you supposed to deal with a murderer in your own family?"

"Assuming they've killed somebody outside the family?" Ed Fitzgerald. Everybody laughs. Ed holds for the laugh, a genial smile on his face. He rocks back in his chair.

"Seriously," Ed says. "When you're talking about how to deal with a sinner in your own midst, among the people you love, the issue isn't the big stuff, because like Bernie says, that's clear-cut. It's the smaller stuff. I mean, like how do you deal with your kid who goes to work for a nuclear power plant when you think that's how we're going to get blown off the earth?"

"Or if your good buddy tells you how he's ripping off the IRS for megabucks a year."

How much more of this do I have to listen to? It's like they're getting graded on class participation. The things that are going on in this church are as small-scale and childish as these Sunday-school chairs.

"The Scripture is fairly straightforward in some ways," Honey says. "We've all grown up with the idea that you get the mote out of your own eye before you bother with the speck in somebody else's."

"Maybe it isn't a speck."

"You should love them." Maria Durden, who brings love into every discussion and has the worst marriage in the congregation.

"That's all very well, but it doesn't tell you whether you should keep paying your kid's tuition after he's got himself into trouble, or whether you should blow the whistle on your buddy, or see him more or less often. That answers no practical questions at all."

"If you love them, you'll know how to handle it."

Ed rolls his eyes. Burton Echols is sitting over on the side, not saying a word.

"If it's somebody you don't love, you don't have a problem,"

Bernie says. "Then it's somebody else's problem. What we're talking about," he says, looking at Maria, "is how do you handle it when the people in your life, the people you love, take off in the wrong direction. I for one think you ought to say how you feel about it and then go on as much as you can with everything else the same. I wouldn't throw one of my kids out of my house because they got in trouble."

He's actually sitting there saying this. After the way he has stayed away from me ever since that night on the phone. For weeks he's been so polite and careful, any time he actually got trapped into talking to me. As if I'm some kind of crazy person he doesn't want to upset.

"You wouldn't throw one of yours out, Bernie, because you have two pretty little girls that are too young and sweet for you to even imagine it. Yet. You wait." Stu Edwards, in his resonant radio-announcer voice. Stu has four teenagers. "They don't stay the way they are at five years old. Mine aren't even the same people."

"It all comes back to which of us is qualified to judge," Honey says.

"I am," Stu says, hitting the center of his chest with both hands. "They're my kids."

Swain clears his throat. He can't stand any more of this. All the eyes are turned toward him. "So am I," he says.

"What do you mean?" Honey is looking at him. They all are.

"John 8:31. 'If ye continue in my word, then are ye my disciples indeed; And ye shall know the truth.'" Nobody says anything. "I'm saying that as a disciple of God, I know the truth."

Bernie turns his head away, faces out the window. A bare branch is stirring just beyond the window sill. Nobody in the room moves.

"Come on, Swain," Stu says, finally, breaking the silence. "It's one thing if you're talking about your kids. But what you're saying —anybody could say that they're God's disciple and then set themselves up as judge of everybody."

"There is that risk," Swain says, and stops again. I'm tired of trying to make it make sense. They can ask me if they want to know.

"That's one hell of a risk," Stu says.

"Yes."

"So what exactly are you saying? Anybody who sees themselves as a disciple—however you decide that—then they can call the shots on the rest of us? Some mad-dictator type, some Quaddafi—"

"What I'm saying is that whatever hold on truth we have comes from our personal direct immediate knowledge of God. Obviously, I'm not going to stone anybody or send anybody to jail. I'm just saying that I have a sense of what is right and what is wrong. I don't have to ask anybody."

Burton staring at me as if I'm some freak he's heard about and he's finally getting a chance to see.

A silence. He looks at his watch. He looks around the room at them. Nobody says anything. Nothing about Hitler, or any of a million perfectly reasonable arguments they could come up with. I've spent all these years trying to persuade them, when I should have just laid down the law. I could tell them I've been chosen and I'm now drafting disciples. I could tell them anything. . . . "I hate to take this moment to leave, but as you know, I need a few moments to finish preparations for the eleven o'clock. I look forward to continuing this discussion with you later."

He stands, looks around at them. My whole life I've been playing to the crowd, and I didn't know what I was missing. This is great. Take it or leave it. Finally I've got some authority for a change. He crosses the center of the circle. Stu slides his chair away from the door so he can get out.

Bernie, watching him leave, thinks, God, if you're really talking to him, set him straight. The boy's getting himself into a lot of trouble.

Swain, stepping into the hall, hears the voices start up again behind him. He'd love to hear what they're saying now.

The following Sunday, he's at the church an hour before the Sunday-school crowd starts to arrive. DeWitt Chambers is struggling through the side entrance with another load of flowers in wet newspaper. It's early, nobody else in the building. The sanctuary is big and cold, with an echo.

"Can I give you a hand?" Swain says across the rows of empty pews.

"Thank you, no. We're doing fine. Last load." He's almost hidden by waving branches of greenery with orange berries. DeWitt is the church's most faithful gardener. He puts his load down on the steps. When he straightens, he's still a little bent.... Swain hadn't noticed before. DeWitt pushes his glasses back up on his nose.

"Hold these," he says, handing Swain a thorny handful of rose stems. "Now you can be useful." Swain takes them carefully, as if he might break them. He has too much to do to be standing around in here this morning. He didn't come in early to arrange flowers, much as he loves to talk to the old guy.

"Now this is my favorite rose," DeWitt says, holding one stem between the tips of his fingers like a glass of wine. Not that the boy cares a fig for flowers, but he does listen so politely.

"White roses and pyracantha. The white and orange are so striking together. I've never seen it done, and I can't think why. Tuesday I woke up in the middle of the night and knew that's what I'd use. With brass canisters. It's going to be splendid."

Swain is still holding the roses. DeWitt is pulling other stems loose from each other and sticking one here and one there into the wet green block in the bowl. Swain holds the flowers and waits. DeWitt is so prissy and old-maidish and everything-just-so.

"You've been bringing flowers to this church a long time, De-Witt."

"I hate to think how long. Thirty years or more."

"I guess I'm just a newcomer compared to you," Swain says and laughs.

"That's right."

Swain smiles. DeWitt complacently snips at the stems. Good thing for Swain to keep in mind, uppity as he's getting lately.

"Has the place changed much in all these years?"

"Not so much. Same sorts of people mostly. Still a lot of the university people. Maybe there's more of a mixture. I'd say you've changed more than the congregation has." He looks over his glasses at Swain. That should get the conversation started.

"Oh?"

DeWitt puts another flower in the bowl and steps back to look at it. Then he looks again at Swain. "I would say so. Since last summer, of course. Since all that came up." Someone has to tell him, and it's perfectly clear by now that nobody else is going to do it.

"What did you make of all that, DeWitt?"

"I've got no reason to quarrel with you over it. I guess you know what you hear. I guess you know who's talking."

"Are people still talking about that? It has been"—he counts—"almost four months."

"They're talking about your being different. And getting more so all the time."

Swain puts the flowers down beside DeWitt and sits down on the steps. "I'm curious about what it is I'm doing that's so different."

"I would have to say that it changes from week to week." De-Witt frowns at the flowers, and makes a readjustment which seems to take an hour. "You know you've been a veritable chameleon of late. That's not an overstatement at all." He gathers up wet newspapers from one bundle and stuffs them into a plastic bag. Swain wants to grab the papers away from him and make DeWitt look at him and answer.

"Will you tell me exactly what I'm doing that's so different?"

His raised voice rings out across the whole big empty space of the sanctuary.

My, my—a show of temper. This is indeed a first. "I don't mind at all. Back in the summer when it happened, you seemed as if you weren't quite with us. Then for a couple of months, I thought maybe you were mad at us all. In your very quiet way, of course." He smiles at the flowers. "Then here lately, you've been in quite a different state of mind. I would say, you have been extremely full of yourself. Full of beans, if you will." He rakes back a strand of white hair. "In some ways, I find it rather"—he waves his hand around, sorting out possible words—"an improvement." Again he smiles.

"I wonder if everyone finds it an improvement."

"Everyone doesn't tell me what they're thinking. My guess is that you still have the support of most of them. But no one really knows what to think. Five months ago now—if you'll consider, Swain—you got up there in the pulpit and made that one rather startling admission, and then that was all."

"Why should I say more? They thought I was having emotional problems as it was."

And right they are, DeWitt thinks. Which is certainly to be preferred to no emotions, which is how you were until all this.

Swain rubs his forehead. A headache is starting behind his right temple. From all the flowers, is what it is. Smells like a funeral in here. "So the whole crew is still keeping an eye on me."

"People do have other things on their minds. But yes, it does come up now and again. I would have to say so. Yes."

The furnace switches on under the floor. There's a vague tremor in the walls that's almost a noise. Swan feels the dry hot blast of heat start again from the vent in the floor near the wall. It should have been running full tilt an hour ago.

"Nobody has mentioned it to me," he says.

"I am now mentioning it," DeWitt says, as he picks up one completed arrangement and adjusts it on the pedestal. Swain stares at the carpet and waits. DeWitt comes back and kneels beside him, opening more wet papers full of flowers. He begins to cut the bottoms of the stems. The scissors make a neat clinking sound, like a spoon against glass.

"DeWitt, I'm having to drag it out of you."

"Since you insist, Swain, I will go ahead and say that I think you're getting a bit"—he searches for the word—"grandiose."

Grandiose. Swain feels heat fill the space between his skin and his shirt, like a layer of insulation. DeWitt keeps his eyes on the flowers, cutting another and another.

Swain looks out across the empty pews, up to the beams that cross two stories above. They're putting on a play in a huge theatre with no audience, their two voices floating out into empty space.

"It's an air you have. A sort of—superiority, arrogance even." He starts to get to his feet, one angle unfolding at a time. He grimaces. "The joints get creaky. Don't ever believe it won't happen. Old age is on us in a flash."

Swain watches him as he looks around for the other canister, as if he hadn't said what he said. He goes over to the wooden pedestal. Swain watches his back. Fucking damn daisies.

DeWitt concentrates on the flowers. Let the chips fall where they may, I've done what had to be done.

"So what's wrong with that, DeWitt?" Swain says to the white shirt back. "Why not be excited, and proud? What more amazing thing could happen to anyone?" He leans forward on the step, until his bent knee is pushing against the leg of his pants. Like nothing he has ever done in this place with all of them here. He looks out at the pews and imagines the faces, all thinking the same as DeWitt, then back at the elbows working, the head bent over the flowers in front of him. Like an orchestra conductor from behind. "A direct experience of God, DeWitt," he says. Still no answer. Piss on the old bastard. He's never had any direct experience of anything.

DeWitt turns. He holds his head up very high, his eyes narrow, his mouth pursed. Now, Swain thinks, his feelings are hurt, it's all going to come out. Swain stays where he is on one knee on the floor.

"The truth is, Swain, much as I have always cared for you, this attitude didn't begin with the experience you refer to. You've always been a trifle smug, I think. Or seemed so. This latest thing has just added to it. I hate to have to say it, but someone should tell you." Try to help and this is what you get. If the boy would stop trying to act like he's not even human, he'd be absolutely marvelous. Just the merest touch of humanity showing, that's all he needs. He steps back and looks at the arrangement, then pokes in another branch where it needs a spot of color.

"I appreciate your honesty." Swain says it slowly and carefully, as he stands. Mark off Bernie; mark off DeWitt. They're all dumping me one after the other. The voice business is just an excuse. It's me they're turning away from, Swain decides. He has to do something to stop it. He wants to call out to all of them, "Come back, don't leave me." He looks at DeWitt's spotted hands, holding the scissors and a stem.

"Honesty is very rarely appreciated," DeWitt says and turns back to the pyracantha. He sighs. Now the man is all in a dither. Of course he'll get over it.

He doesn't look up again that Swain sees. If he would look up, maybe we could start over Swain waits. But DeWitt keeps fussing with the flowers.

Swain turns. I'm not going to beg for anybody's attention. He walks past DeWitt up the aisle, through the big empty cave of the sanctuary, out the back swinging door.

Two hours later, he's sitting in his place behind the pulpit. Latecomers are still filing in. He leans his head against the side wall. His headache is in full force now. Smug. Superior. I ought to get an acolyte to take the flowers out, as soon as the service has started. First one bowl and then the other, while DeWitt sits out there and watches. If he stayed.

If DeWitt had any idea what it takes to look out at these faces ...people I don't want to lose...most of the time...and say that

God has a human voice. If he had any idea...

Why do I care anyway? They sit out there and wait for it to be handed to them, just because they managed to get out of bed by eleven. If the *Times* were delivered before one o'clock, there wouldn't be a half dozen of them here. They'd let the paper fill up their heads instead of Swain Hammond. Superior. Well, there's some truth to it.

I'd be better off teaching homiletics. The pay couldn't be any worse. Then they can find somebody who isn't superior in any way. That ought to make them all happy.

After the service, lunch at the Epworths'. He forces himself to get through the service. He doesn't feel any better, maybe even worse, when he and Julie are standing on the Epworths' front porch. "How long do we have to stay?" he says to Julie, as they hear Hawk's footsteps approaching from inside.

"They just want to talk about Bryan," she says quickly. "You like Bryan. Remember?" The door opens.

"Come in, folks. Julie. Swain. Glad you could come." He kisses Julie's cheek, shakes hands with Swain.

"Sit down, sit down. Janet will be right out." Too hearty, Swain thinks. He sounds like a radio turned up too loud.

At the table, Janet tells them some long story about lobbying at the legislature on an environmental bill. Swain lets Julie do their half of the talking. Bryan isn't here. Swain wishes he were. It's starting to seem as if kids are a lot easier to deal with than their parents.

Swain's head is a little better than it was—after two extra-strength Tylenols that he swallowed without water in the car before they came in. If he'd waited until he came in, there'd be a rumor all over the church by tomorrow that he's on tranquilizers, taking something for his hallucinations.

Instead he's sitting with Hawk Epworth, drinking a cup of coffee so weak it looks like tea. Lunch is over. He and Hawk have moved to the living room. Julie has gone back into the kitchen with Janet. Abandoning me, Swain thinks.

"I've been wanting to tell you that I appreciate the help you've been to Bryan," Hawk is saying.

"I wish I could be better help to him. He's a fine boy, wrestling with some grown-up problems."

"He thinks a lot of you. He really does."

"I'm sorry he couldn't be here this afternoon. Did he talk with you about our recent conversation?" In which he ran out the door as if he'd seen a ghost?

Hawk gets a cagey smile on his face. "He seemed very interested in the things you said to him. Janet and I couldn't quite get the straight of it."

Swain frowns, as if he doesn't understand.

"About the power of God. Having it in you." Hawk looks at his coffee cup, then at his shoe. A wingtip. He waggles it back and forth. We're going to get to the bottom of this, he thinks, right now. "Things like that," he says.

"Certainly we all have the power of God in us."

"Oh, absolutely, no question." Hawk smiles his gummy smile again, rearranges his pants leg. "I'm just curious about that whole subject coming up with Bryan, when you were, you know, talking with him about his problem."

"What is his problem, Hawk? How do you see it?"

"He isn't getting over what happened to the Miles boy."

"Actually, we were talking about that and Bryan brought the other subject up himself. He asked me about it. He reminded me of that sermon last summer in which I talked about hearing God, hearing a voice. Apparently Bryan was still a little curious about that. I've always been surprised that so few people seemed to be."

"I've wondered about all that myself." Hawk forces a chuckle. Here goes: "You know, Swain, I never completely understood back then, maybe I missed it. What did, uh, God actually say?"

"You didn't miss it. At that point there was nothing that I could understand and report. It was—incomplete."

"And now you understand?"

"Now I know that God has chosen me to do his work."

"Chosen . . . you."

"Yes."

Damn. He stares at Swain. He really said that.

Hawk cuts his eyes toward the kitchen, where Janet is. She's not going to believe this. It's as bad as Bill Bartholomew has been saying since last summer. "I guess that's what you preachers mean by being called."

Swain nods and takes a swallow of his coffee. "A bit late in my career. When I went into the ministry, there was never anything I could point to and say 'That was it, my calling.' Most ministers don't. But—I wanted something. . . ."

"You've sure got something you can point to now."

Swain nods. Hawk is looking at him like a prosecutor with a good case. The ingratiating smile is gone. He's got the goods. A shudder of dislike passes through Swain. He puts the cup down on the table before he spills it. Hawk is a shit. I hate him. Not just him, I hate half of them at least, and I'm mad at them all the time. When did I get so mad? Was it always like this? Hawk staring. I used to like Hawk. What has happened? He keeps sitting there waiting for me to say something.

"It's not easy," Swain says. Lately he has felt so confident, powerful. Now suddenly it's crumbled. His own voice sounds feeble. "All this . . . that we've been talking about, it's difficult." Hawk nods. Swain takes a deep breath, looks up at the clock on the mantel, a tall glass globe, like the one that sat on the shelf in his father's study. A big shiny see-through egg. Without looking at Hawk, without looking away from the shine of light on that globe, he says, "There's a story in John about blindness, about a miracle."

He doesn't look back at Hawk at all. There's a quiver in his stomach like stage fright. "Jesus made a blind man see. He put wet clay on his eyes and he could see. And then the man went out into the world, and he told people what happened." Swain's eyes follow the moving clockwork. "They didn't believe him. That's what it says in John: 'They reviled him. And they cast him out.' They thought he was faking, Hawk. They thought he was making it all up."

The weight in Swain's head is beginning to turn, slowly. Like a carnival ride rolling slowly up into its first spiral. Hawk's face is strange, wavery. It's like looking at him through water. The words are going around in his head, riding a Tilt-A-Whirl. I'm going to lose my balance, fall out of the chair. They reviled him. They cast him out. All my life, all I ever wanted God for was so I wouldn't be so lonely.

Hawk is sitting forward, saying something. Swain forces himself to hear it, to slow down his brain. "... not been cast out. People just don't understand. It's—people are frightened of what might be happening to you." Now the words are clear. The clock is ticking. The sun hits the mahogany table. Swain puts his hand up to his forehead and lets it fall to the arm of the chair.

Hawk doesn't let himself look away from Swain for a second. The man looks as if he's just been through something awful. "Are you okay?" he says. "Can I get you anything? A glass of water?" I don't know if he's even hearing a word I'm saying. I should get a doctor. This guy is coming apart, he needs to talk to somebody.

Swain looks over at Hawk, sitting there helpless and embarrassed, not knowing what to do. He closes his eyes. I'm the one who's helpless, weak. Somebody do something to help me. Hawk could come across the room now and touch me while my eyes are closed, and both of us would think we dreamed it and it didn't happen. Put one hand on my hair, like a blessing. Or just put an arm around me for a minute.

But Hawk isn't going to do that. Nobody is. Something about me tells everybody: "Don't touch." And everybody listens. Except for Julie.

Swain pushes himself forward to the edge of the chair. "Hawk, I think the best thing for me is to go on home." He rubs his hand across his forehead. "I'm—I don't know—short of sleep, I guess. Things have been piling up on me lately."

"Sure, Swain," Hawk says. "If there's nothing I can do...?"

Walking down the front steps, when they're finally out of the house, Swain can feel Julie watching him. "You drive," he says. "Please."

"Okay." She nods. She is still watching him.

They get into the car. He leans the seat back as far as it will go and closes his eyes. He says, "Let's go to bed when we get home."

"For sex? I thought you were feeling bad."

"Yes, for sex. And yes, I feel bad." He doesn't open his eyes.

TEN

Somebody should take a picture of this: Swain Hammond holding a three-year-old. The way she's leaning back against his chest, all he can see is her chubby little legs and the top of her head, curls that are too soft to be real hair. Her heart, Kate's heart, is beating against his stomach. It's like holding a puppy that smells good. Is it baby powder or do they naturally smell like this?

"Are you taking the first shift in the nursery, Dr. Hammond?" Shillingburg, Carla. One of the junior highs. They change so much so fast he's forever calling a roll in his head when he sees them, trying to get hold of the names.

"Just helping out, Carla. Patrice is in charge here."

"Right," Patrice says, from one of the little elementary chairs. She's patting an infant that's finally quiet. "Whatever I say here goes." She looks down at the red-faced kid wrapped up in its little blanket. "You hear that, sport?" The baby isn't much bigger than her two hands. She looks so thin now, she and Jakey both.

"Come down here and help us some Sunday, Carla," Patrice says. "We can use a few more volunteers."

Carla has on pink eyeshadow all the way to her eyebrows and a jacket like the ones baseball players wear. She puts her hands in the pockets and leans her head back against the collar. "Not me, man. It's not an age I can relate to."

"You might change your mind sometime," Patrice says. "There are some good things about it."

"Count on it," Carla says, starting to move on. "You guys have fun." She's gone.

Swain looks at Patrice over the heads of half a dozen three-and-unders playing on the floor between them, both of them pinned to their little chairs by the weight of a child. She reaches over to swat the one who keeps hitting kids with his tow truck. Kate, in his lap, laughs. Patrice says, "Jakey's a lot better. The school decision was right. Even Joe has backed off a little and isn't threatening to take him out." She pauses, looking at him as if she's measuring the distance between them.

"I haven't seen Joe in weeks."

"Lucky for you," she says.

"I got the idea when we had that run-in in the grocery that he thinks I'm the one you're seeing."

She raises her eyebrows. "That's completely unfair."

Swain laughs. "Under the circumstances, I would say so."

He watches a kid push a jet fighter with a little man in it across the carpet between them. Kate slides out of his lap.

"Is Jakey home this weekend?"

"He's upstairs in Sunday school. Bryan Epworth is helping him around. I'm down here staying out of their way."

"Great. That's wonderful." He leans back in the chair. The two of them, Bryan and Jakey. "That's the best news I've had in a while."

Patrice fakes surprise. "Since when are you so into kids? Everybody knows they're not your thing. What are you doing in the nursery anyway?"

He makes a wry face. "Last week before the service I tried talking to DeWitt. This week I'm staying the hell away from him." He shrugs, looks at his shoes. "Everybody is right. About me and kids, I mean. But . . . I guess it's the time I've spent with Jakey, or thinking about him. . . ."

"I see." She gets up and puts the baby down in the crib. She looks back at him, still bemused. "Well . . . how about holding the fort here for a few minutes? I need to go down to the kitchen for a bottle." She smiles, and sails out the door.

She didn't even wait for him to answer. He looks around carefully. Maybe they won't notice she's gone. Wrong. They know, every one of them, instantaneously. From all parts of the room, they're watching him, eyeing him, starting to move toward him. Here they come, one after another, heading for him. They're storming the beach, heads hunched, helmets on, running through the surf with their weapons. They're after me. The boy in the overalls toddles over, dragging the steam shovel by its bucket, and gets himself in position right in front of him to stare. Such huge eyes. Swain stares back. Slow motion, the kid loses his balance and falls down.

The look on his face, still aimed at Swain—any second the screaming's going to start. He couldn't be hurt. He's only two feet tall, all he did was sit down. His pudgy face is contorting, getting ready to let loose. Please don't. Wait for Patrice. She'll be here soon. Here it comes. Jesus. A wail of mortal agony, and he never once takes his big wet eyes off Swain.

"Come here, fellow. Come on over here and sit with me." Swain slides off the chair onto his knees on the floor. He holds his arms out to the kid, who continues to sit where he is and pour great huge tears down his face and howl. The tears are so big. Maybe tear ducts shrink when you get older. Maybe they start off adult-sized and everything else gets larger to fit. Swain claps his hands the way he's seen people do and holds them out. It doesn't work.

He knee-walks over to the boy and picks him up like an arm-load of firewood and swings him up in the air. That ought to get his attention. He comes to rest in Swain's arms, silent. He puts his thumb in his mouth and begins to study Swain.

"Do me. Do me, too." Another kid, probably four or five, pulling at his shoulder. "My turn. I'm next."

"One at a time, boy. I need to take care of your friend right now." The baby in the crib is making whiny, cranky noises. Across the room a whole row of tall skinny picture books collapses like a deck of cards and starts sliding off the shelf onto the floor. The one he was holding, Kate. She did it. Now the baby's screaming.

Patrice walks back in with a bottle and puts it in the kid's mouth. Thank God. The baby starts sucking on it like crazy. You can hear him across the room. He's holding onto that thing and staring at Swain through the slats of the crib. See? he's saying. This is what I wanted. How come you don't know anything?— good thing you're not running this show. Those big flat blue eyes. The little shit. What am I doing down here in the middle of this anyway? And Patrice walking off and leaving me with it. He looks at his watch. I have to get upstairs and get into my robe.

"Just walk off and leave me," Swain says. "What are you trying to do?"

She laughs. "I told you. I had to get a bottle. You're a big boy, old enough to baby-sit for a few minutes."

He looks down into the crib. The bottle has slid out of the kid's mouth. Watery-looking milk is lying in the corner of his lips, trickling down his cheek. Aren't you supposed to burp them? Patrice should know. He says, "I think I may be too old."

A whine starts from a little girl playing near the wall. It picks up force and gets shrill, like a burglar alarm. Another girl is trying to pull a toddler-sized table away from her. It's bigger than both of them. They're each hanging on to a leg and pulling. The shrieks are starting to harmonize. "They're getting a divorce," Swain says. "Having a little trouble with the property settlement." Patrice goes over to break it up.

Swain says, "Why would somebody voluntarily bring such a creature into their home?"

Patrice stops, her back to him. Her shirt is so thin he can see a mole high on her back. The kids are still screaming. She's just going to let them kill each other. She turns around.

"As I was saying to Carla, it's worth it, Swain."

"But look what's happened—"

She nods. "Nothing could be worse."

"Do you ever think 'Suppose I'd never had a kid at all'?"

"No." She hesitates. "What about you?"

"What about me?"

"Are you ever going to do it? Have any?"

"I don't know. I never would have considered it until . . . the last few months." He picks up his suit coat off the table and puts it on. "I've got to go," he says.

He walks around the crib, heading for the door, and stops—on an impulse—close to her, and watches while her eyes get wide.

"Swain?"

He takes her shoulders in his two hands and turns her.

"Swain, what are you doing?"

He moves toward her slowly, so she has time to know what he's doing. He leans over and kisses her, his mouth opening into hers. A hard kiss. Then he moves back fast. She's staring at him, her lips still parted. He has to look away. The baby is making whimpering noises beside them. He steps back from her, turns as though it's some kind of military drill, puts his hand on the doorjamb to keep his balance, goes out the door.

He turns the corner of the hall and saunters toward his office feeling as if he's had two drinks.

"Good morning, Dr. Hammond. How are you this morning?" Her sweet old lady voice. I should kiss her too.

"Just fine, Mrs. Helgesen. I hope you are well."

"Good morning."

"Good morning."

"Oh, Swain. I need to talk with you a few minutes today when you get a chance."

"Swain, come look at what we've done in the lower grades."

"I'll be right there. . . . We'll do that. . . . Good to see you. . . . You're looking well. . . . How was your trip?" It's like walking down the hall in high school, the way it would be if you were popular. People speak to me, pull at me. It's like having a bunch of kids saying 'Daddy, Daddy,' at the house when you come home. I'm the big cheese.

And I kissed Patrice, by damn. I up and did it. He smiles brilliantly at Janie Haddonsfield. She stops in her tracks. He keeps walking and leaves her standing there. The hall is full of the smell of women's perfume. He loves it. Once his mother came home from a trip and he went into their room while she was unpacking. When she opened her suitcase, the room was full of that smell.

His dad wasn't home. Swain was standing and watching, not saying anything. She was singing something in Italian, she had been to Italy.

She looked around and saw him.

"Hey, babe," she said. Going to Italy always made her happy. She reached over and rumpled his hair. He put his hand up and felt where she touched.

"Did you have fun while I was gone? Did you miss me?"

He nodded.

"Here, you can help me. Put these over in the top drawer." She handed him a thin folded square of her clothes, a slip or a nightgown, he didn't know. It smelled like trees. He walked over to the bureau, holding what she gave him carefully with two hands. The material looked so smooth and it had that smell, he held it up and rubbed it against his face.

The whole vestibule is full of it, perfume. Wonder who else I'm going to kiss.

In the hall at the top of the staircase that comes down into the vestibule, Jakey and Bryan are trying to decide what to do next.

"I mean, it seems completely stupid to go to church if we can get out of it," Bryan is saying. "We could tell them we want to sit in the balcony by ourselves."

"Yeah," Jakey says, "Mom'll let me do anything if it's with a kid. If I say, 'Hey, Mom, Bryan and me are going to get a couple of Uzis and hold up a 7-Eleven,' she'll say—he makes his voice high—'I think that's wonderful. You boys have a great time.' So where do you want to go?"

"We could go to a video arcade."

Jakey makes a face, kicks one foot against the other. "Naah, they're not open on Sunday."

"Oh yeah. I forgot." He can't even see video games. Idiot. Stupid. Why can't I remember that?

Jakey says, "Do you have any money?"

"Some."

"We could go climb the fence where the football team practices and hit those big padded frames they have."

"Do you think they still have them out on Sunday?"

"They might. We could go check it out."

"Okay. We gotta hurry. All we've got's an hour."

Swain hears something clumping down the upper flight of stairs. They come into sight. Jakey, hanging onto Bryan not by his arm but by a handful of the back of his sweater. Bryan says, "Hi, Dr. Hammond," and nudges Jakey with his elbow.

"Hello, Bryan. Hi there, Jakey." He puts a hand on the shoulder of each one, gives Jakey an extra pat. "I'm glad you're here, boy." Jakey mumbles something.

Bryan looks up at him. "So how's it going?" Swain asks him.

"Okay."

Jakey says, "Fine."

"Look, we got to go," Bryan says.

Go in peace, Swain wants to say to them. And now may the love of God be with you. Happy birthday. Merry Christmas.

"Okay, guys," he says. "See you 'round."

Now it's time, he decides as he's getting ready to go into the sanctuary, to tackle the Bernie situation. While I'm feeling bold, I might as well get that straight. Got Patrice taken care of. The boys are doing fine. I could solve all my problems once and for all.

"Honey? Swain?"

He turns. Julie. He flushes. All I did was kiss her once, he thinks. That's all I'll ever do. That was it.

Before he can speak, she says, "I feel really weird. I don't know what's going on. I've got the strangest feeling in my gut."

Oh my God. "You mean like something's happened? You've got a feeling like something's happened?" All I did was kiss her, he thinks again.

She turns him aside so that they have a corner of privacy away from the stream of people going past "No. I mean, like I'm coming down with something. Some intestinal bug. I just wanted to let you know in case I'm not out front. It's been bothering me all morning. Last night too. I feel kind of uneasy. I may go on home."

"Okay, babe." He puts his arms around her. The people continue to pass, catching sight of them, smiling and looking away. "Do you need me to do anything?"

"No, I just wanted to tell you in case you don't see me and wonder." They let go of each other. She looks up at him for a moment. "I don't think you ever hugged me in the middle of traffic."

"Lots of firsts," he says, smiling, full of confidence and benevolence. Full of beans, DeWitt would say. He kisses the top of her head. "Go home and take it easy. I'll be there in a little bit. I'm sorry your stomach hurts."

He heads off down the hall. Julie taken care of. Patrice taken care of.

Swain doesn't get a free moment to do anything about Bernie until midweek. By then he's not so sure about what he's actually going to say, but he makes himself go give it a shot anyway. He drives over to Bernie's office—no appointment—and presents himself to the receptionist.

"Mr. Morris is on the phone, sir." She acts as if she's guarding the Crown Jewels. "Was he expecting you?" He can see Bernie's feet through the crack in the door, sprawled out in front of his swivel chair, one propped on the other. He keeps jiggling them. He's probably popping a ballpoint pen in and out, or rapping it against the top of the desk. "Sir," she says. "Was he expecting you?"

"No. I'll wait." He sits down on one of the sofas and picks up a *Forbes.*

"I'll let him know you're here."

"Thank you." He closes the magazine, throws it back on the pile.

His hands are shaky all of a sudden, as if he's had too much coffee. He can hear Bernie's voice, the tone but not the words, bringing the conversation to a close.

Back in his office, Bernie puts his phone down. Beth buzzes him and says, "Dr. Hammond is here."

"I'll be with him in a minute." So the great guru finally comes to see me, thinks Bernie. Terrific. What are we supposed to talk about now? Here it is the middle of November. The eighteenth of November. He should have been over here talking to me back in July when all this started. Now what does he want? He wants me to sell him a site out on the highway where he can build a shrine for all his groupies to come worship him? Near the airport for easier access. Maybe he'd like me to donate it.

I don't have to see him. Beth could get rid of him. He just walks in with no warning, and expects everything to stop. Maybe he's gotten himself straightened out, that's what he's here to say.

He stands up goes over to the door. "Swain."

Swain stands and crosses the waiting room, as if he has just been summoned to stand trial. All his bravado is gone. Bernie's face looks professional and businesslike. It was a mistake to come here. I should turn around and walk out now.

They go into his office. Swain closes the door.

"You just over in this neighborhood?" Bernie says.

"No, I came to see you." They sit in the two plaid armchairs. "I was thinking that we're overdue for a talk."

"Well—" Bernie touches the edge of a metal ashtray on the table, gives it a spin. "Nice of you to come by."

"You and I have been friends a long time. We've been avoiding each other lately. I know it's as much me as you. But I don't like it."

Bernie nods. "Things have gotten in the way." He picks up the ashtray and holds it in front of him in both hands.

"When it really hit me was back in the summer. That session of the elders."

Bernie nods, keeps his eyes on his fingers and the ashtray.

"I know you meant well," Swain says, "but it was a blow. I didn't like the way you handled it either. Even on the phone, it was like you weren't looking me in the eye. You haven't ever since."

Bernie looks up. "What was I supposed to do? You told me nothing about any of this. I have to find out in a meeting that you're hearing voices."

Swain stares at him. He sounds as if he's the one who's mad. "You could have talked to me, Bernie."

"You're the one who had something to say."

Swain is silent. Then says: "I should have. I was confused. So much was going on. And then I got that phone call, that the session thought I was crazy. And you one of them."

"I was the one who called."

"I know that wasn't easy."

"Fucking straight." Bernie pissed off? This is not what I expected.

"I kept thinking that if I'd had a chance to tell you what it was like . . ."

Bernie takes off his glasses and rubs his face. "Did you ever . . . I don't guess you ever went and talked to anybody about it?"

"No."

"Why not?"

"Didn't need to."

"Swain," he shakes his head. "You expect me to believe that what you heard was really the Top Banana?"

"Seems like you—at least the way I've always seen you— would at least consider it."

"Me?" Bernie looks around his office. He holds out his hands, palms up. "For Christ's sake, Swain, I've got two real flesh-and-blood kids and a wife. I've got a business to run, a bunch of meetings to go to, a lot of routine daily stuff to take care of. I don't talk to angels, they don't talk to me."

"But you used to—"

"Used to what, Swain? What is it you remember?"

Swain shrugs. "I don't know. I could always talk to you. We were always on the same wavelength."

"That's the very reason I knew you'd taken a wrong turn. Because voices from God don't break in on my frequency. If it happened to me, I'd turn myself in for nuts."

Swain stares. He's really mad.

Bernie goes on. "I just never thought you'd do anything like this—make up a spooky song-and-dance like this. You were the only preacher I knew of that wouldn't. I thought that was really something."

"Yeah?" Swain says. He feels his whole face lift. Bernie thought I was really something? "When I've seen you lately, you've looked away as if I was a wino panhandler."

"I never thought you would do this," Bernie says. "You think I like watching you get up in front of people and say what you've been saying? How do you think it feels to watch somebody going down the tube? I don't like it, Swain. I've known you too long." He glances over toward his desk, at the coat rack, the wall. "Look," he says, "I should tell you—Joe Miles called me. He thinks the elders need to bring it up again, this same business. Says you tried to do a miracle with his kid in the hospital."

A wash of heat pours over Swain's chest and arms. Bernie's waiting, no expression, completely blank.

Swain swallows. "He's right. I did." Don't let him look like that. "Just listen to me for a minute, Bernie."

Bernie doesn't say anything. Goddamn him for doing this. Goddamn.

Swain stares at him and waits. It's too late, that's what his face is saying. Finish and get out of here. You blew it already.

"Bernie, what happened was, for about two seconds, I had this feeling that something could happen. I stood next to Jakey's bed and prayed. All I did...I prayed for what I really wanted to happen. I don't even know exactly what I said. My heart was beating all the way up in my head. It felt like a fire hydrant had cut loose inside me. Bernie, I just wanted none of us to be there. I wanted

Jakey to be outside playing, like he was before. I wanted him to see. I'd have done anything. . . ."

"Joe said you lost it. He was right."

"I may be losing it. But that was—"

"Miracles, Swain?"

"You've got to understand—"

"I don't have to understand anything." Bernie leans closer. "This whole business makes no sense to me at all. I don't want to even think about it. I thought—I hoped Joe was imagining things, with what he's been going through. I wanted it not to be true."

"For one minute, give me a break, Bernie. I have to get it across to you—"

"I'm not the Supreme Court. If I was all that big a deal to you, you'd have said something about it in the first place. I just think you ought to be warned. . . ." He looks down at his watch, looks back at Swain.

"Joe's really going to pursue it?"

"Sounded like it."

"I don't care. There's nothing I can do about that. It's out of my hands."

Great, Bernie thinks, terrific. He wants to play it that way? From now on, Swain Hammond is out of my hands.

Bernie's face is flushed dark. His neck looks as though it has suddenly gotten razor burn. It's no good trying. I'm just tired. I want to go lie down over there on the sofa. Swain says, "There are a few people I wish were . . . I don't know, on my side, I guess. You're one of them. I suppose because we go so far back. The rest of them, the way I feel now . . . I can't make myself worry about it. I don't want to pester you about it—I just wish you could understand. I really. . ." He did it again, he looked at his watch. "Okay," Swain says. "I'm going to take off now. I don't know what else to say."

Bernie stands up and holds out his hand. He looks old, thick around the middle, middle-aged. "Bernie, maybe I shouldn't say this, but I feel if I lose touch with you—you and Patrice Miles—

then I'm losing the whole first half of my life."

He puts his hand on Bernie's arm. Bernie watches, doesn't move. Swain lets his grip slide off of Bernie's arm until his fist is closed only on the sleeve of his coat. This is the way Jakey was holding on to Bryan. This is how it would feel if somebody were leading you around. He squeezes the material into his hand.

"Swain?"

He looks up. Bernie's face—why does he look . . . ? What am I doing? He drops his hand from Bernie's coat sleeve. "Look, Bernie, don't worry. I'm okay."

"Take care of yourself," Bernie says. "We'll be in touch." He steers Swain toward the door. Swain is saying, "I'm sorry I didn't call you and you had to hear it first in—" Bernie shuts the door and goes back around and sits down behind his desk. He rings Lynne, she's not at the house. He sits with the receiver in his hand while he tries to think of somebody else to call. He looks at his calendar. An hour and a half before he's scheduled to be any-where. I'm not going to sit here and beat myself over the head with this all afternoon. You win some, you lose some. But Swain? He was the one person in the world you knew would always be solid.

For two days after his talk with Bernie, Swain feels wounded. He sits in the armchair in the living room pretending to get some paperwork done, his great surge of confidence gone as fast as it came.

Things are falling apart on me, he thinks. One more thing, that's all it would take. One more person to defect. The edges of me breaking down the way a grocery bag gets soft when some-thing spills inside. One more bit of pressure and my guts spill out. What's everybody going to do then?

Julie's no help at all, sitting there with her book. He looks over at her. Staring at me like I'm not really here.

"Why do you keep looking at me like that?"

She sighs. "Was I looking at you? I didn't even know it. I'm going to go nuts if I don't start getting some sleep. I still don't feel good. I still have that funny burning way down in my stomach. I don't know what it is. I keep feeling like if I could go to the bathroom, it would help. But then I do and it doesn't."

"Stress," Swain says, an edge in his tone. "The pain of having to live with me. I'm terribly sorry to be such a liability."

"Probably that's exactly what it is. Anyway, you know perfectly well why I was looking at you. Anybody in their right mind would be worried to death about you, Swain. You can't expect me to just go on my merry way."

"Why not?"

"While you're waiting for your orders from God?"

"Okay. Fine. Worry, then. I don't care."

A̲t lunchtime now he goes out for a run, from the Y up Airport Road, into the center of town, then back. Two immense hills. This is supposed to make him able to cope with the rest of the day. A trickle of sweat runs down his back. He didn't need this sweatshirt, even though it is almost December.

On Rosemary Street, he dodges a row of students filling the whole sidewalk. Hops off the curb into the street, back on the sidewalk in front of them. Wonder if any of them notice him at all. He pushes the headphones back up on his head. "Take your car to Bucky's Car Wash. Take it today." He switches stations, looking for music.

One more block and it's time to turn around and head back. A girl up ahead in jeans. Big heavy butt swinging back and forth ahead of him. He's losing steam. Half a block. Passing Big Butt. She moves to the side. Shows a little respect for an old man. Strange getting old in a college town.

Over the top. Halfway home. His head falls forward, his arms swing loose at his sides. He's made out of limp pieces of rope.

"Swain."

"Sam." Swain lopes to a stop. "I didn't know you're a runner."

Sam looks as if he may not make it. He bends from the waist, his hands on his hips, waiting to catch his breath. He's carrying a lot of stomach.

"New," Sam says. "Last week." He pauses for two more slowing breaths. "Doctor said I had to do it. Said if I wanted to make it to fifty, I better do something different." Sam laughs, still out of breath. "I can't say that the world's any better for my having made it to forty-nine."

"I'm glad you're paying attention to him. It's good to see you."

"Good to see me sober, you mean."

"That too."

He grins. "That also started last week."

"Good for you." Swain sticks out his hand. Sam shakes it. "Congratulations." Sam was the one person who was coming apart worse than me.

"Don't take it too seriously, Swain. It isn't going to last. I've quit a bunch of times before."

"What got you to do it again now?"

"My ex-wife said if I didn't, she'd go to court to keep the kids away from me. I could have gone one way or the other at that point. Gotten it together for a while to get her off my back. Or I could have said the hell with the kids and everything and let it all go. Which is what I meant to do, to tell you the truth.

"On top of all that, there was my boss calling me in one morning. He said, 'Patience and sympathy in these matters goes only so far, Sam.'"

Swain thinks, Which one of the members is going to say that to me? Bill? Joe, with the victory shining in his black eyes? Maybe Bernie. "Patience and sympathy goes only so far, Swain."

Sam shrugs. "So here I am. Running up and down the road like it's good for me. The truth is, it'll probably kill me sooner."

Swain forces a smile. "Still seeing the friend that you introduced us to at the cafeteria?"

"Yeah." He laughs. "You could almost say I saw her for the first time last week." A warning look crosses his face. "She's okay," he says. "A fine lady. A little different from what you might expect. But she's real decent, she's been good for me."

"Maybe that's part of why you're laying off the sauce."

"No. Can't anybody else get you to do it. Anyway I'm going to fall back into it."

"You know that even now?"

"Yeah, I know. I can tell I'm not done with it, I don't feel like I've made any big decision."

Swain feels weight lift off him, like a deadline taken away. Somebody will still be worse off than I am.

Sam says, "It hasn't been hard enough for it to be final. Not that it's so easy. But I can tell you I'm starting to think one day I'll do it, dump it completely. I'm as sure of that as I am that the time isn't now. Does that make any sense?"

"No." Swain laughs. "Can't say that it does." Sam is shaking out first one leg and then the other. His calves are big muscular triangles. "I'm glad things are going better with you now, Sam."

"Thanks." He taps the bend of Swain's shoulder with the bottom of his fist. He says, "You take care of yourself."

On his way back to his office, Mildred stops him. "Dr. Hammond, *Westside This Week* is ready for you to look at."

Swain takes a copy with the couple of fingers he has free. He's carrying boxes of art supplies Margie DeLissa handed him out her car window for the Prison Ministry Group.

He dumps it all on the front-office counter. "You know where these things go, Mildred?" She takes them away.

He starts down the hall, reading the newsletter. "Etta Jones will lead a discussion on freedom of choice in suicide and euthanasia.... Our new group of motet and madrigal singers will sing Orlando di Lasso's: *Ave verum corpus....* Ushers: Marilyn Williams, Ed Fitzgerald, Rudy Haddonsfield, Bernie Morris, Michael Woodhouse...

"...Handbell choir rehearsal...Family seminar: Living with Preschoolers...Divorce Adjustment Group will meet....Come to the Village Ministry Center's Forum Series on Poverty....Join us in an experience of worship through journal-keeping.... Book-of-the-Month Discussion will be on Hinduism, as described in Huston Smith's *Religions of Man*. This book is available in the church office." Presumably, Mildred knows about that.

So much stuff. He kicks his door shut, throws his file folders onto his desk and sits down in the armchair. That's only the first page. He scans the headings: New Members, Upcoming Small Group Experiences, Report on Asian Indian Ministry, Westside Soccer Team. Too much. These can't be "the works of my Father." But if they're not, then what? What have we not thought of to do?

Maybe dump the Hinduism books and instead make God available in the church office. Or have a box where grace is collected like canned goods from people who have enough of it. Or maybe God could use the Westside newsletter as a mouthpiece, to send him his instructions, right under the Westside Soccer scores. "Dear Swain, report for duty." Then tell me exactly, please, what that duty is.

ELEVEN

"Relax into the wholeness of your mind-body-spirit," Louie the yogi says. Swain lets his head fall back to the floor. Current is racing through his arms and legs. They want to do something, maybe get up and walk out of here.

He raises his head and cranes his neck around to get a look at the whole scene. The corpse position. Twenty corpses. It's the first time he's seen the assembly room from this angle. The bottom sides of chairs, the legs of the tables. This is what it's like to be a high school principal, walking in and out of classes, trying to find out what it is you're running. The more I see, the more I wonder.

"Find a peaceful place deep within yourself," Louie moans from the front of the room. His voice is like wind coming around the corner of a house. Swain stares at the ceiling. Somebody used one of the leftover paper pumpkins to dim the overhead light. A murky orange glow tints his feet, as if he had on shoes that got wet and bled. The paper pumpkin: is it going to catch fire, should I lie here and worry about it? This is not working, this yoga business. No point in looking for any answers here.

He twists around and looks at Louie, who sits with a conspicuously blissful expression on his face, smiling like a skinny little Buddha. Swain puts his head back down, tries to relax his jaw, his tongue, his eyeballs. He can't relax. He's like frayed wire pulled tighter and tighter every day.

"Now," Louie says. The silence around his voice is like a layer of cotton. Swain closes his eyes. The darkness still has the same pumpkin glow. "Breathe...inhale deeply," Louie says, sucking a square yard of dusty close-to-the-floor air into his skinny little chest. Marilyn Williams is lying nearby, I haven't done a thing about her mother being sick.

"Breathe out all your cares in one great sigh." Silence. Everybody's waiting for somebody else to do it. Somebody does it: a big exaggerated blast of air. Swain lets the breath leak out of him: that one was for Marilyn and her mother. He takes a deeper breath and lets it go. That was the unreturned phone calls. Another big puff for finding people to fill spaces on three committees. What are the chairmen doing anyway? I shouldn't have to worry about that. He imagines the list of phone calls floating in the air above him, hovering, suspended by his breath. As soon as he inhales, it will fall down on his face.

The door shuts at the back of the room. He turns and looks. Julie. She made it. Her ankles and feet, blocked by the rungs of a chair—his eyes follow the line of her leg to the bottom of her green coat. Taking off her coat, quietly, moving carefully, laying it across the table. She sees him. He waves, lifting one hand off the carpet and letting it back down. He rests his head back again. I'm more relaxed than I thought. That was a major exertion.

"Sit up, please, if you will." Just when I was getting comfortable. Swain sits up and looks around to see where Julie is. There, on the far side. She missed the relaxing part, she's just in time for the contortions.

Julie sinks down onto an open space on the floor. At least it's quiet. I need to be quiet. I could put my coat over my head. . . .

I'm not going to do any yoga, just lie here. I should have gone home. It was crazy to come. She turns her head a little to the side and sees Swain's back, long and familiar in his white undershirt. He looks the way he does sitting on the side of the bed putting on his socks in the morning. If nobody were here but us, I could tell him now and not wait anymore. I could lie right here where I am and not have to move, and say across the room to him, "Swain, there's something I have to tell you."

I'm putting it off. That's all I'm doing. I could have gotten hold of him.

She turns her head away and rests back on the floor.

Louie says, "Now I will demonstrate for you the sun salute." The way he speaks English sounds to Swain as though it's his second language, which it's not. He's as American as anybody here, probably from Tarboro or Pine Grove. Wonder if yoga gives your eyes that glow.

"Traditionally a disciplined practitioner will perform the sun salute a hundred and eight times." He waits for the inevitable ripple of laughter. "We will not try to do this. But if you begin your day with these asanas—no more even than three or four times—then you will have more joy in your day, more lightness."

Swain looks around for Julie. She's the one who is lightness. She should be teaching this group how to float through their days. Unless she's forgotten how, with all I've loaded onto her.

Louie begins standing, stretching his arms slowly high above his head. Still breathing so his breath is loud. It's like listening to a hospital patient on oxygen, you hear their life. He bends forward, his hands touch the floor, his back straight. Now he's down on the floor, moving like a snake, like wave motion passing through a rope. This is the way you salute the sun? Swain's not going to move like that. He has bones that prevent it, unlike this little fold-up Louie, who is coiling back up into a standing position.

"Now together." They all raise their hands above their heads, fingers locked, stretching for the ceiling. "Reach to the sun," Louie says. Swain reaches toward the paper pumpkin over the ceiling light. He's tall enough to pull it down. I feel like such a cynic. Like a ten-year-old at ballroom-dancing class. All I want to do is make a joke out of the whole thing.

"Now lean forward, arms extended." Louie's walking through the rows of them, all bent over. "Backs straight," he says.

Julie lies motionless on the floor. This can't be happening. All these people doing exercises, like there's nothing else in the world.

Swain thinks he had problems before. I could tell him, "Swain, I've got your assignment from God. This is it." See how he acts then.

"Make the vertebrae deeply embedded in the back. Do not let the backbone come up like a ridge." Swain reaches back and touches the knobby row of bones down the center of his back. Louie is wandering from one to another, touching, readjusting here and there. The tension in Swain's legs is building to a burn.

He feels Louie move past him, not touching or commenting. Maybe my negative attitude shows. "Please slowly slide your feet backward, extending your legs behind you." Relief. Swain eases out into a push-up position. They lower themselves to the floor. Once again, blood is flowing everywhere it's supposed to be. Where is the spiritual value of all this? What is the point?

He hears himself, what he's thinking, and freezes, his palms pressed against the floor. The way I feel about Louie . . . this is the way Bill Bartholomew and Bernie and Hawk Epworth feel about me: "Surely, fellow, you're not asking us to believe that God talks with a voice . . . that sun salutes really do anything?"

The people around him push up from the floor, arch their backs backward. Swain lies prone. He turns his head around toward Louie: there's that same placid permanent smile. He's not worried. It doesn't make a bit of difference to him whether Swain Hammond buys his act. He doesn't care what anybody thinks about his spiel, whether they believe it, whether they think he's crazy.

He pushes up and arches his back like the rest of them. I'm not going to be caught not giving the guy the benefit of the doubt. Three contortions later the class is over. He looks over and Julie is still lying there relaxing.

The lights come on, and the place is too bright. He watches her sit up, rubbing her eyes. She stands, not speaking to anybody, picks up her coat and looks around for him. What's with her? I'm usually the one who's in a hurry to leave.

She walks over toward him. He gets up from the floor. "Come

on," she says. "Can you leave now? We need to go."

"I have to find my shoes."

"Find them and come as quick as you can."

"What's going on?" People are milling around them, asking Louie questions, looking for shoes and coats. "Is something wrong?"

"I'm ready to go home."

"Okay." He looks at her close. Her eyes are puffy, she's pale. He goes to the table along the wall, gathers up his stuff, steps bare-footed into his shoes without tying them. He goes back over to her.

"You're going to freeze," she says. "It's cold."

"I thought we were in a hurry. Come on." He looks around the room once. "Good night," he says in general to whoever is near. They slide out the side door, before anybody can stop them. Down the hall, out the side exit. He pulls her to a stop at the edge of the streetlight shadows of the trees. "What is it? What's the big hurry?" A heavy branch keeps blocking the light from the street. He can, then he can't, see her face. People are still calling out through the dark, "Good night."

"Let's go, Swain."

"Tell me now. I can't stand this."

Her face looks as if it's had Novocaine. The whole thing is dead. "Julie..."

She says, "I'm pregnant."

"What?"

"I'm pregnant, Swain."

Lights hits her face again. He watches her breath coming out in a cloud. Looking at me like that, like I'd hit her. He looks away down the street. Cars at the intersection, tail lights starting to move. I'm in one of those cars, little, in the back seat, in the dark, somebody driving me away from here. She did it on purpose.

"You're not even late—you hadn't said a word—"

"Four days."

"That's absurd, that's nothing."

"I bought a test at the drugstore. I did it in the bathroom at the hospital. That's what the burning, the funny feeling was."

"A test like that can't be reliable."

"Swain, I know it. I knew when I woke up this morning. I'm pregnant, there's no question."

"I don't...I can't even make myself think..."

Silence.

"Why didn't you call me? Why didn't you come get me out of there?"

"I don't know. I couldn't yet." She stares straight ahead at a button on his shirt, then leans her face to touch his chest. "I wanted to see you when I told you." He looks past her head, across the street, into somebody's dark yard. He pulls back from her. She wanted to see me, let her.

She stares at him in the white street light. If I told him I had cancer, this is how he'd look.

I knew it would be this way. I knew.

I have to give him time. I could kill him for looking like that.

"I don't believe it," he says.

Her hand on his arm, her touch so light he can barely feel it, she's touching his coat. He stares down at her hand in the glare of the streetlight. She says, "Let's go home."

In the house, Swain goes from room to room turning on all the lights. Already it's as if there's somebody else here, hiding. He comes back and finds her in the kitchen. "Have you had anything to eat?"

"No." She sits down at the table and puts her head in her hands.

"I'm going to fix us an omelet."

"I'm not hungry." She doesn't raise her head. She could go away for a while. Let him get through this by himself, not come back until he says he's decided.

He breaks eggs into a bowl, watches a yolk sink down into the gel, rips it open with a point of the fork.

His back is to her. She isn't making a sound. The whisk rasps at the sides of the bowl. He counts. It would be early August. He pours the eggs into the pan. If she had ever really wanted a kid, she'd have said so, as old as we are. More than just "someday."

Toast pops up. He spreads it out to butter. As long as I keep moving, don't look at her, I don't have to think about it. The knife scrapes across the bread: a rake dragging across pavement. He turns the omelet, puts it all on two plates and brings them to the table.

He sits down, and the smell of butter and eggs comes up at him in a greasy wave. He turns sideways in his chair. She slowly pulls apart a piece of toast, watching her fingers.

"It could be wonderful, Swain."

"Julie, I'm not going to start taking this seriously. Not until I've heard it from a doctor."

She looks up at him, her eyes hard on him, her hands stopped motionless. "I've told you. It's true."

"Okay," he says. "Okay. But tonight's not the time to think about it. We're in shock. We can't expect to make sense."

She looks down at the table. I could wait forever, he's never going to want this baby. Anybody that didn't even like being a child...

She feels her stomach swell like that high-speed photography where you can watch flowers open. Seeing herself out there where she wasn't before. Now she's holding the baby, putting it in Swain's arms, feeling it just as real as if it's already born, wrapped up snug in a blanket, both our arms around it. *Our* baby, Swain. Ours.

"Julie, look at me. You never wanted children. That's always been clear. You'll see when you can think again."

"I've been thinking all day."

"Tell me what could change what's been true for thirty-seven years."

"Swain, it was never real before now."

"Jesus, Julie, what were you going to do, just wait until it happened accident—" He stops. "Julie, *is* this pregnancy an accident?"

She stares at him. Does he really think . . . ? "Yes, it is," she says in the coldest voice she has ever used in her life. "You think I would want to get pregnant with anybody who's acting like you've been acting lately?"

He stares at her. "I see."

"And thanks for trusting me," she says. "I can't believe you would even imagine I'd do that."

He shrugs. "I'm sorry." She thinks, he doesn't look the least bit sorry.

They sit in silence. Then he says slowly, one word at the time, "Julie, we never wanted to have children."

Her face flushes, darkens. She doesn't look at him. Now she's going to cry.

"Julie, think about it. How good things are between us. I know it hasn't been easy lately. But think about—"

Her sitting there crying is not going to change anything. "Have you thought about what it would do to our lives? To your life? There goes your nice little dream world. You wouldn't have time to go around with your head in the clouds anymore. I'm nearly forty years old. We both are. I'm not spending the rest of my life with a kid."

There's no point in saying a word. I won't listen. Just keep my mouth shut and wait. She feels the baby stirring in her arms. Little squinched-up red face, his hair straight and dark like Swain's. He yawns like a kitten. She rocks him back and forth.

She's turned so he can't see her face, the light shining down hard on her hair, so it makes streaks of shadow across her head. He saw a fetus once, in a jar. A little seahorse. Nothing more than that.

"Julie," he says, quiet now. "This isn't doing us any good. Let's call it quits for now and go to bed. We're both tired. I think you need to get some rest." He looks past her at the black panes of the window, while he waits for her to speak.

She gets up, not looking at the plates of cold eggs and the crumbled toast. I hate him. "Get some rest." Like he's talking to some crazy person. He's the one who's crazy. I can't talk to him, not while he's like this.

She passes him without touching him or looking at him. He stares at the cold omelet. Yellow poison, a cloud of yellow smoke that smothers everything in its path. He looks away from it, stands up and turns off the kitchen light.

The line is moving forward slowly. Swain inches toward the steaming pot with his green plastic plate. Wednesday night youth group roars around him on all sides. It's hot as a restaurant kitchen, Ragu sauce spattered all over.

It's the kind of plate that has dividers in it, like traffic bumps, so your applesauce won't run into your meatloaf. He turns it in his hands. Like the ones they had had at his elementary school. Or a baby food plate—he stops the thought but it comes anyway. A plate with a clear plastic bottom and toy fish or clowns rattling around underneath. Eat your way down to the clown.

The doctor confirmed it. Nobody's talking about it. She hardly even looks at him. All he wants to do is eat. Boxes of Krispy Kreme doughnuts. Peanut butter. A whole can of enchilada dip— the cruddy-looking tin still in the trash in his office. His hands feel greasy from food. She acts as if she'd been hit on the head.

A kid rushing through the line bumps him. He knocks into the back of what's-his-name Wyrick ahead of him. This is the same bunch that had the hayride last month and mooned a Winnebago. Some of them are probably still on restriction. I should be talking, not just standing here.

A hand is reaching for his plate. "Hi, Dr. Hammond."

"Hello, Carla." No pink eyeshadow tonight. Maybe she's changed her mind about children too, and she's helping Patrice in the nursery. Maybe she's pregnant. He's kicking himself for ever even thinking of having a child...what possessed him to ever think it? It's as if he had brought this all on himself by those moments of weakness.

"A lot of sauce or a little?"

"A lot. Doesn't everybody like a lot?"

"I guess some people are on a diet." She shakes Parmesan on top. He watches her move from the steaming pot to the counter. She's an attractive little thing, he thinks.

He says, "I'll bet you're not." She smiles into the pot.

He picks up his tea and silver. Now—a place to sit. He stands at the side of the hall and looks across the tables.

"Over here, Dr. Hammond."

He heads in the direction of the voice. A long table with an empty space on a corner. "Hello, Ike. Brenda." He puts his stuff down, looks down the table at the rest of them. They're probably all kicking Ike under the table for calling him over. "How's everybody?" He does his camp-counselor smile. The Ellsworth twins. Suppose it's twins.

"What's happening with you guys?" he says. He looks at Ike. A ninth-grade jock. The sleeves of his T-shirt are pushed back to show off the scabs on his arms.

"Not much," he says. "I got a job for Christmas vacation."

"What are you doing?"

"Working at Oak Ridge Camera Shop."

"Take my picture." Ellsworth Number One widens her eyes, parts her lips, tilts her head to the side.

"Sure. Come to my studio and take off all your clothes." Ike bares his teeth and laughs like Dracula. Swain jumps.

"You're pretty young to get a job like that," Swain says, ignoring Ellsworth One, who's rolling her eyes at Ellsworth Two.

"My mom knows the guy that owns it. I don't care, as long as I get a discount on lenses."

"I'm getting a camera for Christmas," Brenda says. She has pinched features and a wide face, like an owl. "A Nikon."

Swain says, "It was just Thanksgiving."

"I told my parents what they can get me," Ted says. "A kayak, a pair of Rossignol skis, a confiscated trawler full of mind-altering substances. . . ."

"Your mind needs altering," Ike says. "I'm serious."

Ted remembers Swain, and sinks down in his chair.

Ellsworth Two snickers. "What are you getting for Christmas, Dr. Hammond?"

He stares at the center of the table. This whole room is full of noise and glare. He feels light-headed, dizzy. He fumbles for some even slightly funny answer that will let him get by. "I don't know," he says. "I haven't thought of anything yet."

"Okay, let's think up some stuff for Dr. Hammond for Christmas," Brenda says. "How about a . . . I know, a"—she stares at him—"a sailboat." She laughs apologetically. "I mean, you're like, the quiet type."

"How about your own library," Ellsworth Two says, "with, um, a big chair and some cigars, stuff like that?" Both Ellsworths start giggling.

Jesus, these kids are irritating.

Ike is shaking his head. "You've got it all wrong. He needs something totally different. You should get a Maserati, Dr. Hammond. I'll tell your wife that's what she should get you."

"I see." His wife who now won't talk to him or look at his eyes . . .

"You could drive around in it and nobody would even believe you were a preacher."

"Ike," Brenda says, pursing her mouth in a warning.

They're pushing their luck.

"I just mean it would surprise everybody," Ike says.

That's what I need to do, surprise everybody.

"So what do you think, Dr. Hammond?"

He works his face into some kind of pleasant expression, as though it's all a good joke. "I'm not feeling like I want any surprises just lately," he says. She has never once in all these years actually come right out and said she wanted a baby. Not once.

"I'd settle for a tennis racket. Or getting my old one restrung."

"Boring," Ike says.

"I didn't know you play tennis," Brenda says. "If you want to, I'll play you sometime. I'm on the tennis team."

"I'm sure Dr. Hammond really wants to play tennis with you," Ellsworth One says. Helen—she's the one with the mole close to her ear. Which makes the other one Dana.

"I think that's a great idea," Swain says to Brenda. "I haven't played in years, though. I'm not very good."

"That's okay."

"I met my wife playing tennis. At least she was playing, I was just walking by."

"What did you do," Ike says, "run out in the middle of the court?"

"Her ball came over the fence. She came looking for it."

"That's so romantic," Helen says, gazing at Swain. She almost seems sincere.

He smiles a tight smile, not looking at her. "Yes," he says, "it was."

Ike snorts. "Romantic." He tilts his chair back, stretching his arms back behind him, faking a yawn, looking at Helen. "Is that all you ever think about?"

Good. Maybe they will talk to each other awhile and not to me.

The next day he is too low to care whether he goes through the motions at all. Whatever anybody wants to do is fine. She can have a baby if she wants to, just take it somewhere else. Just leave me alone.

He sits in his office in a listless funk all day, up until Sam arrives. Sam, drunk again, actually climbs up onto Swain's desk, and that is the point when his patience runs out.

"Sam, get down from there."

"Not just now, thank you."

"Get off my desk."

"I am trying to demonstrate something to you which is an extremely important point in what I am telling you." His hand waves close to the buzzing light fixture.

"Get down from there now." Sam was wanting somebody to kill him. That's what he's going to get.

"What time do you have, please?" It's nice up here. It changes everything. Looking down at Hammond from up here, he's a kid, he's ten years old, bent over to look at his watch. Something else Jakey can't do, look at his watch. Wonder if Swain has anything in here to drink: that's the rule, whenever the kid gets on my mind. . . . Wouldn't be surprised if old Swain didn't have him a little something in here somewhere.

Swain says, "Three-eleven."

"The afternoon is flying by," Sam says, teetering and catching himself. "Seems to me that we have just begun this conversation."

Swain looks at the dirty Hush Puppies planted on his blotter. His eyes follow the saggy line of Sam's pants up to where his stomach is hanging over his belt. If he keeps on, he's going to wind up on a bench in a park. The image comes to mind, won't go away: Sam, stinking, bleary-eyed, holding a bottle in a crumpled paper bag, asking for quarters. I'll find him and sit with him, keep him company. The two of us'll go to hell together.

"Okay, Sam, stay there. Just don't fall." He moves the framed pictures, the stack of mail. Then he steps back and sits down in the armchair.

"What I need is a pulpit like you have, good buddy," Sam says.

Nobody listens to me, not without getting that patient look on their face. Screw 'em. How many of them know what it's like to destroy a life? They've got business to listen.

"Yeah? What would you say?"

"I would explain that there's not a damn thing anybody can do about anything. Look at you—" He leans over and points a stubby finger at Swain. "Look at you, you can't even keep me from walking on your own desk."

Sam kicks at the little stand-up calendar and misses, waves both arms trying to get his balance. Swain lunges toward him, to where he's going to fall. A suicide hangs on to the ledge of the building, and the firemen with the net rush back and forth, forty stories below. Sam hangs there, tilted, not falling, not standing. Then he drops to his knees, crouched on the desk, so his eyes are level with Swain's.

"I went over to the blind school to see the boy," he says. "I hadn't seen him."

"How did it go, Sam?"

"Went bad." Swain's face is huge, up close. "He sat there in a chair in front of me, his face turned away. Waited for me to say what I had to say and go. I said it: I said I was sorry. Then I got out." Everything is weaving. Swain grabs hold of his arms.

"I said I'd die right now if it would undo it. There's not an hour of the day I wouldn't. I didn't know what else I could say. He said, 'Yeah, well, that's okay.' Then he waited for me to leave. Sat there cracking his knuckles.

"I said, 'I guess I'll be getting on back' and he stood up like he'd been let out of jail. He said, 'Bye' and shot out of that room. First stuck one arm out and waved it around. Then he was out the door."

Sam tries to unfold his legs. Cramped. They won't unbend. He looks down at the floor, like being up on a mountain. Far down there are highways and buildings. Kids going blind. I'm God looking down on everybody. Laughing. He feels his shoulders shaking. Then Swain's arms around him.

"I'm glad you went to see him. I think it will help—"

"Nothing's going to help, Swain." Slowly he gets off the desk, wiping his eyes, holding on to Swain.

"Sit down, Sam."

"I've taken enough of your time."

"Sam, you can't drive."

"I'm fine. I have a ride."

"What ride? Let me take you home."

Sam shakes his head. "It's okay, Swain. Nothing to worry about. Don't worry about a thing." He goes out the door.

Swain puts his stuff back on his desk, shakes off the blotter where Sam was standing. Sam is going to wind up killing himself. And he's right—there's nothing I can do.

The telephone buzzes. Swain sits down in his chair, makes himself change gears, get Sam out of his mind. Then he picks up. "Swain, glad I caught you." It's Rudy Haddonsfield. "Look," he says. "A couple of us have been meaning to talk to you about replacing the swing set in the elementary play area. That thing that's in there now..."

Swain fades out of the conversation. He's reaching up toward a small boy, a toddler, crouched at the top of a sliding board. The kid is so scared he's quivering. He's going to start crying any minute. How did he get up there in the first place? He feels his hands go under the boy's arms, his fingers wrapping around that little chest, he has on a T-shirt. The boy's face lightens each half second as Swain brings him closer to the ground.

Imagined. It didn't happen. He didn't even think it. This subliminal advertising, flashing across his brain, that keeps coming back. Rudy is saying, "... Those pipes that are rusted out." Rudy has a kid that age and an older one. Swain now has another two calls on hold.

It happens again and again: on the phone, in the sanctuary, in counseling sessions.

A crash, at his arm. Light metal. A bicycle, thrown to the ground. He sees the wheels still spinning, the spokes throwing off light. Then the child. In two steps she's next to his chair, both hands on the arm of it, lifting all her weight off the ground, jumping up and down. "Guess what we saw," she says. She's out of breath, her cheeks flushed. She pushes her face up next to his. She's so rosy and new-looking. The whites of her eyes, her lips are so new. Her breath touches his face. "Guess. You'll never guess."

Then: gone. His arm lies on the arm of the chair, nothing else there. He's in his office, the couple across from him on the sofa, still arguing: Eleanor leaning forward, "It's because you expect me to do everything," she says. Howard is shaking his head, looking toward Swain, impatient for his say. Swain rubs his eyes.

Julie is shelving journals, the ones that have been left out on the tables. The loudspeaker says, "Dr. Hathaway, 3215. Dr. Hathaway, 3215." If God talked to me, it would be on this speaker, twice. The voice would say, "Ms. Hammond, this is God. Ms. Hammond, this is God." And I wouldn't even hear it, I'm so used to it. She slides a journal into its stack: *Plastic and Reconstructive Surgery*. It would say: "Have the baby. Have the baby. Stick to your guns. . . ."

Progress in Cardiovascular Diseases. American Journal of Nephrology.

When she found out she was pregnant, in the bathroom down the hall, the little doughnut shape showing up in the cup just as the package said, you could see it from across the whole long room, sitting there on the shelf where she left it. Then she walked back into this library. First thing that caught her eye was the book display that said: "Look What's New in Gastroenterology."

Look what's new. She hasn't told anybody but Swain.

It's dangerous to be in this room. You ought not to come into a medical library pregnant or with anything wrong with you. You can't not look up whatever it is, and then you find out how awful something can be.

It was like that when she first got into medical in school, flipping through books, seeing color plates of things she wished she hadn't seen. It hasn't bothered her in years. Until this morning, when she checked in the new books: *Surgical Decision Making, Cancer and the Oral Cavity,* and then *Blood Disorders in Pregnancy.*

Blood disorders. A little early to be worrying about any of that. The baby hasn't even got a father yet. I don't even have morning sickness. Nothing but tiredness and a little queasiness, and that funny indigestion way inside. The doctor said it was true. Being pregnant doesn't feel like I thought it would. It's not what I expected at all.

Swain lying there asleep this morning like everything's normal. Then in the kitchen watching me, whenever he thinks I'm not looking. Nobody saying anything. I can't stand it much longer. She leans her head against the spines of books. I miss him, I can't help it. But if I don't have this baby, that'll be the end of it. It'll be over. I won't love him anymore.

She makes herself stand up straight. She puts him out of her mind, the way she has had to do with a lot of what she has seen in this hospital. That scene last year as she was getting out of the elevator: doctors and nurses running, pushing a stretcher with a woman on it, hugely pregnant, screaming, the sheets falling off of her, while they ran with her to surgery, the light from a window catching on the tube of the IV swinging. And the man: her husband, standing there in the middle of the hall, his eyes never leaving her for a second all the time he was crying as if his life was being taken away. She makes herself not think about it.

You can't decide between your husband and your child. It's not human to have to do that. The speaker comes on again: "Dr. Sanchez, 6204. Dr. Sanchez..."

At home that night they sit in front of the TV. A woman comes on with a big box of detergent. Swain gets up to change the station. "You don't want to see any more of this, do you?"

"I don't care. Go ahead and turn it off." He turns it off and sits back down in his chair. The way they're sitting he can't see her face.

"Maybe we should go to bed early," he says. "It's been so hard to get up."

He sees her move one leg. She heard him. She doesn't say anything.

"Julie, will you at least sit up and look at me?"

She turns so she's facing him.

"What is this?" he says. "Are you trying to force me into it?"

"No." She looks down at her hands. "I just don't feel like talking. I don't know what there is to say."

She sits there. The silence is so solid it's pushing him backward away from her.

He closes his eyes. This is my father's final revenge on me. That's what it is. That I have to do it too; that same destruction all over again. I'd hate a kid even worse than my father did. Dad would look like a prince by comparison.

Julie gets up slowly. There's no point in both of us sitting here being miserable, she thinks.

He looks up. She says, "I'm going to bed."

On Tuesday he drives down to the school to see Jakey. Alone. He walks across the campus in the cold. Kids are out playing, real children, and not his. Their voices ring down the quad. They're climbing on a big wooden fort. He gets closer. The boy in the blue jacket is trying to push the other kid off the ladder. Ladder Kid clobbers Blue Jacket, without losing his hold. Dark eye sockets— but he seems to know where to hit. A woman sitting on a bench over near the tree gets up to go break it up. Only a couple of weeks now until Christmas. Surely these kids will all have somewhere else to go for the holidays.

He takes the left turn in the sidewalk down toward the dorms. Two boys, sixteen or so, are sitting on the steps of one of the houses. They raise their heads toward him as he approaches. His footsteps on the pavement sound loud in the cold air.

"How you doing?" one of them calls out. Which probably means "Who are you? Send out your signal."

"Doing okay," he says across the open space to the boy. The boy stubs out a cigarette on the cement step, leans back, draping his hand across the knee of his jeans. Swain walks past. Their conversation resumes.

Swain squints at the number on the next house. "Up here." It's Jakey. Where is he? Swain goes up the steps. On the glider at the far end, in a red ski jacket. "Hello, Jakey," Swain says.

"I heard you coming." He slams the glider backward and forward, pushing off hard from the floor. Swain reaches over and touches him on the shoulder, gives him a pat on his red jacket.

"I'm glad to see you."

"You came down here just to see me?" He makes the glider stop. Dr. Hammond drove all the way down here by himself, not even with Mom. He always mostly liked Mom.

"Yes."

Jakey takes a nickel out of his pocket, throws it up in the air, straight up, and catches it. He says, "That's a long way."

Swain sits down on the glider. "How're things going? Did you just get out of class?"

"Yeah. Gym." He snorts. "If you want to call it that. Somebody has to tell you every single little thing to do."

"What were you doing today?"

"Uneven parallels." He shrugs. "They're okay."

He says I should call him Swain. I can't call him that. Are you kidding?

Swain thinks, should I say something about the nickel? Would that insult him? "I'm impressed you can throw something up in the air and catch it."

"Oh yeah?" Jakey shrugs, grins. "No big deal." He says, "I can't hang around here long. I have mobility this afternoon. I forgot about it when you called."

"What's mobility?"

"You know. Learning to walk." He makes a face. "How to get around by yourself and not run into things."

"I'll bet you're pretty good at it."

"I guess."

"What if I went along with you for a while? Would I be in the way?"

He hesitates. I've been doing good for weeks, but you never can tell. "You better ask Mrs. Satterwhite. She's the teacher."

"If it's okay with you, I'll come with you and ask."

"Well... I guess." He pictures himself speeding down the sidewalk, walking around people, crossing streets, stepping over bumps, no problem. Dr. Hammond and Mrs. Satterwhite can hardly even keep up with him. "Yeah, it's okay."

"Great."

They start down the steps. "This is my dorm," he says. Swain looks up at the red brick upper story. Pigeons walk back and forth, cooing, in the gutters.

"Looks pretty nice."

"Over there's the gym." Swain looks where he's told to look.

They head down the sidewalk, passing kids in groups and pairs, some of them leading each other. Jakey zips up his jacket. They leave the row of big brick houses and come to a long low building with a portico and a warm smell floating from around back. It smells like crumbly yellow cake with an inch of icing. "This is the dining hall. The food sucks." He stops, remembering Swain. "Except Friday nights, if you don't go home, they have cheeseburgers or pizza."

On the brick wall of the building is the school's seal, around it a circular banner that says—Swain twists his head around to read it—"By Faith, Not By Sight."

Jakey says, "This is where I'm supposed to meet Mrs. Satterwhite."

Swain can see Mrs. Satterwhite coming, a big fiftyish woman, hurrying across the grass. She arrives flustered, embarrassed to be running behind when the pastor has come for a visit. She hustles them into a car and they drive a few blocks toward the center of the little town.

Swain looks over into the back seat at Jakey. The long white cane lies across his lap. It's like a pole that tightrope walkers use, except for the lightness and the red tip. He turns it over and over in his fingers, his face facing out the window.

"I'm planning to take us down to Hooper Street, Dr. Hammond, if that's satisfactory with you. We need to do a little practice today on intersections."

"Fine. Whatever you'd ordinarily do. Don't let me interrupt a thing."

"You might possibly be acquainted with my pastor, Reverend Eldritch. My family has always gone to over to Mill Ridge Presbyterian."

"I know his name."

"He's one of the finest men. We're lucky to have him. And been such a help to us at the school."

"I'm sure he is."

"Has Jakey told you all about what he's learning in mobility?"

"He told me a little." Swain reaches back and pats Jakey's leg. He keeps feeling guilty, as though they're leaving him out.

"We have three or four different courses we follow to learn all the skills," she says.

"I've seen you," Swain says. "Driving into town I notice pairs of people out walking, one with a cane."

She nods and sighs. "People will look. I keep expecting us to cause somebody a wreck one day when they're driving by and craning their necks."

Jakey says, "They could have a ten-car collision and all pile up on top of each other. I can hear it now." He starts making explosion noises, as if he's playing war. His whole body jerks with each explosion. Cars slamming into each other—Trans Ams and Corvettes all crammed together with smoke coming out.

She turns the car onto a long empty block and pulls up next to the curb. "We'll start here and head down in the direction of where there's more traffic. You might not be able to tell it," she says to Swain, "but this street is a hard one. All the children think so."

"You're not kidding," Jakey says. He's ready to get out and do something. They've been riding forever. Finally she pulls over and they get out of the car.

Swain looks down the wide empty street. Cold sunlight sparkles off the chips of glinting rock in the pavement. Christmas decorations on some of the houses. "Round corners," Jakey says. "How can you find which way to cross if the corner just goes around in a circle? They're killers. Unbelievable."

Swain buttons his jacket against the chill. Mrs. Satterwhite gets Jakey started in the right direction, then drops back beside Swain.

With the cane in his hand and nobody close, Jakey slows down.

"You remember, Jakey."

He swings the cane in a small arc, taps it down to the pavement.

"Good," she says. To Swain: "You move it back and forth. It clears the way for each foot to make a step. It's a rhythm."

"Tap, tap, tap."

"That's right," she says.

The red tip swings back and forth up ahead of them. He's picking up speed; he starts to move easier. Good. Swain looks out around him at the terrain up ahead; the sidewalk is full of jutting buckles and cracks. The sound of the cane echoes against the houses. Now where's he going? Swain leans forward to trot up there and stop him. He's heading right out into the street. Swain looks back. A car is creeping toward them, a block and a half away.

Mrs. Satterwhite puts her hand on Swain's arm. "Wait, Dr. Hammond," she says.

Jakey stops, feels around with the cane, poking it at the pavement and the air. How can she let the child stand out there in the street? He wants to go over there and steer him with his hands on the two shoulders of that red jacket back to the sidewalk.

"He has to learn to notice when the slope changes," she says. "He should have been paying attention to that."

"Jakey," she calls to him. He's walking three feet in one direction, then three feet the other direction, jabbing at the asphalt with that cane. "Follow the line of pavement to your left, Jakey. Let it bring you back over to the sidewalk."

That seems to mean something. He feels his way back, as if he's crossing a rope bridge, hand over hand. The car that was coming up behind them moves past, the driver bent forward to look up on the porches for an address. Somebody could have been driving through here fast, not looking—or zooming out of a driveway.

Jakey's back up in front of them again, his shoulders slumped down. The cane drags a little every time it touches.

"Jakey, you're doing fine," Swain says. "Don't let it get you discouraged."

Jakey mutters something, without turning back, that Swain doesn't hear. The collar of his jacket pushes up against his hair. You can tell just from the way he holds his head that he's blind. The angle isn't quite right for watching where he's going. He looks a little too high, and he faces all the time straight ahead, not looking to the left and right. Something else for the kid to learn —how to hold his head.

Oh God. There he goes. Off in the rough again. I'd have broken the cane in half like a golf club by now. He wants to anyway, as if it's the cane that's doing this to Jakey. Now Jakey has walked up to a tree. He finds it first with the cane, then his hand.

Jakey's face has turned a deep pink. He stands with his hand on the trunk of the tree, a little out of breath, his mouth set hard. He says, "Shit," just loud enough to be heard.

"Seems like we're having a little more trouble than usual today," Mrs. Satterwhite says.

Jakey leans his forehead against the inside of his arm.

She says, "I know it can be hard when you're most especially wanting to do well."

Swain thinks, no wonder Patrice couldn't teach him. How does anybody endure this? That's what Julie needs to think about, while she's sitting and staring and punishing me.

But if we were going to go ahead and have it, if I could pick the kid out in advance . . . Jakey's coming forward now, the tip of that cane feeling at the gnarled roots all around the tree. It's like an obstacle course. The way he's got his mouth set and his shoulders pulled together, he's racing a car, making turns fast, whipping it through a course. The end of the cane stubs up against the edge of the sidewalk. His shoulders let go, he's crossed a finish line.

"Bravo," Swain says, loud, and it echoes down the street.

This is the kid I want. This is the kind of kid I should have been—gutsy, toughing it out on my own. Not like I was, standing in their house like a shadow, waiting for them to see me.

"Now you know where you are, Jakey," Mrs. Satterwhite says in her fake-soothing voice. "You're doing fine. Don't you think so, Dr. Hammond?"

That night, as usual, he can't sleep. Julie, for a change, can. Lying there with her hair all over the pillow, her face turned toward the window. Swain walks around to her side of the bed instead of getting back in on his. There's no point in trying to sleep. He sits on the arm of the chair next to the bed and looks at her. The blanket bunched up under her chin. Her mouth open a little. He can almost see her breath, coming and going, so slow he feels his own insides slow down to the rhythm of it. Her lips look fuller, her eyebrows farther apart than in the daytime. As soon as she wakes up and remembers, she won't look like this anymore. He wants her back. It seems like a thousand years since this began. Ten days. All she does is stare at me like she doesn't see me, or stare off somewhere else. I want her back like she was. He tries to remember it. Her smiling. He looks away from her. It's like looking at a picture of somebody that's gone.

It's stupid to blame her. She didn't do it. We just got on the wrong side of the percentages. But I always thought you were supposed to be relaxed and unstressed when you were trying to get pregnant. I've forgotten what that feels like, if I ever knew. Maybe the two of us did it on purpose, as if we didn't have enough trouble.

The moonlight makes her face so white and dark, takes all the color out. He wants to whisper something to her that will make her wake up and be with him, but not remember the rest. If he could just call a time-out. He tried. Two nights ago he lay on the bed and held her, he just wanted to be touching her. She lay in his arms as if she didn't know he was there.

We'll get over this, he tells himself all day, and then he knows they won't. She'll never forgive him for not wanting their baby. He's lost her. Julie's never coming back. A wave of pain goes through him. The best thing there's ever been in my life. If a baby is what she wants, I can't keep her from it. I *had* been thinking about it. Some part of me wants it. That must be true. He watches the pulse in her temple, the movement of her eyelashes against her cheek. He has always been scared she would get cancer and die. He never expected this. He looks over at his own empty side of the bed, as if his sleeping body were lying there.

In the morning, I won't be sad. She'll be shitty to me; I'll be mad at her. It'll be just like it was today.

In the morning, they eat breakfast in silence.

She looks up at him. He's like a stranger. Sitting there in his suit and tie, little dabs of tissue still stuck to his neck. What is he thinking? He knows how I feel. He's the one who's going to have to say.

She makes herself keep eating. I'm eating for two, she thinks. She puts her fork down. How can I eat? How can I even walk around, when I don't know? She wants to scream and scream at him: "Am I having a baby? Tell me something." She picks up her napkin and carefully wipes her lips.

If I just give him time . . .

At work, all Swain wants to do is hang around in the front office where people are coming in and out. People who have had children and lived through it. But they're different from him, people who might not even think twice. He flips through the manila files in the top cabinet drawer. "I'll be glad to find whatever you need in there, Dr. Hammond," Mildred says. She wants him out of her files. She doesn't seem to realize: this is praying. Dear God, tell me what to do.

"Thanks, Mildred. I think I can find it." He doesn't need anything that's in this cabinet. But if he goes back to his office, he won't write his sermon or return his calls. This is where he wants to be, flipping slowly through stacks of paper. We should throw out the whole drawer and start over, there's nothing in here anybody needs.

If I go back there by myself, I'm going to call Julie and tell her: okay, let's have it. I'm crumbling, I knew it last night. I can't believe it's happening.

I have no business being a father. I'll wind up hurting our child. Has she ever considered that? I can't love a kid. I don't know how. How do you love anybody you can't go to bed with? All these years of preaching God and love, I've pretended I knew what I was talking about. Our baby would die of loneliness. Julie can't do it all by herself.

I'm caving in, and it's going to be the worst mistake of my life.

He wants to run toward the place he sees an accident happening, yelling, "Stop! Wait!" But it's too far away. He would never get there in time.

Finally, the day ends. He hasn't called her. He drives home, halfway knowing what he's going to do. It's as if he's bringing her flowers. But he can't think about it, he can't yet start to face all the things it will mean.

He finds her in the living room, turning through a magazine. She puts it down. He sits down on the sofa across from her chair.

"You're home early," he says.

"A little." She hesitates. "Swain..."

"I know," he says. "This can't go on."

She says, "I have to have it."

"I know." I should have called this afternoon. I wanted to bring flowers. I don't want her to get to be the one to decide.

"Swain, say something."

"We're going to have a baby. You and I are going to have a baby."

Inside him a weight is—so slowly it's barely noticeable—starting to rise, coming up through the middle of him. It's over, done. "Julie, we're having a baby. You said it—there's nothing else to do. You want it. In some way . . . I suppose . . . I want it." He picks up a pillow from the sofa and wipes the sweat off his face with it. He leans his head back, stares at the wall, the swirls in the plaster. We'll have to fix a room for it, and get a crib. Pick a name. She'll get fat. She'll walk funny. He hasn't thought about any of it. Not one single detail.

She looks at him, his legs sprawled half across the room. She takes a huge long breath. So—that's it, we're going to do it. She feels her whole body relax, get lighter and larger. The lamp on the table suddenly looks so warm, the plants so glossy green. All the color flooding back into the world from wherever it's been all this time. I'm hungry. I could eat a whole package of bacon. I can smell it frying. The life coming back . . . Swain hasn't moved.

She wants to go over there and gather all of him up in her arms. Poor fellow, it hasn't been easy. . . . She gets up to go to him. "Swain, it'll be—you'll be a good father. It won't be like you think."

His eyes closed, he feels the blood going out to his fingers, circling, coming back. His pulse beats deep in the center of his head, in his neck, in his legs. Then he hears her moving, crossing the room, and the anger leaps back up in him. "Stay there," he says, his eyes still shut. "Don't come over here now."

Silence. She is standing motionless somewhere in the room. Let her stand there, he thinks. I don't care.

Then the fire in his chest dies down again. It isn't her fault. He wants her beside him.

"Can you feel it yet?" he says, from wherever he is. "The baby?"

"Not exactly," she says. "But in a way." Now she's moving toward him again. She knows: he wants her over here.

He feels the sofa sink. Now she's beside him, the warmth and rustlings of her along his side. Help us, God. If this is what I'm chosen for, you chose wrong. His eyes still closed, his lips pressed together hard, he reaches out for her hand.

TWELVE

"I understand you're soon to be a father," DeWitt says.

"Not so soon, but yes." The traffic in the hall is loud around them; it's almost time for Sunday school.

"Congratulations. I wouldn't have thought you'd have wanted to do that. I'm supposing it was a surprise."

Swain looks him over carefully. His mottled sun-spotted old face. "Yes, it was. No one else has thought to inquire."

"No one else has opened his mouth, that's all." He narrows his eyes and looks at Swain carefully. "It's going to be good for you."

"I'm sure it will be. Of course, I'll have a lot to learn. But everything's going to be fine." Swain smiles and puts a hand on DeWitt's shoulder.

"You don't mean a word of that, but it's true."

Swain laughs. "It's very hard to lie to you, DeWitt."

"If it weren't for me, who'd shake the truth out of you?"

"Maybe having this kid around will."

DeWitt nods, "I look forward to seeing how you turn out."

This morning, in front of everybody, he is faced with the real thing. A baptism. This, Swain, is how it's going to be.

The three of them stand at the baptistery. Louise holding the baby, a boy, dark like Miguel. A tiny little red-faced thing with fine black hair. Miguel reaches out, as Louise passes the child to Swain, puts another layer of arms below theirs. The child is trailing blankets and lace. Swain stands quiet with him for a second. The kid waves his scrawny, wrinkled arm. He's not even old enough to be fat.

"Almighty God, we present unto Thee this child. Look with favor upon this dedication. May Thy light preserve him from error, and Thy power maintain him in perseverance. Make his life fruitful with good works..."

This drafty alcove. Somewhere in a box is the christening dress they put on me. I'll stand here and hand my own child away. Miguel hasn't taken his eyes off the baby. Swain is talking to him, "...that in every way, you shall seek to lead him in the love of God and the service of our Lord Jesus Christ." Swain feels the intentness of the congregation, some of them leaning forward, raised up in the pews to get a view of the baby. He's saying it, doing it all, smooth as could be. It's easy—the water, the ritual words—but it's happening without him. His mind has stopped. He's flying on automatic pilot. He can't think. He doesn't want any baby. He wants to get out of here.

"Do you solemnly promise to fulfill these duties...?"

They say, almost together: "We do." When it's my turn, I'll stand here and make the same promise. I'll lie. I can't promise anything about this child. We're having it. That's all I know.

"I baptize thee in the name of the Father, and of the Son, and of the Holy Spirit."

The words, the feel of the child stirring in his arms, close a door inside him. He can't think "baby" at all.

Tuesday, coming back in from a meeting he barely made himself sit through, Swain stops in the door of the fellowship hall. "What's going on here?"

"We're fixing the greenery." A girl with a piece of holly stuck behind one ear sits back on her heels and holds up a length of evergreen rope. The Suderman child. Mary? "The sixth-graders are doing all the decorations for the Christmas service. It's going to look much much better than last year. It's going to look great."

"I'm sure it will be wonderful. It smells good. I could smell pine trees all the way down the hall."

"Dr. Hammond, they're not pines, this is spruce. And we got some mistletoe." She points across the sheets of newspaper and the clumps of kids to another heap of green. There's a chipped dab of red polish on her fingernail. "We were going to hang some of it over the door, but Mrs. Miller said we couldn't. I thought it would be pretty funny."

Swain forces a smile. "What's the lumber for?"

"Frankie's father is going to build a real manger."

"I haven't heard about any manger."

"We have to have something for the baby Jesus."

"Where's that going to go?" What do they think this is—the class play?

"I don't know. Mrs. Miller does, she could tell you." She holds out two ends of twine, wrapped around a bundle of branches. "Hold this a minute. Somebody took the scissors." He takes the strings, squats holding the bundle together, and waits.

Then she's back, flopping down on the newspapers beside him with a big sigh. "Somebody is always taking the scissors." She cuts the twine and ties it. "Next year when you have your new baby, it can be the baby Jesus. Is it going to be a boy or a girl?"

"We don't know yet."

"Oh yeah. I guess it's too soon to have those tests. But I think it's good to know up ahead, so you can get the right kind of clothes. I hope it's a girl. If it's a girl, I'll baby-sit. I only charge two dollars an hour, because my mother said that's enough, even though everybody else gets more, which is not fair, if you ask me. I'm very responsible."

"I'm sure you are." No one could leave their child with this little smart-mouth. "We'll certainly be looking for sitters."

"I bet Christmas is very special for you and Mrs. Hammond this year. I mean, think about it. Christmas is about a baby, and you're having a baby. It makes me cry even to think about it." The holly is starting to droop and slide down her face. She takes it off and throws it into the pile. "I just think it's terrific, and so do all my friends."

"I guess it's pretty terrific." I sound like I'm reciting memory lines, he thinks. Dead voice: I guess it's pretty terrific. Surely people notice.

"You should know, you're the one who's doing it. Or your wife is, anyway."

"Well, it's scary too, you know." His knees are starting to hurt. He sits down on the floor. "I'm not so sure about how I'll do... being a father."

She nods. "I can understand that. I'm never going to have any children. I'm going to be an archaeologist. I don't think I'll have time to have children too."

"An archaeologist." Arrowheads, that's probably what she knows about archaeology. When they buried his parents, there was so much machinery around their graves you couldn't even see dirt. You couldn't see it was a hole in the ground. What it really was was hidden. Somebody had been there and dug a hole that was big enough for two people.... He feels dizzy. The smell of the pine is getting to him. She's still going on. "...I think the past is so fascinating. Especially ancient man. The only thing I don't like is the chemistry part. You have to take that in school so you can do carbon-testing and stuff like that...." Fading in and out. Does she think he's listening to this? He told his parents he was going to be a minister one day when he was ten or twelve and someone who had come for dinner asked him what he was going to be. It was as if he hadn't said anything, or what he said didn't count. His mother laughed her lilting laugh and said, "Oh, Swain." She always acted as if he was a painting: all you had to do was look at him every now and then and he would just hang on the wall and wait for hundreds of years. His father asked the guest, who was British, whether he wanted ice in his drink.

"...But I think being an archaeologist is very important, because if we don't know about our history, then how can we make any progress? That's what I think."

Nine years since he went to their graves. He never wanted to hear the word family again in his life. I have to get out of here or I'm going to get sick. "I need to get back to work," he says. She stares up at him, noticing him now. He says—maybe she didn't hear him—"I have to go."

Julie is standing in the narthex, people coming in talking just as if it were Sunday morning. At eleven-thirty at night. Christmas Eve is the only time we come over here at night, except for now and then a wedding, or some youth thing in the basement. I could go on in and sit down. I've already done my ten minutes of standing out here speaking to people. She looks around. I'm not ready to go in. I'd rather stand out here and watch everybody. Sit up front like I do and it's so hard to see anybody without being obvious. I wouldn't have expected so many children here so late. Was it like this other Christmases or am I just starting to notice? Lately she has stared and stared at parents and children, looked back and forth between the one in the stroller and the one pushing it, trying to see however she can what's going to happen, how it's going to be.

Janet Epworth is heading for her, steering Bryan.

"Merry Christmas."

"Merry Christmas to you."

Bryan stares at her. He looks at her stomach, it doesn't look bulgy.

"You're up pretty late tonight, Bryan."

Janet says, "We're hoping that this will inspire sleeping a little later in the morning. I'd like to have one Christmas I could sleep past 6 A.M." She smiles indulgently, pats his shoulder. He looks embarrassed, turns his head away as if he's watching something intently on the opposite wall.

Julie thinks, I'm going to let mine speak for himself. How would Janet like it if somebody answered for her?

Janet says, "We're all so delighted for your good news."

"Thanks, Janet. I'm very excited."

"I know Swain is just delighted."

"He seems to be getting used to the idea. I think he's going to make a wonderful father."

Janet nods. "He has been such a good friend to both Jakey and Bryan. I don't know how any of us could get through all this without him."

A compliment, about Swain. Julie feels a rush of warmth. Nobody has said anything nice about Swain in six months, not to me. And about the two boys, that should please him.

"Thanks, Janet. I'll tell him you said that."

She carries it with her—maybe things are changing—as she moves toward the door of the sanctuary. "I don't know how any of us could get through this without him": that really is nice. The Epworths have probably given him the benefit of the doubt as much as anybody here has. She walks down the side aisle, instead of the center, to her place near the front. Even so, every single one of them who's already seated turns to stare at her. She catches an eye here and there and nods, smiles. Mrs. Eastwood, Joe McDougall, the Fitzgeralds. Pregnant, is what they're thinking. There's nothing to see, I look the same as usual.

I should look more different. The minute I was pregnant, I should have. Whatever could change me overnight into a person who has to have a baby ought to show. If hormones could do that, they could change anything. Maybe Swain's hormones are out of whack.

At least me being pregnant ought to take some of the heat off him. They couldn't fire somebody whose wife's pregnant, even if he does try to do miracles. They're just lucky they've got somebody brave enough to try.

The Christmas Eve service itself is enough to keep Swain in the ministry if nothing else will. Whatever else is troubling him always goes away, at least for that hour. Now he is past the opening music and stirrings. Quiet has settled over the congregation.

He talks into almost-darkness. The candles behind him on the altar flicker on the faces out there. "... To rekindle our sense of wonder in Thy majestic ways and to look to the Christ as our Star of Hope." It is only minutes until midnight. The dark makes it a campfire circle, drawing them all in. The eve of Christmas. Christ has never been his Star of Hope. Only God. Not God the Father. Simply God. Yet he is so moved by it all ... seeing them all out there.

The church is full of the long looping ropes of evergreen. He reads: "And lo, the angel of the Lord came upon them, and the glory of the Lord shone round about them: and they were sore afraid." Now the kids begin to read. From the balcony, Bobby Burroughs: "And the angel said unto them ..." Now Melissa, standing beside her mother, down near the front. Her voice is like a wisp of dandelion puffball on the air, it's so light. Her mother moves her own lips with the words. Near the front, Jakey stands and recites: "Behold I bring you great tidings. ..."

Swain watching him, feels his chest actually swell. He tries to meet Julie's eyes, but she's turned toward Jakey. The sanctuary is silent. Swain thinks, They're all out there feeling proud of him like I am. The silence goes on: Swain jumps. It's his turn to read. He scrambles to find his place, "And all they that heard it wondered at those things which were told them by the shepherds."

Bill Bartholomew keeps his eyes on Swain reading. He shakes his head. The man doesn't even know when it's his turn to read. Even the smallest children are picking up when they're supposed to. Not Hammond. Standing there with that odd disoriented look he has. Anyone as intelligent as he is has some responsibility. ...

The reading ends. They rise to sing. As the congregation stands out there in the semidarkness, Swain sees more clearly the faces. No one bends over a hymnbook; everyone knows the words.

"Silent night, holy night, all is calm, all is bright." He looks at all of them: Frances Eastwood, with her whole family; the Haddonsfields, the Morrises; kids with dates; people jammed in together on crowded pews, half of them people he doesn't know. It's like a homecoming—he loves it. He doesn't even like the rest of Christmas. He just wants this, to hold them all here in this moment through tomorrow.

Bernie has his arm around his youngest, who is standing next to him on the seat of the pew. He almost didn't come. He didn't even want to think about what kind of performance Swain was going to put on at Christmas.

Then that thing in my office, Swain pulling on the sleeve of my jacket. Broke my heart, seeing him do that.

But he doesn't even have to do anything, or open his mouth. You still know there's something real wrong there. Look at his face right now, that far-off look, it's like looking at some wild animal's eyes, something that doesn't care about anything civilized. Maybe having a kid on the way will help straighten him out.

Swain says in a voice softer than his usual pulpit voice, "Will each of you please light the candle you hold and carry it with you as you go from here, as sign of the light that has come into the world anew again tonight." Now there is only darkness and candles and the hint of a face in the shadows above each flame, as the flame is passed from candle to candle up and down the rows.

The quiet deepens. He looks out at hundreds of flickering lights, and raises his arms. He would give them everything he has. He doesn't hate anybody in the world. "The grace of the Lord Jesus Christ and the love of God and the fellowship of the Holy Spirit be with you all." If he could just hang on to the way he feels now...

I don't want a kid in my house—not my kid, not Julie's brother's kid, not any kid. If they're going to come, they could at least go through the motions of going to my service. Not that that would make up for it.

"Now can we go see our Santa Claus toys?" Eddie says. He looks first at his father, then at Swain.

"Not until everybody else is up and ready." Murph yawns and scratches his stomach.

"I'll put on some coffee," Swain says. He pushes Eddie's little shoulder, steers him into the breakfast room with his father, gets him out of his way. It's not even seven o'clock yet.

"Black is fine," Murph says, settling into a chair.

"I remember."

Eddie slumps into another chair. "Not coffee," he whines. "Coffee takes hours."

"You want your presents—you stop that," Murph says. "Your mother may put up with that, but I don't."

Why doesn't Julie get herself in here? She can't leave me with these two jerks. This is the way it's going to be . . . a little snot like Eddie interfering with the whole rest of my life.

"Eddie," Swain says. "How about a bowl of cereal for you, to hold you until everybody gets up?"

"Cap'n Crunch?" he says. His face brightens, he sits up straight in his chair, as if he had just won a million dollars in a lottery.

"Sorry. All we've got is Shredded Wheat and All-Bran." Eddie's face falls into ruins, his happiness utterly destroyed. So easy—to make or break his little world. What's it going to be like to have so much power?

"How about some cinnamon toast, then?"

"You don't need that son, not good for you teeth. You eat too many sweets anyway," Murph says.

"Come on, Murph. It's Christmas morning. Time-out."

"Okay. If you want to make it."

"Yeaay, cinnamon toast." Eddie waves his arms over his head. "Soon can we go open the presents?"

Swain says, "Soon."

"Good morning." Helen. In a puffy blue bathrobe all the way to the floor. Her hair still looks as if she just got out of bed. She's much more like Julie than Murph is.

"Good morning," he says. Down the hall, another door opens and shuts. Julie comes in. "Merry Christmas." Julie's the first one of all of us to say it. "Merry Christmas," he says and goes over and kisses her.

"Let's go see what Santa Claus brought," Julie says. "Is everybody sitting here waiting for me? Come on, Eddie." Murph looks annoyed, as if he could have waited all morning, as if he'd rather have breakfast.

Julie says, "You go first, Eddie." Eddie races past her, knocking against her, then the door. They stand in the breakfast room for that half second and look at each other as Eddie, in the living room, starts to yell. "Wow. Come look. You're not going to believe this. A Robot XQK and laser gun. I don't believe it." Even Murph smiles. He didn't give the kid dental floss for Christmas after all.

Murph gets slowly up from his chair, acting as if it's a lot of work to stand up. Still grinning, he says, "Come on, come on. Let's get in there. Helen, do you have the camera?"

THIRTEEN

Swain balances his plate on his knees and reaches over to the coffee table to get his drink. Everybody's so quiet, eating. This is a house I'd like to live in. Big windows onto the woods, a porch around two sides, miles out in the country, away from Chapel Hill. The trees are so thick that even in late February you can't see through them to a house or a road.

For the last two months, Swain has withdrawn into a quiet that has lulled everyone into thinking that all is finally well with him again. He has gone through the motions of work and home in a comfortable trance, smiling pleasantly out at the world from a daydream about nothing in particular. It is a way he learned to protect himself from loneliness in his childhood. It feels like being rocked slowly in someone's lap in a rocking chair. It is the form of time-out he gives himself still, and he has never needed it more. Julie is not fooled by this, but she is relieved. It has been nice to have a break from all the turmoil. When the baby comes, he'll love it. She's sure of that. In the meantime, let him dream.

They are at the Haddonsfields'. It's their turn for the South of Franklin Street potluck.

"What can I get anybody?" Janie's standing in the entrance from the dining room.

"A lifetime supply of this green stuff," Bernie says. "Who brought this?"

"I did." Gladys Henby. She says it so quietly you can hardly hear her. She says, "I grew it myself. I put a little greenhouse just outside my mother-in-law's bedroom window. She's so sick, you know. I can hear her if she calls."

Patrice comes back into the living room. "That was Joe on the phone. He's going to be late, but he's coming."

Swain's fork stops.

"He had an all-day meeting," she says.

What's he doing showing up? The two of them going somewhere together? Impossible. Swain puts down his plate, feeling the comfort of recent months starting to slip away. He looks over at Julie. She shrugs. She has the gall to think Joe is attractive.

It takes Joe twenty minutes to arrive. Swain waits for him the whole time. The doorbell rings, Janie is handing around the cream and sugar. Swain looks at his watch. What can happen in front of this many people? It's almost time to go home anyway.

Joe comes in, taking off his coat, a draft of cold from outside rushing in around him. He says his hellos to the dinner crowd scattered across the floor, jammed onto the sofa.

Swain glances over at Patrice. She's smiling, waiting for Joe to thread his way through the people and find a place next to her. What is going on? Swain stares at her. She looks as if she's in love with him, for Christ's sake. It's an act. Maybe she's just being nice because she's finally decided to leave him.

Janie is bringing Joe a plate. "I know you must be starved." Patrice looking at Joe as if she can't get enough of the sight of him. I can't believe it, Swain thinks.

He watches Joe stepping over people to get to Patrice. Not a trace of self-doubt in him. She wouldn't have looked twice at Echols if she hadn't been crazy. She wouldn't have looked twice at me either.

Joe, with his fork poised above his plate and somebody talking at him, is slowly surveying the crowd. He's going to see Julie first. There. He stiffens, it's unmistakable, a flicker across his face. Then it's gone, the smile is back. He looks nowhere but at Julie.

He pats his belly as if he's the one pregnant, and smiles. She laughs. She thinks, He *is* charming. She mouths across the heads of a dozen other people, "How's Jakey?" Joe makes a circle with his fingers. Why couldn't Swain have just yelled at him, instead of hitting him? Julie puts her plate aside, her stomach feels not good at all.

Joe's eyes start around the room again, looking for Swain, all the warmth gone. It's like waiting for a killer serve to come across the net at you. There's nothing you can do until it comes.

Here it is. Joe nods. Very slow. Very cool. Loud talk is going on in the space between them. He says, loud enough to be heard by all of them: "Reverend Swain, nice to see you. It's been a long time."

The other conversation stops. People look up. There's something in his tone...

"Good to see you, Joe."

"Congratulations on your happy news."

"Thank you. I guess we're about half the way there now." He looks at Julie.

She nods. "Almost."

Joe says, "I want to apologize for the way I behaved the last time I saw you. That day in the grocery store. Months ago. Back in the fall. You remember." At this point, nobody is even pretending to pay attention to anything else. The two of them are out in the middle of a stage.

Bernie's heart sinks. There's no way Swain's going to get through this. Joe will eat him alive.

"Nothing to worry about," Swain says. "What you were going through...Actually I don't blame you for evening up the score."

Julie winces. He has to bring it up? Why can't he leave well enough...?

"No excuse," Joe says. If it weren't for his eyes, Swain might fall for this.

Patrice puts her hand on Joe's shoulder, squeezes hard. He ignores it. Why does he have to stir this up now? It was all settled over. She glances around the room, Julie looks as if she's going to be sick.

Joe wrinkles up his forehead as if he wants to look perplexed, squints at a vase up high on a shelf. "One thing I've been meaning to ask you, Swain. About when you came to see Jakey in the hospital." He looks innocently wondering at Swain. "The word going around is that you actually tried to do some kind of healing trick on him . . . a miracle, that's what people have been saying, Swain. That you told that to one of the kids. You know how rumors distort things. I can't get Patrice to tell me anything about it."

He smiles. There is complete quiet in the room. Somebody, a woman, shifts her legs. One stockinged leg slides against the other.

Bernie thinks, Please Swain, say it's a rumor, say you don't know what the hell he's talking about. Come on, Swain. You're not going to like selling real estate.

Swain takes a deep breath, holds it for a second. "I don't know exactly what you heard, Joe, but what happened was nothing to be upset about."

Joe's watching him like a hunter with a gun. Here it comes.

"I'm upset all right. I don't like the idea of anybody trying out their magical miracle powers on my son."

"Joe," Patrice says. "Please—"

Faces all around Swain blur. All he can see is Joe lit in warm yellow lamplight, Patrice leaning toward him, so gently saying "please."

Swain says, "Joe, there was a source of power in the room . . . for a moment I thought something was really going to happen, that it could . . . the boy was lying there. . . . I had to do anything I could."

Joe's face is a seamless wall. Not a flicker of expression.

"So much for your source of power," he says.

Swain shrugs. "I was wrong. It didn't work. Somehow or other I didn't let it work. I'm not sorry I tried."

There is silence in the room. Nobody is breathing. Swain is looking down a long tunnel straight to Joe.

"Oral Roberts," Joe says. He laughs a sardonic laugh. "Not what

I ever would have expected to see at Westside." He lifts his eyebrows. "Not what I would have expected from you."

"What did you expect from me?"

"Not much. More of the same. A lot of talk."

Swain's eyes narrow. He can feel his fist connecting with the side of that face.

He says, "Joe, I hit you. With my fist. For no reason, at the worst possible time there could ever be." He feels the sudden stirring of everyone in the room and ignores it.

Julie puts her head down in her hand, rubs her forehead, her eyes. Why is he doing this to us?

Then she slowly lifts her head and looks from face to face. Shock. Every one of them so shocked, they can't believe they're hearing it. DeWitt, Rudy, Janie, both Fitzgeralds. Even shy little Gladys, much as she adores Swain, sitting there staring at him and blinking. Bernie with the wind knocked square out of him, as if he had just got hit himself. Oh my Lord, Swain has really done it now.

Joe says, "I remember."

"Why haven't I been called before a special meeting of the session to explain that? Why didn't you send your lawyers after me? You just let it go. That's not what I ever would have expected from you."

Joe's face is suffused with blood. He looks at Swain steadily. "I didn't give a fuck about that, Hammond. I hit you first, don't forget that. You hit me back. Fights I can understand. Miracles I can't. You've got some kind of voodoo going that I don't buy. I don't think anybody at Westside is going to buy it either."

"We'll see," Swain says.

Julie is dead silent on the way home. "So what was I supposed to say?" he asks her.

She murmurs something. He looks over at her. She has her eyes closed.

"I think you're trying to escape," he says.

"I wish I could." Her voice is flat. Neither one of them says anything for the rest of the drive.

At home, she goes straight to bed and is out in a minute.

Lying beside her, he isn't having such an easy time drifting off. His body is tired, but his mind is so clear, like a power plant lit up and running all night.

His legs are motionless under the covers. They're mine, but I can't move them. Joe took it all out of me. It doesn't matter. Nothing matters. They're going to run me out of the church anyway.

I'd be better off if they did fire me. Probably they'll just look the other way again, act like nothing happened, tolerate my little quirks. They'll never get rid of me. We're all stuck, including me.

Why do I even care? There's not one of them that matters. I hate every one of them. They don't listen. Narrow-minded, petty . . . He can feel the blood vessels inside his brain getting tight and small. Joe, Bernie . . . all of them . . .

This is what God picked for a mouthpiece. Swain Hammond, full of nothing but hate and fury. I'm the one who is narrow and closed-down.

Listen to this: Your message will never get through. Do you hear that? Swain Hammond is a clogged drain. He hates everybody. He's even scared to love his own child. Scared to be a father . . .

. . . Everything in him pauses, stops. A thought runs through him like a drug speeding into every vein: who he really hates, who he's really mad at. He lies for one moment in total stillness while the knowledge takes him over. Then his legs move. He pushes up on his elbows, pushes the covers back, sits up in bed. I'm going to go tell them. Now.

He pulls his clothes on in the dark. Julie doesn't stir. He finds his way through the house in the dark.

The car starts with a roar loud enough to wake up the whole neighborhood. He doesn't care.

All the stoplights are blinking yellow. He doesn't slow down. He leaves the car parked on the roadside and climbs the hill on a diagonal, the shortest route to the gate.

A chain loops across the entrance. He steps over it. It's frozen. Each big metal link covered with ice. His leg brushes it, stepping over, the whole thing creaks back and forth. It's trying to warn them I'm coming. Nothing can stop me.

The cold makes his eyes water. The sun is almost up. Everything is so gray; all the stones make big long shadows like black stripes. He can't even tell when he's stepping on a grave, the paths are hardly even paths. Doesn't anybody come here?

His legs are freezing. His stomach is queasy. I should have eaten, at least gotten some coffee. No, if I ate, I'd get sick.

He's done burials here, but he tried not to see their plot. The way you avoid somebody at a party. The last time he actually came to their graves, he stood at a distance as if he was called before them, forced to stand at the foot of their bed, while they whispered back and forth about him and he couldn't hear.

There . . . His chest draws in hard. There they are. That's the back of it, their stone. It was here . . . you can almost see across the road to the track field. This is the place. The morning they were buried, the trees were shorter, there were guys out running laps. He watched them go around and around. That's the stone. A rectangle with ragged edges.

"I'm here," he says. He wants to grab them both by the arm, hard. The air is full of them. They're here. This is the place. He walks around to the front of the stone. He's walking on them, standing on their necks. Someone should be here to see it.

He stands motionless in the cold, his feet planted on them. They were going to the beach when it happened . . . flying. Always going. Once they both went away and didn't even tell him. . . . Both of them called and left a message for the other—to do something about Swain—they had to be away a few days. Neither of them got the message. He didn't tell anybody. He was old enough—ten or eleven. He made sandwiches. He watched TV and rode his bike to school. He didn't really think anything bad had happened to them, they just forgot him, that was all. His mother reappeared first, after two nights and two days. She couldn't believe it had happened. He felt sorry for her when she cried. Felt bad because he had made her cry. His father came back a couple of days later. He never mentioned anything to Swain about it at all.

The two of them . . . they deserved to drown. She could cry and cry and I wouldn't care now. God, what a fool I was.

"It was you," he says, leaning over, standing on their two graves. He's talking straight to the stone. HAMMOND—cut in deep. "You did this to me. You turned me into something that hates everybody, that's terrified of his own child." He wants to stomp down harder until their bones break.

He leans over and grabs hold of the rough top of the granite and pushes. It doesn't move. It's anchored in the center of the earth. He can't pull it loose. "I hate you." His voice shakes. "Both of you." He's crying. All the bones in his chest are breaking. "You should never have had me. I wish you had died before I was born." He is on his knees, his hands across the top of the stone, still pushing at it, pulling it toward him. It doesn't move. His wrists burn. He lets go of it and falls. Julie, somebody, help me get away from here. Please, God . . .

He gets to his feet. Over to that tree. He'll hold onto the tree. He takes a step toward it. Everything is blurred. . . . A cry starting way down in him grabs hold of his insides, doubles him up, like a cramp. His hands hit the grass. His wrist is scraped from the stone, there's blood on it. "You did that to me, you bastards."

He's on his hands and knees, getting away from them. If he can just get over to that tree . . . "Why?" he yells. It echoes and shakes the air. "What was wrong with me? You couldn't stand me. You acted like I was nothing and invisible." He looks up to where the bare tree branches cross, tries to yell all the way up there, to the sky that looks yellow-gray. "What was so terrible?" His voice won't go that far. He gives up, collapses down on his hands and cries.

The dead grass rubs against his cheek. He pushes his face against it. If he pushes hard enough against the ground, he'll get down to where it's warm. "I loved you. I did the best I could."

He lies still on the ground, his breath slowing. The cramp in his chest is letting go. His crying rocks him, slower and slower.

He opens his eyes. Dead leaves. Somebody pulled all the leaves off. Loves me, loves me not, over and over, a million times. Loves me not. I'm so tired. If they would just go away now and leave me alone.

He gets up to his knees, slowly rises to his feet. He's ten feet from their graves. His head feels light and empty. He looks around. Everything gray and frozen. Nobody here. Chatwin . . . the name on the nearest stone. He looks back at the one that says Hammond, makes his eyes focus on it. Hammond—that's my name. Julie's name. The kid's name.

"You'd think I would want to have a kid, and do it right." He can't look away from that rock. He shakes his head. "I can't do it right. I don't even want to." His eyes fill up again, but he doesn't cry. He hears his own voice calling out inside his head—"Mama." Waked up at night, had a bad dream, calling her to come. I will not say it out loud, I won't call her—his breath catches, he says the rest of it, a blank for her name, he whispers, "I am so scared."

FOURTEEN

His eyes squinch shut. Too bright. Where are the covers? He twists around, tugging at sheets, waking himself up. Goddamnit. Pulling the sheet up around him.

Too late. He's awake. A wave of pain starts below his ribs.

I don't hate them. Why did I do that? I never hated them. Jesus Christ. Going out there in the middle of the night...?

As if they could hear me... They're dead. I didn't say it. He presses his face against the mattress. He wants to find them and say he's sorry. He wants to take it all back. He lies still, tries not to think. If nothing moves in him anywhere, he won't hurt.

This is how Sam feels. Guilty. Welcome to the human race. The worst he has ever hurt in his life.

Which is absurd. Nobody heard me. Nobody was there. There are plenty of real problems in the world, if I want something to hurt about.

He opens his eyes, turns in the bed. Pants. I have clothes on. I came in and lay down. The memory of it sweeps over him again. One time when he was sick, before he was even old enough to go to school, both of them came in and sat on his bed, one on each side, and Dad sang a song for him, so softly, Mom all the time brushing her hand across his forehead, and then when Dad finished and was quiet, he remembers her saying to him, "My little boy."

They loved me. I always knew that. They did the best they could. It goes round and round in his head: they did the best they could. They gave me everything.

It sends another wave of pain through him to think of hurting them, either one.

He thought he would wake up different this morning. On the way to the cemetery, driving fast on icy roads, somewhere in his haste and confusion, he was thinking, It's going to be over soon. I'll stop being mad.

But this is worse. I'm still mad and I don't want to be.

He sits up, stands, wavers a moment, upright by the bed. Then he walks into the kitchen.

Julie is putting her coffee cup in the sink, getting ready to go. She looks up. "Good morning," she says. "I tried to wake you."

He walks over to her, puts both arms around her, holds her tight against him. He leans down and brushes the side of his face against her hair.

"Are you okay, Swain?"

"I don't know." His face is numb. It feels strange to talk.

"Is there anything I can do?"

He shrugs, but she can't hear that. "No. Just stay around, keep ... being patient with me."

She looks up at him. His face looks gray. His doctor said there was nothing wrong. Stress, maybe.

"I'm okay. Julie. I am. Don't worry."

She doesn't look convinced. He switches into briskness. His usual self. "Look at the time. You need to get going. I've got to hurry."

He hears her car drive out as he steps under the shower, and then there is only the roar of the water echoing around him. I'm going to pull myself together ... I'm going to get through this.

What I'd like now, what would solve everything, is some instruction from God that would be so huge and different from everything that's happening that it would drown all my other problems, make them seem small, make me forget them. The way a war could. If you were going off to war, you'd quit worrying about the fact that your car needs fixing and you're about to flunk out of school. He lets the water pour and pour over his head.

When he gets to the office, he decides what to do: deal with Joe Miles the way he knows best, from the pulpit. The party episode will be all over the church by Sunday anyway. At the very least, it will take his mind off his pain.

On Sunday morning, he adjusts his notes on the lectern and waits for the congregation to settle. He wants their full attention for this. He begins: "Everybody knows that party small talk is the least meaningful of human conversation. It is empty and trivial and meaningless.

"This morning, I would like to tell you about an exception to that rule, about a conversation I had at one of our church potlucks this past week that has been very much on my mind.

"Joe Miles asked me at that gathering about something that he heard happened last summer. It was after his son Jakey's accident. I was visiting the boy in the hospital. Jakey was groggy, he wasn't long out of surgery. I stood there in his hospital room beside his bed, overwhelmed, knowing what he had lost." Patrice in a pew close to the back moves so she's hidden behind Mike Woodhouse. Her face disappears from his view.

"That afternoon, standing in that room, I started to pray. As I prayed, I felt a surge of such force moving in me that it seemed I would lose my balance. I didn't fall. What I did was pray that Jakey Miles would see again.

"I didn't think. I felt that rush of force, like a pump, a pipe broken and spraying in every direction. I didn't stop it, I prayed for it to keep on. And I said what I said: I asked God that Jakey be healed, for him to sit up then and there and take his bandages off and see. For one moment in that hospital room, I believed that that could happen." He pauses, looks down at his notes, and waits.

Bernie, seated alone halfway back, shakes his head.

Mary Elgar, two seats behind Bernie, thinks, Lord Almighty, he's at it again.

"Miracles are a dangerous subject in this day and age," Swain is saying. "We don't believe in them. We're embarrassed by the stories of miracles in the Gospel. It's a part of our Christian heritage which we go to great trouble to disavow.

"I'm not here to propose that we begin to take these stories as literal truth. I'm certainly not going to offer myself as a miracle worker. I didn't do any miracles—hard as I tried that day.

"The New Testament is full of miracles, of the lame who get up and walk, and the blind made to see. But the Scripture is also clear that Jesus did not want to be known as a magician. In Mark 5, when he told the child to rise and walk, he turned then to the others who saw it happen. 'And he charged them straitly that no man should know it.' He did not want his teachings to be lost while miracles got all the attention.

"But we humans are dazzled by the thought of the miraculous. We face death and disease and great suffering, in the present or in the future. It is inevitable. What teaching could ever compete with the power of immediate healing?

"The most incredible truth is that Jesus offered a teaching that could. That may be the strongest statement that anyone could make about the Kingdom of God. We don't see many miracles these days. Not one of us gets the help we want in our day-to-day lives. No one steps in when we are hurting and makes it all right. Yet when we acknowledge the power of God, we are confronting a force and a promised life that makes the healing we long for grow pale.

"I'm saying to you this morning that I believe in a force that unbalances and overwhelms me with its power and life, that makes miracles seem both possible and small."

Gladys looks at him, standing up there in that pulpit, stepping down now. She watches his head and shoulders still showing over the rail as he goes back down to his seat next to the wall. He really does know, she thinks. I know he knows. She feels the hope swell up in her. Please, Lord. A promised life. Let every word Dr. Hammond is saying be true.

The organ begins. All around her people stand for the hymn. She gets her hymnbook and finds the number. Thinking about it all makes her want to get up and sing.

At the close of the service, Swain goes to stand at the side door to greet anyone who wants to shake hands with him. Maybe it's his imagination, but it seems there are a lot fewer handshakers than usual, the rest of them going out the other door, avoiding him.

When the last ones are gone, he goes back to his office. Julie has already gone home. He's ready to be there himself. Everything he's doing now feels like a charade. His heart isn't even in it now, it's just the right thing to do. There is nothing in his head now but his own parents . . . stuff that happened a hundred years ago. Good thing for them that they died and never had to actually hear any of what he said at the cemetery, any of what's going around and around in his mind now.

I'm too old to be going through this. Near forty, them dead fifteen years. It's embarrassing, and yet he feels as bad as he can ever imagine feeling. He keeps thinking about Sam. Sam knows about feeling bad.

He opens the door to his office. He stops short. Bernie, on the sofa, staring at the floor between his own feet. Bernie looks up. Swain walks past him, unhooks his robe and puts it on a hanger.

"So what is going on, Swain?" Bernie is standing now, talking to Swain's back. "That's all I want to know."

Swain turns around. "What do you mean?"

"What are we expected to do? What are we supposed to think when you throw something like this at us?"

Swain looks out the window.

Bernie says, "I'm talking about your sermon, in case you've already forgotten."

Swain nods. "I haven't forgotten. You didn't waste any time getting to me."

"Neither will anybody else. Do you think you have some kind of audience for this stuff at this church, that there's anybody in the whole bunch that wants to get into this holy-roller healing thing?"

"If there is, they haven't let me know." He drops into the chair.

"Then why, Swain? Why are you going full speed toward self-destruction? I'm asking you as a friend. I don't want to see this happen."

"It's my job."

"It may very well wind up being your job this time, that's what I'm trying to tell you."

Swain nods. "I'm aware that I'm taking a chance. Though I can't see why what I said is so outrageous, frankly. I didn't feel like I was sticking my neck out. Well, not very far, anyway." He smiles. "It was a good sermon, Bernie. Come on. Admit it." It was a sermon Dad would have loved. I had them all listening, no doubt about that. He feels the sadness rising in him, and forces it away.

"For Christ's sake, Swain." Bernie lets his head sag.

"What to do with crazy Swain," Swain says. "I'm glad you're at least talking to me."

Bernie looks up slowly, as if he took a break from listening and now he's coming back. "What I want to know is . . . are you all right? You've got us all worried sick."

"I'm all right." Swain pauses. The look on Bernie's face, tight-lipped, dull-eyed—he *is* worried about me. "Thanks, Bernie."

Bernie doesn't look at him or say anything.

Swain says, "I still wish I could get across to you—to somebody—what it is I'm trying to say."

Bernie looks at him wearily. "Okay," he says, "tell me again. Straight to the point. One sentence, Swain. What are you trying to say?"

"God's as real as a station wagon."

Bernie shakes his head. He tells himself for the thousandth time, The old Swain isn't coming back. "That was to the point," he says.

"A lot of things have happened to me, Bernie. I've got too much going on now. But none of it—gut-wrenching as it is—has electrified me like facing God." Bernie's face: he's looking at Swain the way you look at a dog with a hurt foot. Some poor pitiful creature that was dumb enough to get himself run over. "You're not going to give it the benefit of the doubt, are you, Bernie?"

"Tell me this one thing, Swain. Has it helped you out any? Is anything any easier?"

"Not a thing. I have never been more miserable." He looks at his feet.

Bernie says quietly, "Maybe if you'd take a break from some of this... the miracles business, God... get it all off your mind. Maybe you and Julie could—"

"Bernie, what kind of church is this? What are people actually doing here if they're not interested in this?"

"People are interested, all right, like it was the cover of *The National Enquirer*. They just think it's horseshit and don't want anybody to catch them looking at it."

Swain shakes his head. "Maybe I just don't belong here."

Bernie says, "Swain, I don't know what to think."

Swain stays in his office a few minutes after Bernie leaves. He doesn't want to walk out with him. He'll wind up talking about his parents, lambasting them again, to Bernie, who actually knew them. He doesn't want to do that. He has been disloyal enough already.

There's one car left besides his, when he gets out to the parking lot. DeWitt, getting ready to leave, stops when he sees him.

"Aren't you the brave boy." DeWitt shuts the car door he was just opening and turns around slowly.

"Hello, DeWitt," Swain says. He pulls his coat collar up. Harsh March wind is coming straight across the empty parking lot.

"Miracles. Really, Swain."

"All I said—"

"I heard every last carefully considered word of what you said. It is true that you could have gone further. But in this setting, as I'm sure you know, what you said was quite enough. Whatever are you up to? I hardly know what to imagine will come next."

"I'm not up to anything. And it wasn't all so carefully considered. I'm getting tired of tiptoeing around."

"God been talking to you lately?"

"Haven't heard a word. Not in months."

"Too bad."

"Yes. It is." He looks at DeWitt, stares without saying anything, the way DeWitt always looks at him. "You seem to be enjoying this whole spectacle," Swain says.

"I have to admit it's certainly more interesting than if you were romancing one of the sopranos, the sort of church scandal one usually gets."

"Is this a scandal?"

"What could be more scandalous? You're trying to talk an extremely reasonable group of people into magic, which is a little—I hate to say it—embarrassing."

"Embarrassing." Swain shakes his head. He pushes his hands down into his pockets and looks up at the sky, closes his eyes. Embarrassing. "DeWitt, that's so incredibly trivial I can't believe I'm hearing it."

"You tend to forget you're dealing with humans."

"That's what people say when they're making excuses for the worst kind of behavior."

"What's so terrible about our behavior, Swain? Would you believe these things you've been saying if I got up and said them to you?"

"DeWitt, I don't know if it's me and I just don't have what it takes to talk anybody into anything, or if it's something that no one can tell anybody else. But I feel like the building is on fire and I yell fire and nobody even looks up. I've got too much to cope with now, anyway. I don't know—I'm beginning to lose the point of it. I don't know why I keep trying. I'm in the wrong place. I don't know how it happened."

DeWitt looks down at his car keys. He doesn't have on gloves.

The cold makes his hand a mottled lavender. He takes a breath and lets it out slowly.

He feels a wave of protectiveness for the boy come over him. He touches the inner corners of his eyes with his thumb and forefinger, as if he were pushing up his glasses. He looks up and says, "Don't take it all so hard, Swain."

FIFTEEN

When he gets into the office, Gladys is standing in the hall next to his door with a tissue wadded up in her hand. She's damp around the eyes. Her nose is red.

He fumbles with his key. "Come on in, Gladys," he says, touching her shoulder, steering her in, flipping on a light. "I'm sorry I'm running late." The office smells like old coffee.

"Sit down," he says, "I'll be right with you." Quickly he glances through his messages from Mildred. Then he comes back over to the wing chair. His usual position. He sits here and listens and no one seems to notice that he's dying slowly in front of them. Am I invisible, he thinks?

Gladys has huddled up in a corner of the couch, up toward the edge, toward him. Her pocketbook in her lap. There's something squirrel-like about her, that plump little body and her hands gathered up in front of her. He has to make himself listen. I need a break, he thinks. Maybe I'm already taking one, just going through the motions. It is May—ten weeks since he got up and tried to tell them about miracles one more time. Since then, he has grown a little more depressed every day, and this time he has been unable to retreat into his own inner world.

"It's getting worse and worse, Dr. Hammond," Gladys says. She lifts the damp wad of tissue toward her eyes. "I don't know what I'm going to do."

"What's happened, Gladys?"

"All day she calls me. My mother-in-law. All day. She says her pillow isn't right. And it's the same as it always is. She says there wasn't enough ice in her orange juice, or it's too big and she can't swallow it. I crack it with a hammer, wrapped up in the dish towel, just the way she says she likes it. All I ever do is crack ice, winter and summer. Not that she knows what day it is."

She sighs and looks away from him. "Oh, sometimes she does. Sometimes she makes good sense and that's even worse. When she's crazy and making things up, I can just ignore it. She says terrible things to me, I couldn't even tell you. If Walter were alive, maybe I could stand it better. I try to do it for him, that's the only reason." She cries softly into her hand with her face turned away.

Swain focuses on the corner of a picture frame. I didn't do her any good the last time we went through this. It's not going to be any different today. Give us strength, O God, for the task which is ours.

Gladys dries her eyes and looks at him and waits. Her eyes search his face. What does she think I can offer? I haven't helped anybody yet.

"I'm sorry you're suffering with this, Gladys. I know it's hard."

She swallows and nods. "I'm so grateful I can come talk to you. I feel terrible even thinking the things I think about her."

This lady deserves a refund. She ought to be asking for forty years of tithes handed over to her right now. She doesn't even get to come every Sunday now, it's too hard to get anybody to nurse. I should offer her a complete refund. She'd be surprised. I owe her a favor. For the moment, she got me out of my slump. Swain feels reckless, what-the-hell.

"Why don't you take a vacation?" he says. "It's May. It's almost summer."

She straightens up and looks at him carefully. What is he suggesting? Surely he must understand. . . . "Where would I go?"

"I don't know. Philadelphia."

"Philadelphia?" She frowns. All those things people have been saying about him . . . He does look so very tired.

"Anywhere. It doesn't matter. Tell one of your kids you have to have a break and to come stay with her. Then go somewhere, do something."

"I don't even know where I'd go."

"Or sign up for a course in something."

"In what?"

"Italian."

She squints at him. "Italian?" People *have* been saying all this while that he's gotten a little...strange. She looks at him again, praying not to find anything....She wants to tell him: "Don't talk about Italian, Dr. Hammond, don't say anything crazy. I need to believe you...."

"It's a beautiful language. Do you like opera?" He feels drunk. As long as she doesn't think he's making fun of her...

"Well, I always did enjoy the choir," she is saying.

What am I supposed to do? he thinks. If God were living in a tree in her backyard, it wouldn't help her. It didn't help me. What's the point of my being here anyway? I'm a piss-poor social worker, and nobody listens to me about God. It's a waste. You can't tell anybody about God.

"Gladys, I don't know how to help you." Fill her now with Thy Holy Spirit. He thinks it in spite of himself. May Thy love bring light. It's a habit, like rubbing the side of his chin. She's such a dear old soul.

"Gladys, look. I'm not—what if—Gladys, I'll come sit with her, your mother-in-law, this afternoon and you go to a movie, or go get a beach towel and sit out in the sun. I can put off what I had planned. You get out and do something, anything. That's all I can offer you. I'm sorry."

She stares at him. What on earth is he talking about? "Dr. Hammond, thank you, that's not necessary. I certainly can't let...I couldn't even think of...I don't even know where I would go anymore. I don't know anything I want to do."

"Get a friend and walk around in the mall. I'll be there at two-thirty. I'll stay until six." Whatever I have ever done, this ought to be ample punishment. "Write down anything you think I might need to know."

"You surprise me, Dr. Hammond. You certainly do." If this is what they mean by crazy, then there's not any need to worry another minute.

"Why are you surprised? What did you expect?"

"I don't know." She stops and thinks. It all goes so far back. "I've been a member of this church since Walter and I got married, even though it's not a bit like the church I grew up in. Walter liked it, so now it's my home. When you take up your membership, you're faithful to it, that's the way I was raised. Now I keep taking up your time. You're a fine young man, I've always thought so. I certainly never expected this."

She stands. Swain stands. She looks up at him. He looks so strained and tired, especially right around his eyes. Somebody needs to take care of him, not the other way around. She hesitates. "It's so kind of you. But I shouldn't let you."

"Let me. Please."

She's a raving lunatic and mean. Swain is sitting in the big blue-flowered armchair with its back to the window. The terrible old creature in the bed gets the view of whatever backyard is out there behind him. The nurse, whoever is sitting in this chair, faces pill bottles, dozens of orange plastic bottles on the bedside table. And the water glass that looks as if it has sat with the same water in it for years. And the gaping mouth of old Mrs. Henby. She is in much worse shape than he imagined.

For fifteen minutes she was awake and knew what was going on. Thank God that's over. Now he sits motionless. He barely breathes. He doesn't cross his legs. He doesn't get up and walk out of the room — he might wake her. Three hours and ten minutes to go. This is not what ministers do, sitting here listening to that long whistling breath and a clock ticking. She looks like the old man in *2001* when he turns into an infant again.

When he first came in she stared at him the way a kid looks at a doctor who has come to give her a shot. Her eyes so far back in her head her skull showed. That's what he saw when he walked in, not the pale blue lace night coat or the watercolor of camellias or the bottles of pills. When Gladys was gone and it was only Swain, she said, "I don't know why she would do this. I never understand. Young man, get me that silver hairbrush." Swain looked around. There wasn't any hairbrush. "Get it. What do you think you're being paid for? Worse than the colored girl she left me with. I can't understand it. I fired her. I'll fire you too. You can look sharp, young fellow, if you expect to do any work for me. I'm not like most people these days. I don't put up with anything and everything."

"I don't see your hairbrush, Mrs. Henby." On the dresser top all he could find was a crocheted place mat and a glass bowl with powder in it and some big fat pearls too heavy to wear around that scrawny little neck. "Maybe it's somewhere else in the house and Gladys can find it when she gets back." By the time she gets home, he'll probably have a long list of things for her to do. That'll really be a big help to her. He turned back around to the woman in the bed. She was staring at a portrait on the opposite wall. A girl in a shiny blue dress with a wide skirt and hair like Loretta Young.

"That's my daughter," she said. "She passed away."

"I'm sorry."

"You have no idea. None at all."

Swain gave up on the hairbrush and sat back down in the chair.

"Are you just going to sit there the whole afternoon? You might make yourself useful since you're going to be here. Go cut some wood. Mow the grass if you still need something else to do. Sitting there doing not one thing in this world. I can't understand it."

"I'm here to keep you company and see that you have everything you need."

She laughed, a derisive hoot that quavered a little at the end, and her harangue was over. Everything she said after that was crazy. Sleep talk. Pieces of sentences about the terrible heat this summer and somebody named Roger and the chrysanthemums and the window that's stuck.

Now she's quiet, lying there breathing louder than the ticking of the clock. He can't take his eyes away from her mouth. Her cheeks sink and tremble a little with every breath she draws in. Suppose I were sitting here with a woman who had been plaguing my life every day for years. Suppose I were Gladys and at this moment the minister walked in.

He sees himself come in the door. He's smiling, not broadly, not a grin, but gently with closed lips. But there's a light in his eyes. He can see it, his own face. Not bad. It's a plausible, fairly presentable facial expression for a person with his job to do: bring hope and relief and then go. If you stay here long, you can't look like that.

He watches himself go to the bedside, touch her hand, lean over her face, into that breath that could pull a live person in. Come die with me, it says. There he is, standing by the bed. There's compassion on his face, the real thing. He's felt it a million times, standing beside a bed, being glad it's not him, not him in the bed and not him having to live beside it. He walks out of houses sometimes as if he'd just been grazed by gunfire. He thinks again, What if something terrible turns out to be wrong with the baby, if it's retarded or something?

Mrs. Henby stirs beneath the covers, shifts her legs. Her mouth moves like a baby's. Breast-feeding seems so bizarre and primitive, somebody getting food out of your body.

I should have brought some work, a book. If I get up to go look for one, she'll wake up. Why did I put myself where I had to sit three hours and think? Put off thinking, that's what he'd like to do.

He never in his life considered being anything but a minister. It was a mistake. From the beginning. He can't deal with the people. He never could. And now, what is there to say about God? "No one can tell you. Listen to yourself." They don't need me to tell them that every Sunday for the next thirty years. A light dizzy sensation comes up the back of his neck and spreads into the bottom of his head. He has known it without thinking it for three days, for three months, for the whole terrible spring he has known: he has to quit.

The words sit there in front of him. He waits for them to do something terrible to him, to turn him inside out with grief. I have to quit. It's unavoidable. It's the only conclusion.

The light feeling fills his whole head. It doesn't hurt, it's not so bad. It's going to be okay. What did I ever like about it anyway? It was all just my wanting and wanting, of God, or something to be there.

I could still take Communion. Under his knees is the soft carpet of the chapel where he went when he was a kid. The tiny glasses dropping into the slots of the altar rail. God of God. Light of Light. Very God of Very God. He won't lose that.

Or the benedictions. He loved the benediction. He wanted it for himself, not to stand there with his arms raised in front of them, but to be on the other side. He wants it now. Someone to touch his hair gently and say "Go from here in peace."

In peace. Relief. It's over.

Maybe this is the instruction I've been waiting for: to quit. I can do that.

He looks over at the bed. Lying there with her mouth open, the air whistling in and out. She's scary-looking. He feels like a six-year-old left alone at night. He wants to pull a chair over and climb up to reach the telephone and call the neighbor's number. I shouldn't be the one to stay with somebody who is dying.

When he gets home, there's a note on the table. "Call Bill Bartholomew."

Great. Bartholomew. This is it. They're coming to take me away, not that it matters now. I'm leaving. What a joke on them.

"Julie," he yells from where he stands. He hears her in the back, hiding from him, not wanting to tell him to his face that Bill called. Or crying because she thinks she's not pretty anymore. Being pregnant is making her crazy. It's been weeks since Bill has called. That's been one nice thing about all this, him leaving me alone.

She comes into the kitchen. Her breasts so big they look as if they hurt. He can't get used to it. He forgets and expects her to look the way she did. "What does Bartholomew want?"

She kisses him. "I don't know," she says. "He didn't say."

"Well, I can guess. But it doesn't matter. Julie."

She was already looking at him.

"Yes?"

"I've decided I'm going to leave the church."

"Westside?"

"The ministry."

She leans toward him as if she can't see well and she's squinting her eyes hard to figure out who he is. Then she straightens, her face smooths out. "Swain, everybody feels like that sometimes."

He shakes his head. "I'm serious."

She looks at him hard again. She goes over to her chair at the table, slowly sits down. "Swain," she says. "Oh, Swain."

She's staring at him, stunned. He forces himself not to look away.

"It's the right thing, Julie. I swear it is. I can't go on pretending I'm doing anybody any good."

"I know you're going through a bad time. . . ."

"The bad time is almost over."

She looks out the window. "Julie . . ." If I talk fast and explain it, she won't start crying. "Look, I promise it's all going to be all right, it's what I need to do." She keeps her face turned away and her arms wrapped around her. All I ever do is hurt people, he thinks.

"Julie, I don't want to make you unhappy." He pulls a chair over and sits down in front of her. He puts one hand on her leg.

She won't look at him. He watches the tears start down her face. "Please understand."

"Understand what? I'm tired of understanding everything. This is not fair, Swain. This is sabotage. I was doing all right up until now, but this is too much. It's like you're trying on purpose to pull the rug out from under us."

Doing all right, hell. She starts crying and pouting over nothing every other day. The dishwasher breaks and she goes in the bedroom and slams the door.

He shakes his head, looks at the floor. "I'm not trying to pull any rug—I told you earlier, I told you Sunday—"

"You didn't say one word about quitting."

"Not exactly. It took me a couple of days to catch on."

"Catch on to what, Swain? You act like you think you're making some kind of sense. This is the craziest thing yet. I can't stand it anymore. Here I'm trying to get the house ready for the baby—"

"And I'm not? Is that what you're saying? I've done everything you said you wanted. Except for one time, Julie, one time I forgot to pick up something at a store—"

"You don't care about anything but your own stupid craziness. It's all you think about."

"And what are you thinking about, Julie? Nothing but whether your hand is too swelled up to wear your rings. Whether your hair—"

"You wouldn't care if you couldn't wear your ring. It would be fine with you if nobody even knew you were married."

"That's right, Julie. Nobody knows I'm married. I've been keeping it a secret all these years." He gets up and lies down on his back on the bed. He says, "Maybe there's not a lot of point in our trying to talk about it right now."

"Fine, Swain. You just let me know when you get everything figured out."

He waits until the morning to call Bill Bartholomew back. He is within days of being through with church elders and what they think. Julie's going to like the idea when she gets used to it, not being a preacher's wife anymore. She's been more irritated than I have with the way they've acted. It's the pregnancy that's got her so upset now, that's all. It's absolutely reasonable, I just have to expect that.

Bill is with a patient. Finally, in midafternoon, he returns Swain's call.

"I'll get straight to the point," he says. "I and several others have become increasingly concerned. We feel that there is a need to discuss some questions. Speaking for the other elders and myself, we would like you to appear in session next week to address some of these matters. Since you will be otherwise involved in the meeting, the Reverend Frank Witherspoon from St. Andrews has agreed to come over and preside."

"I'll be happy to. That's fine. What matters in particular, Bill?"

Bill pauses. "Your recent positions on charismatic religion. Also"—he clears his throat—"your behavior toward the Miles family, specifically toward Joe Miles, in the emergency room at the hospital on the day of his son's accident."

"Bill, I look forward to the opportunity for clearing the air." Swain swivels his chair like a kid playing in an office. Bill Bartholomew and his band of elders can't hurt Swain Hammond now. I am free. He stifles the urge to laugh into the phone. He says, a tone of magnanimous warmth in his voice, "Bill, I think this discussion will be very useful for all of us."

He puts the phone down, leans back in his chair and rubs his chest and stomach with both hands, as if he had just finished a good meal.

The phone lights up again. This time it's Sam.

"Hello there, Uncle Reverend Swain." Swain puts his feet on his desk and leans back in his chair. The metal pedestal squeals like bad brake lining. Somebody told him once they could tell whether he had time to talk when they called by whether they heard that squeak in his chair.

"How's it going, Sam?"

"Fair. Not too bad. You all ready to have that baby yet?"

"Got a couple of months still to go."

"That's not very long. Best get cracking."

"What is it I'm supposed to do, Sam?" Wonder if Sam will still call.

"Damned if I know. Sleep a lot, maybe. You won't get much chance afterward."

"So I hear."

"Just checking in, Swain. Wanted to let you know I still haven't jumped off a bridge."

"Good. Sounds like maybe things are going a little better for you."

Sam laughs. "Anything would have been an improvement."

Swain twists in his chair just to hear that scrape of metal. "I wish I knew how to be better help to you, Sam. I don't feel like I really have been much."

"Hey, don't go to running yourself down now, got to set a good example for the kiddo. You've done just fine, what could anybody do?"

"Not much."

Sam's quiet.

"I'm not meaning you, Sam. I just meant in general..."

"Well, I like to talk to you. You're at least harmless. Which is more than I can say for most of these counselor types."

Harmless. He should have pushed Sam off his desk that day: Sam flying backward through the window, into the bushes, wide-eyed, his mouth open. People are going to quit saying things like that to me. Harmless. That's exactly what I've been for too many years.

"No offense," Sam says.

"How would you like to be thought of as harmless?"

"I'd give anything."

The next week Swain attends the last Tri-City Ministerial Association lunch of his entire life. No more basement lunches, iced tea, canned beans, tear-away rolls. Valeria is down the table. Her voice, telling some funny story and laughing, makes the ice in his glass shake.

He makes himself listen to what's going on where he is. "You're performing quite a service to the community here with this program, Brother Robbins." Jerome Douglas is pushing his bread around in his gravy, talking in his pulpit voice.

The room is full of tables of people, talking and eating, the place is full of noise. Every Wednesday: lunch and twenty minutes in the sanctuary for people working in downtown Raleigh. The two-dollar lunch is bound to be part of the draw.

"You've every right to be proud," Jerome says. "This is quite a turnout. This pretty typical?"

"Give or take twenty-five," Ed Robbins says. "When the weather's pretty, people want to stay out on the mall. A little rain like today and we get a good number."

"Well, I think your program here is a fine offering," Jerome says. "You are certainly to be commended." Swain and Dave Branson murmur something and nod.

He only came because it was his last one. If he hadn't been running late, he'd be sitting down there with Valeria. This way he gets a full dose of the kind of thing he'll be glad to be rid of.

Swain says, "How long you been in the ministry, Jerome?"

"I have worn the collar for forty-one years," Jerome says in that voice. Maybe it's the collar, it's choking him.

"Did you ever think of getting out? I don't mean the daily ups and downs, but seriously."

"No, I never have, I am grateful to say. Oh, I have had my moments of doubt. I have been tested, but never so severely as that. The Lord has been easy on me." May you be easier on the Lord, fellow. Swain has heard Jerome preach.

From down the table, Valeria catches sight of him. Poor old Swain, stuck with that Jerome.

Jerome points his hawkish eyes at Swain and purses his lips. "We all descend into our valleys of shadow. Why do you ask?" Valeria keeps watching. Maybe one day I'll invite Brother Jerome to come preach. See what happens then. It tickles her to think about it. What was mighty good for Swain would be the living end of Jerome. That old fart. Now, Swain, he always had it in him. Good-looking boy, too.

Swain is laughing. "No," he says. "Don't misunderstand. In fact, I've never felt more secure in my own faith."

"Oh, the pleasure of those times," Jerome says, leaning back in his chair and rubbing his stomach with both hands.

"Yes," Swain says and smiles. "Indeed. The most memorable of times."

Valeria finishes her lunch and tells all of them around her she's sorry she's got to leave early. Then she comes down and stops behind Swain's chair. He needs a little more attention from this old girl, he looks kind of droopy today.

The first thing Swain knows she has an arm around his chest, under his chin, and her face down next to his. The two of them facing Jerome, who is working hard at smiling. Swain is completely surrounded by her. She's bigger than he is. He feels silly. How long is she going to do this? Her cheek warm against his, her chest pushed up against his back. He wraps his arms around her arms. Who cares if it looks ridiculous, Jerome can go to hell. He starts to grin.

"This boy is some fine preacher," she tells the people across the table. "He says the Word right out." She rocks him back and forth. He feels the first stirring of arousal in his crotch.

She says, "This man is a blessing to behold. Yes, sir."

"I'm certain you're right, Valeria," Jerome says. "I hope to have the pleasure of hearing him. . . ."

Valeria is letting go, smoothing down his hair, patting his back, moving on down the table. She looks back at Swain, says, "I'll see you, boy." He watches her departing back, still feeling her arms and cheek against him. She manages to embarrass me every time she sees me. And it'll cheer me up every time I think about it all afternoon.

When he leaves the lunch, he goes to the Y, changes clothes and goes out for his run. Running makes him feel as if he's leaving it all behind. Jerome and everybody like him. The breeze pushing through the weave of his T-shirt, wet now in the warm summer drizzle. He is flying, cutting through the thick air. At the top of the hill, he can see the big white steeple of the Methodist church, the whole skyline of downtown.

The sermon is coming along. The one where he announces the big news: Swain Hammond is calling it quits. He has written it ten different ways in his head, between phone calls, driving around town. He wishes Valeria would be there to hear it. She's right: he does know how to preach. There's no question about that. His shoes beat against the pavement.

I could cite the oracle at Delphi: "Summoned and not summoned, God will be there." I could line up quotes like evidence at a trial. "*Non foras ire*"—I'd love to get up there and say that—"*in interiore homine habitat veritas.* Go not outside. Truth dwells within you." He moves over for a car that picks up speed as it gets past. He's out of breath. The Latin rings through him like a bell outside a monastery.

"And Jesus said, Is it not written in your law, I said, Ye are gods?" Who will they ever find that's less of a god? Since that's what they apparently want. They don't even want to hear the word God.

I ought to forget writing a sermon and just get up there. That's the way Valeria would do it. All this obsessing with words and here I am with a kid on the way, and no job in sight. Everything I've ever relied on shot to hell, at least changed so much I can't even recognize it: my marriage, religion, my own insides. I was right that night on the patio. It *was* the start of my destruction. My life has never been the same again, and never will be. And now on Tuesday I have to go to session and try to explain to the jury what happened.

On Monday night, he is calm. There is nothing to prepare. They'll ask him questions. He'll answer them. He starts to think his way around the table of people who will be there. So familiar, some of them so dear. He stops with Mary Elgar. It hurts to think about. He'll see them tomorrow, no need to put himself through it twice.

Julie comes into the bedroom where he's sitting in the dark. "How's your back?" he says.

"Terrible. I think he's lying on a nerve."

There's somebody in there alive now. He has felt it move under his hand and against his own body, lying in bed next to her. He saw the fuzzy blurs in the dark picture she brought back from the doctor. She showed him the head. When they were at the movie, the baby jumped when the cars crashed in the car chase. Nervous like his dad. Swain pictures a gnomish old man in a cave, hunched over because the ceiling is so low, muttering at the cramped accommodations. Then sometimes he worries about it not having air, in there drowning. He looks at her stomach and takes a deep breath for the kid.

"Why don't you lie down?" he says.

"I'm going to."

He gets up and lies down on the bed beside her.

She says, "Swain...I'm going to ask you one more time, and then I'm not going to say anything else. Please think about waiting a little while before you do this."

He shakes his head. He doesn't look at her, he can't. He tells himself once again, I'm doing the right thing. I have no choice. He says, "I'm going to give enough notice so I'll have time to find something to do. Then I'll start making some kind of plans. I'm not thinking straight about that part of it now. My brain just won't do it."

"Your brain," she says. She has even lost the spirit to fight. Every night she has terrible dreams about something happening to the baby. That's the only way things could get any worse, if something happened to the baby....

Swain says, "I don't want what comes next to influence this decision. Can you understand that? If I found out my choices aren't much, then I might hang on to this when I shouldn't. It would be wrong, Julie."

Wrong to take care of his child doing the only kind of work he ever meant in his life to do? "I guess there's nothing more I can say," she says.

"Say you're not going to run off somewhere and leave me."

She laughs a sarcastic laugh.

He says, "You could make it fine without me, pregnant or not."

I can't sit, I can't lie down, can't half breathe. What does he think—I'm going to waddle off into the sunset with some medical student? She says, her voice cold as she can make it, "I'm not going anywhere."

He can hear her breathing. Almost see her in the dark. She's still with me, he thinks, right here beside me. We'll get through this. Just take it one thing at a time.

If he walked into Paul Hammond's study and told him what he was doing now—the way his mother sent him in to confess a couple of times in his early years—his father would look up and let his eyes fall on him and a long time would pass before his eyes would focus and he would completely know it was Swain. They were brown eyes with a lot of loose skin over the top that fell down toward them and made what he said seem to come from far back in a cave. He would take off his glasses and wipe them and then put them down on the blotter and he would look again at Swain as if that by itself would answer any questions.

"Leaving, are you?" Swain imagines him saying.

"Yes, sir."

His father would nod. "I'm sure you know what you're doing."

"Yes, sir."

"Good, then." And his father's eyes would wander back to whatever was on his desk. He would smile politely at Swain before he turned finally back to his work. That's the kind of answer he got out of his father. Now he's in the even less desirable position of waiting for answers from God.

SIXTEEN

"Close to 75 percent of the membership data cards have been returned," Charlie March says. Bill Bartholomew nods. They've decided to torture me, taking up the routine business first. Swain tips his chair back, steadies himself with one hand against the row of books behind him. The spines feel good against his hand. He used to play with his father's books, sitting on the floor of the study at home, lying between the bookshelves and looking up past all those rows to the ceiling. The room smelled good. Dad made little noises, lighting a match, turning pages, leaning back in his chair.

"We need to offer a reminder to the others, perhaps during the eleven o'clock," Bill says, looking over his little black reading glasses at Swain. Swain nods and makes a note. Apparently they're not going to ask for a resignation effective today.

Frank Witherspoon, who is officially presiding since Swain is in disgrace, sits quietly. He glances over at Swain when Bill does, then he looks away.

Swain ignores him. He thinks, I'm quitting. They can't fire me. However it happens... I'm getting rid of a few problems very soon. Cleaning the slate, starting life over again. The thought hits his brain once again like an ounce of Scotch. A new life. Starting today, he looks at his watch, the second of June.

Then he looks around the table. I'll miss them. Even if they did, half of them, avoid my eyes when I walked in. They're all nervous, trying to pretend they're paying attention to what's going on.

Bernie. Maybe he'll keep on arguing with me at least.

Mary Elgar, his defender, reaching under the table to scratch her leg, saying, "I don't know what it is we're so eager to find out with these cards. Seems like a lot of trouble to me, for what we get out of it. I don't like the idea anyway. Nobody's business is what it is." He'll run into Mary now and then on the street, maybe at the post office. He wants to put his arm around her and lean his head against that big solid shoulder.

Who's going to be left? Maybe nobody. All this time he's been like the telephone repairman. People let you into their house, but they don't interrupt their conversation. Like being a waiter. He looks down the table at Hawk Epworth. How would a person go about making friends with Hawk? Or anyone? How do grown-ups do it? Being a minister, he's never had time to find out.

He can't imagine being buddies with DeWitt outside the church. Patrice will stay in touch, surely. Maybe there'll be surprises: somebody like Ike or one of the other junior high kids. Or Bryan Epworth on his bicycle.

". . . One important matter before us tonight," Bill is saying. Witherspoon is supposed to be doing this, not Bartholomew. Swain turns toward Bill, sits up in his chair. "Many of us have expressed our concern"—that word "concern" again—"about some of the positions that Dr. Hammond has taken in the pulpit and about other matters. I've suggested to him that this gathering would be a proper forum for talking over some of these considerations."

His chin jutting, he looks over his glasses, down his nose, at the others at the table. Swain's heart starts to beat so hard he feels it against his own arms. This is stupid. I'm quitting anyway. I could just tell them, but this is my only day in court. Maybe finally somebody will understand. . . .

He nods. "I welcome your questions and comments. If anything, I have wished to have more feedback from you and other members of the congregation." He smiles, his confidence returning.

Bill says, "May we begin then with a matter which may be no more than unfounded rumor." He looks at Swain. "It cannot be true that you struck Joe Miles on the afternoon eleven months ago when his child was blinded."

Swain's mouth is dry. He says, "It is true and I have no excuse for it. That regrettable incident is in a category apart from the others I expect you will want to question me about tonight. I can offer some explanation, but I will say again: there was no excuse."

Hawk shifts in his chair. Out of the corner of his eye, he can see Mary drawing rows of lines on a page of her notebook. Bars. She's already decided to send me to jail.

"Please explain, if you will," Bill says.

"In a family waiting room in the emergency room, Joe shoved me repeatedly, backing me up against a wall, blaming me for what happened to his son. It was behavior understandable for a man in his position. But it came at a time when I was pushed to the edge myself. It was like a reflex. He hit me; I hit back. For all my life up until that day, I had turned the other cheek as we have been told to do. But on that day, or maybe some day weeks before, without being aware of it, I had reached my limit. For one regrettable moment, it seemed to me that the time had come to start hitting back. I behaved in a way that was, I think, both human and inexcusable."

He stops. Hawk is watching him, his head lowered a little, like a teacher looking up from calling the roll to find out who's causing the disturbance. Charlie, as if he's just had a piece of bad news. He doesn't look at Bernie. Bill waits. He can keep right on waiting. That's all I have to say.

"If there are no questions about that at this point, we'll simply move along," Bill says. "Another item I have listed here in my notes to myself, Dr. Hammond, I refer to as 'miracles.' Most of us heard you make reference to an incident with Jakey Miles—"

"That's right. And what I want to ask you," Swain says, looking around the table, "is whether any of you, looking at that boy with the bandages fresh on his face, would have passed up what seemed like a chance at changing what has happened to him?"

"That's not the issue," Hawk says. "It's thinking you could do it in the first place that is sort of hard for some of us to understand."

"Hawk, it wasn't me."

"Who was it?"

"I think you know what I'm going to say. It was God."

Silence. He looks at each face, blank. They just sit there and stare at him like they're waiting.

"God," Swain says. "The reason for the church. The focus of our worship. Has everyone forgotten that?" They continue to stare.

Swain stands up and walks to the other end of the room. He turns around and looks at them, still watching him. He turns back again to the dark window. If I could show them . . . If any one of them had heard that one word "Son," ringing down the empty hall . . .

He puts his hand to the glass. Cold. He leans, lets his head hang. This is the end of the row. There's no way to tell them. This is why I'm quitting.

He starts to push away, stand up straight, turn around, say it: I'm leaving, guys, it's over. But his hand . . . the glass . . . it's humming. He doesn't move. He doesn't breathe. Under his hand, the glass is trembling. It's moving. He feels his spirit leap, a match touched to paper.

He reaches both hands up to the window, his arms reaching high, pressed against the panes. Yes. Now is the time. God. He sees the white reflection of faces at the table behind him, then that fades as he looks past out into the darkness. The force is alive against the palms of both his hands.

"Father," he says. "Appear to all of us now."

He says it again in silence. Father. This is a plea. I am begging. Aloud: "Be here in this room now."

He feels the force against the glass, all the darkness that's out there pressed up against his hands.

Nothing. God does not speak.

"Some sign."

There is no answer.

Once more: "Father."

Silence.

He is standing at a dark window. Nothing is going to happen. He is alone, empty of everything, falling through space, in a plane turning end over end.

Then—a weight of warmth descends on his shoulders, his back, pulling at his arms.

He turns. Mary, Hawk, Bernie. Surrounding him. Arms supporting him. Hands reaching for him. He stares at their faces, one and then another.

He lets go of the window, the wall. Tears rise in his eyes. They're carrying him.

He is a baby in a blanket, surrounded by arms. He is falling into a warm net. He holds onto the shoulder that is under his hand. Carrying him. He wants them to. He lets them lead him, lower him into a chair.

At the Sunday service, he goes into the pulpit to give his notice. They sent him home that night, weak, as if he had been sick. A final terrible embarrassing proof that he's not able to lead people to God.

Then he called Bartholomew and told him what he was going to do. On behalf of the session, Bill posted a notice that the congregation would meet at eleven o'clock and take up urgent business. He bent the rules a little by not saying exactly what.

Since then people have called, those same three: Mary, Hawk, Bernie, a couple more. Bernie talked to Julie, told her to get him to a doctor. She said she'd already tried.

Now the ushers stand in front of him, four of them, the first notes of the doxology humming up through the organ. Rudy Haddonsfield, Michael Woodhouse, John Ferrando, Mary Elizabeth Franklin. John collects the plates and gives them to Swain. "Praise God from whom all blessings flow," the singing rises like a high wall of water behind Swain as he turns to face the altar and puts down the offering.

Then they're taking their seats again behind him, the ushers filing offstage. Swain turns back. It all works like a dance, like a music box of tiny moving figures wearing frock coats and powdered wigs who come out and dance as long as the lid is open. So orderly and small. The movements of the machinery bring him into the pulpit, make him say what he has to say.

"I have come to tell you this morning that I am leaving the ministry." Not asking them to petition the presbytery to remove him, as he should. Just telling them: I am leaving.

For the first time in their marriage, Julie is sitting near the back of the church. She almost didn't come. Why should she? He has quit listening to anybody, needing anybody. Why should I come over here and sit under his nose for him to say he's through with all of us? Now he's told them. She looks around. It's as if he just slammed a door or flung something on the ground in front of them. They stare up at him. And they don't see what he's like at home.

Joe and Patrice Miles. Patrice catches her eye, frowns, and looks away. Joe looks as if he's watching a good car chase on TV. He always looks like that. Mrs. Helgeson, Joan Woodhouse, all of them looking back and forth at each other. Except for Bill Bartholomew, sitting there not moving a hair. I'm tired of worrying about what they think. People keep noticing I'm back here, and whispering to each other. Why can't some of them do something to stop this? He's spent all these years going to see them in the hospital, now he needs somebody to help him.

"On a Sunday almost a year ago, I came to you," Swain is saying, "reluctantly and in great confusion, and told you I had heard a voice that I knew to be the voice of God." He rehashes it all, reminds them.

"I was angry then, disappointed that no one seemed to understand, or even was curious about what had happened. The only curiosity, it seemed, was about what strange behavior I was going to come up with next.

"But I don't come here today to accuse you. The difficulty did not lie with you.

"Neither does it lie with me. For a long while I blamed myself. I asked myself what it was that kept me from getting it across. Maybe, I thought, it was because I wasn't a good enough speaker, I didn't say it right, I didn't get the words right. Or maybe because I hadn't built the kind of relationship with each of you that would allow you to trust me. Or maybe because I was in some way holding back.

"So I blamed myself. But that's over. That's not why I'm leaving the ministry.

Gladys sits with her hands clasped tight against each other. Don't do this, Dr. Hammond. Please.

"I have decided that it was neither my fault nor yours. I give my notice as a minister today for this reason: I have come to believe that the experience of God is not something that one person can tell another about. It is an experience that no one can truly communicate to anyone else. God cannot be summoned, no matter how hard we try."

He could ask for a leave, Bernie thinks. Get a little rest, find out what's wrong with him. People could understand that. No, he has to go overboard and dump his whole career. Just do me a favor, God, don't ever say anything to me. And leave my friends alone.

"This morning I come before you to tell you that in a matter of weeks, a couple of months, at the pleasure of the elders and the presbytery, I will be moving on. Because I don't know how I can serve any good purpose here. By what I now believe to be true, this career is a contradiction. I can't stand in this pulpit week after week and pretend there's some hope for my doing what I'll never do." His heart is picking up. Beating not faster but harder. Each beat comes down hard on his ribs. A shudder, a chill passes over him. He thinks, I'm doing it. I'm leaving.

"So I stand here for one of the last times and offer to you my hope that we all find what we are seeking.

"I cannot call myself a generous man. In so many ways, I don't reach out. But I have known since I was a young boy that there is a God, and that something about that astonishing fact is the most important thing in the universe." A flush rises to his face. He's trying again. It's time to give up. "I think now that the ministry has never been anything for me but my own search for God. And I can no longer deceive myself that I'm doing anything more than that."

Tears fill his eyes. His last real sermon. The sanctuary is a blur, if he blinks, the tears will run down his face. He doesn't want to see. "With all my heart, I say to you one more time"—raising his arms, one sleeve catching—"may the love of God be with you. The grace of the Lord Jesus Christ and the love of God and the fellowship of the Holy Spirit be with you all."

SEVENTEEN

S wain is lying face down on the bed. It's hard to breathe except on one side of his nose. He doesn't feel like turning over.

Julie moved his stack of clothes off the chair to sit down. He hasn't hung up a pair of pants or a shirt since he took off what he wore a week ago to quit. Julie hasn't touched them either, except to move them to sit down.

"I can't think," he says toward the open door of the closet. "My brain has stopped." For a week he hasn't met with anybody. He put them all off, anybody who wanted to talk with him.

Julie isn't saying anything. He can't see her sitting over there behind him. What is she doing? "Why aren't you talking?" he says, mostly into the bedspread. He hears her start to say something, but she hesitates.

"I already said, Swain, I still wish you would go talk to somebody about all this."

"Yes, you did say that." He sighs. "My last defender gone over to the other side." He rolls over on his back, stares at the ceiling, finds the familiar water stain in the plaster, stares at it until the usual shapes—a tiger, faces in profile, the hook of a scythe—appear. "I think I'll see if Jakey can come over." He smiles at the ceiling, it sounds like something a six-year-old would say. "Mrs. Miles, can Jakey come out and play? Can he come over to my house?"

"Good idea," Julie says. If Swain had the maturity that Jakey has, we wouldn't be in this mess. Maybe some of it will rub off.

He looks over at her. Reading a book about babies. "What

should I tell him we're going to do? We don't have anything for kids to do here. He can't play Scrabble." She looks up from her book. He's asking me that? Why can't he decide, since he's so good at making big decisions?

"We could go swimming, do something fun. It *is* summer, you know."

"I'm very aware of what season it is."

He sits up, suddenly eager to move after a week of lethargy. He says, "We'll come up with something." Julie watches him, stares at him the way she does these days, while he finds his shoes, looks up the number, makes the call.

"Okay," he says. "Jakey said fine. I'll be back in a few minutes."

He stops, rubs his chin, thinks about shaving. Hell, it's Saturday. I've already given notice, I don't have to worry about that kind of stuff anymore. I'm through being the town clock. He smiles to himself, goes out and gets in the car.

At the Mileses' house, he rings the bell and waits. No answer. Then he rings again. The car is in the garage. The door opens. Joe.

"Come in," he says. "Patrice isn't here. You're stuck with me for a minute. Jakey's in the bathroom. He'll be right out."

They stand in the hall. Joe hasn't shaved either. Swain hears the toilet flush in the back of the house.

"So you got up there and quit."

"That's right."

Joe nods, staring at him, the same wondering way Julie does, except with a little bit of a grin. "I was surprised to hear it," he says.

"Probably a lot of people were surprised. And relieved."

"Not me," Joe says, the smile widening a little. "I was beginning to enjoy our little debate."

Jakey is coming down the hall. "Dad, I can't find my running shoes."

"Hang on. They're in the den." Joe goes looking for shoes.

Jakey says, "So what are we going to do? We could go to Toys "R" Us. That would be okay."

"Let's go back to my house. Julie's expecting us. Then we'll see."

Joe comes back with the shoes, hands them to Jakey, looks over him at Swain. "You boys have fun," he says, smiling that same taunting smile.

Outside, Jakey lets his hand trail along the hood, unobtrusively finding his way around to his side of the car. Swain smiles. Every time I see him, the kid does new things, little stuff you wouldn't think of if you weren't paying attention.

Jakey changes radio stations, beats time against the door all the way back to the house.

When they come in, Julie is sitting in the armchair in the living room, patting a scruffy stray cat.

"Hey. Where did that thing come from?" Swain says when they get in the door.

"What thing?" Jakey says.

"A big yellow cat, Jakey," Julie says. "I don't know where it came from." She looks up at Swain and then back at the cat. I'll just take care of the cat until the baby comes, since there's nothing I can do anymore about Swain. She watches her hand running slowly over its back. Stiff spiky orange hair, the color of strained carrots. "She's been hanging around the back step every night for days."

"Ratty-looking thing." Swain comes over and reaches out a hand toward it. It blinks. Doesn't move, but it's getting ready, way down under its skin. It's going to jump on me, Swain decides, even if it's not showing yet. "Why did you bring it in? It's so ugly." The cat looks at him with its piss-colored eyes. "Probably has terrible diseases."

Jakey comes over and stands near, not certain which way to reach. Julie says, "Put your hand over here, Jakey." She leads his hand to the cat. He pats it a couple of times, steps back. "Cats are

REVELATION ☐ 287

for girls," he says. If you just stick your hand out, it's hard to know if something is going to bite you. You can't even tell.

The cat turns back toward Julie, walking carefully on her lap as if her legs were a bridge across a pond. It settles down around the lump of her stomach. Julie smiles.

The cat raises its tail slowly and brings it down fast. It blinks, raises its tail again and looks over at Swain.

Julie laughs.

"What?" Swain and Jake both say.

"The baby's jumping around in there. Wants to come out and play with the kitty." Jakey makes a move toward her to feel around and see what's happening. Then he stops. The baby's still inside her. You can't just go putting your hands all over people.

Swain stares at her belly. There it is. He can almost see it, the little drop in her big plaid shirt. It falls as if the earth had shifted underneath. The cat is staring at the spot. It waits and waits. It starts to move toward the place, advancing toward the other side of the bulge. There it goes. Out of the corner of his eye, he sees Jakey step close to the chair again.

Jakey thinks, they're being so quiet. Why doesn't anybody tell me what's going on?

The cat puts a paw out, touches where the baby kicked and jumps away. He inches forward and swats and draws back. He comes forward again. Brave now, he doesn't back off. Two soft cat paws pressing down on the baby. Julie looks down at all this as if none of it has anything to do with her, as if she's watching something on TV.

"Jakey," she says, "do you want to touch where the baby is moving?"

He hesitates. Touch a baby that's still *in* somebody? "I guess."

She takes his hand—he looks as if he's worried about what's going to happen to it—and puts it on her stomach. Then his face lights. He laughs.

"Jeez," he says. There it is, thumping around. Amazing. Far

out. "He hits pretty hard. It's definitely a boy. He's ready to be born."

Jakey with his grubby little hand on my stomach. And this big old stray cat—everybody touches a pregnant woman. Too bad Swain can't get pregnant. He'd love it. Now the cat is pushing with one paw against her, then the other, then the other, kneading her. The way kittens do with their paws when they're nursing, bringing the milk out. She tries not to laugh.

"I've seen them do that," Swain says.

"Shhh," she says.

He thinks, the same motion they make with their paws all their lives, even when there's not any more milk. The way I'm still making whatever motions it was I made as a child. The cat is pushing and pushing, staring at the spot with its vacant feline eyes. That same hopeless lifelong tune.

"Look." She says it without moving, not to disrupt.

Jakey says, "What's happening?"

"The baby is pushing back. I can't believe it." She is staring at this thing that's happening to her, her lips parted, the lamplight shining on her eyes. He sees her face, how she's going to look, when the doctor hands her the baby, her eyes and her arms reaching for it, so happy that he feels that his chest will explode with joy to look at her. He reaches over and puts an arm around Jakey.

Julie says, "Every time the cat punches in, the baby punches back. It's like they're talking to each other."

Swain watches. Do I see it? Yes. There. "Amazing. From one world to another world. They're sending messages across Outer Space."

"What you're calling Outer Space is me."

He can't take his eyes off her stomach and those silent cat's paws. Maybe the baby thinks it's talking to God. Or the cat does. Maybe I'm hearing God through something as hard to talk through as a swollen stomach and a plaid shirt. No wonder nobody can explain it.

Jakey says, "Put my hand there again." Swain looks first at Julie, then he guides the boy's hand onto her stomach.

Jakey pauses for a moment. Then he laughs. "That's out of sight."

Now Julie is laughing like she can't stop. The cat backs off from her swollen belly and looks up at her face. "I can't believe that happened," she says. She picks up the cat and sets it on the floor in front of her chair. It stares at her and swings its tail and blinks.

Probably glad to be let off, Swain thinks. It's heard all it wants to from the other side. Too late now. Life as an ordinary stray is over. You've got a mission now, cat. Try to figure out what it is.

"Come here, kitty," Swain says. "Come on over here. " He keeps his eyes on the animal. See? It's dazed, doesn't know what's happening. It doesn't move toward him at all, just sits there.

He reaches over and puts a hand under its bony chest and picks it up. It flops over his hand like a length of chain. It hasn't been fed much, or picked up either.

"What do you think of that, sport?" Swain leans his cheek down next to the animal's face. "Pretty amazing, hunh? Looks like there's nothing there and then it starts to jab at you." He looks at Julie. "This animal will never be the same again."

Julie rolls her eyes. Jakey says, "Still feels like a cat to me."

"I'm serious," Swain says, clutching the cat. I'm never going to let go of this cat in my life. The stupid stunned expression on its face, blinking and looking around. He buries his own face against the long scrawny neck of the cat that is starting to twist in his arms. Finally I've found an ally.

Jakey says, "Have you thought up any good names?"

On Monday morning, he starts to face them all again, everybody who wants to talk with him, starting with Bill Bartholomew, who says, "I believe you're being very wise to take a sort of breather, if you will."

They sit at the table in the library where the session is always held, the very spot where he failed to produce God. Swain looks over at the window. He doesn't feel the least apologetic. "A breather isn't exactly what I had in mind."

"Mmmh," Bill says, making a note in a pad he has taken out of his inside jacket pocket. He doesn't explain the notation. He looks up at Swain, as if he had just remembered him. "What are your plans for the future?"

"I have none."

Bill's eyes widen slightly. "I'm sure you'll find something that suits you very well."

"Shall I expect the elders to take any action? To deal with the presbytery?"

Bill smiles. "A formality. It will be taken care of."

"I'll be glad to be as useful as I can in your search for my replacement. As I mentioned before, I'm willing to remain here as much as two months full-time, perhaps into the fall part-time if you need me."

"Thank you. We'll be moving as quickly as we can." Bill looks at him clinically, as if he were a symptom that couldn't look back. He says, "I won't pretend that I'm not relieved that this is settled. As you know, I've felt you've been heading in a direction that is not right for us here. But I'm sorry as well. You have an interesting mind. I felt personally let down when you involved yourself in all this." He pops his ballpoint in and puts it in his pocket. "I wish you well. I hope you get . . . everything worked out."

Bill Bartholomew wishing me well. He looks carefully at that familiar face, the worst pain in the ass in eleven years in the church. A little overliteral, overprecise. But not such a bad guy.

Swain stands and extends his hand. Right now, I don't hate him at all. "Bill, I hope you find a bang-up good minister who's just what you want." They shake hands. Bill says, "Thank you, Swain." He looks a little embarrassed.

Patrice is on next, scheduled for lunch. They're sitting side by side on the counter stools at the greasy spoon three blocks from the church.

"Sudden," she says.

"Not really."

"I guess not, I suppose something like this has to have been building up for a while. I just didn't know."

Swain puts his coffee mug down on the counter. "I don't guess anybody did. Maybe I should be relieved it wasn't any worse. I didn't go into a McDonald's with a rifle and start firing on people."

"And you didn't run off with another woman."

"True."

"Are you still going to come see us?"

"Absolutely." An advantage of sitting this way is that you don't have to look at each other all the time. It's like talking while you're driving or lying on your backs in bed.

"That's a relief. I did wonder."

"You needn't have." I'm not saying good-bye to her. There's no reason to start feeling depressed.

"Do you know what you're going to do?"

The waitress, one he doesn't know, mops the counter at the place next to him with a gray rag. There's a smear of grape jelly across her white dress, level with the counter.

"I don't have any idea," he says. "I can't get myself to start thinking about it."

"Something will come up."

"So everybody tells me. Better come up pretty quickly. But I'm not worried. I don't know why." He takes a sip of his coffee, puts it carefully back down. "You tell me something. How is it with you and Joe?"

"Good." She smiles, makes her eyes get big and wide. "Hard to believe, isn't it?"

"A little surprising. I'm glad. What happened to what's-his-name?"

She makes a face, regretful, embarrassed. "He really is a very decent guy."

"You were going through a lot then."

"I still am." She looks back at him. "Joe and I decided the way we were going wasn't doing anybody any good."

"Did he know—"

"Not exactly. Not who. But he knew something was going on, and he wasn't exactly home by the hearth himself. So we just decided to mark off whatever was happening for that few months last winter and start over. I did make sure he knows that none of it involved you."

"That's why he was willing to let me in the door."

"Actually I think Joe sort of likes you."

"He picks some strange ways to show it."

She smiles. "Joe is an unusual man. Like you."

"Swain." Called out from behind him.

He turns. Bernie is trotting down the Sunday school annex hall. Swain waits, as he catches up.

"Hey," Bernie says. He stands and looks at Swain for a second, then smiles and hits him on the side of his shoulder. "You're full of surprises, fellow."

Swain puts out his hand to shake hands. Bernie extends his without looking away from Swain's eyes. "Look," Bernie says, "I haven't exactly given you a break . . . about all this. I could have cut you some slack."

"You did all right at the session."

Bernie hesitates.

"I'm talking about when you and the rest of them pulled me down from the window." Bernie looks as if he'd rather they didn't mention it.

Swain says, "Not that I have any apology about what I did there. Ministers are supposed to try to bring people closer to God. That was my last try."

Bernie nods. He says, "I've quit blaming you for trying." He shrugs. "I guess being there made the difference."

"You've quit thinking I'm nuts?"

Bernie looks away, scratches his head. "Swain, now that I think about it, you've always been nuts."

He isn't getting off the hook that easily. "You think it was the Top Banana or not?"

"I don't know. But a guy like you doesn't get up and make a scene like that for nothing."

Swain feels the color rise in his cheeks—that's about as close as Bernie Morris is ever going to come to a profession of faith. He remembers Bernie's face that night. "Thanks," he says.

"Yeah," Bernie says, tapping him lightly on the shoulder with his fist.

One by one, or in groups standing in the sanctuary or before Sunday school, they all say their piece to Swain. Mary Elgar reaches up and puts her arm around him and says, "Gutsy fellow. Your daddy would be proud. Matter of fact, he might actually understand what possessed you to think you have to leave. The two of you, only people I ever knew that would try to reason your way out of a traffic jam."

His daddy would be proud. He still aches every time he thinks of them.

"By the way," she says. "One thing about your new reputation —this church is full of people that aren't a bit sorry you punched

Joe Miles, under any circumstances. He's not exactly a humble man."

Swain grins. Every day should be like the days when you're leaving.

Mary gives him a pat and says, "Boy, you stay in touch with me."

Then DeWitt, who just nods, as if he's listening but isn't convinced.

And Hawk Epworth, who says, "I was very sorry to hear that you're leaving, Swain. My boy Bryan was too. I don't know why, but somehow or other," he laughs apologetically, "he feels like it's his fault."

Swain frowns. "It's not his fault." Bryan pacing up and down his office, telling him he'd be a not-too-bad father. He makes a mental note to give the boy a call.

One person, and then another, and another.

Frances Eastwood says in her sweet reproachful way, "You have always been a help to me."

Ed says, "You've got it figured all wrong, buddy. We heard you. I heard you. It's just not our job to stand up and say so, maybe it shouldn't be that way."

It's turning out to be fun. He's enjoying it all. That's the strange thing. After the first shock of feeling unclothed, after the dizziness wore off, he likes what's happening. People, one after the other, coming to him, and almost all of them saying something nice, that he had acted right, or that he had somehow done some good. But nobody trying to talk him out of it. He mentions that to Julie one night, saying, "That's what proves that behind all the rest of this, they're glad I'm leaving. They love me to death as long as I go."

Gladys eases her big old Cadillac slowly along the street, peering up at the house numbers. She went to the Hammonds' house once years ago, but it has been so long since she has been able to go anywhere much. Now which one is it? What kind of car does Dr. Hammond drive?

There it is—1136. Plain as day. She pulls up to the curb. If he's not here, I'll sit and wait. She looks up in the rearview mirror and adjusts her hat. She puts on some lipstick, and adjusts the collar of her blue linen jacket.

She puts her pocketbook over her arm and walks just as fast as she can go up the sidewalk and up the front steps. The bell chimes back in the house somewhere. She can see through the panes in the door a china plate catching the light on a side table. Another day she might want to see what his house looks like. But this is an emergency.

She hears footsteps inside. She feels her face flush. I should have combed my hair. Don't be silly, Gladys. Think about why you're here. He opens the door.

"Gladys, what a nice surprise. Come in. Julie's in the back, I'm sure she'd like to say hello."

"It's you I need to talk with. And I'll only stay a moment. I have something very important to say."

She walks past him over to the sofa and sits down. He watches, amazed. Is this the same Gladys who sits and cries in my office? She killed the old lady and she's come to confess. He looks at her shoulders, standing up straight as a ramrod. She's not here to confess anything. He closes the door and follows her into the living room. He sits down in the chair opposite her.

She looks at him for one second. He is looking like a teenager in a T-shirt, and his hair is a mess. Then she fixes her eyes on the mantel and says what she has come to say: "You must not leave the church."

Swain's shoulders relax, he smiles, glances at the carpet, then back at Gladys. "That's kind of you. I appreciate your—"

"I'm not just trying to say something nice to you, Dr. Hammond. It's very important."

Sitting there in that suit coat when it's ninety degrees outside. "Can't I take your coat?"

She shakes her head. He says, "I'm sorry. I didn't mean to interrupt." He sinks back into his chair.

"I know what you said in your sermon. You think you can't tell anybody about God. Well..." She looks at her hands on her pocketbook. Swain leans forward, suddenly wanting...feeling his heart start to pick up speed. What, Gladys?

"You came over and sat with my mother-in-law. I was surprised at myself that I would let you do any such thing, but I did. I was glad to get away. And now, ever since you did that, it doesn't seem so bad. Seems as if I can stand it. I have had a girl come in on Tuesdays, but that isn't the same. I don't know why. When you did that, said you'd come stay, it seemed like all at once there might be things I could still hope for. The way I had been feeling, everything was over for me." Her voice starts to tremble a little, then she gets herself under control. "I don't know the Scripture like you do, Dr. Hammond, but I was raised on it. The Bible commands that we love one another. 'By this shall all men know that ye are my disciples....'"

The tears rise up in her eyes. "It was a very loving thing you did. I can't just keep silent and let you go away."

Swain feels heat spread across his chest and down his arms like burn. He leans toward her farther, crossing half the space between them. She hasn't finished. She says: "Dr. Hammond, you are a good disciple. You mustn't stop now."

He mustn't stop now.

He tries to clear his throat to speak, but nothing catches. The house creaks in the quiet. Gladys says, "That's what I came to tell you."

"Gladys, I already—"

"Go back and tell them. Everybody is allowed to change their mind."

"Dear God..." His pulse is hitting now against the insides of his head. He puts his head in his hands. Have I been through all of this just to get somebody to pat me on the back?

She says, "Swain, it's not too late."

The Scripture is pouring through his head, he's seeing it on a computer screen, rolling by, turning too fast. "A new commandment I give unto you that ye love one another...By this shall all men know..." Is she right? He needs to stop and think. Just sit still by himself and think.

His head down, he sees her feet in their old-lady shoes start to move. He looks up. She's standing, taking her keys out of her purse, snapping it shut. "I have to be going now," she says. "I hope that you will talk to the Lord about this some more."

He lets his head sag again. He doesn't get up. Now she is walking toward the door.

He doesn't even look up to see her go. He hears the door open and shut, her footsteps, and then the car starts up out near the curb.

I mustn't stop.

What does she think a minister does? I hated sitting with her mother-in-law. It was the worst three hours I ever spent. I'm not going to spend my life doing that. People can get their own baby-sitters.

The room is quiet, the light coming in the windows slanted. I wish she hadn't come. She's wrong. It's too late for her to come over here and tell me this. I made my decision. I never in my life wanted to be that kind of disciple.

He sits straight up in bed. It's still night. Julie's beside him. He looks over at the clock: 3:12. It was a dream.

A big cat, a mountain lion. So silent and huge. He can smell it still in the room, a circus smell, rotting sawdust and shit and heated fur.

He lies slowly back down. It's okay. There's nothing here but us. He hears Julie breathing. He feels his heart beating. It was nothing but a dream.

Then he sees himself again walking down a street downtown

and there it is beside him, its shoulders working slowly back and forth, back and forth, with each long step. It's leading him, pulling him. He can't escape.

In the sanctuary, crouched on the carpet, licking, yawning, stretching its big jaws, making little flicks with its tail. Waiting for him. Everywhere he goes it's there. It's here in this room now.

His eyes shut for one moment, he smells its hot breath on his face, the darkness closing over his head. He pulls himself upright, breathing hard. He looks around the room.

There's no sound at all, not a car creeping down the street, not a branch rubbing against the house. Julie hasn't stirred.

His heart pumps in the silence. He feels the other heart pumping stronger there in the dark. Feeding that terrifying effortless power.

There's no getting away.

That day when he sat on his balcony, all those years ago, and saw for a moment through the surface of it all. The dark trunks of the backyard trees, the water standing on the mud, the falling-down shed, his own legs in front of him. And all of it part of one huge creature, all-encompassing. He should have known then. There's no getting away.

Where are its eyes? he thinks. I want to see the face of God.

He strains to look into the darkness and find the shape hidden there. Darkness inside of darkness.

The smell of it fills the room again. Hot flesh and fur. It is all around him. He is breathing it, drowning in it.

The Lord is my shepherd. I shall fear no evil.

The rolling darkness engulfs him. He is inside a huge living animal, bound into its muscle. Somewhere a heart beating close to his head. All the force of that beating suffuses him. Every beat calming him, stroking him.

Go with me, he thinks, get me through it.

He feels a gentle rocking motion. The creature is moving. He is a part of its moving, its incredible force.

When he wakes again, it's morning.

REVELATION □ 299

Julie's in the bathroom running the blow-dryer. Light from the window is killing his eyes. His head is starting to clear. Then he remembers: the dream. His heart stops. He lies still, remembering how it felt, letting his strength slowly gather, until all of that huge animal power is his. Start now, he thinks. He gets out of bed and goes to find her.

She's standing in front of the mirror, under the light, half-dressed. Thin white nylon hanging over the bulge of her stomach. He comes up behind her. She looks at him and shuts off the dryer. "Good morning," she says. She can tell already it's not any ordinary morning.

He leans his hands on the mirror in front of her, high above their heads. He looks from his face, to her face, to the baby. And back. His shoulders, his bare chest rising like a wall behind her. This is where it begins again. Their faces, their two bodies in the mirror, all they've got ahead of them: it goes straight to his heart. He puts his face down next to her hair, his hands pressed hard against the mirror. He says, "Julie, with the kid... I'm going to do the best I can."

She nods, watching him so closely, she is hardly breathing. He can't feel her moving at all. Then she leans her head back against him. She says, "I'm counting on it."

He closes his eyes. She reaches her hands up behind her, behind his shoulders, draws herself closer to him. Hands... on his shoulders, his back. This is the way it was when he pressed against the humming window, his own hands against glass, begging God. And then the other hands coming to find him, lifting him away from there. They carried him so gently. He closed his eyes and let them.

Carry and be carried. That's all God and Gladys are asking me to do.

He says, "Julie, I'm going back to ask them to take me back. I guess you know."

EIGHTEEN

The telephone light is blinking when he gets into his office. He reaches across the desk, putting his stuff down and picking up on the line. "Swain. Joe Miles."

Swain walks the phone around the desk to his chair. He sits down. "How are you, Joe?"

"Fine, thank you. I'm calling to see if you and I can get together late today for a drink."

A drink. Swain glances down his calendar schedule. "Sure, Joe. We could get together earlier, if it's something that—"

"How about six at the bar in the Continental."

"That's fine. Is everything . . . is Jakey okay?"

"Nothing to do with Jakey. He's okay. We'll talk this afternoon."

"See you then."

All day Swain is extravagantly cheerful. He hugs Mildred, who then steps back and looks him up and down and says, "Lord o'mercy, Dr. Hammond." He walks down the hall, throwing a pencil up in the air and catching it. Six end-over-end flips it does. He catches it every time. They've got to hire me back. They couldn't not do it. A prize like me? They couldn't make such a mistake.

That night after work, Swain gets to the hotel first and wanders around the lobby, catching glimpses of himself in the mirrors on the columns, wandering among the sofas and the waist-high urns of flowers. He's excited, terribly curious about this business with Joe. It's a little like being in school and waiting in a dorm lobby for a girl to come downstairs. At two minutes to six he goes into the bar.

Joe walking in, sees him at a small table over by the window. Swain looks like everybody else, a regular guy stopping in for a drink, not a preacher. Swain raises a hand, Joe nods, then doesn't look at him again as he crosses the room. Swain must be eating his heart out to know what this is about.

Swain stands.

"Hello, Joe." They shake hands and sit down.

Joe nods to the waiter. "Good of you to make time on short notice," he says to Swain.

"No problem."

"I must say I'm curious," Swain says, after they've ordered their drinks.

Joe laughs. "I'm sure you are," he says. "Most of our get-togethers have been...well, we could have sold tickets and done very well." He looks for a moment at Swain. He could be good for something, now that he's got this church stuff behind him. "I won't keep you on hold. I know you're leaving the church. I want to make you an offer."

Swain doesn't move.

"Just listen to the whole idea before you make up your mind. It's nothing you've ever considered before." The drinks arrive. Joe picks his up. Swain waits. An offer? Blackmail. That's what it is. He fights off the urge to laugh.

"You know I've been at the business school and consulting in recent years. I used to be in the brick business...." Swain nods. "Okay, you know about that. I'm getting antsy with academics is the main thing. I'm ready to get back into something, ride a wild horse again for a while. A new business."

"Yeah?"

"I'm working with several people on this. The financing is worked out, preliminary engineering plans drawn. Still fairly rough at this point." A careless gesture with his hand, as if he and Swain have been doing business for years. "The basic idea is—we're putting together a town. Down on the central part of the coast. The land is available. Nothing there but a few fishing docks and some guys taking a netful of shrimp now and then." He leans back in his chair, takes hold of the table by both corners. "What we're going to do down there is incredible, Swain. It's going to be beautiful. A whole town. Solar houses, good-looking. We're not going to touch all that scrubby live oak, we're just going to leave it right there. Water and sewer first thing, no septic tanks."

I have to stop him. . . .

"It's something every one of us involved is proud of, Swain. I want you to talk to some of the other guys, and look at the plans. I want to take you down there. But first I wanted to tell you what I have in mind." He leans forward. Here's the clincher; he can't say no. "We need you to talk for us. As soon as you got up there and said you'd quit, it jumped into my head.

"We're going into a rural county where a preacher is king. We need somebody out front for us that has credibility with these people."

"Look, Joe . . ." Swain says.

Joe says, "A temporary thing, while you're making up your mind about where you want to go." Swain Hammond isn't the only one who can talk. "Swain, I know this is sudden. Think about it. I know this was probably the last thing in the world you would have expected from me lately. I've been torn up over my boy." He's not going to leave me sitting here high and dry.

"But even before the accident, Joe, I was not one of your favorite people. We've always rubbed each other wrong."

Joe shrugs. "I thought you ought to be out doing something. Working full-time at least. I can't see a man spending his life handing out Kleenex. It's nothing but a way to get next to women and then pretend you didn't."

"Whatever you think of the value of it, it's more than full-time."

"I'm not here to argue. You've made your decision about that."

"Actually, Joe, Sunday I'm going to ask for my job back."

Joe sets his drink down. Goddamn. Then the whole thing was nothing but one big grandstand play. Leading us all on. He stares at Swain. Pretty clever. "What makes you think the preacher job's still open?"

"I don't know that it is. I'm going to reapply. Are you going to stand in my way?"

"No. If you're crazy enough to want to do it . . . Forget I ever said anything."

"Tell me why you want to hire me, Joe."

"I told you. We need a preacher."

"You want to be my boss."

"I already am. If you're real lucky, I'll continue to be."

"I mean my only boss. Not one among four hundred."

Joe smiles. "It's true. I like that idea."

Swain keeps his eyes on him. We're getting somewhere now.

Joe says, "I want you under my thumb."

"Why? What are you going to get out of that?" All these years he's watched Joe as if the man were a beautiful powerful circling shark. . . .

Joe shrugs. "Just strikes my fancy. A man has the balls to get up and claim he hears the voice of God—I don't know. Take it as a compliment. I don't want you running around loose."

Something like straight bourbon is spreading through Swain's veins. This . . . from Joe Miles. A whole battalion, an army has just saluted him.

"Okay," he says. "A compliment then. Thanks."

Joe says, "If I were you, I'd watch out for Bartholomew. I'll keep the offer open, just in case."

On Sunday, the place is packed. The word has gone out: there's going to be a spectacle. He looks away from the congregation, across the front of the church. The burgundy altar cloth sways a little as people stand. The thought of standing makes him

dizzy. Hawk Epworth is saying "...join together now in the
singing of Hymn 256, 'Be Thou My Vision,' all stanzas, if you
will."

Gladys looks around at the crowd. You would think it was
Easter. All these people! Just look. And Swain up there as calm
and quiet as ever. It's going to be fine. There's not a bit of reason
to worry. None in this world.

If it doesn't work, Bernie thinks, there's a lot of stuff a guy like
him could do. Plenty of things. He doesn't have to hang around
with a bunch of clowns like us. God, it's hot in here. He wants to
take his jacket off. He fans himself with the lid of the hymnbook.

Swain turns to the page. The black dots of the music swarm.
He flips it shut. There's a sick feeling at the pit of his stomach.
This whole thing may not fly. I may have handed them one thing
too many. He wants to get up there and say it and get it over with.
The sweat has stuck his shirt to his back, his chest, it's hanging on
to both his arms. He's trapped in this shirt.

I will not leave you desolate. I will come to you.

He says it over and over. He hears the great sigh of the congregation sinking back into the pews.

He starts to move. Seven steps in a semicircle, around the
wooden post. In a few minutes, it's going to be over.

Julie is seated on the side to get as wide a view as she can.
There weren't this many people here Christmas Eve. I've never
seen so many. Mary Elgar, over there dying to get up at the front
and tell everybody what to do. Bill's face from the side, blank and
cold as it can be. DeWitt looking as if he's the one who's God.
And my stomach turning somersaults. It's worse to look than not
to look. The problem with sitting over here is they can all see me.

Swain, in the pulpit now, faces out across the rows of them, to
the back of the room, then forward again. "On the night of the
Last Supper, Jesus said to the disciples, 'A new commandment I
give unto you, That ye love one another; As I have loved you...
By this shall all men know that ye are my disciples.'

"And then Jesus was arrested, betrayed, crucified. And ordinary men were left with the commandment to love one another . . . as Jesus had loved them.

"Twelve men. Think of them as a committee. Men as different as Peter and Thomas, as different as any two or twelve of us here in this room.

"What more difficult assignment could they have than to love as Jesus did? What more difficult challenge do we have today? To find such love in our hearts is to me the most intimidating of God's challenges. The impossible commandment.

"How can God, knowing the human heart, knowing all our hates and angers and fears—how can He ask such a thing? How could anyone imagine that any of us is up to it?"

He pauses. The queasiness is gone. It's okay, whatever they do, it doesn't matter.

"There is an answer to that in the Scripture. In a very familiar story. One we all know—about the fishes and loaves." He tells them the story, fleshes it out, turns it into a Charlton Heston drama, while they wait to hear him say what they came for. "Five thousand people gathered in the desert," he says. "And Jesus told the disciples, Feed them. And what did the disciples say? 'We have here but five loaves and two fishes.'"

He looks across the congregation. "Five loaves for five thousand. A meal multiplied and multiplied as it was shared."

He stands quiet for a moment and looks around the room. "When I think of loving as Jesus commanded, I am a man faced with a very large crowd and a few pieces of bread. A little is all I have." His eyes move slowly across the rows.

Julie, looking around as he does, suddenly knows, It's settled, it doesn't matter what he says now. They've already decided something.

"You are all aware that I asked this congregation to petition the presbytery for the termination of my time here. I made this request from this pulpit three weeks ago today. This morning I have come to ask you to take me back. I made a mistake."

There's no gasp, just a great rustle of movement. Finally he said it. Gladys smiles, puts a hand up and pats at her hair.

Bill Bartholomew looks away. A mistake. On and on about his personal life. The man doesn't know when to stop, he's going to turn this thing into another maudlin scene.

"I gave up the ministry because I had come to believe that in this search we're all making, there's very little one person can do to help another. In the past week, you—many of you—have convinced me otherwise. You have reminded me of the times in which we have helped each other, perhaps not in the ways I had hoped or intended, but still with so much force for good that I am touched and amazed. It was feeling this, in my heart, in my gut, that made me know I had done the wrong thing."

"So I come back to you today, because I want to do whatever it is I can. I want to go on as your minister. I want to take my few pieces of bread and make them go as far as they will. We are promised in that story of the fishes and loaves that, as we share, the little we have will go a long way."

It's all said. He looks across the rows, lets himself see them, face by face. They're all here: the Mileses, all three of them; Gladys; Bernie. His glance moves fast across the room. Bryan Epworth and Hawk; Bill Bartholomew; Mary; DeWitt; Ed Fitzgerald; Sam, bless his heart.

"The elders are scheduled to meet in session a week from Wednesday. As always, they will be advised by your wishes. I will look forward to hearing your decision."

That's it, Sam thinks. He was going to make a good drinking buddy. So much for going to hell together. They can't turn him out. Who else do they know who even might have heard God? He looks around. Hawk Epworth is about to pull a muscle in his neck straining himself to see what everybody's going to do. You can't tell a thing from looking. Sam sits back and smiles up toward the front, so if anybody looks at him, they'll know which way he's going to vote.

Swain feels himself start to turn, almost in slow motion, his muscles sliding back and forth against each other, like the shoulders of the lion. Every move is easy. He steps back in the pulpit, lets his hands fall from the lectern. Another step and he is going down the stairs.

He pauses at the bottom step. It's too quiet. The silence behind him is bearing down like a train. He looks back. A blur of colors, rows and rows of faces, coming in and out of focus. Why are they waiting? Now he sees. Bill Bartholomew is coming down the aisle, the same impatient annoyed look he has when there's some emergency and his beeper goes off and he goes out the side door. Swain stands where he is and watches him approach. The light from the stained glass shines blue on Bill's forehead. Swain glances once around him: the choir sitting motionless, the director's mirror hanging above them, the surgical table of the altar, the windows climbing behind like a set of spires. Bill comes up the steps. Swain goes to meet him. They stand together in the center of the front.

Bill nods to Swain and then turns to face the congregation. "As an elder of this church, I am happy to report that a special session was held this morning. Based on a rumor that surfaced yesterday, we believed that we might have the opportunity this morning to get our minister back. To be prepared for that, we passed a resolution to commend to the congregation that the earlier resignation of Dr. Swain Hammond not be accepted. This church has always been known for taking stands, some of them unpopular. It's in keeping with this tradition that we offer our continued support to a pastor with the courage to say things many of us don't want to hear."

Bill turns to Swain. Now you see how it should be done, he thinks. A man can get up and reverse himself and do it with some dignity. He looks at Swain. Why does God make such choices? A man like Hammond, when all he's going to do with it is talk and cry and try to do miracles that fail. He says, "If you will call a business meeting of the full congregation, I think we might put this matter to a vote now and find out the will of the church."

Swain steps back into the pulpit before the microphone. So they're going to keep me. The mike whistles as he starts to speak.

He feels solid, steady, calm. He waits for the whine to die away.

Julie, over on the side, brings her arms close around the baby. Without taking her eyes off Swain, she thinks, we'll tell you about all of this someday.

"This assembly of the congregation of Westside Presbyterian Church is now gathered to take action on church business. I turn the floor over to Bill Bartholomew."

Bill says, "Do I have a motion?"

Sam gets slowly to his feet. "I move that Dr. Swain Hammond remain minister at Westside Presbyterian, that the congregation not take any resignation from him."

"Second." It comes from all over the church. Second. Second. Second. They want me. He looks up at the top of the church, at the high dark beams, expecting to see red spirals of confetti coming down slowly on all their heads, catching in their hair. It's Times Square on New Year's Eve. Julie's crying. So are Mary Elgar and Frances Eastwood.

Bernie stands. "I call for a vote on the motion." He thinks, eight times seven is fifty-six, eight times eight is sixty-four. I'm not going to start bawling in front of the whole bunch of them. He looks at Swain for one second—when is he going to stop looking like a nine-year-old who hopes you'll like him—then he looks again. Swain is standing there steady as a rock, not rattled at all. Come to think of it, he's looked like that ever since he got up there. When did the boy stop worrying? Well, it was high time the Top Banana did something nice for him for a change.

"All who are in favor, please say—" Bill stops. Swain looks where he's looking. Across the congregation, people are starting to stand. One and then another. Bernie, Mary, Hawk. Gladys. Old Mrs. Lampley, coming up slowly, holding onto her cane. Now DeWitt.

Jakey starts to elbow his mother and say, "What are they doing?" But he can tell what they're doing, they're standing up. You don't have to have eyes to know that. He gets to his feet. Everybody is tall all around him, he can feel the shadows of them on him. Swain won't even be able to see me, he thinks. He climbs up on the pew and stands up higher than anybody. He plants his feet, so he won't lose his balance, and crosses his arms. If it weren't church, he would yell, "Yeaaay, Swain."

Patrice, beside him, watches Swain up there seeing it all happen. Every motion in the room registers on his face, which seems to give back light, to return the warmth the congregation is sending to him. This is how he was meant to be. I always knew it was there.

There's no sound but the quiet shuffling as they get to their feet, another and another, all the way to the back of the church, Jakey on his pew standing a little above the crowd. Swain feels the tears rise in his eyes and start to spill over. Then the rustling sounds stop. The last one is standing. The room is silent to the top of the roof. No one moves, there is not a whisper. He feels all their eyes on him.

Then Gladys steps out of her pew, begins to come toward him, up the aisle, like the Queen Mother arriving at a grand state occasion. Now she is at the front. She did this. It was all her doing. He feels a rush of warmth for her. She doesn't say a word, she takes his hand in both of hers.

Then the rest of them, every one of them, follow. People begin to pour into the aisles. Not a sound but footsteps on carpet. He thinks he can hear their hearts beating, it is so quiet, as each of them, one by one, takes his hand. This is what it feels like to be touched by a column of light.

When they leave the church, maybe an hour later, Julie is at his side. As they go down the front steps to the car, suddenly it seems almost like the moment when the bride and groom leave the reception. Though almost everyone has gone, and none of the few remaining have any rice to throw.

She lowers her weight slowly into the front seat. He gets in on the other side. Each of them waits for the other to say something.

He says, "Well?"

She says, "I'm not worried anymore."

He smiles, starts the car.

He pulls out, looking pleased with himself. Nobody says anything. She thinks, This is the kind of quiet we used to have before all this started. After fourteen years of marriage, our first round of problems. Guess we got through it okay.

He feels himself relax, his neck muscles starting to let go. Driving is like slow swimming. Easy. Things are going to be easier from now on. Then the thought comes again, the one that behind everything else, still hurts him all the time.

He says, as they near the turn. "I want to make a stop. At the cemetery."

He can feel her looking at him. "Okay."

She stays in the car as he walks down the path between the low stone walls. The chain isn't up today. There's a potted plant at a grave next to the path that's blooming such a rich buttery yellow it looks as though the color would come off in your hand. He doesn't pause. He goes, as if he could do it with his eyes shut, to their graves.

There are people around, a woman on the next row making a spot for a vase of flowers to stand up. He didn't bring any flowers. He wishes he had. He sits down on the wall and looks at the headstone, the sun hot on his back and shoulders. Hammond. He says to it softly, so nobody can hear him: "I'm not mad anymore."

He saw his dad once walking by himself across campus late on a windy gray day. Swain, in high school then, on his way home in the afternoon, caught sight of him from a distance. It was still winter, getting dark early. His father was gripping books and papers under one arm, leaning into the wind, his coattails flapping around his legs. He looked so lonely, with his shoulders hunched over. He looked by himself, and old. Swain didn't run after him. He'd been mad too long by that time.

Now he wants to run and run, crossing the sidewalks and grass, to catch up with him and then act like it was an accident, walk with him to his car or wherever he's going. His father would start talking then, telling some story, his whole chest would expand with what he was saying and he would seem bigger. He would even forget Swain was there, but that wouldn't matter. He'd be distracted and excited, talking. He wouldn't look so forlorn and alone.

And his mother. Once he dreamed she came and stood by his bed. He was sick and in the infirmary at school. It was in the year after they died. He woke up in the night, turning over and over, not knowing whether he was awake or not. There was the dim shape of the guy in the next bed. A water pitcher on the table beside him. Then he knew she was there. He closed his eyes. He dreamed how she straightened the covers around him, brushed back his hair. She was so pretty. She always was. He has pictures. Now if he could straighten the covers around her, put his hand on her hair...

"Let's go sit outside," Julie says at home later, after they've eaten.

He is still exhilarated, but starting to slow down. "Okay," he says. "Lead me to a chair."

She laughs. The screen door slams behind them. They walk up the hill at the back of the yard and sit down next to a tree. She leans back against the tree beside him, it puts them a little bit at angles, looking different ways out on the slope of yard, where the weeds look like the bank of a creek.

"Did you ever think about planting flowers back here?" he says.

"I like it the way it is. It's okay with me if you want to plant some."

He smiles. "Maybe I will."

He hears a metal jingle and twists back to look behind them. It's Tex, the Gustafsons' golden retriever. Tex comes around and stands a few feet in front of them, watching, panting, his tongue hanging halfway to the ground.

"Hello there, fellow," Swain says and stretches a little to scratch Tex's chest with his foot. Tex lies down between them, his head on his paws. Swain reaches over and rubs behind his ears.

Julie watches. Swain doesn't even like pets. What is he doing? First he makes friends with a cat, and now this. She looks down through the trees of a whole block of backyards. It's so peaceful back here. This is where it all started.

Swain hears her start whistling, softly, something that is familiar. It takes him a minute to recognize it. *The Moldau.* She's nearly worn out the record. He leans back and listens. She has it right, as right as one soft whistle can make something written for a symphony.

Listening, he can picture the river the music is about. He can hear it. Running from high up on a mountain in Eastern Europe, a creek turning into a river, two creeks joining together, making a bigger river that's picking up force and rolling over rocks and sending spray up into the sun. He hums it with her. He is floating over that valley, flying, looking down into a confetti of light and spray.

He closes his eyes and the river is in him. This is how it feels when a river lets itself go to the ocean. He can feel the music in all his limbs, in the place where Julie's hand is on his leg. Two creeks become a river, flowing home.

"Did I put up much of a fight really?" he says.

She stops whistling. "You were never easy." She smiles, her eyes on his, then goes back to her tune.

Swain does hear the voice of God again, a couple of weeks after that Sunday, a little more than a year after the night when it first happened. This time, it is as a note of music, as he is just waking up. Julie lies beside him asleep. They lie like two spoons, his chest against her back, his arm draped over her, his hand on the warm globe of her belly. It's early, still twenty minutes before time to get up. He knows before it happens that it's coming. He doesn't move. He waits, while the note emerges from a sound too deep to be heard. Then it's audible, filling the room, humming against his bare skin, like the warm touch of a hand. In the same moment, it begins to diminish, a dwindling vibration of piano strings.

Swain lies still. He doesn't cry as he did the first time, or soak the sheets with his sweat. He doesn't wake Julie. The morning light on the far wall shifts with the shadows of tree branches. He watches the triangles and splinters of light, forming and re-forming, and feels the slow rise and fall of his own chest, and then of Julie's, her shoulder stirring slightly beside him. Her hair has fallen back away from her face. His own face lies so close to her: her ear, the freckles on her neck and shoulder, the fine down of her cheek that shines in the light from the window. We are breathing together, he thinks—Julie, the baby, and me.

He listens. Everything is quiet: the room, the yard beneath the window, the sidewalk out front. He thinks of the houses up and down the street, and who lives in each one. The Gustafson kids next door. The old fellow up at the corner who's probably already out walking with his stick. All the people, house after house. He can see it all in his mind now, one surface, one skin, that same world he saw years ago from his balcony. In the silence, he can feel the living hum. He thinks, It is breathing...with our same slow breath—mine, Julie's, the baby's, all of us.

What he feels then, flooding the whole space of his being, is joy, undeniably joy, though none of it has come as he would have expected. It is not what he looked for at all.